Praise for *Legends of the Nor...*
A JUNE 2021 INDIE NEXT PICK

"[Evison's] strength as a fiction writer . . . is his knack for locating telling depths within small canvases and finding compelling drama in workaday lives." —*The Seattle Times*

"Jonathan Evison's *Legends of the North Cascades* is a beautifully rendered and cinematic portrait of a place and its evolution through time; it is also— pure and simple—a story of survival and the love and devotion between parent and child." —Jill McCorkle, author of *Hieroglyphics*

"Evison's majestic and panoramic latest conjures the beauty, power, and unforgiving nature of the Cascade Mountains in alternating narratives separated by thousands of years. Evison masterfully delivers a subtle yet pointed commentary on how society marginalizes veterans and how we profess to admire yet distrust the individualist ethos while also offering a profound meditation on the human spirit." —*Booklist* (starred review)

"Only a writer of Evison's talent could so brilliantly weave the struggles of a PTSD-stricken veteran and the ghosts of an ancient family into such a powerful social commentary. Wildly original and breathtakingly bighearted." —Willy Vlautin, author of *Don't Skip Out on Me*

"Engaging . . . This modern back-to-the-land story feels like Jon Krakauer's *Into the Wild* meets Jean M. Auel's *Clan of the Cave Bear*, a combination that makes for a compelling read in its appreciation of the monumental properties of nature and recognition of the history of humans in the North Cascades." —*Library Journal*

"Evison weaves the prehistoric past and the troubled present together with imagination and tenderness in this haunting, timely meditation on the redemptive power of love."   —Hillary Jordan, author of *Mudbound*

"Bella, resilient beyond measure, is the heart of this tale, her vivid mind imagining a conduit between eras, a story of survival thousands of years old, that parallels their own."   —*Addison County* (VT) *Independent*

"Under the daunting and impassive mountains of the title, two dramas, one ancient and one contemporary, intertwine to become a greater story of parent and child attempting to survive in the harshest of circumstances. For me, the heart of this fine novel is Bella, a young heroine whose courage and steadfastness are a timely reminder of how human decency can prevail in the darkest of situations."

—Ron Rash, author of *Serena* and *In the Valley*

"Evison (*Lawn Boy*) delivers an intimate . . . story of grief and parenthood with characters from two distant millennia . . . Evison's empathetic vision offers much to consider about the limits of parental authority and the capacity for both physical and emotional survival."

—*Publishers Weekly*

"What a great storyteller [Evison] is . . . After exploring themes of what it is to be human, this tale has a very satisfying ending."

—*The San Diego Union-Tribune*

Praise for *Lawn Boy*

"Mike Muñoz is a Holden Caulfield for a new millennium . . . Evison, as in his previous four novels, has a light touch and humorously guides the reader, this time through the minefield that is working-class America . . . [His] subject matter and wit are a welcome departure from self-conscious MFA trust-funded prose—one of his many comic targets, along with Walmart, puppy mills and inbred, rich white folks. As he chases the American Dream, Mike loses two teeth in a kitchen extraction scene (no insurance), but gains so much more—a social conscience, romance and his niche in life. Not to mention a laughing, sometimes teary audience who stay with him until the very last page."

—*The New York Times Book Review*

"Jonathan Evison takes a battering ram to stereotypes about race and class in his fifth novel, *Lawn Boy* . . . Full of humor and lots of hope . . . An effervescent novel of hope that can enlighten everyone."

—*The Washington Post*

"Evison excels at finding the humanity in his characters . . . This tender bildungsroman follows Mike from one setback to another, each interaction involving slyly observant and brilliantly witty dialogue that also poignantly conveys vulnerability . . . In his bighearted portrayal of Mike Muñoz, Evison has created an indelible human spirit content to live authentically."

—*Booklist* (starred review)

"A roller-coaster ride of a novel . . . Moving, evocative and beautifully written . . . Evison meticulously evokes a richly detailed marginalized world."

—*The Providence Journal*

"Moving . . . Evison convincingly evokes the small disasters and humiliations that beset America's working poor . . . Evison's quiet novel beautifully considers the deterioration of the American Dream."

—*Publishers Weekly* (starred review)

"It's a difficult thing to write uproariously humorous fiction that has heart, passion, and inspiration rolled into it as well. The life of Mike Muñoz is a comedy of self-inflicted errors and familial obstruction, but his positive outlook . . . is infectious and inspiring and will make you laugh and cry, often on the same page, sometimes for the same reason."

—*The San Diego Union-Tribune*

"This book has one of the best first chapters that one could ever read. It is compelling, tragic, and funny at the same time. It is worth buying the book just for that wonderful chapter with its masterful writing . . . A very timely novel that rings very true to life." —*Manhattan Book Review*

Praise for *This Is Your Life, Harriet Chance!*

"Infused with Evison's characteristic empathy and heart and humor . . . [Evison's] got a talent for character, emotion and pacing."

—*Los Angeles Times*

"[This] is a book that speaks to all of us, whether we're young enough to check Facebook fifty times a day, or old enough only to have a vague idea what the internet is. The themes Evison presents—disappointment, delusion, redemption—are universal, and he deals with them beautifully in this wonderful novel. This is your life, Harriet Chance, but it's ours, too."

—*The New York Times Book Review*

"It's hard to imagine a family member of any family who won't see something familiar in Harriet's quest to understand her spouse, her children and herself . . . It's hard to imagine the reader who won't be moved by this lively, lovely work."

—*The Denver Post*

"Evison writes with his typical unflinching honesty about a life that is not what it seems . . . Poignant reflections on aging, parenting, friendship and marriage constantly surprise with their quiet truthfulness."

—*The Toronto Globe and Mail*

"Openhearted, effervescent . . . Evison handles the jaunty tone with aplomb."

—*The Washington Post*

"Thank heaven for surprises, especially of the Jonathan Evison variety . . . Sure to become a book club favourite this fall, *This Is Your Life, Harriet Chance!* is a pleasurable mix of the crazy escapades, changing relationships and thoughtful reflections that make up a life."

—*Toronto Star*

Praise for *The Revised Fundamentals of Caregiving*

"With its extremely cinematic plot and collection of quirky scenes, the novel might remind you of *Little Miss Sunshine* meets *Rain Man* . . . *The Revised Fundamentals of Caregiving* is even-keeled, bighearted, and very funny, and full of hope. Through Ben, missteps are made, and human foibles are exposed. But we also glimpse that distant shore of hard-earned redemption. For that, Evison's novel is worth the voyage."   —*The Boston Globe*

"Grimly hilarious . . . The novel culminates with a classic road trip across the American West. Mr. Evison injects a wonderful amount of feeling into those empty highways and dingy rest stops."   —*The Wall Street Journal*

"An entertaining picaresque and a moving story of redemption."

—*The New Yorker*

"Evison is one of the sharpest writers around, and proves it in pretty much every line of this funny, brassy, unflinching tale . . . Nothing sentimental about this book, just good, honest, punch-to-gut emotion, with amazing adventures and revelations along the way. You'll get your heart broken several times over in this book, and yet, if you're like me, you'll end it with a full heart and a heavy sigh, and maybe a smile. How did he do that? Dunno, but I'm damn glad he did."   —Ben Fountain, for *The Millions*

"[An] engaging book . . . The journey is reckless and wild, infused with the sad rage that makes good comedy great . . . As this carload of misfits moves east, relationships are broken and forged, and Ben recreates a kind of family. This could be horribly clichéd and yet it isn't, because Evison never bows to what we expect from happy endings."

—*The New York Times Book Review*

"*Revised Fundamentals of Caregiving* is a journey back to life . . . It's moving and funny, and, my God, how refreshing it is to read a story about someone caring for a disabled person that isn't gauzed in sentimentality or bitterness . . . Evison once worked as a personal care attendant himself, and this novel is dedicated to one of his clients. The experience seems to have taught him just what true caregiving is all about, and that insight along with his plaintive sense of humor had me alternately chuckling and wiping my eyes through much of his book."

—Ron Charles, *The Washington Post*

"The comic novel may be the hardest work of fiction to pull off well . . . Evison proves that some of the best comedy emerges from lives that have jumped the rails." —*Minneapolis Star Tribune*

Praise for *West of Here*

"[An] expansive, century-spanning novel . . . *West of Here* is the kind of work that begs to be called sweeping, with its large cast of characters encompassing multiple eras, sturdy American themes of community and nature, and a style that could be called cinematic . . . The big picture is pretty impressive."   —*Entertainment Weekly*

"A voracious story packed with daring folks who dream of carving lives onto the last frontier."   —*The Washington Post*

"A fresh and contemporary approach to the historical genre, tying the present realities of our great but truthfully young nation to the attributes of our pioneer days . . . [This] big, sprawling, entertaining story brings us face to face with the ecological and social consequences of those early days. Without moralizing but with plenty of heart [Evison] pulls the past and the present together into a celebration of American spirit."
                —*New York Journal of Books*

"*West of Here* has it all. It's a literary page-turner (no oxymoron) of epic sweep and elegant syntax—a novel so splendid that its 486 pages seem sorely insufficient."   —*The Louisville Courier-Journal*

"Evison has created a vibrant, richly populated community that doesn't need any help seeming fully realized . . . Reading *West of Here*, you feel as at home among the mountain men, prostitutes and crusaders of the nineteenth-century mudscape as among the parolees, bartenders and former high school basketball stars of the twenty-first."   —*The Oregonian*

"Big and unforgettable . . . *West of Here* is a sprawling tragicomic novel about identity—national and personal—that's as entertaining as it is insightful." —*Miami Herald*

"*West of Here* is a tale of a journey, where humans are made heroic by circumstance and by often accidental choices. Not all the choices are right or good, these people aren't superheroes . . . This is a novel that a reader can settle into, a work that is, most of all, a darned good story." —*The Denver Post*

"Brilliant . . . Evison skillfully and beautifully weaves together vignettes (often riotously funny) of the lives of P[ort] B[onita]'s residents, bringing together a wide variety of voices in a chorus of humanity and ultimately showing us how thin the veils between generations really are." —*The San Diego Union-Tribune*

ALSO BY
JONATHAN EVISON

All About Lulu

West of Here

The Revised Fundamentals of Caregiving

This Is Your Life, Harriet Chance!

Lawn Boy

LEGENDS

of the

NORTH
CASCADES

A NOVEL

Jonathan Evison

ALGONQUIN BOOKS
OF CHAPEL HILL
2022

Published by
Algonquin Books of Chapel Hill
Post Office Box 2225
Chapel Hill, North Carolina 27515-2225

a division of
Workman Publishing
225 Varick Street
New York, New York 10014

First paperback edition, Algonquin Books of Chapel Hill, January 2022. Originally
published in hardcover by Algonquin Books of Chapel Hill in June 2021.
Printed in the United States of America.
Published simultaneously in Canada by Thomas Allen & Son Limited.
Design by Steve Godwin.

This is a work of fiction. While, as in all fiction, the literary perceptions and
insights are based on experience, all names, characters, places, and incidents
either are products of the author's imagination or are used fictitiously.

LIBRARY OF CONGRESS CATALOGING-IN-PUBLICATION DATA

Names: Evison, Jonathan, author.
Title: Legends of the North Cascades : a novel / Jonathan Evison.
Description: First Edition. | Chapel Hill, North Carolina :
Algonquin Books of Chapel Hill, 2021. |
Summary: "After his wife's death, a man brings his young daughter to live in a cave
he has found in the Cascade mountains. Once there, his daughter begins to
sense the presence of other people in the cave, a mother and son who retreated
there during the last ice age in an effort to survive"— Provided by publisher.
Identifiers: LCCN 2020040903 | ISBN 9781643750101 (hardcover) |
ISBN 9781643751719 (ebook)
Subjects: GSAFD: Historical fiction. | Mystery fiction.
Classification: LCC PS3605.V57 L44 2021 | DDC 813/.6—dc23
LC record available at https://lccn.loc.gov/2020040903

ISBN 978-1-64375-248-8 (PB)

10 9 8 7 6 5 4 3 2 1
First Paperback Edition

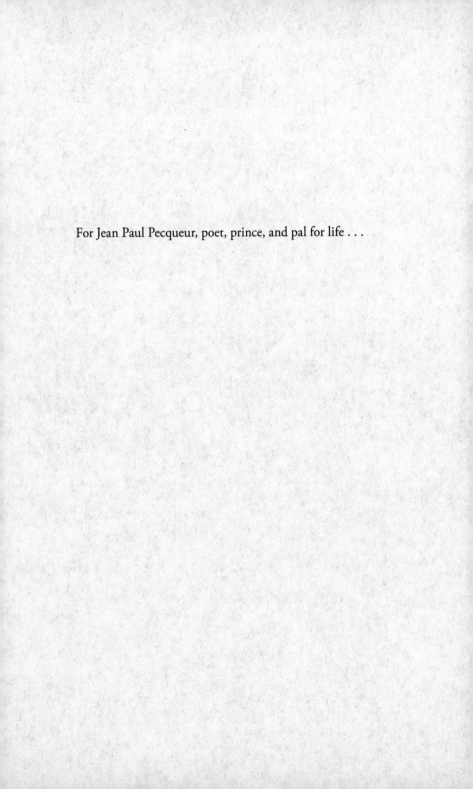

For Jean Paul Pecqueur, poet, prince, and pal for life . . .

A Brief History of the North Cascades

Eight million years ago these mountains began pushing their way through the earthen crust of the continent, born hundreds of millions of years earlier as a jumble of tertiary rock, sediment, and basalt from beneath the ocean floor, all of this castoff material trucked along upon the shifting plates of the earth until it collided in a geological mosaic here, on the northwestern edge of the North American continent.

These are the North Cascades, west of the Skagit River and east of the Puget Sound, extending north to the Fraser Valley, still volatile and ever changing. As recently as twelve thousand years ago, this entire wilderness was covered in a massive ice sheet, from the eastern divide, extending south and west to the Olympic Peninsula: a great, barren world of white, frozen and wind-ravaged. The people who lived here hunted mammoth and bison. They lived in caves and burrows, imprisoned by ice. Enduring the constant perils and malevolent moods of the shifting ice, they managed to abide in their small clans.

In time, the great sheet of ice retreated, freeing the rivers and exposing the waterways and marooned alpine lakes. Thousands of years before European explorers arrived to "discover" this new world, before the trappers and loggers came to impose their wills and claim their fortunes, before the corporations came to reap their profits, the Nooksack, and the Skagits, and the Wenatchis wintered on the banks of these waterways, fishing, and hunting, and telling stories by the light of the fire about the beginnings of the world, about The Time Before Everything Changed, and about the great spirits who lavished upon them all the natural wonders that sustained them through the epochs. And about the spirits who still walked among them.

LEGENDS
of the
NORTH
CASCADES

I

———

The Book of the Dead

The Time Before Everything Changed

Maybe Nadene was right; maybe their marriage wasn't worth saving. God knows she'd tried twenty different ways already. Dave couldn't begrudge her now for wanting to throw in the towel after fifteen years. Still, lingering there in the driveway, five minutes after she'd sped off in the Dodge, leaving a rooster tail of gravel in her wake, Dave nursed a small hope that cooler tempers would prevail, and that she'd come around. This time would be different. Dave would quit running from the damage, and take ownership of his own shit, once and for all. No more excuses, no more obfuscation, no more avoidance. He'd finally get the help he needed. He'd go back to the damn desert and relive it all if that's what it took to win Nadene back. He was ready for the fight.

Though it was hard to account for Dave's optimism, there it was. Maybe it was that fine day. That first hint of spring warmth in the air, the mountains finally beginning to shed their snowy cover, bristling green with cedar and spruce in the morning sunlight. After a long winter, it was hard not to be hopeful under all that blue sky. He made a pot of coffee and began drinking it on the front porch, hopeful that she would return soon.

If they could not find another convincing reason to save their marriage, they'd save it for Bella. For all their failings, they'd always done their damndest to provide a good and stable environment for Bella. They'd fed and clothed her to the best of their means; they'd tried to nourish her burgeoning interests every step of the way, tried to allay her fears, and reward her enthusiasm, and instill Bella with confidence, and a sense of possibility. They'd always done their best not to argue in front of her. And mostly, it seemed, they'd succeeded. Bella was nothing if not bright, and curious, and quietly confident. Though she was only seven-and-a-half years old, she read at a fifth grade level. She communicated easily with adults. She had an emotional IQ higher than Dave, but she seemed to be taking the world more personally than ever.

In the truck after school Friday afternoon, on the way to drop her off at Nana's, Bella had started in with the questions again.

"Do you still love Mommy?" she said from the passenger seat.

"Of course, I do, baby. I love you and Mommy more than anything in the world."

"Are you gonna get separated?" she asked.

"No, baby," Dave said.

"Promise?"

"I promise."

Bella eyed him evenly. "I don't believe you," she said, turning to peer out the fogged-up side window.

Dave reached over and patted her on the knee.

"Baby," he said. "Look at me."

Bella complied, a little dubiously.

"Adults sometimes have issues they have to work through," Dave said. "They have patterns that develop in their relationships, not-so-good habits, and sometimes they're hard to break."

"What kind of habits?" she said.

"Well," he said. "Like a lack of communication, things like that."

"Like how you never talk about Iraq?"

He winced inwardly, and patted her knee once more.

"Baby, I don't want you to worry about anything," he said. "Everything is going to work out fine."

"You're lacking communication again," she said, turning back toward the window.

Though Bella had him dead to rights, Dave couldn't help but swell with pride a little bit. Surely, he must have done something right to produce such a perceptive kid?

The fact was, Dave used to be good at a lot of things. He was good with his hands, good at solving problems, good at staying calm in a crisis; he was clutch, when you got right down to it. Above all, he was good at belonging: belonging to his mother, belonging to Coach Prentice and the team, belonging to his platoon, belonging to Nadene. Hell, there was a day when it felt like he belonged to all of Vigilante Falls. So, who turned their back on whom? An honest accounting always yielded the same conclusion: Dave, Dave had turned his back. Though as freely as he could admit this state of affairs, as clearly as he could see it, he still could not begin to understand it.

So, how was he supposed to talk about it?

After two hours of alternately sitting on the front porch and pacing the driveway, after an entire pot of coffee, Nadene still had not returned. Dave managed to get his truck started on the third attempt, and drove to his mom's to pick up Bella. Where would he be without his mom? His mom was the definition of clutch, always pulling through in a pinch. How could he ever be anything but a mama's boy, when his dad left him, still wetting the bed at three years old? His baby brother Travers had no memory of their father at all. Dave mostly remembered what he'd seen in the handful of pictures his mother had kept in a shoebox in the laundry room, so they didn't even feel like real memories. Funny how the memories he wanted to summon were so elusive, but the unwelcome ones were relentless. Anyway, he doubted his mom even had the pictures of his dad anymore. Why should she preserve her husband's memory, when he left her with an infant and a toddler, and disappeared somewhere east of the mountains? Still, in the thirty-six years since his dad ran out, Judy had never spoken ill of the man, despite the fact he never paid child support, never called on birthdays, and never even looked back, let alone apologized. Whatever happened between

Dave and Nadene, Dave hoped he could expect the same from her, in spite of everything.

Dave skirted the center of town as usual, but couldn't avoid the high school. Vigilante Falls High School was long overdue for a facelift. The old brick building looked all but abandoned, empty as it was on a Saturday afternoon. The purple-and-gold VFHS insignia emblazoned on the side of the gym—*HOME OF THE FIGHTING VIGILANTES*—while still legible, had faded in recent years. The adjacent grandstand was riddled with graffiti: "Lundgren blows," "Itchy Boy '16," and Dave's favorite, "Satin Lives."

The old gridiron was still patchy from winter, the goal posts a little worse for wear over the decades since the Vigilantes' glory days, a run of three consecutive 1A state titles in the late nineties. If Dave let himself, he could remember the thrill of Friday nights under the sodium lights like they were yesterday; the cagey, heart-pounding promise of the locker room, as Coach Prentice delivered his gruff, pre-game address, invariably ending with the crux of Coach's personal philosophy, in football, if not in life: *play for each other*.

If Dave allowed himself, he knew he could still recall, and quite palpably, the readiness and rowdiness of the crowd: the friends, and neighbors, and family. If he let himself, he could still recollect the dizzying adrenaline of charging onto the field just as the band started blaring the Vigilantes' fight song, the kettledrum and the tuba rattling in his chest, stirring virtually every emotion he'd ever felt all at once. If only Dave would give himself a break, he could live it all again, at least in his mind. But these were comforts that Dave had not allowed himself in years. Maybe if he got the help he needed, if he could make amends, make peace with himself, straighten out his marriage, his career track, and his emotional health, he would once again allow himself to dwell for a time in that cocoon of nostalgia.

But first things first.

Dave pulled in behind his mom's LeSabre in the driveway, hopped out of the cab, and strode up the walkway and the front steps, wishing he'd taken time to shave. After a cursory knock, he let himself in before his mom could answer. She was busying herself in the kitchen, dressed in an oversized gray sweatshirt and baggy jeans.

"Hey, Ma," he said.

"Davey," she said. "I was wondering when you're were coming. You hungry?"

"Nah."

"Can I get you some coffee?"

"Already drank a whole damn pot. Thanks, though."

"How about a razor?"

"Leave it alone, will you? It keeps my face warm."

"Your brother was by," she said.

"Yeah?"

"Wanted to borrow my chainsaw."

"Ah," said Dave. "Does he even know how to use it?"

"Apparently."

"Mm," said Dave, mildly impressed. "How's your back?"

"Better today," she said. "What about your hip?"

"Sleeping on the sofa sure isn't helping," said Dave.

"Aw, Davey, honey," she said. "Sooner or later you two will straighten things out. Be consistent, that's the important thing. Consistency is everything."

"I know," he said. "I'm trying, I really am."

His mom clasped his hand.

"I know it will all work out," she said. "I keep praying."

"I appreciate that, Ma. I know it will."

"I wish you'd go to service with me once in awhile. Everybody is always asking about you. It's like you're a ghost."

"Yeah," he said. "I can see that. Maybe one of these days."

"Reverend Hardy used a football analogy this week. You would have liked it. He said the modern world was looking at third and long."

"At least," said Dave.

"You are loved, Davey."

"I know that, Ma, thanks. Where's Bella?"

"She's in the back room."

Dave was about to call for her when his jean pocket began to vibrate. Maybe it was Nadene, ready to lay down her ground rules going forward, ready to assign her conditions. Maybe it was her brother Jerry wanting to take him fishing, so they could talk. Hopefully it wasn't Jasper at Terminix trying to trade out his Monday shift again.

Whoever it was, Dave didn't recognize the number.

"You gonna take that?" said his mom.

Dave sighed. "Hello?" he said.

"David Cartwright?"

"Take me off your list, please," said Dave.

"Not a solicitor, sir. Harlan Dale, here, Whatcom County Sheriff's Department."

"Oh?"

"You sitting down, Mr. Cartwright?"

"No."

"Well, maybe you ought to."

The rest of the call was a blur, as Dave stared stupidly at a six-inch strip of yellow linoleum curling up near the foot of the fridge, while the information washed over him. Tanner Creek Road. Big bend at mile marker two. Must have been doing sixty-five.

"I'm sorry, Mr. Cartwright," said the sheriff.

"Thank you," said Dave.

His ears were ringing when he pocketed his phone.

"What is it?" said his mom, fishing her reheated coffee out of the microwave.

"It's Nadene," said Dave.

Just the way he said it was enough for his mom to catch his meaning.

"Oh, Davey," she said, setting her coffee aside, and clutching him tightly.

When Everything Changed

———

Not five minutes after Dave got the call, still numb with disbelief, he was tasked with breaking the news to Bella. They perched side by side on the foot of his mom's guest bed, Bella clutching her pack, feet dangling a half-foot above the carpeted floor, a seven-and-a-half-year-old vision of her mother: the long black hair, the green eyes, the placid face, and the native complexion.

"What's wrong?" she wanted to know. "Am I in trouble?"

"No, baby," he said.

"Did you quit your job again?"

"No, baby, it's not that. It's . . . well, baby, it's Mommy."

"Is she sad again?"

"No, she's not sad," he said.

Dave held his breath momentarily, and clenched his fists as though he might squeeze an answer out of them.

"Mommy had an accident," he said at last.

"Is she okay?"

"Mommy was hurt very badly, baby."

"Is she at the hospital? Can we go see her?"

"She's not okay, baby," he said, his voice catching. "I wish she was."

"What's wrong with her?"

"She's didn't make it, honey."

"Make it where?" she said.

"Mommy . . . she died in the accident, baby."

The silence of Bella's incomprehension filled the room like a vacuum.

"But Mommy's not old enough to die," she said finally.

"Baby, not everybody dies of old age. Accidents can happen to anyone."

"She can't be dead," said Bella. "You're just saying it!"

When Dave tried to wrap her up in his arms, she fended him off angrily at first, pounding at his shoulders and chest. But after a moment, her body went limp, as she allowed Dave to absorb her, and began sobbing into his armpit.

"It's gonna be okay, baby, I promise," he said, stroking her head.

But Dave couldn't see how. He could hardly remember the last time anything was okay. Bella must have been in diapers.

For two days afterward, Bella refused to say a word, no matter how Dave and his mom tried to draw the child out. Though uncommunicative, her bewilderment was written clearly enough in her silence. She clung to Dave's side virtually every moment of the day and night, as though permanently fixed there. Meanwhile, Dave moved about in a fog of disbelief, while Travers graciously handled most of the arrangements.

The seven grand it cost for the preparations, the plot, the casket, the marker, the memorial, and the reception nearly cleaned out what was left of Dave and Nadene's savings. They had no equity in the house after the last re-fi. Neither one of them had life insurance. There was no nest egg anywhere, no safety net beyond his mom, and how, at thirty-eight-years-old, could he ask any more of his mom? As it was she cared for Bella at least three nights a week. Not to mention all the Red Apple gift cards, and the meals she sometimes left in the refrigerator. Of course, Travers would never refuse Dave a loan, but Dave could never take his little brother's money on pride alone.

In spite of the cost, Nadene's memorial was a drab affair at Saint Barnabus. Dave sat up front in his musty black suit with the unfashionably wide lapel, as Reverend Hardy delivered a brief message to the half-empty church about redemption, and salvation, and earthly grief, all of which beaded up like water off of Dave, who could feel twenty sets of eyes boring holes in his back.

Bella sat at Dave's side in the darkest blue dress Dave could find for the occasion, silent and befuddled, and like Dave, unable to summon tears.

The reception was held in the fluorescent-lit environs of the basement, generally reserved for Bible study and charity bingo. Thirty or forty people were in attendance, more than half of them belonging to the Charles clan. Travers hired a caterer from Mount Vernon for the affair, though nobody but Travers and Coach Prentice exhibited much of an appetite.

Despite the countless handshakes and hugs he dispensed, Dave may as well have been somewhere in orbit around Neptune for how present he felt at the proceedings. The gravity of the occasion could not hold him there. The only thing that kept him tethered to the world at all was the perpetual presence of Bella stationed at his side, fiercely clutching his hand.

Holding On

If Bella had to explain it, it was like the dull, heavy feeling of being half asleep. Like when her dad carried her into the house from the truck late at night. The heavy feeling settled in her bones like a numbness. When she was not clinging to her dad, Bella moved about the house in a state of slow-witted confusion; eating and drinking mechanically, sometimes pausing in one spot to stare into space, as though she'd forgotten her way to wherever she was going. Wherever she was going didn't seem to matter anymore. She felt disconnected from the world and everything in it, like she was haunting it. She looked for comfort in the everyday things that once gave her life shape: her stuffies, her pearler beads, her little ponies. But she couldn't stay engaged for long. She turned to her books, but even her favorites, *The Curious Cat Spy Club*, *Ophelia and the Marvelous Boy*, *Flora & Ulysses*, failed to hold her attention for more than a few pages at a time.

Her dad, meanwhile, slumped on the sofa much of the time, half-dressed in front of the television, though he never seemed to really be paying attention to it. On the fifth morning after the funeral, Bella found him there, sleeping with his eyes open, or so it seemed. Bella must have stood between him and the TV for a good five seconds before he registered her.

"Hey, baby," he said, finally.

"Since you're not working, can we go somewhere?" she said.

"You want to go to Nana's? Go to the park?"

"I want to go on vacation," she said.

Picking up the TV remote, he muted the sound.

"Baby, it's not a good time to go on vacation. You've got school."

"I hate school," she said.

"Aw, baby, don't hate school," he said.

"Well, you hate your job."

"That's different," he said.

"Hate is hate," she said. "Nana said so. I don't like it here without Mommy. I wanna go somewhere different."

"I don't like it either, baby," he said. "But we're stuck here. At least for now we are."

"I don't want to be stuck here, Daddy."

"Neither do I, baby."

He set the remote aside and opened his arms to her.

"How about a hug?" he said.

Bella plopped down on the couch and fell into his arms.

He ran his fingers through her hair and held her close.

"Right now, we just gotta do what we gotta do, okay, honey? We gotta keep on doing the things we've always done. Otherwise, we might get lost."

"I'd rather be lost," she said, fighting back tears.

And in the days to come, Bella managed to lose herself. Actually, if she had to explain it, it was more like she emptied herself, and filled herself back up with other people. Like on the bus to school, where she sat silently, faced pressed to the cold window, as she let the squabbling and chattering of the other kids wash over her. Watching the houses and trees blur past through the rain-streaked glass, Bella exhaled herself like a breath, and almost instantly she began to absorb the other kids. It was like they entered her through her ear holes all at once. Soon, she could hear their thoughts, and feel their anxieties, and know what it was to be somebody else. It was at once frightening and comforting, this lack of self, this otherness. And every day it seemed to get stronger.

Fortifications

———

Though Terminix had been damn generous in offering Dave a month's paid leave, he had no intention of going back to his job. He no longer had the stomach to kill anything he didn't intend to eat. Not even cockroaches. That, and he was done wearing uniforms. He was done with affiliation in any guise. As friends and neighbors reached out with meal trains and condolences, Dave yearned only to escape their pity and concern, tinged, as it seemed, by morbid curiosity.

Once Bella had broken her silence and returned to school, Dave escaped into the backwoods almost daily, hiking fifteen and twenty miles at a go, in spite of his lousy hip, up the canyon, and over the rock-studded ridge, into the sprawling high country of the North Cascades, their precipitous peaks and cornices buttressed by glacial ice, white and windswept against the late winter sky.

As long as Dave was moving, putting distance between himself and the world, he could endure living in the moment.

One afternoon, while taking refuge on a small plateau high above the canyon, he paused in the clear, cool, afternoon to eat a heel of bread and a tin of sardines, taking in the remarkable panorama through the cloud of his breath; the great, yawning jaw of the canyon, and the ruffled blanket of spruce and fir sprawling clear to the bottom of the basin and beyond. Behind him, the peaks of the Picket Range reared up like spires: Ghost, and Phantom, and Fury. To the west, beyond the frozen silence, lay the inland Pacific, with its labyrinthine waterways.

Here, in this spot above it all, he lingered as long as the day would allow, basking in isolation. When he finally hefted his daypack, and turned to resume his progress, his eyes lighted on a narrow cleft in the side of the mountain.

In a world that seemed all out of mysteries, the gash in the hillside demanded his attention. Tentatively, he poked his head in, sniffing the chalky air, wary of bear, or cougar. Sensing no danger, Dave entered what amounted to a stone chamber, the size of which was difficult to ascertain at first. By the paltry light of his phone, he eased his way along the near wall for four or five steps, until the rock began to close in on him from above. After a few more steps, he arrived at the rear of the cavern. Stooping, he doubled back along the opposite wall, feeling his way along the cold rock, before stationing himself in the very center of the space, which he estimated to be roughly four hundred square feet. The stillness of the place was overwhelming.

Dimming his phone, Dave sat down upon the cold, hard earth in the darkness, only a narrow blade of sunlight slicing the foreground diagonally in front of him. For the first time in weeks he drew a deep breath, and clutched it in his chest, and stared at the back of his eyelids for a good fifteen seconds. Rather than exhale the breath deeply, he absorbed what he could of it, letting it pass slowly through every pore of his body, his shoulders slackening, as he released it gradually.

He spent the next twenty minutes repeating this exercise until finally, he let go a deep sigh. While the experience did nothing to buffer him from the future, he found comfort in the stillness, and in the tomb-like depths of the cavern, which immediately took on an almost holy significance. Here was sanctuary, and shelter in the realest sense; a divine cathedral of rock to soothe the aches and pains of the temporal world.

Dave would visit the place again and again in the weeks that followed, hiking eighteen-mile days for a few precious moments of shelter from the outside world.

It was upon Dave's third visit to the cave that he began to consider and calculate the possibility of leaving his life behind and taking shelter in the inexhaustible wilderness of the North Cascades. Yes, to turn his back on the world was a rash course of action, but what was left for him and Bella down below? Their lives were a smoldering heap of rubble. The only woman Dave ever loved, the only mother Bella would ever know, was two weeks in the grave. And in spite of Bella's naïve insistence, she wasn't coming back. The days of his employment at Terminix were numbered. The prospects for future employment were fraught with unknowns. He was down to nineteen-hundred dollars, roughly a third of which would be eaten up by the mortgage payment due in two weeks. Each possibility he contemplated for the future seemed bleaker than the last.

To leave the civilized world behind seemed like a natural extension to the escape Dave had been gradually charting for a decade, a course that had accelerated in recent years. He started tuning out the news cycle before the last election. He shut down his Facebook account shortly thereafter and taped over the camera on his laptop. He stopped engaging in political discourse of any kind. Eventually, he stopped returning calls, or paying social visits, or attending the occasional Sunday service at Saint Barnabus to appease his mom.

Now, with Nadene in the grave, life in V-Falls had become altogether untenable. Dave no longer wished to be around anybody, except for his daughter. And what was left for a child down there but a world that would likely forsake her, a world that would wring the wonder and humanity right out of her, as it sought to reduce her life force to an algorithm? The modern world held no more promise for Bella than it did for Dave. Reverend Hardy had it wrong: It wasn't third and long. It was fourth and forever. Time to punt.

It only took a matter of days for Dave's unlikely speculations to harden into a conviction; to live in isolation suddenly seemed like an imperative, and the only future he could bear to contemplate. The decision itself proved to be a morale booster. If not hope, it gave Dave's life new purpose and direction. Thus began the six supply runs in two weeks; through the steep canyon and over the wooded saddle, thirty-five hundred vertical feet up the mountain, eighteen miles round trip, a third of it in snow shoes, to town and back, packing sixty and seventy pounds per load: vintage hand tools—two saws, a planer, a drill, a mallet, a hammer, a coffee can full of hardware. Fishing tackle, rods, a pair of Winchesters, .22 and .458 Magnum, a hundred and thirty-six rounds. Skinning knife, nylon rope, parachute cord, binoculars, butane lighters, wooden matches, three flashlights, three headlamps, and five pounds of batteries. Topo maps, bear spray, fire starter, ibuprofen, a first aid kit. A pair of old Coleman lanterns to be used sparingly, three gallons of kerosene, a hatchet, a wedge, a shovel, three pairs of work gloves (two large, one small), two sleeping bags, two inflatable Therm-a-Rests, four wool blankets, four tarps, clothing for all seasons, a transistor radio, and every trip, two or three empty water jugs. Oats, flour, rice, sugar, and books, cumbersome, heavier than tools, awkward, backbreaking books. The least he could do was improve himself with all the time he'd have on his hands. He devoted one whole trip explicitly to the printed word: used books, new books, library books, children's books, textbooks, medical books, survival books. In two weeks' time, Dave hauled anything and everything a body could think of to survive in the backcountry of the North Cascades.

Almost everything.

One Crummy Backpack

———————————

"What about my stuffies?" said Bella. "They don't weigh hardly anything."

"I thought you were too old for your stuffies," her dad said.

"I changed my mind."

"But baby," said her dad, kneeling down to eye level, which was his new way of being convincing. "They take up so much space."

"Not Snorax, he's tiny."

"Okay, baby, you can bring Snorax."

"What about Stitch?"

"Of course, Stitch," he said, patting her head, and folding her into an embrace. "Stitch is family."

"I don't wanna leave all my toys," she said. "You get to bring a whole bunch of stuff, all those books, and tools, and flashlights, and all I get is one crummy backpack."

"I brought other stuff," he said. "I brought some LEGOs, and your Hello Kitties."

"But not their house," she said.

"Baby, it's way too big to haul up there."

"They won't have anywhere to live," she said. "Just like us."

"Baby, everything will be safe at Nana's, I promise. You can play with it when we come to town."

"Why can't we just leave it in my room?"

Her dad fell silent, freeing her from his embrace to hold her at arm's length and look her steadily in the eye.

"We're not gonna have this house anymore, baby. You know that."

"Why?"

"Because we're not."

And that, as far as Bella could tell, was the logic of adults. They didn't need a reason, or at least they didn't need to give you one.

"But it's not fair," she said.

He pulled her into another hug, squeezing her tight.

"I know it's not fair, baby, I'm sorry," he said.

Life was never fair. That's what it meant to be seven years old. You never got to make up your own mind. People dragged you on errands, or passed you off to somebody else to watch. You were a responsibility. You lived by their clock and adhered to their plans and ideas. They made you eat things you didn't like. They made you go to sleep early and miss all the action. They talked about you like you weren't even there. Your whole life was following orders and eating cottage cheese. Then your mother died, and everything around you unraveled so fast that you began to miss taking orders. Your dad, he disappeared. He walked around like a zombie. Except on those occasions when he turned to jelly, and he held you close, desperately, it seemed, and he squeezed you so hard you could hardly breathe. And he sobbed and sobbed, and you could feel his tears running hot down the collar of your blouse and feel them drying on your back.

"I love you so much, baby," he would say with a croaky voice.

"I love you, Daddy," she would say.

And as badly as she wanted to be strong on those occasions, she could not control her own grief, and she began to sob, too, until both of them were just a big unraveled mess, and there was nobody left to comfort anybody. There was only the two of them, broken and confused.

A Hole in the Sky

Bella could hear her mom's voice, which was how she knew she couldn't really be dead. As long as she could hear her mom's voice, she must be alive somewhere. She must have just run off like she threatened to do at least five times when she thought Bella wasn't listening.

On Bella's last night in the nearly empty house, while her dad was still packing, and checking, and double-checking, and quadruple-checking his pack, Bella lay on her bed alone in her soon-to-be old bedroom, pretending her mom was in bed beside her, like she always used to be right before lights out. That's when she told Bella stories about Raven, and Xa:ls, and Chichel Siya:m. About the old basket woman, and how she stole children, and may or may not have eaten them. About Kulshan and his two wives. About Crow and her son and her daughter. About fair Mouse and ugly Beaver. About how Salmon freed the rivers and saved the world.

"Tell me again, Mommy, about The Time Before Everything Changed," said Bella.

"That's before Salmon freed the rivers, when all the Salish Sea was just ice, as far as the eye could see."

"But there were mountains."

"Yes, these same mountains."

"And there were giants," said Bella.

"Yes, there were giants who walked among the people; fanged beasts that stalked the people by day and haunted their dreams at night. And there were giants who fed the people and clothed them, too: the bison, and the mammoth. But there was no Raven, no Coyote, no Salmon in The Time Before Everything Changed. There was only the Great Provider, who, in her fickleness and cruelty, had banished the people to live on the ice with fire as their only friend."

"The Great Provider was a 'her'?"

"Of course she was," said her mom.

"What were the people called?" Bella said. "Were they Nooksack?"

"The people didn't have a name for themselves, then. They were just the people. And for thousands of years the people lived in the frozen world, hunting the bison and the mammoth. It was a hard life, but they survived."

"Then everything changed," said Bella.

"Yes, the whole world as they knew it began to change. First, the giants began to quarrel amongst themselves, and soon their numbers began to dwindle. Until one day, the giants disappeared without a trace. The people had never lived without the giants. They felt betrayed by the Great Provider. They had grown tired of her cruel and fickle ways. What had the people done to deserve this suffering? It wasn't enough that the Great Provider had marooned them in a frozen wasteland, then she stole the mammoth and the bison from them and left them to starve."

"Did the people die?" said Bella.

"Some of them, yes," said her mom. "But the people that lived, they got together and decided to defy the Great Provider. If you will not provide for us, we will provide for ourselves, they said. We will find a new paradise. So, early one morning when the Great Provider was still sleeping, the people rose, and crept quietly across the ice, and tore a hole in the sky with their spears. And then they passed through the hole in the sky, looking for a new home on the other side."

"Did they find it?"

But her mom didn't answer.

"Mommy, did they find it?"

But Mommy was no longer next to her.

"Who are you talking to in there?" called her dad from down the hallway.

"Nobody," said Bella.

The Only Hospitable Place

If there was one place in Vigilante Falls that Dave would ever miss, it had to be Dale's Diner, a fixture in V-Falls for years before Dave was born. As a kid, his mom waitressed at Dale's. She'd come home at night with her smock smeared with ketchup, bringing cold burgers and soggy fries. In high school, Dave and his linemen would crowd into a booth in the evenings after practice, gorging themselves on two-dollar sides of hash browns and toast. They'd loiter for hours, poring over the playbook, drinking Pepsi, and generally horsing around. Even in his waning days with Terminix, Dave ate breakfast at Dale's at least once a week.

The polished fir countertops had lost their luster over the years, and gone to splinter and tarnish. The vinyl seats had lost their springiness, and the grease-stained wallpaper was as brittle as old parchment. But the storied past abided at Dale's, the rugged spirit of V-Falls abounded on the walls in black and white photos depicting extravagantly mustachioed men, mud-plastered and grinning, straddling big timber, or squatting on massive stumps; giant crosscut saws, and axes in their clutches. The menu too was a survivor of a bygone era. Dale was still serving chipped beef and chicken à la king and shrimp puffs and cottage cheese with canned pineapple.

But like most V-Fallers, Dave mostly only went to Dale's for breakfast, and this was sure to be the last time. Travers had been waiting for him with a cup of coffee when Dave arrived with his loaded pack and oversized cat carrier, Bella in tow. A stranger would have never taken them for brothers: Dave, lean and hard in blue jeans and checkered flannel shirt, a week's growth of beard blanketing his angular face, and Travers, soft around the middle, dressed in a khaki suit of western cut, an outsized, black suede cowboy hat, and boots that had never been within two hundred yards of horse manure. No doubt he had a wallet full of business cards in his jacket pocket, and a phone full of contacts.

It was shortly after the rush. Darla, her unruly black hair wrestled into a defiant bun at the back of her head, still wearing that wrist brace on account of her tendinitis, seated them in an ancient orange-and-umber booth by the window, overlooking the muddy parking lot.

"I'll warn you, the shop's a little crowded," said Dave. "And the ventilation isn't great, so you're best off leaving the bay door open if you plan on working in there."

"This is dang crazy," said Travers. "This is not how things are supposed to go. Everybody understands what you've been through, Dave, but c'mon."

"Do they?"

"You know what I mean," says Travers. "Things feel upside down, right now, they must. I can't even imagine what you're going through. So, why not take a break? Go camping for a few days. Take my fifth wheel, drive to the dang Grand Canyon if you need. But this is not right, what you're planning here, Dave."

Dave looked down at Bella, gripping her crayon a little too firmly as she decorated her children's menu with waxy swirls of black and blue. Like bruises, thought Dave.

He slid the house key, the truck key, and the keys to the shop across the table to Travers.

"You'd be wise to sell off the tools. Otherwise, they'll just liquidate them when they come for the house."

Travers stirred two packets of Sweet'N Low into his black coffee.

"This ain't over, yet, Dave. You can still save this."

"Save what?"

"Save your house. Save yourself. Save Bella. You're just not thinking straight, that's all. It doesn't make a goddang bit of sense what you're planning here. You two will freeze to death up there before winter."

"The hell we will."

Travers sipped his coffee and shook his head woefully.

"Why, Dave? Why can't you just grieve like a normal person? Get drunk, cry, sleep all day, eat a whole cake, and go make an ass of yourself down at Doc's?"

"Travers," he said. "We're dying, can't you see that? It's not just Nadene; it's the whole world. We've gone past the tipping point. We're too far gone, little brother."

"Nothing is gone, Dave. We're sitting right here at Dale's like always, drinking weak coffee, and wondering if Darla's ever gonna pluck that hair on her upper lip."

"You'd be wise to hunker down yourself, Travers. Maybe start preparing for you and Kris and Bonnie."

"Dave, you just sound paranoid. And what can I do if the world ends? How is living in the goddang mountains gonna save you?"

Dave looked down at the tabletop and drew a long breath through his nose.

"This isn't just about saving me, Travers. They already got to me."

"Then what the hell *is* this all about?"

"The truth is, I don't know exactly," said Dave.

"Well dang, Dave, maybe you ought to know the answer to that one. Otherwise, what the heck's the good in walking off into the wilderness with a seven-year-old girl?"

"She's almost eight."

"Damnit, why don't you leave her at Mom's, or with Kris and me? Why are you set on doing this?"

"I want to go, Uncle Trav," Bella said.

"She's my daughter," Dave said. "You understand? I want her to have a good life: a true life, a pure life. There's nothing left for her here. Nothing but sickness, and greed, and useless outrage."

Travers pushed the keys back across the table. "That's not true, Dave. There's a lot more than that."

"Like what?" said Dave. "Deals to be made? Hills to be bulldozed?"

"Well, now," said Travers. "I don't see where you get off begrudging a man supporting his family. Not everybody wants to live in a cave. Look, I know things look bad right now, but they're bouncing back, they are. The economy is recovering already. Eventually, you'll be able to see past Nadene. Pretty soon, things will be better than ever."

"Keep telling yourself that," said Dave. "That maniac is gonna kill us all. Maybe what you ought to do is start preparing for certain eventualities."

"Eventualities?" Travers ran a hand through his hair wearily. "What are we even talking about here, Dave? I'm sorry about how things have worked out, I am. We all are. But none of this is forever."

Dave took hold of the saltshaker and gripped it tightly, rolling it with his thumb along his palm to his fingertips. He looked briefly at Bella, greasy-haired, nails bitten to the quick, worrying her bottom lip with her front teeth, green eyes piercing the page as she worked her black crayon savagely in circles. A brief but unruly throng of guilt crowded in on Dave, but he chased it away before it could take over.

"Dave, it ain't no place up there for a little girl."

"I told you, Uncle Trav, I wanna go," she said.

"Well, Trav, it ain't no place down here, either," said Dave.

Still gripping the saltshaker, Dave looked out the window, across the empty lot, riddled with potholes and food wrappers. He looked out beyond Highway 20, past the veterinarian's office, past the video store, now vacant and shuttered, past the dingy Chevron, and the little gem shop that was hardly ever open, past The Golden Dragon Chinese restaurant where Nadene got food poisoning, and Dave left his wallet. Farther still, Dave gazed over the wooded bottomlands, beyond the bulwark of checkered green foothills, beyond the power lines, and cell towers, and housing developments, and past his brother's vacant plats spreading rash-like into the wilderness. And farther still, Dave gazed into the open maw of the great, rock-studded canyon, rising precipitously to the pinnacles of the North Cascades. And it seemed to Dave that it was the only hospitable place left in the world.

Home

Trudging across the highway, Dave and Bella jumped the guardrail just past mile marker 62 and ventured into the wilderness; Dave loaded for the final time to the tune of eighty pounds, pulling Bella along by the wrist as she clutched her dirty Snorax to her chest. In his other hand, Dave balanced the bulky cat carrier with Betty inside, the three-year-old foundling, black as oil, and fit-to-burst with her first litter.

After a mile or so, Dave's hip finally warmed up, and stopped aching, and he was moving well, despite all the extra weight. Bella managed a steady pace through the densely wooded bottomlands, though not without Dave's constant persuasion. He distracted her with games, I Spy, and Pick A Number, and I'm Thinking Of. When that didn't work, he finessed her along with promises of magnificent things to come: waterfalls, and deep crevasses. Finally, when promises of grandeur no longer sufficed, Dave resorted to threats.

"You want to get eaten by a bear?" he said. "Have at it. Betty and me are moving on. Remember to play dead if he gets hold of you."

That one was good for about a mile. But eventually, even the possibility of being eaten alive was not enough. Around mile four, still a mile from the mouth of the canyon, Bella quit on him; she sat on the ground sulking, refusing to go another step.

"Aw, honey, c'mon, now," he said. "I know you're tired. But we're almost there."

She clutched her chin and hung her head in silence.

"Baby, we gotta keep moving."

After five minutes of this, Dave finally reversed his tact, and kneeled down beside her, setting down the cat carrier, and unburdening himself of the pack.

"Sweetie," he said. "I'm sorry Daddy's making you walk this far. It doesn't seem fair. But we have to."

Tilting her chin up, Dave saw that her little green eyes were filled with tears.

"Aw, honey, I'm sorry," said Dave

"I don't want to go any farther," she said. "Why can't it just be here? Why does it even matter?"

"We're almost there," he lied.

"Then, why do we have to hurry?"

Dave wrapped her in his arms and hugged her until he could feel her little heart beating behind her ribcage like a scared rabbit.

"Sweetie, look at me."

He held her at arm's length and looked her in the eyes.

"Do you want me to take you back? If you really want to go back, I'll take you, right now."

"No," she said emphatically.

"Do you want to stay with Daddy?"

She pursed her lips and nodded.

"You want to stay with Betty and her kittens?"

She nodded again.

"Then we gotta keep moving, sweetie. Just for a little while longer, I promise."

Dave was grateful when, a quarter mile later, a big orange Tomcat picked up their trail and started following them, much to Bella's delight, and Betty's unease. What the cat was doing out there, two miles from the nearest house, was anybody's guess, but it was clear after a mile or so that the Tom had chosen them with a devotion Dave could not question.

"Can we keep him?"

"I'm not sure we have a choice, baby."

By the time they entered the craggy jaw of the canyon a half-hour later, Bella was already smitten with the big orange cat, whom she named Tito.

You see, Dave told himself—already we're making connections, already our lives are getting fuller. The orange cat was like a sign, his sudden presence and apparent devotion was an assurance that everything was as it ought to be.

Through the broad canyon they passed along the broken trail, still patchy with snow, until the steep, wooded walls closed in around them. Tito pulled up the rear, darting in and out of the ferns and salal, occasionally falling back out of sight, only to hurry forward again in bursts, a repeating cycle that kept Bella occupied for miles.

In a sunny meadow near the south end of the canyon, they stopped for lunch, in the shadows of the broad-shouldered foothills. In a few short hours, they had already achieved a degree of remoteness. Bella soon fell asleep against Dave's leg, clutching her peanut butter sandwich. Dave leaned back against a big fir and tried with little success to empty his cluttered mind.

Tito slunk around the perimeter, inching closer to Dave and the carrier by the minute, until he was within two feet of Dave, resting tentatively on his haunches.

"What?" said Dave.

The cat tilted its big, orange head, kneading the ground with its forepaws.

"You might want to re-think your plan, buddy. Bound to be a hard life up there for the likes of you."

Tito took this as a cue to move in closer and was soon pressing his side firmly up against Dave's thigh, executing a half circle, his tail parading proudly behind him.

"You have no idea what you're getting into, cat," said Dave. "You didn't think this out."

It was as though Dave was talking to himself.

Dave let Bella sleep for an hour or more, knowing there would still be ample light to reach the bluff, and knowing too, that the sleep would serve her well going forward. Fiercely, she slept, mouth slightly open, her fingers creating a permanent impression in the soggy wheat bread of her sandwich.

Having ingratiated himself to Dave, the orange Tom turned his attention earnestly to poor, pregnant Betty, tucked deep in the carrier, pressing himself firmly against the side of it, his swishing tail aloft.

"Cat, you're even dumber than I thought," said Dave.

When he reached out to pet the Tom, the cat backed off warily, out of arm's length.

A half-hour later, Bella awoke, rested, but slightly confused.

"Are we there?"

"Not quite, sweetie."

With some effort Dave managed to rouse Bella back into action, and they plodded on through the walled corridor toward the high country. The butt of the canyon proved as ever a steep and grueling affair, with Dave making two trips at every juncture; first to convey the supplies, fifty and a hundred yards at a time, then doubling back for Bella, who never left his sight.

Midway up the south face, they arrived at a wide, bald escarpment, the site of a recent slide, which scarred the mountainside for several hundred feet vertically. Here, Dave was forced to carry Bella up and over the loose gravel, his feet scrambling for purchase.

"My God, you're getting heavy," he said, grunting.

Finally, in the late afternoon, with Dave carrying Bella the final leg, Betty mewling urgently from within her hold, and Tito following at a distance of forty feet with relative ease, a pale but determined sun beating down on them from the west, they crested the wide saddle, still covered with snow.

From this perch, now familiar to Dave, but new to Bella, the whole of the alpine wilderness lay seemingly within their grasp. The saw-toothed pickets marooned in ice, the wedge-shaped valleys awash in shadows, and the plunging canyon below, the river snaking through it, until the rock gave way to the sprawling forests to the north.

"We're home, sweetie," he said.

But Bella was already fast asleep again.

S'tka

S'tka's earliest memories were of warmth and security. Swaddled in hides, eyes wide, she peeked out at the great, white world from the shelter of her mother's arms. What anxiety she knew was immediate and lingered only so long as she remained outside the reach of her mother. At night, bathed in the flicker of the flames, hushed voices washing over her, the icy wind moaning in the darkened hinterlands, her thoughts arrived formless and fluid, radiant, like the warmth of the fire.

All she knew for certain, all she could grasp that had shape and meaning, was that this was where she belonged. This was home. The mountains, huddled together against the chill, the mountains, with their wooded folds, and craggy seams were home to the people, a sanctuary from the frigid wind that swept across the sea of ice, a refuge from the beasts of the lowlands, a retreat from the cold, flat realities of the outside world. Like her mother's persistent clutch, like the ever-warming flame, the shelter of the mountains was eternal.

Young S'tka and her people lived by the promise of the eternal. Even when they didn't thrive—which, through the long, lean seasons of bitterness and ice, of, privation and peril, was more often than not—they clung to the notion of a benevolent design. The Great Provider, she who created the world and everything in it—though she tested their will frequently, pushing them to the edge of starvation with cruel regularity, when she wasn't freezing, goring, trampling, or infecting them to death—would not forsake the people. For this was The Time Before Everything Changed.

Thus the people believed that they belonged there, that they did not come to this place from elsewhere, nor were they prisoners on this ice. They were survivors, now and forever.

But the icy world was not an agreeable host, far from it, and not everyone survived it. If the bloodthirsty beasts of the wilderness were not enough, if the relentless exposure to the ravaging elements, the ever-lurking shadow of sickness, nor the unwelcome visitations of the hostile clans from the south were not enough to seal their fates, there was the land itself: violent, unpredictable, and ever-changing.

The spring of S'tka's seventh cycle, while lagging well behind the women as they foraged upon a grassy hillside just below the snowline, everything changed. It began as an angry rumbling that rose up from the center of the world, a thunderous report so loud that it seemed to envelop everything. S'tka glanced up just in time to greet a frigid blast of wind rushing down the mountain, pelting her face with granular ice. And in its wake came a terrible wall of white that rolled up the forest in front of it like a mat of reeds, engulfing everything in its path.

"E'ma!" she shouted. "E'ma!"

But S'tka could scarcely hear her own voice above the roar of the collapsing mountainside as it tumbled over the rock, churning the trees to splinter, and cleaving the mountain practically in half. In a terrible instant, S'tka watched as the torrent of filthy snow swallowed her mother and the others whole.

"E'ma," she whimpered.

And then, like frozen rain upon the ice, there came a hiss, which seemed to last an eternity before finally relenting, followed by an awful stillness that took hold of everything. And there came a silence like no other, a silence so complete that even the world, and the sky, and everything in it were small by comparison.

Honey, I Can't

Flat on his back, Dave stared dully up at the wash of stars, ears ringing, face burnt to a crisp, desert air ravaging his sinuses and clawing at the back of his throat.

What the fuck just happened? Where is everybody? What am I doing on my back?

The questions circled the inside of his skull like dazed houseflies.

Think, Dave, think.

One second they were at the head of a convoy barreling hell-bent through the desert of Al-Qa'im, adrenals pumping, senses tingling. Smitty was moving his lips silently in prayer. Baxter was gripping his rifle fiercely, sweating like a boxer, as the desert night blurred past.

The next thing Dave knew, he was on the ground, his teeth mired in the grit of sand. Numb from the shock, he couldn't tell whether he was hit.

He tried to call out to Barlow, but blood pooled in the back of his throat. Dave's heart was starting to pick up speed. Feeling was creeping back into his hands.

Breathe, Dave, fucking breathe. Stay calm, man, let the world come back into focus.

Every ten or fifteen seconds the sky flashed red, just long enough to see the tendrils of smoke wafting east, away from the city, quickly followed by a string of percussive thuds, reverberating as though from deep in the earth. Through the ringing of his ears he could hear the ragged cries of those he assumed to be his brothers. But how far off? A hundred feet? Thirty feet?

Is that Baxter? Smitty?

"Duane," he tried to call out, but it was a garbled and breathless effort, as the blood again caught in the back of his throat.

He grit his teeth with a crunching of sand. Bit by bit, he swallowed the blood, as the sky flashed hellish red, and the mortar blasts thrummed like drumrolls in his chest.

He could feel most of his body, eventually. The mental fog began to lift. He clenched a fist and swallowed some more blood. It was time to move. Time to sort shit out. Time to throw his life back into peril and help his brothers.

So why couldn't he move? Why was he stuck on his back in the damn sand like a capsized tortoise?

"Daddy," Bella said with breathless urgency from outside his dream. "Daddy!"

Dave bolted upright, and drew a shallow breath, appraising the cool, musty darkness as he surveyed the cavernous space, broken only by the weak light of dawn puddled at the entrance.

"Daddy, wake up."

"What is it?"

"Betty. She's sick. I think she's dying, Daddy."

Dave's heart contracted like a fist. Groping in the darkness, he located the lantern and lit the pilot, summoning the shadows, which sprung to life like genies on the stone wall. In the glow of the waltzing flame, Dave and Bella arrived hunched at the carrier in the corner, squatting to peer in at Betty's dark figure, as she wheeled restlessly within, mewling in a pinched and urgent manner.

"It's okay, Betty," said Dave. "Just do what your body tells you."

Raising her hackles, Betty arched her back then mewled again, pushing the length of her body forcefully up against the wall of the carrier.

"Daddy," said Bella. "What's happening?"

"Sshh, baby," he said. "It's okay."

Betty slid onto her side, where she spread her hind legs and licked irritably below her abdomen.

"Why is she doing that, Daddy? What's wrong?"

"She's preparing."

As he said it, Betty loosed an uneasy squall.

"Help her, Daddy."

"Honey, I can't."

Betty yowled again on cue, then positioned herself on her back. And just like that, it began. A few more fervid licks between the hind legs, one last miserable mew, and the first kitten crowned, emerging moments later, pink and writhing and impossibly tiny from between Betty's splayed haunches, cord and placenta attached.

"Daddy," said Bella, after a moment. "Why is she eating it?"

"It's not what you think, honey. C'mon," said Dave, rising. "Let's give Betty some space."

"Is she going to die?" said Bella.

"No," said Dave.

"Are the kitties going to die?"

"No," said Dave. "Betty will take care of her kitties."

"What about us?" she said, as Dave led her from the cave into the pale light of the new day. "Who's going to take care of us?"

"We're gonna take care of ourselves, baby."

Actually it was not that Dave couldn't move, it was not that he was physically paralyzed, though he could feel he was hit in the hip, but that wasn't holding him back. The will to move had simply left him. He could feel his whole body, it just refused to move. Just this once, his body had decided it was not going to move. It was not going to do what was expected of it, it was not going to fulfill its duty. He was going to lay right fucking there in the desert, and he was going to close his eyes, and he was going to blot out the miserable cries. Even through the hood of his eyelids he could see the sky flashing crimson, as the mortars drummed in his chest. But goddammit, he was not going to move. He didn't care if he died. But in the end, whether it was his training, or his conscience, he moved mechanically to the aid of his brothers.

Now, a purple heart and over a decade later, Dave was ready to live again, if only for Bella. With expert efficiency, he built a small cooking fire out on the bluff and set a pan of water to boiling. He'd stockpiled over thirty gallons of fresh water from the creek in the weeks leading up to the final transition, four and five gallons at a time, up the steep wooded bank, and through the little glen, then up again the crumbling hillside to the plateau.

Twenty minutes after the coals flattened out, Dave and Bella were eating oatmeal with raisins around the windswept fire.

"Why this place again, Daddy?" she said.

Every day, she reminded Dave more of a young Nadene, with those absorbent green eyes.

"Well, for starters, we have to name all these mountains," he said, encompassing them with a sweep of his spoon.

"The sort of pointy one is Mt. Kiss," she said of Phantom. "Because it looks like a white chocolate Kiss."

"What about the fat one?"

"Hmm, let's see," she said, scrunching her nose.

Soon she'd named them all, though Dave knew there was a good chance she wouldn't remember most of the names the next day, which was good news, because she could name them again.

When they returned to the cave to monitor Betty's progress, they found her recumbent in the rear of the carrier, anxious and alert, engulfed by an indeterminate mass of kittens, all jostling for position at her deflated belly; the pink one, practically hairless, two or three gray ones, one orange, two, possibly three black.

"Ooooh, look, Daddy," said Bella. "Can I pet one?"

"They're not ready," he said.

"Why?"

"They're too young, honey. They need more time with their mommy."

"But Daddy, I want to pet one, they're so cute."

"Soon, Bella."

"But Daddy."

Bella spent most of the day in the cave by candlelight, watching Betty groom and feed her litter. Over and over, Dave reminded her to give them space, not to touch them, not to alarm Betty, who seemed somewhat distressed by Bella's constant attention, or maybe it was the big orange Tom, never far off, who was putting her on edge.

Meanwhile, Dave busied himself around camp; stowing the last of the supplies and staking out a small garden on the plateau. At midday, he paused in his labor to coax Bella away from the cats, into the light of afternoon, where he revived the cooking fire, added water to the leftover oats, and reheated them.

"We already had this," says Bella.

"You liked it this morning."

"That's because it's breakfast."

"Touché," said Dave. "How about this, how about for dinner we have something different?"

"Like what?"

"How about kitty?"

"Ew. Daddy, gross!"

In the afternoon, Bella watched from a stony perch as Dave split wood. He set, swung, split, and tossed like a machine, outrunning his thoughts until the wood was piled three feet high. Together, they stacked the quarters neatly beneath the natural overhang at the mouth of the cave. When they had completed that task, they rang the fire pit with stones.

"Not too close," he said. "They get too hot and they can explode."

The constant engagement, the clear and urgent sense of purpose these tasks provided Dave were a blessing. This was what control felt like. Here,

Dave knew what outside forces were at work, and what perils were lying in wait. Weather, and famine, the kind of forces Dave could prepare for, and protect against. Not like the forces they'd left behind; those political and financial and social and emotional forces that conspired against them daily.

By the fire, Bella sat rapt late into the evening, green eyes aglow, reflecting the flames, as Dave told her of the forces that shaped these mountains, of the glaciers and volcanoes, and the mighty sheet of ice, a mile thick, that once covered the region farther than the eye could see.

"It looked like the north pole," she said.

"Yeah," he said. "I guess it probably did—if you mean white and frozen and flat."

"It wasn't all flat," she said. "There were mountains. And it was colder than now."

"Much colder," he said.

"There were people."

"Yes, there were."

"They looked different, but they were pretty much like us," she said.

"It's true," he said. "They had the same brain as us, the same capacities."

"What's 'cacapities'?"

"Capacities means they could do the things we can do; problem solve like us and also think abstractly."

"What's 'abstrackely'?"

"It means thinking about things that don't exist physically. Like ideas, or stories."

"The people were hunters," she said, matter-of-factly.

"Yes, they were."

"But the girls didn't get to hunt," she said. "The girls took care of the children, and prepared food, and made clothes, and stuff like that. Why do the girls always get the boring jobs?"

"It's a fair question, baby. It's not like that anymore. Especially not for you. You can do anything you want."

"Can I hunt?"

"Of course, and you will hunt, you'll need to hunt out here," he said. "When you're older."

"Aw," she said. "Why do I gotta be older to do anything good?"

Smiling, Dave reached across the fire and mussed her hair.

"That's not true," he said. "Look around. You get to live in the most beautiful place in the world. Look at these mountains all around you."

"Duh," she said. "I can't exactly see them in the dark."

"But you can feel them, can't you?"

"I guess so," she said.

Bella sipped her licorice tea, turning her attention to the glowing coals, her little mind apparently working on something.

She will thrive here, Dave thought. A natural life will offer her all the right challenges to keep her engaged, to keep her spirit connected to all that was wild and wholesome. There were books to be read, adventures to be had, there was all the bounty of nature. What cause for loneliness? They had each other, they had the cats, and they had the town at their disposal when they needed it, which wouldn't be often.

"The people from back then lived in caves," said Bella. "Or shelters dug in the ground."

"Did you learn all this from Mrs. Rundgren?" he said, impressed.

"No," she said. "It's just stuff I know."

"Mmm," he said.

My God, who was this child? If only Dave could summon an ounce of that curiosity, that sense of possibility, or that childlike certainty, he might feel alive again. Where along the line had his child cobbled together such poise? When Dave was seven years old his curiosity revolved mostly around things and experiences he wanted: toys, and video games, and Seahawk jerseys. His knowledge consisted mostly of sports trivia and Spiderman comics. But not Bella; her mind had scope. Her imagination was seemingly boundless. Her facility with language alone was astounding. Think of the potential, in ten and twenty years.

Another pang of guilt prodded Dave at the irrefutable knowledge that he was limiting Bella's possibilities by forcing her to live in exile.

"Daddy, what do you think happened to the ice people?"

"The world changed."

"How did the world change?"

"The climate, mostly," he said sleepily.

"I hope it got warmer for them," she said.

"Eventually, it did."

"Maybe they left," she said. "Maybe they found their paradise behind the hole in the sky. What do you think?"

Dave yawned. "I really couldn't say, baby."

"That's what I think," she said. "But how could there be a hole in the sky?"

"Aw, baby, it's so late, it's time for bed," he said. "We can talk about it more tomorrow."

"Promise?"

"I promise."

"Can you carry me to bed?" she asked.

"You're so dang heavy these days, do I have to?"

"Please, please?"

"Fine," he said with a sigh.

Hefting her fifty pounds, he wrapped her up and held her close. He could barely fathom how big she'd gotten, seemingly overnight. To think only yesterday, Dave could cradle Bella in one arm, a wobbly-headed little tub of adipose, helpless and drooling. Now, look at her: lean and poised, and fully awake to the world.

"Daddy?" she said, as he ducked into the candlelight of the cave.

"Yeah, buddy?"

"Why did the world change?"

"I wish I knew," he said.

Dark All the Time

Living in a cave wasn't so bad, really, once you got used to the low ceilings and the hard, lumpy floors, not to mention the fact that it was dark all the time, and the space was so crowded with supplies you couldn't do a somersault if you wanted to.

Her dad was always busy those early days, which left Bella to herself a good deal of the time. Sometimes she read by the fire. Not her old favorites so much, but books her dad brought along about geology, and weather, and survival in the wilderness. Not that she understood a lot of what she read. There were words she couldn't even begin to pronounce, words whose meaning she could hardly guess at. But there were big words, too, that she was starting to recognize, and Mrs. Rundgren said recognition was the first step in learning a word.

Sometimes she played with her Hello Kitties, who had taken up residence in the woodpile. But somehow Kitty and Mimmy and Pachacco and Dear Daniel and Mr. White didn't speak to her like they once did. Her dad still wouldn't let her play with the real kitties, because he said they were too fragile. Betty didn't want anything to do with her, and Tito wasn't much of a playmate, always coming and going as he was.

Although the impulse to handle the kittens almost got the better of her a few times, Bella contented herself by shining the flashlight into the crowded carrier to watch them wiggle and squirm and suckle at Betty's teats. She wanted so badly to name them all, but as it was, all crowded into the carrier like one big, furry blob, she could hardly tell how many there were. One of them, the one with the white spot on his forepaw, she would call Sugarfoot, she decided, and another one, all black, Boris. She knew her life would feel much fuller once she named them all, and her dad would finally let her play with them.

"How much longer do I have to wait?" she asked him daily.

"Just another week, baby."

"When is that?"

"In seven days."

"I know that. But how many hours?"

"Quite a few, baby. But they'll go quick, I promise."

It was hard to tell how long anything was anymore. Time didn't pass the way it used to in her old life. There was hardly anything to give her days shape; no 6:45 alarm clock, no 7:25 bus pick-up, no first recess, no lunch recess, no final bell, no 2:55 bus drop-off, no waiting for Daddy to get off work, no 6:00 dinner, no thirty minutes of TV, no storytelling with her mom in bed before lights out.

Instead her days were broken up only in the most basic of ways: day or night, asleep or awake, bored or not bored, reading or not reading. In the darkness of the cave, sometimes she couldn't even tell if it was night or day. Sometimes she couldn't tell the difference between awake and dreaming. Sometimes it was like Bella was living outside of herself, or actually more like the outside was living inside of her.

A Very Brief History of the Clan

———

And then there was Ek'lil, who dropped her baby on the ice, and carried it around for many days, refusing to believe it was dead.

And He'pa, who could not see, and did not last long in the world.

There was A'kai, the old man. He went slowly, but none too gracefully; devoured by wolves, as the rest of us fled to safety.

A'kai was surely not the first martyr in the history of our clan. Nor the last.

Then there were Yq'mat, Kt'ak, and Ok'eh, wolves themselves.

There were the elders, Ee'tsa, and O'qu'a, weak-eyed and fading with every moon, a cold, white fate nipping at their heels.

There was the child never named. Many children never named.

There were the sick left behind.

There were stories going back too far to remember, kept alive like sacred flames, out of habit and vulnerability as much as anything else.

They clung to the familiar; they clung to all that they could control.

They buried their dead in the ice, never guessing that their bones would be scattered far and wide in some future epoch, to be ground to dust.

S'tka was swollen with baby when the elders decided that the clan would leave the mountains for good. *Destiny* they called it. As if it were some plan hatched from behind the sky, and not the desperate design of shortsighted mortals. The elders assured S'tka and her people that their destiny lay somewhere out of sight, beyond the mountains, and beyond the ice. They told them if they listened, they could hear it on the frozen wind. Oh, how they dazzled with their hyperbole, how they hypnotized the people with their vagaries, all their grand promises of a new home, somewhere unknowable, someplace more kindly and promising beyond the far-flung horizon.

But such delusions were not for S'tka, who dreamed of meat; fresh, pink meat she could sink her aching teeth into, meat that she could gnaw until her jaw was sore. S'tka dreamed of blood dripping down her chin. And a bed made out of something softer than ice. She dreamed of safety and security, and shelter from the cruel elements and bloodthirsty giants of the frozen world, forever vying for her flesh. Safety seemed like a practical purpose given the world they lived in. So why tempt the elements? Why risk the unknown?

In the end, it was not for S'tka to decide. What choice had she but to follow them? And follow them she did, with tiny, hard-won steps, her aching bulge out in front of her, but not before looking back one final time at the mountains that had been her curse and savior.

Signals

———————

Out on the bluff after meals, when the fire was not quite enough to warm them, Dave and Bella found themselves leaning into the transistor radio for warmth. Depending on the atmosphere, the weather, the interference, and which way the antenna was pointed, sometimes they were lucky enough to tune in the lonesome strains of a pedal steel guitar on the classic country station out of Blaine, or maybe some Patsy Cline, singing about the wayward wind, or Ray Price, singing about the glow of city lights.

And how far the city lights seemed from up there on the bluff, surrounded by the enormous cathedral of the North Cascades in all its green and white and gray wonder, not a soul within miles. With some additional tweaking and a little luck, maybe Dave could tune in the chunky chords of a rock ballad out of Vancouver, BC, playing "classic rock from the sixties to the nineties and beyond." Maybe some Thin Lizzy, or some Pink Floyd, or some Pearl Jam.

Feeble though the signal was in the high country, tinny and crackly as the strains sometimes arrived to Dave and Bella's ears, the music was a revelation. A few notes rendered with feeling cut through the frigid air like a heat source. The simple act of humming a chorus went a long way toward thawing the frozen silence, toward shrinking the immense wilderness around them. Dave was forced to wonder why he'd maintained barely any music in his life since he was in high school, back when Weezer and Bush were in heavy rotation on his bedroom boom box, or blaring on the sideline at VFHS, while he ran his morning drills in the dewy grass. Or on the stereo of the '86 Buick Century sedan he inherited from Coach Prentice, with Nadene Charles riding shotgun, their hands intertwined, their unknown futures gleaming pink and golden somewhere beyond the horizon.

Back when his life had a soundtrack.

So, why did the music die? What did it say about Dave, about what his life had become, that in all the endless hours of planning, listing, and anticipating every conceivable human need, it never once occurred to him to bring a guitar up the mountain, or even a harmonica to learn how to play? If ever the opportunity to learn an instrument presented itself to someone, here it was.

But it was more than just the music. Over the course of two decades, Dave had all but given up on his faith, his country, and his marriage. That Bella even existed was practically a miracle.

Sometimes Dave and Bella could tune in a high school basketball game from Bellingham, or a junior hockey game from British Columbia, and Dave got a vicarious thrill, remembering the excitement, the adrenaline, the immediate promise of competition, the triumph, and frustration, and grace of it.

Unfortunately, the easiest signal to access on the transistor seemed to be some form of news. News! Ha! More like propaganda in the post-truth age. What did that even mean, post-truth? Dave had not brought Bella up here to shelter her from the outside world, so much as to avoid the toxicity of it altogether. Though she ought to have had the benefit of his knowledge, he evaded her frequent questioning as long and as far as possible.

"What's a terrorist?" she wanted to know.

Dave's mind went about eight different ways before it arrived at the vaguest destination he could apprehend.

"It's just a label the they like to throw around in the media and politics," he said.

She worked on the information for an instant, knitting her brow.

"I don't understand," she said.

"Aw, honey, it's all so confusing," he said. "It's not even worth explaining. See if you can tune in some music."

"But, Daddy—"

"Just hand me the radio," he said irritably.

"But, Daddy!" she scolded. "It was you who told me I should always ask questions."

Dave sighed. As usual, she had him in a vice.

"Okay, let's see," he said. "A terrorist is somebody who does something violent, or something meant to scare people or intimidate them for the sake of a belief, which is usually religious or political. What a terrorist looks like depends on where you're standing."

"Like how?"

Dave wrung his hands. How to tell his daughter that many would consider him a terrorist, sanctioned by the United Nations to violate a people he knew nothing of, with whom he had no connection or particular disdain for, owing to reasons he was never given to fully understand?

"Well," he said at last. "Like if you're on the side of the person doing the violent act, you wouldn't consider yourself a terrorist. But if somebody was doing something violent to you because of something they believed in, then they would be a terrorist."

"What if you agreed with them?"

"I suppose that happens to some people. A lot of times the violence happens to innocent people, and it doesn't really matter what they believe. I guess in that case, you'd still have to call the person a terrorist."

"Okay, I get it," she said. "You can change the station now."

Gordon "Gordy" Prentice; Football Coach

—————

"**D**ave played varsity as a sophomore, and that's when we started stringing those titles together. It was Jerome Charles who brought Davey to my attention. Kid couldn't have weighed a buck-thirty, but he was tough. Bulked up after his sophomore season, and after that I could literally put Dave Cartwright anywhere on the football field at any given point in the game. Offense, defense, special teams. I could put him at wideout, in the slot, put him in the backfield. Hell, he kicked a couple field goals senior year. On defense, I could put him in the middle, or anywhere in the secondary, for that matter. Not that I did, but I could have. Probably could have put him at nose tackle and he would have held his ground against guys sixty and seventy pounds heavier than him. He was the ultimate Swiss Army knife in terms of matchups. Not because of his size or his athleticism, but because of his will and his field awareness and his football instincts. And on top of all that, he was very coachable.

"Personality-wise, he was damn near unflappable—until he wasn't. You weren't going to get inside Dave Cartwright's head, you weren't going to take him off his game. He kept an even keel. Until he was angry. And look, I'm not gonna lie to you, I liked him angry. It took a long while for him to get there, but when he got there, it was a focused anger. And if you were the unlucky SOB that was the focus of that anger, lookout.

"I'll tell you why the Division One scouts didn't like him—besides the fact that he was 5'9" and played at a 1A school in Nowhere, Washington. They didn't like what Dave Cartwright couldn't do. Dave Cartwright couldn't run a four-four forty, but he got good jumps, and he had great closing speed. He couldn't jump three feet in the air. He didn't have thirty-two-inch arms or ten-inch hands. What the scouts missed out on was that Cartwright had all of the intangibles, all the immeasurables, all the white-hot passion, and awareness, and instincts, and the will to play at any level.

"It breaks my heart the way things went—I mean with him not pursuing junior college. His pride caught up to him, that's part of it. If UW or Oregon had come calling, I'm betting everything would have ended differently. He never would have gone to Iraq. But when Dave Cartwright got something in his head, nobody was going to stop him."

Barely a Sniff

Twenty-seven rushing touchdowns senior year. Twelve more through the air. Nearly three thousand all-purpose yards, not to mention over a hundred and twenty tackles and three interceptions at linebacker. First team all-league, second team all-state. Three consecutive 1A state titles. Two undefeated seasons. 3.4 GPA. Yet, barely a sniff from the recruiters, Division One or Two. Only three contacts senior season, and one visit (unofficial) from Coach Childress at Missouri S&T, a school that wasn't even on Dave's radar until the night Coach Childress showed up.

Coach Childress happened to be in Everett for a funeral, which was probably the only reason he drove the sixty miles to V-Falls to watch the Vigilantes destroy Lundgren.

It wasn't hard spotting Childress beneath the bill of his Miners cap, standing at the chain link fence, the lone black visage amidst the two hundred or so people gathered that Friday evening under the lights to see their undefeated Vigilantes have their way with the lowly Tigers. Dave could feel Childress's eyes on him for most of seventy-five snaps.

Despite the weak competition, Dave did his best to impress. He ran for a pair of TDs, caught another, made a dozen or so tackles, and almost picked off a couple of balls in coverage.

After the game, Coach Childress, bald beneath his green Miners cap, a fit and toned fifty-five, the slightest shadow of salt and pepper beard, a half-foot taller and fifteen years younger than Coach Prentice, caught up to Dave in the parking lot after the game.

"Mr. Cartwright," he said, catching Dave's attention.

"Oh, hey, hi," said Dave.

Childress extended a sturdy hand. "You looked really comfortable in coverage," he said. "Especially on that third and three, midway through the third quarter—you showed good instincts."

"Thanks," said Dave.

"Or maybe it was just a lucky guess."

"No, sir."

"How'd you know to drop back into coverage, then?"

"His eyes," said Dave.

"Whose eyes?"

"The quarterback, Fulton. He telegraphed it—didn't even check-down to the right side. It was obvious he was looking for the tight end in the seam."

"You could see over those linemen?"

"Yessir."

"How tall are you, anyway?" he said, looking down on Dave.

"5'11"," Dave lied, wishing he were still in cleats.

"You still growing?"

"Yessir."

"Well, that's good," he said. "You've got good vision. You ever play any free safety?"

"No, sir."

"At your size, you ought to take some reps there. Think you're fast enough to cover that much ground?"

"Yessir, I do. But in my opinion, it's not just about straight-line speed, sir. In the backfield, it's that first step that's most important, that break. Anticipating and committing to your target."

"Oh?" said coach Childress, genuinely delighted. "And how do you do that?"

"Mostly I watch, sir, and I listen, and I get to know the schemes, and the route trees, and the spreads at the line of scrimmage and so forth. Then I look for tendencies."

Coach Childress smiled. "Student of the game, I like that."

"Thank you, sir."

"What's the biggest crowd you ever played for?"

"I couldn't say, sir."

"Eight thousand?"

"No, sir," said Dave. "Not even close to that."

"That's what Allgood-Bailey holds. Phelps County loves their Miners, let me tell you. Ever spent any time in Missouri?"

"No, sir."

"Beautiful," he said. "God's country."

"I'd like to see it, sir," said Dave.

And Dave wasn't lying, not even a little. From that moment in the parking lot forward, he'd just as soon have seen Phelps County as Palo Alto or Berkeley. Never mind that he'd never heard of Phelps County or Rolla, Missouri, before that night. He was already in love with them.

Dave could hardly sleep that night. After meeting Coach Childress, Dave was ready to commit, Pac-10, Big Ten, and SEC be damned. All Dave needed was a chance to prove himself on a bigger stage, and to that end, playing for Coach Childress at Missouri S&T seemed like his deliverance. Dave was okay with being undersized. He'd always anticipated being the underdog at the next level. He understood that Vigilante Falls was a small place, that there were ten thousand bigger places out there in America, with bigger and faster guys than him, that played in tougher leagues, against stiffer competition. But Dave also understood that on a football field he had the ability to see things happen before they actually happened, and he possessed that rare ability to slow the game down. He also knew that he hated losing, and that those two qualities in tandem could make for something special, just as Coach Prentice had always taught him.

But neither Coach Childress nor anyone else at Missouri S&T ever followed up with Dave. Looking back, that was the first domino to fall. It was tempting to curse the universe for making him 5'9", or for consigning his origins to the little backwater of V-Falls, where he could never distinguish himself to the larger world against "real competition." But Dave never once cursed his fate, or his humble beginnings, for they were who he was, the forces that put the fire in his belly and the chip on his shoulder. Even after walking away from football, Dave felt lucky for having enjoyed the privilege of strapping on those pads, and excelling at the thing he loved to do more than anything in the world: to lose himself and find himself all at once, to know his role, and surrender himself to the larger cause, and, most importantly, to engage fully in the act of play, to embrace the concept of winning in a world that was mostly about losing. And to do it all in front of most everyone he'd ever known or loved, how could he consider himself anything but lucky? To make his people proud, to gratefully accept their adoration, even their financial contributions, to absorb their hopes vicariously, it was never anything to be taken for granted. No, it was something to accept gracefully, like his mom taught him, whether on the sidelines, in the hallway, or in the supermarket.

Even through the quiet, unsure days of summer, when the calls and the letters didn't come from colleges far or near, Dave knew he was lucky. Not that he wasn't worried sick about his future. Not that the panic didn't keep him up most nights. Not that he had any idea what he'd do with his life if opportunity never came knocking. Dave did his best to hide this anxiety from his mom and his little brother and Nadene, and her brother, Jerry, and Dave's friends and teammates and boosters, and pretty much everybody but Coach Prentice.

Coach Prentice was a rock through the dark days. Dave called him almost nightly through summer, even as the window was closing.

"Still nothing from Coach Childress?"

"Nothing new, I'm afraid. But this ain't over, Dave."

"It feels over," said Dave.

"That's no way to talk, boy."

"Coach, I appreciate all you've done for me."

"Well, I'm not done yet."

But that's where the winning ended. Coach Prentice may have been the last person to ever believe in Dave. Then came fall, that dreadful, unimaginable season of dying light, and Dave, with no plans, still at home with his mom and his little brother, with no foreseeable future in Rolla, Missouri, or anywhere else. Not even in V-Falls, not so much as a job at the Texaco, or Vern's, or washing dishes at Dale's.

Coach "Gordy" Prentice

———

"I guess you could say I took on Davey's collegiate prospects as a personal crusade. Hell, he was the most talented and coachable kid I'd had in eighteen years of coaching. That boy was a coach's dream. Not only was he willing to do anything you asked him to, on or off the field, he was good at all of it. You didn't have to tell him a thing but once, and he never made the same mistake twice. And he was always accountable, always taking responsibility for the team. No offense to Nate Tatterson, who wasn't a bad quarterback, but Dave was the unquestioned leader of that team.

"So, I kept putting in the calls: Boise State, Eastern Oregon, Tulsa. I wrote letters. I raved about Davey's motor. I told them over and over, ignore the measurables, this kid is 5'9" going on seven feet. Look at the tape, I told them. Look at the awareness and the instincts. He's got all the intangibles, I told them, all the qualities of a winner.

"Damnit, it's all my fault. I should have had him transfer to Hale after sophomore year. He could've lived with my sister in Lake City. Probably could have found plenty of folks to sponsor him. Then, we wouldn't have had to hear all that 'quality of opponent' baloney—never mind that we beat 'em all 46–3.

"But I was too damn worried about my own legacy. I let Davey down, and all these years later, I can't say how sorry I am about that."

Grander Things

Even before the fifty-five-minute drive, a sense of significance had attached itself to the recruitment meeting in Bellingham; a formality. This was bigger than football. This was about the rest of Dave's life. The moment he walked through the glass door, and into the non-descript recruiting center, with its queasy overhead light, he sensed an intensity on the part of the recruiter who, with a slight limp, met him halfway across the foyer. The marine bore a certain respectful gravity epitomized by his dress blues, and his clean-shaven square jaw, which had not gone even the slightest bit jowly in spite of what Dave guessed to be his fifty years.

As Dave sat down opposite the recruiter, Dave once again wished he were in cleats and a helmet.

"Well, let's not beat around the bush," said the recruiter flatly. "What do you have to offer the United States Marine Corps, Mr. Cartwright?"

"Well, sir. That's what I'm here to find out. What I can tell you right off the bat is that I try to excel at whatever I do. And that I always give a hundred and ten percent."

"And why is that?"

"Well, sir, because I feel like I've got a responsibility to try my hardest."

"Was your daddy a marine?"

"No, sir."

Leaning back slightly, the recruiter reposed in his chair, considering Dave through steely gray eyes.

"While we're at it, tell me a little about your daddy," he said.

"Not much I can tell, sir. He left when I was three years old."

"Left who?"

"My mother, and me, and my baby brother, I guess."

"Left where?"

"Just left, sir," said Dave. "In Idaho for a while. I'm not really sure."

"What about you?" said the recruiter. "Do you see yourself providing for children someday?"

"Someday, yes, sir."

"But not right away?"

"No, sir."

"You want to travel first, probably. See the world, accrue some experience, figure out a plan, is that it?"

"Yes, sir. One thing I know is that I'd like to have a game plan in this life, sir."

"And why is that, Mr. Cartwright?"

"I believe in preparation, sir. I think a person ought to mind whatever might possibly be within his or her control, so as to better the chances of success."

"So, you've been preparing yourself to be a marine?"

"Not exactly, sir."

The recruiter considered this information, as though it may or may not be significant.

"Do you have a girlfriend? A wife?" he said.

"A girlfriend," said Dave.

"What's her name?"

"Nadene, sir."

"What does Nadene think about you up and joining the US Marine Corps?"

"To be honest, she doesn't love the idea, sir. But when I explain the long game to her—"

"The long game?"

"Yes, sir, the benefits of enlisting."

"Mm," he said. "The steady paychecks, eh? The reimbursements?"

"Yes, sir."

"You'd like to own a home some day?"

"Absolutely," said Dave.

Once again, the recruiter considered him with steely gray eyes.

"Tell me," he said. "What does the word responsibility mean to you, Mr. Cartwright?"

"Well, generally speaking, sir, it means that you fulfill your commitments."

"And to whom or what are you committed?"

"For starters, my mom, my little brother, Nadene."

"What about your country?"

"Yes, sir, of course."

"And why is that?" said the recruiter, looking him in the eye.

"Because I love America," said Dave.

"Oh?"

"Yes, sir."

"And why do you love America?"

"Because it's the greatest country on Earth, sir. Because in America you can be anything you want to be if you work hard enough."

"Anything?"

"Well, I suppose almost anything," said Dave.

"And how can you serve America in return, Mr. Cartwright?"

"However it asks me to, sir. Whatever my job is, that's what I'll do."

"Mr. Cartwright, can you tell me about a time when you demonstrated leadership?"

"Yes, sir, I can," said Dave, thrilled at the opportunity to talk about the thing he loved most.

"I played football in high school, sir, both sides of the ball. On defense, I played linebacker, sometimes end, depending on the opponent, and how we matched up. Either way, sir, it was my responsibility to set the defense on the fly, to delegate in the event of an audible, or a formation that was unfamiliar. It was up to me to tell the safety to drop back, or cheat in, or tell the linemen what to look for and so forth, based on what I was seeing."

The recruiter looked mildly impressed, nodding his square head twice.

"So, you guessed?"

"Not exactly guessed, sir. It was always an informed decision."

"And what if you were misinformed? What if you decided wrong?"

"Well, sir, then you got beat. And it happened from time to time, but not very often, if you prepared."

The recruiter nodded his head gravely.

"It's an observable truth, Mr. Cartwright," said the recruiter, "that sometimes you just get beat."

"Yes, sir. And when that happens, you learn from it. You don't get caught off guard twice the same way. At least not if you play for Coach Prentice."

"You liked playing for this Coach Prentice?"

"Yes, sir, I loved playing for him."

"And why's that?"

"Well, sir, it wasn't just that he was a great coach, he was a great man."

"Almost like a father," said the recruiter.

"Yes, sir. Now that you put it that way."

The recruiter silently appraised him for a moment.

"So, no football scholarship?"

"No, sir," said Dave, feeling his face color.

"Why not?"

"Well, sir, they're looking for bigger players is what it mostly amounts to."

"If you're not good enough for college football, what makes you think you're good enough to be a marine, son?"

Dave was blushing harder than ever now.

"With all due respect, sir, I believe I have some very good qualities to offer, beyond leadership."

"Like what?"

"Like commitment, sir. And determination. What Coach Prentice calls grit."

"Grit, huh?"

"Yes, sir."

"Well, I suppose that's something," said the recruiter.

In the coming weeks and months, Dave came to know the recruiter as Sergeant Sanderson, with whom he met on four more occasions to talk, and once to work out, and once to play a game with little plastic chits marked by printed words such as "responsibility," and "opportunity," and "travel." But the fact is, Dave's enlistment was a foregone conclusion after the first interview, and maybe even before it. As it was with the Miners of Missouri S&T, so it was with the Marines.

Dave was nothing if not decisive.

What Dave remembers most about these meetings with Sergeant Sanderson was the weight and formality of them, the sense of legacy that surrounded the USMC, the quiet self-assurance of Sanderson himself, who, unlike Coach Childress, never once tried to wow Dave with the promise of heroism. The USMC was about grander things than football. It was historic. It was about building a solid foundation for life, about seeing the world, about finding a career, about buying a house, and someday starting a family.

At the time, fresh out of options, and looking for a game plan, joining the marines didn't seem like a Faustian bargain to Dave. On the contrary, it seemed like the most practical, honorable, and rewarding opportunity available to him at nineteen.

The Otherness

———•—•—•———

In the morning, Bella's imagination was immediately back to work where it left off by the fire the previous night. She dreamed again of the great sheet of ice, stretching out forever, felt the grip of its frozen silence, felt the frigid air burning her lungs and nostrils, as the distant cries and whimpers of wolves sounded somewhere in the distance.

These dreams, they were not normal dreams. Bella did not imagine them; it was as though she was remembering them. And yet how could she remember them? How could she possibly know what it was to be a grown woman living in the ice age, to have a baby growing inside of her, to understand a language she did not speak? If these were not memories, how could Bella comprehend with such clarity things so far beyond her experience?

Bella did not linger on her bedroll that morning. Instead, she proceeded straight to the bluff, where she knew for near certain she would find her dad, tending the fire.

"So, when the world changed, what do you think happened to the ice people?" she said, in lieu of good morning.

"I don't know, they adapted, I guess," her dad said, presenting her a tin of clumpy oats, an offer she received with something less than enthusiasm.

"What's 'adapted'?" she said.

"It means they changed their behavior to conform to the new world."

"What's 'conform'?"

Her dad set his oats aside. "Conform means to follow the rules, baby."

"What rules?"

"In their case, the rules of the natural world."

Bella considered the explanation for a few moments.

"Daddy, do you believe in ghosts?" she said.

"I'm not sure," he said. "Why?"

"No reason," she said, unconvincingly.

"What is it, baby? Are you scared?"

"No, not scared," she said. "I just think this place may be haunted."

"Why is that?"

Bella considered telling him about the otherness, but decided to talk around it instead.

"I just do," she said.

"And that doesn't scare you?"

"Not at all," she said. "Daddy, can I go explore?"

"Just don't go beyond the meadow," he said. "Or out on the ridge."

"Can't I please go farther?"

"No, baby. No farther than I can hear you," he said. "And bring the bear spray with you."

Unlike her dad, forever chopping, or digging, or planning his next move, Bella preferred to let her day unfold on its own. After breakfast, she wandered as far as she was permitted. A minute's walk in any direction delivered her to the edge of somewhere entirely different. The forest, with its birdsong, and its playful sunlight, and the trickle of its streams, the craggy rim of the upper canyon, with its prehistoric-looking knobs and rocky outcroppings, the meadow with its shady willow, its whispering grass, and its birds of prey wheeling above, all of these places converged on their little bluff, though she never dared to venture beyond them on her own. But surely she would have, given the permission of her father.

Unable to explore the world she lived in, Bella gave herself instead to the otherness, which filled her up like an empty balloon. Unlike the school bus, brimming with the noise of humanity, out here, in the silence and solitude, she was able to reach further, much further than Kirk Halliday's anxiety about wetting his pants, further even than her mother's voice. That afternoon, Bella lived again in the brutal but uncomplicated world of the prehistoric ice sheet, which seemed to demand her presence.

At dinner that evening, Bella was compelled for not the first time to share her revelation.

"I don't think the ice people came here from somewhere else," she offered, over a tin of rice and stinky sardines from a can.

"There's not really a definitive answer to that, baby. Eat up."

"What's 'definive'?"

"Definitive means clear, reliable. Some people think the ice age people came over a land bridge fifteen or twenty thousand years ago from Asia, and some people think they came from the south. It depends who you talk to, I guess."

"I think once a thing is alive, it never goes away," she said.

Bella felt a little proud of herself when her dad lowered his fork, and gave her that blank look again, and began to shake his head as though he was stunned.

"Baby, you are really something else, you know that?"

And again, Bella felt pride coloring her face.

Deb Coatsworth;
Public Librarian, Vigilante Falls

"I'm not at liberty to say what materials Mr. Cartwright checked out. Even if I wanted to, I couldn't go back and find out—not if you put a gun to my head. Because no such history exists. As in, there's no record of it.

"And I want you to think about that for a minute.

"In a world where everything is for public consumption, in a world where our every inclination is fastidiously catalogued and turned into algorithms, a world where our TVs listen to us; the poor, underfunded public library that turns away nobody is your last bastion of confidentiality. If you want to see liberty and freedom at work, go to a library.

"So, the answer is no, I can't tell you what he checked out. And I wouldn't if I could. Knowing what little I knew about the man personally, it's safe to say he liked his privacy. All I can tell you is that his materials were quite numerous, and he frequently brought them back wrapped in a large plastic garbage bag. On several occasions the materials were warped, or water damaged.

"He was always polite, and quiet, too, which made him quite popular around here, in spite of the damaged materials. I will say that he had a smell about him like wet dog, though as far as I know, he didn't have any dogs up there, only cats. And quite a number of them, from what I understand."

This Many

———

Dave skirted past the platinum rewards members in his alphas, clutching his duffel, chin up, as the blood suffused his cheeks. He didn't enjoy being a spectacle, but at least they didn't bump him to first class. In spite of his upright posture, his damn shirt stays were riding up on him as he walked down the jetway alone, and rounded the corner, ducked into the aircraft, where the male flight attendant's courteous smile morphed into something graver as he greeted Dave.

"Welcome aboard, sir. And thank you for your service."

Dave crammed his duffel into the overhead compartment, and slid into his window seat, where he gazed out across the tarmac. As the rear of the plane began to fill up, it seemed that every set of eyes found Dave on their way past: old and young, male and female. A few older men nodded meaningfully. There were a handful, too, who could not hide their disdain for Dave and his service. Either way, he would've done anything to get out of that uniform.

Eventually, a somewhat frantic young mother, whom Dave put in her mid-twenties, clutching a wailing infant, and towing a curly-haired boy of maybe three or four, paused in the aisle at row seventeen. Dave promptly stood and assisted her with the two overfilled carry-ons threatening to slip off her shoulder, stuffing them in the overhead with his duffel, as the middle-aged couple in 16B and C winced at the caterwauling infant.

"Would you like to sit by the window?" Dave said to the boy.

In his final gesture of shyness, the big-eyed toddler with the curly hair silently nodded to the affirmative, whereupon Dave hoisted him over the high seatback and lowered him into the window seat.

"Shush, now, it's okay, sweetie," the mother consoled the infant. "Thank you, that was very kind of you," she said to Dave, as he slid past her into the middle berth.

"Do you want to switch seats?" said Dave.

She managed a beleaguered half-smile. "To tell you the truth," she said. "I'd rather have you in the middle. He'll just keep the baby awake, otherwise."

No sooner did the young mother take her seat and buckle in than she expertly emancipated one of her breasts from beneath her cotton blouse, and offered it to the infant, whom, much to everyone's relief, stopped wailing.

"There you go," said the mother, stroking the infant's downy head.

When the mother caught Dave watching her sidelong, she only smiled sweetly, and Dave blanched as he turned his attention to the toddler, face pressed to the window.

"Is this your first airplane ride?" said Dave.

"Yes, but I'm not scared," said the child.

"Well, that's good."

The aircraft was still taxiing when the infant fell asleep, and the young mother extracted her nipple and replaced her breast in one fluid movement. Before they even reached cruising altitude, she fell asleep herself.

Watching her almost-pretty face at rest, Dave wondered at the young mother's story. She was wearing a wedding band, maybe she was flying to meet her husband. Was she a military wife? Why was she traveling alone? Dave imagined Nadene in the not-so-distant future, clutching a baby of her own. Maybe it would be a boy, and they could name it Gordy, after Coach Prentice, or Jerry, after Nadene's brother. Already, he yearned for fatherhood, an endeavor in which he aimed to be everything his own father was not, to do all the things with his children that his father never did with him and Travers. Dave liked kids to begin with, but the thought of having his own someday was thrilling. Not right away, of course, not until he was ready professionally and financially. In the meantime, he still had some boxes to check: travel, save, plan.

"Are you a policeman?" asked the young boy.

"Nope," said Dave.

"Then why are you dressed like that?"

"I'm a marine."

"Like an army man?"

"Better," said Dave. "But kinda like that."

"I'm gonna live above a gas station when I grow up," the boy announced.

"You might as well aim high," said Dave.

"I like the smell of gas," he explained. "Don't you like it?"

"I kind of do," said Dave.

For the next half hour, Dave and the boy—mostly the boy—talked of many things; of the boy's recent train ride. They spoke of the boy's favorite colors—black and green, and blue and yellow; his favorite meal—chicken burritos with ketchup and no lettuce; and his favorite movie, *Monsters, Inc.*, even though Sully still scared him sometimes.

"Do you ever get scared?"

"All the time," said Dave.

"About what?"

"About the unknown," said Dave. "The things I can't see coming, I guess. Sometimes I get scared that my life won't be everything I want it to be, that I won't be able to do all the things I've planned out."

"Aren't you scared of getting killed? That's what I'd be scared of."

"Yeah, that, too, I guess."

At the end of the flight, Dave helped the young mother with her bags, the infant still fast asleep on her shoulder, as she shuffled slowly down the aisle. Halfway to first class, the young boy tugged on Dave's pant leg.

"Remember," he said. "My mom says it's okay to be scared."

"I'll remember that," Dave said, giving the boy's curly head a final mussing.

Little Black Lies

———

Dave awakened at dawn next to Bella to find one of the tiny, black kittens pinned lifelessly beneath her sleeping figure. Carefully, Dave pried its oddly contorted body out from beneath her hip, and stole out into the gray dawn to dispose of it deep in the brush, beyond the ragged tree line to the south.

Bella was still sleeping soundly when Dave returned. Still, he was ninety-nine percent sure she'd notice the missing kitten.

Full morning arrived gray and cool, with their little perch above the canyon cloistered in the clouds. Though the peaks and high ridges that all but surrounded them were invisible, Dave could still feel the immensity of them there, lurking beyond the mist, buttressing him from the outside world. It was ten degrees colder than the previous morning as Dave busied himself with the cooking fire. Though he missed the vistas, in some ways he preferred the cloud cover. There was a sense of security to be enjoyed under a shroud. Among other things, it hid the smoke of his fire. Ultimately, Dave had not chosen this place for its grand vistas, or its spiritual benefits, but for its strategic sightlines, and its clear view of potential interlopers.

Eventually, Bella emerged from the cave and sat by the fire, eyes downcast, as when she knew she was in trouble.

"What's the matter, baby?"

"Daddy, I did a really bad thing," she said, casting her eyes down.

"What did you do?"

"I let a kitty get away. One of the little black ones. I know it was bad, I'm sorry. I just . . . I couldn't help it, Daddy, he was so cute. Now, I can't find him anywhere. He's so tiny, Daddy, he can't take care of himself."

"It's okay, honey," Dave said without hesitation, even as his heart ached a little. "I put him back in the carrier with the others."

"But there were only two black ones when I checked, Boris and Sugarfoot. There's supposed to be three black ones."

"You must have counted wrong, baby. Betty only had two black ones."

"No, Daddy, there were three!"

"Well, all I know is, I put him back in there," said Dave.

"Are you sure?"

"I'm sure, baby."

But Dave was not at all certain that Bella bought the explanation. He knew it was probably a mistake lying to her. Instead of trying to protect her from the grim reality of her actions, maybe he ought to have been using this as a teachable moment about the fragile nature of life, about how everything died, and how it wasn't always fair, and didn't always make sense. But he couldn't do it. God knows, she'd had enough reality already.

"Baby, just wait until I say it's time before you handle the kitties anymore, okay?"

"Okay."

Dave stirred the coals and repositioned the iron skillet at the edge of the pit, then patted Bella on the head.

"I know it's hard, baby. I never had any impulse control myself."

"What's 'impulse control'?"

"Well, just, waiting is hard sometimes, even when you know you're better off doing it."

"I love you, Daddy," she said, crowding in next to him, and clutching his arm. "Thanks for putting him back in."

Every time she said "I love you," it damn near broke his heart. But knowing he lied to her broke his heart even more.

"I love you, too, baby."

Beyond Earshot

———

With only the cats and thrice read library books to occupy herself, and with precious little freedom to roam beyond earshot of her dad, Bella lived outside of herself much of the time, escaping into the ancient, ice-strewn world which seemed to summon her with increasing urgency, as though it were her duty to host it.

Lying flat on her back in the meadow, or seated upright on her rocky perch above the canyon, or huddled in the dreary depths of the cave on a rainy morning, Bella answered this call to duty, emptying herself so that the otherness could fill her up.

"What are you thinking about, baby?" her dad said, startling her from one of her reveries in front of the dying fire.

"Nothing, really," she said. "Just thinking."

"About what?"

"About different stuff," she said.

"Like what?"

"I don't really remember."

"Is there anything you want to talk about?" he said.

"No," she said. "Not right now. Unless there's something you want to talk about."

In spite of the temptation, Bella had now determined once and for all not to share her secret life, for fear she might lose it. Then, there would be no adventure left, no escape, nothing of consequence to fill her days. What was more, her attendance in the icy past now seemed to be required, as though she were called there as a witness.

"You sure you're all right, baby?" said her dad. "You need anything?"

"I'm okay," she said, lying. "But Daddy, can I please go down to the river?"

"Not by yourself, baby. But I can go with you a little later, after I'm finished with my work."

"How about the edge of the canyon, can I go there?"

"What's at the edge of the canyon?" he said.

"Nothing," she said. "I just want to go somewhere, I want to do something different. Everything just feels the same, Daddy."

"You can go down to the meadow if you bring the bear spray."

"But I've been to the meadow," she said. "Like every single day, I've been there. I've been to the smokehouse, and the little stream, and the tall grass at the edge of the woods."

"Baby, I'm sorry, but you need to stick close to home."

"Why does home have to be so small? What's the use of living in the mountains if I can't even explore them?"

"We've explored a lot, baby," he said. "You've been to the river, you've been up and down that canyon with me. Heck, you've been just about everywhere you can see from here."

"Exactly," she said.

"Look, if you want, we can go somewhere together a little later. Maybe if we ate an early dinner we'd have time to hike up to the—"

"Daddy, I wanna go places by myself. I want to be independent."

"Baby, you will someday. You're seven years old."

"I'm almost eight."

She folded her arms, pouting.

"If I was a boy, I'd be called Gordy, and you'd let me go, I know you would. You'd probably let me hunt, too."

"That's not true," he said. "How would you know that?"

"Because it's always been that way," she says. "Girls always get a crummy deal."

S'tka

— · — · —

Oh, how they raged, the filthy hypocrites. Jumping up and down, thumping those hairy chests, foaming at the mouth, scratching their dirty nethers and armpits, then smelling their fingers when they thought nobody was looking. And the other women, they weren't much better: retreating out of sight, skulking in the shadows with their animal skins and their suckling infants, as if they never would have attempted the same offense in S'tka's situation: half-starving, her stomach feeding on itself, the thing growing inside her protesting at every step, stoop, or bend.

What was a scrap of meat for a ravenous mother?

The nerve of them. Especially when no less than three of those stinking, hairy protesters, those not named U'ku'let, could just as easily have been responsible for the growing bulge at S'tka's middle. Look at them, the gallery of buffoons. That any one of them would beget her a child was a nauseating thought.

Looking at you, Yq'mat, with your massive brow ridge, and dim, deep-set eyes.

Looking at you Kt'ak, with your chafed lips, and flat nose, and tiny, misshapen ears.

Looking at you, oh wise one, Ok'eh, courageous leader, with your stupid fantasy of another world beyond the ice.

And what of poor, hapless, U'ku'let, with the harelip, and the bulging neck? U'ku'let, who couldn't grow a decent beard, or bag even the most beleaguered of diseased bison without the aid of another hunter. U'ku'let, maybe never quite as clueless as the clan suspected, but forever a follower.

That among all people it was the coward U'ku'let who found the courage to defend S'tka's honor, even as she gnawed on the filched hindquarter in question, blood dripping down her chin, was nothing less than a wonder.

But so it was.

Bony chest thrust forth, exposed nipple stiff from the frigid air, U'ku'let stepped between the offended mob and S'tka's bulging belly.

"She's carrying a baby!" he proclaimed.

A proclamation by which the clan was less than moved.

"Just what we need, another mouth to feed," replied one of the elders.

Hard to argue with that. But consider the indignity of her condition. All those months swollen with child, and so little to eat, S'tka had carried the load of two men down the rugged, snow-packed mountains, away from the security of home, and over the endless ice, as they made their way toward a horizon that never seemed to get closer, a sun that only seemed to grow weaker. Why ever had they undertaken this journey? Clearly, there was nothing beyond the ice. It went on forever, anyone could see that. They should have stuck to the mountains. Better to starve there in the relative safety of their den than to freeze to death in this barren wasteland.

S'tka, however, had little choice but to follow them on their futile journey into the new world. And despite her condition, she worked dutifully through the months, until every joint in her body ached. See her disemboweling and dressing the animals, see her scraping the stinking, bloody pelts for curing, see her urinating on them to cure them, carrying them over her shoulder for miles on end. S'tka had scrubbed the bugs and the stink from the men's furs, always wary of exposing her backside, lest Yq'mat, Kt'ak, or Ok'eh decided to take liberties as she knelt at the banks of icy streams.

They took whatever they wanted, the men. They viewed all that they saw as something to be possessed or conquered. They walked about scratching their chests as though they were the masters of this icy hell. They acted as though they were not beholden to the Great Provider for the game they took, or the light that shined down on them. These men acted as though they themselves were the great providers. Though each of them was born out of a woman, each of them had suckled at a woman's breast, each of them owed his life to woman, still, they treated a woman as something less than themselves.

Someday soon, all that would change.

Curse them, the stinking hypocrites. S'tka was entitled to fresh meat; her body demanded flesh and blood. She'd shouldered more than her share of the burden, so why shouldn't she have meat? Was it S'tka's fault that the food was so scarce this season? Had she decided their fortunes would be better out on this ice? Did they suspect she could live on such meager rations as bones without flesh?

Oh, but the clan elders were angry for her trespass. Their sanctimony knew no bounds.

"Thief! Thief!" they shouted.

"You can't let them starve," U'ku'let protested, indicating S'tka's swollen abdomen.

"She would have the rest of us starve," they insisted. "By stealing, she has betrayed us. Go, both of you."

And just like that U'ku'let and S'tka were cast out of the circle, banished to the endless ice, essentially condemned to death.

Still, they could not pry the bloody hindquarter from S'tka's grasp in the end. S'tka would have her meal. When Ok'eh attempted to wrest the shank back from her, S'tka sunk her teeth into his hairy forearm, delighted when he cried out like an old woman! To hear him screeching, to see him hopping up and down as though on a bed of hot coals—that was almost worth the price of banishment.

Almost, but not quite.

The wind was bitter cold away from the fire. The flat, white world offered no shelter, nor much in the way of variety. Without discussing a course of action, U'ku'let and S'tka mutually agreed to reverse their course, and abandon the possibility of a new world. They found themselves moving with the wind at their backs, away from the fading sun as they began their journey back toward the distant mountains from which they came, a barely perceptible ridgeline along the eastern horizon, three, maybe four days across the ice without the security of the clan, with little sanctuary, and the slim possibility of survival.

U'ku'let, stonily silent, walked ten paces in front of S'tka, never once looking back at her. For many hours they trudged along at a measured pace, collecting windblown sticks, whose journey across the ice may well have been as long as their own. S'tka continued to gnaw occasionally on the stringy remains of her bloody ration.

"I didn't ask you to stand up for me, you know," she said.

But U'ku'let did not answer. Nor would he partake of the picked over appendage when she offered it to him.

"I don't need you. Go back if you wish," she said.

At last he stopped and swung around to confront her, his face contorted with anger.

"Back to where? Back to what? You have doomed us, woman!"

From there they retreated into silence once more, plodding on over the ice, as the sun sunk below the edge of the world. They were doomed from the start, thought S'tka. People were never meant for this world. Why would the Great Provider have made them so scrawny and helpless, so dependent upon one another for survival? Why would she maroon them in this ghastly, frigid nothingness? More each day, S'tka found herself angry and disillusioned with the Great Provider. It almost came as a relief to be cast outside of the circle, away from the collective struggle, and the desperate impetus to survive.

Let this wilderness swallow her, child and all. Take her now, and end her useless suffering, spare her unborn child the agony of birth. S'tka would mourn the loss of nothing this stingy world had to offer. How could she even call the provider great when she provides but the bare minimum?

Eventually, U'ku'let glimpsed a tiny smudge of black awash in the endless white, presumably the remnants of an abandoned fire, smoldering weakly on the ice. They hurried their pace over the barren ground.

Upon arriving at the dying fire, they fell to their hands and knees, and began to heap the ashy remnants into a mound at the center, blowing desperately on what little that glowed, until they managed to revive it, nurturing it back to a nearly respectable state of insufficiency. They camped on the ice beneath the moon, hunkered around their paltry fire, accompanied only by the sucking and smacking and gnawing of U'ku'let, who had finally consented to take the giant femur and suck it dry of marrow. With this, along with the low hiss of the glowing coals, came the moaning of the wind blowing in from the north, and in the distance, the baying of wolves.

Funny, how quickly S'tka appealed to the Great Provider for her safety now, when only hours ago she'd been ready to forsake her altogether. Why had the creator made her so weak? U'ku'let was right, she had doomed them. They could not possibly survive outside the circle. Soon enough, they would become food for the ravenous wolves, a certainty she felt in her bones.

Rocking gently forward and back on her haunches, S'tka cradled her swollen belly against the cold, as the wolves bellowed in the darkness.

Ha'act too ha'act too ha'act too, she chanted beneath her breath. *I am you.* A song to appease the Great Provider. But the howling, and the yelping of the wolves, and the crippling sense of vulnerability never ceased. It didn't help that U'ku'let soon fell asleep sitting upright, leaving S'tka alone to ponder all that was terrible and unknown.

H'act too ha'act too ha'act too, she chanted.

Finally, she succumbed to sleep, and dreamed of more ice.

U'ku'let shook her awake with the weak sun, and the first thing she heard was the baying of the wolves, closer now than the previous night.

"We must go," he said.

Without another word, S'tka was on her feet, her great belly thrust out before her, trudging east for better or worse into the great, white world.

Nothing or No One

When she was not living outside of herself on the ancient ice, Bella belonged to the mountains. Now that her dad had finally permitted her to explore farther and wider, extending her range as far as the upper rim of the canyon, and the forested hill on the far side of the meadow, Bella's days were much fuller. See her frolicking in the high grass with the kitties, see her scrambling up hillsides like she was born to it. Hear her identify the trees by name: silver fir, and hemlock, and maple, and red cedar. And the fish: coho, and king, and sturgeon. See her dart sprite-like in dirty tennis shoes between the evergreens. Hear her say how she loves what she calls the "whistley" call of the white warbler, and how she thinks the song of the varied thrush is "sad and beautiful." See her observe, hear her question, watch her explore. Listen to her talk excitedly of her discoveries and adventures. See her dirty little face rapt in the glow of the fire.

As for Dave, he had good days, and he had bad days. On the good days, he was able to breathe deeply and stay ahead of his anxiety. On such days, he was able to connect, able to ground himself in the physical world, to exist in the present moment, at least some of the time. On the bad days, it felt as if he belonged to nothing or no one. Though he was alert and observant, he could not seem to access a sense of curiosity or wonder. He did not yearn or seek to expand his interior life on the bad days. It was a room he preferred to keep unfurnished: a window, a mattress, dingy white walls. Better yet, a cave. Never mind the natural wonders that surrounded him. On the bad days, nothing stirred his appetites. Still, he knew he must abide for Bella's sake. And so, Dave planned. He acted, he taught and protected, maintaining the smooth surface of his patience at all times as he dutifully went through the motions.

In the fall, with any luck they would smoke salmon and sturgeon, deer and perhaps even elk. And so, Dave busied himself completing the little smoke house hunkered amongst the firs, along the wooded ridge a hundred yards south of the cave. As he was caulking the slat roof—the slats made of fine wedges hacked from cedar—and stuffing the gaps with moss, Bella appeared suddenly at his side, something she'd done on a number of occasions lately. Either Dave was losing his edge, or Bella had mastered stealth.

"You scared me, baby," he said.

"Sorry," she said. "Daddy, how do you know if something is real?"

"What do you mean?"

"I mean, how do you know the difference between real and obstruct?"

Dave mussed her hair.

"You mean, 'abstract'?"

"Yeah, abstract."

"Well," he said. "If it's abstract, you can't touch it, baby. It's just an idea."

"Can you see it?"

"In your mind you can," he said.

"But what if we're just in our minds?" she said. "What if I'm imagining you, like in a dream?"

"Then you'd be dreaming."

"How do you know?"

Dave paused in his labor.

"Because you couldn't touch me in your dream."

He reached out and squeezed her hand.

"See," he said. "I'm right here."

"So then Mommy isn't real anymore?"

"Mommy's still real," he said.

"But I can't touch her."

"No, you can't, not anymore."

"How is she real, then?"

"Because she lives inside of you, baby."

"How?"

"You remember her," he said. "That makes her part of you."

"What about in thousands of years?" she said.

"What about it?"

"Will she still be part of me then?"

"Nobody lives thousands of years, baby."

Again, the explanation was apparently not to her satisfaction.

"What if people keep remembering somebody, like in stories?" she said. "And what if the same stories kept getting told over and over? Would they be real, and not ab-structions?"

"They'd still be abstractions, baby," he said. "But they'd be as real as any Bible, I suppose."

Dave was hoping this consolation would be enough to put an end to her speculation. But it was not, and he ought to have known.

"What if the person remembering the person never knew them?" she said. "Or they never even heard the stories, they just knew them, anyway?"

Dave spent a moment trying to unpack her logic, but finally grew impatient.

"I wish I had all the answers for you, baby, but I'm not sure I even understand the questions sometimes."

S'tka

For two days they plodded onward across the ice field, through the frozen haze, hunger gnawing at their insides, guided only by the dim prospect of the mountains on the eastern horizon, with the occasional black smudge of a fire pit to comfort and protect them from the wolves, should the beasts ever decide to overtake them. What option did they have but to keep going, to keep trudging back from where they came? Where else was the promise amidst that flat, white expanse? What else was beyond that frozen haze that hung like a gauzy curtain, obscuring their progress into . . . where, if not what they already knew?

Doomed outside the circle of the clan, with nothing of their own to burn, S'tka and U'ku'let soon learned that even in their solitude they were beholden to the castoffs of others for their survival, their strewn scraps, and their dying fires. To come upon another living person, another outcast, someone else to strengthen their numbers would've have been a relief.

It was not until the afternoon of the third day, clear but frigid, that the mountains finally appeared to be drawing nearer, their jagged peaks and snowy cornices discernible against the relief of pale blue sky. Sharp and opposing, frozen and treacherous, they remained a welcome sight, a relief from the flat, one-dimensional world of the ice.

During S'tka's sleep the previous night, the baby had dropped inside of her. It now pressed against her entrance with urgent force. The terrible cramping slowed her pace, much to U'ku'let's annoyance. S'tka could feel the baby wanting out with every step. Surely, it would not be long.

Please don't let it be long. Only long enough to find shelter.

S'tka was determined not to have her baby out there, exposed to the perils of the ice. They must make the mountains before her time came, and find a den or cave, or some sanctuary from the elements. They must have more than measly sticks of kindling, they must have wood to build a real fire. And above all, they must have the one thing that got them in this mess in the first place: meat. Bloody, warm, glorious meat to gorge themselves on.

Despite their determined progress, U'ku'let and S'tka did not make the mountains before the sun dipped beneath the ice. Without a fire, they could not afford to stop, so they slogged on beneath the moonlight for miles, the temperature dropping so low that S'tka's breath all but crystalized in the air before her. So tiny amidst this sea of ice they must have looked to the moon above. That the baby had not moved inside of her all day was troubling, though the pressure on her opening was now crushing. S'tka began to worry that something had gone wrong inside her. As her mood nosed toward panic, the moon ducked beneath the clouds, leaving them vulnerable, and all but blind in the darkness. Still, they muddled their way forward.

When it seemed they could not possibly continue under these conditions, a tiny orange glow to the east beckoned them. The promise of warmth compelled them onward another half-mile.

When they drew close enough to the fire, S'tka could make out a lone figure stooped over it, feeding sticks to the flames. It was impossible to tell whether the figure had registered their approach. Even as they drew within thirty feet, the figure gave no sign that he saw them.

"We are cold," said U'ku'let to the stranger, who straightened up with a hissing.

"We mean you no harm," U'ku'let assured him.

The little stranger squatted back down wordlessly at the edge of the flames. He was a hideous sight to behold in the firelight; his cheek covered in angry boils, patchy with facial hair, his head and brow singed hairless, and a raised, pink scar across his neck. Even draped in fur, it was clear that he was gaunt, starved to the edge of death.

"Where are the rest of your people?" said U'ku'let, warming his frozen hands over the flames.

But the stranger said nothing, and only spit into the fire.

It occurred to S'tka that the little man was probably mad with starvation. He scratched constantly at his patchy scalp, once pulling out a tuft of hair and lobbing it into the fire.

"So you are alone?" said U'ku'let to the little man.

But again, the little man refused to speak. He would not so much as look them in the eye as he stirred the flames, a plume of embers rising orange into the night.

"Hmph," said U'ku'let with a shrug.

And so they all consented to the silence and the warmth. When it became clear that the little man was no threat to them, U'ku'let and S'tka surrendered to their exhaustion.

S'tka dreamed of warmth and shelter, of shadows ducking and dodging on the walls of a cave, of security, and the luxury of laughter, only to awaken by a dying fire in the blistering cold.

The ugly little stranger was gone without a trace.

"Let's go," said U'ku'let gruffly.

And soon they were up and trudging east toward the mountains, the pressure between S'tka's legs unbearable.

By midday, they had reached the low hills, and slowly they trudged up and over them. In two hours' time they reached the patchy forests and stony outcroppings that they never should have left in the first place.

Shortly before the sun dipped out of sight behind the hills, they found pitiful shelter in a burrow at the base of a rockslide. The space was so cramped that S'tka was forced to crawl in on her hands and knees, a task rendered nearly impossible with her fit-to-burst belly.

U'ku'let gathered sticks for a fire at the mouth of their shallow warren, where he finally roosted sullenly, just as the snow began to fall. S'tka, sprawled beneath her shelter of stone and earth, without so much as an extra hide to comfort her from the frozen rock, gasped for breath as she was wracked with her first contraction.

Let it come stillborn, she prayed. Spare us another life to sustain in this frozen wilderness. But such was the agony of childbirth that even prayer was beyond her reach. It seemed that all she could access through the pain was bitterness and contempt.

Bah, the Great Provider! What do you provide us but cold and misery? Why must we forever scrape, and wrestle, and beg you to spare us? Why saddle us with the capacity to care? Why not let us die off mercifully, freeze in our slumber, rather than face your unending burdens? What is the reward, this? To cleave a woman in half, to rip her apart for the unwanted opportunity to perpetuate the misery in the form of a helpless lump, to pass along the agony and struggle through the generations? Oh, Great Provider, it's hard not to wonder at your wisdom.

The torturous spasms were getting closer together. S'tka's pelvis raged, her heart galloped, her breathing came in shallow fits. Though she yearned for a hand to clench, a concerned face to gaze up at, she knew better than to call for U'ku'let for support. She couldn't help but wonder why he ever chose to defend her in the first place? Was he really so naive as to believe that he alone might have planted the seed that caused this? Why did he wait to claim her until it would cost him the only life he'd ever known? Oh, Great Provider, you are a fickle master.

Once the contractions were so close that they came one after the other, S'tka's thoughts glazed over and hardened like a sheet of ice. The thing told her to push, so she pushed with every bit of strength she could muster.

Outside the rocky hollow, the snow gathered round U'ku'let as he stared into the fire, cursing his fate.

After hours of struggle, an exhausted S'tka finally managed to push the baby free of her, only to gather it up in her arms. A profound relief washed over her at the sound of its pinched and phlegmy cries.

U'ku'let soon ducked his head into the crowded space.

"Has it come? What is it?" he said in the darkness.

"A boy," she said.

"Ahya! Haha!" he said. "A boy! He will be N'ka."

And so the boy was to be called N'ka, named for the fearsome wolf of the north. May he grow to be fearsome like his name, S'tka thought, for he would need to be in this cruel, frozen place. N'ka the wily survivor, N'ka the fearless hunter, N'ka whose name struck fear in the hearts of his adversaries.

"N'ka," U'ku'let said again, and S'tka could actually feel him smiling through the darkness.

And for the first time in so long she couldn't remember, S'tka felt herself smiling, too.

"N'ka," she said as much to herself as to her whimpering son, as she stroked his tiny head.

As soon as U'ku'let ducked back out into the night, retreating to the fire, she heard him let loose a hoot into the snowy heavens.

"Ahya! Haha!" he said. "Oya N'ka."

Oh, Great Provider, I have doubted you.

The strain of S'tka's effort had chased the chill from the enclosed space around her.

"You are N'ka," she cooed, as the rooting infant groped to find its mark. With a little coaxing, it arrived there with a snuffle and a sigh.

S'tka nestled N'ka close as he suckled, shielding his little ears from the chill air. Outside the warren, U'ku'let laughed giddily at the falling snow. In an instant, the whole frozen world had changed.

A Sticky Burden

The moths arrived on the bluff like a pestilence. The night air throbbed with them. Ravenous for the pale light of the fire, they flitted desperately about, their thousand wings thrumming and pulsing around the little camp on the plateau. Of all the natural discomforts Dave planned for—the bitter cold, the relentless wet, the mud, the snow, the ice, the chapping and chafing and blistering—moths were nowhere among them.

In recent weeks, Dave had sensed Bella's optimism waning somewhat. The pitch of her excitement when she talked about the natural world was not what it had been a month ago. A month ago, she hardly ever came in before dark, scurrying and climbing and stalking butterflies until the sun dipped below the hump. But in recent days she'd been spending more time within the stuffy confines of the cave, flipping impassively through books, scratching patterns in the dirt floor, or simply idling. Of late, Bella seemed to have turned inward, and Dave could only wonder if it was because he, too, had retreated further within himself.

Sometimes she seemed to be living somewhere completely outside of herself. Several times Dave caught her staring wall-eyed out over the canyon, or fixedly into the candle flame. While not alarming, the behavior spoke to a developing habit of disassociation that could be problematic if not checked.

"Let's go to town tomorrow," he said, as they sat around the fire, long after dinner, the inexorable moths bumping the sides of their faces.

"We'll leave bright and early," he said. "You can go see Nana. I can go to the library and get some new books."

She brightened immediately.

"Can we go to the park?"

"Sure, we can go to the park. Nana can take you."

"Even if it's raining?"

"Of course. Nana's not afraid of a little rain, is she?"

"Can we stay more than one day?"

"We'll see," he said, knowing he was lying.

Two nights would feel like a defeat, three would be suffocating. He wouldn't stay at all if the hours of the day would permit it. But how could he possibly expect Bella to hike eighteen miles in a day?

"Can we have pizza?"

"Yeah, okay."

"The frozen kind?"

"Sure, baby, we can do that," he said.

A familiar guilt prodded Dave at the thought of all he had denied Bella, all the things she'd been forced to relinquish through no choice of her own. The least he could do was let her indulge in these estranged comforts now and again when the opportunity presented itself, though he knew it would only make their paths more difficult in the end. In an ideal scenario, they would cut themselves off from the world completely.

In the morning, the weather gods smiled upon the North Cascades. Dawn arrived without a cloud in sight. The purity of chill mountain air exhilarated with its crispness. The jagged spires of the high country seemed so close, stood in such sharp relief against the deep blue sky that it seemed you could reach out and touch them. To the west, beyond the succession of wedge-shaped valleys, still engulfed in shadow, the straits and channels of the Salish Sea shone like hammered steel, clear to the horizon, broken only by the cluster of San Juan islands rearing their humped backs, as though to warm themselves in the morning sunlight.

Dave and Bella loaded up on carbs by the fire, oats with walnuts and dried huckleberries.

"We should get moving," he said, scraping the pan clean.

Upon their departure, Dave kicked out the cooking fire and hoisted the empty external-frame pack on his back.

"Baby, put your coat on," he said.

"But I'm not cold."

"Honey, you've gotta wear a coat. At least until it warms up."

She wouldn't catch a cold on Dave's clock. In all their time there, neither of them had contracted so much as the sniffles. They ate well, if a little light on protein, supplementing their diets with chewable multi-vitamins. They stayed warm, they got plenty of sleep, they exercised, and they hydrated religiously. Most important of all, they had no contact with anyone. You had to be around other people to get sick.

The trail was mostly dry and clear as they wended their way down the rocky face of the mountain and into the canyon below. It took the usual twenty minutes or so for Dave's hip to warm up and stop popping. Though the river was still running high, already the alders and maples were beginning to change colors. The air was beginning to thin with the approach of fall. By mid-morning, they'd put two thousand vertical feet behind them, and reached the bottomlands, where the mosquitoes began to swarm them.

"I'm tired," Bella said, a whine in her voice.

"We're almost there, baby."

The promise of frozen pizza and jungle gyms had worn thin by the time they reached the highway, jumped the culvert, and began hiking west toward town. By the time they reached Dave's mom's house, Bella was officially cranky. His mom was not at home, and both doors were locked.

"I'm thirsty," said Bella.

"So am I."

"And hungry."

"Me, too," said Dave. "Be patient, baby."

Dave considered jimmying a window, but ultimately decided against it. It shamed him that he was annoyed with his mom for not being home, though he'd given her no notice, not so much as a hint that they might appear at her doorstep. But of course there was no way they could. So they sat on the steps, where Bella fell asleep in Dave's arms, a sticky burden, until his mother returned home an hour later, smelling of flowery perfume and candle wax.

As it turned out, his mom had been at church, where she'd stayed late to fold chairs, sweep up scone crumbs, and throw away coffee cups in the reception hall. She gossiped, a little nervously it seemed, as she readied her patented sandwiches in the kitchen: thawing the sourdough in the microwave, gathering the generic mustard and mayonnaise from the door of the fridge, the bread-and-butter pickles, the wilting iceberg lettuce from the crisper, and the thick sliced turkey she always got from the deli counter at Red Apple that invariably looked dried out, and a little off-color, like dead human flesh. Not that Dave didn't appreciate his mother's efforts, not that Bella didn't think they were the best sandwiches ever.

Watching his mother execute the same sandwich routine he'd watched a thousand times, from his earliest youth to this moment, Dave was itchy to get moving.

"I wish I would have known you were coming," she said.

"Sorry, Ma, no phone."

"Among other things," she observed nonchalantly, plating the sandwiches, which she'd carefully cut into quarters.

When she circled back to the fridge for the orange juice, she whispered in Dave's ear.

"What on earth did you do to her hair?"

"She wanted it," he said. "It was getting tangled all to hell. She looked homeless."

"Well, she is, at least as far as anyone but you is concerned," she whispered.

"Look, Ma, I don't need to hear it, okay? I've got a lot to do in town. Can you take her to the park?"

"Of course," she said, averting her eyes.

She didn't bother to ask him when he'd be back for Bella. Whenever it was, it would be too soon for everybody involved.

Underdogs

———

Watching Bella dismount the monkey bars with a smile and a wave for her nana, it was hard to see any deficit in the child from where Judy was sitting, beyond that dreadful haircut Davey had given her. To hear Bella's laughter, to listen to her imaginary play, to behold her politeness, and her curiosity, one would have to conclude that somehow, some way, she was well adjusted despite everything.

"You shouldn't smoke, Nana!" she called from the jungle gym. "It's bad for you."

There was a reason Judy sat upwind from the jungle gym. Though she was down to two cigarettes a day, she'd been dying for this one since midway through Reverend Hardy's sermon that morning, which wasn't half as comforting as she might have hoped. Travers would kill her if he knew she was smoking again, but her nerves were shot. What toll was two measly cigarettes a day going to exact compared to the anxiety Davey and Bella caused her on a weekly basis with their absence from her life? She kept telling herself it was temporary, that this crazy notion about living off the grid would run its course, but she was finding it harder each day to persuade herself.

As normal as Bella seemed drinking diet soda and eating frozen pizza in front of the TV, there were moments, like a few minutes prior on the drive to the park, when Judy caught the girl in a thousand mile stare, as though she'd totally checked out of reality, lips silently at work, almost like she was praying, which Judy wished she was.

"Bella? Are you okay, sweetie? Bella, honey?"

"I'm fine, Nana, I was just thinking."

Judy was glad Travers wasn't there to see the child lost in her thoughts like that, because Travers and Kris had already determined to take matters into their own hands, and Judy was not so sure that was a good idea, the two of them putting themselves between Bella and her daddy. Judy had prayed about it, but the Lord had been none too forthright in providing any answers. She just wished Davey would come to his senses. She knew the old Davey was in there somewhere, the Davey who used to be a light in the world, who'd had that generosity of spirit you could lean into like a campfire. He could absorb. And he had so much to give. But every time he came back from that business in Iraq there seemed to be less of him: less laughter, less warmth, less patience. Whatever it was that wrung it all out of him, he never talked about it, and everybody, including Judy, was afraid to ask. Seemed to Judy the least the damn Marine Corps could have done was help Davey get his old self back.

"Nana, can you push me?" Bella called from the swings. "Please, please, please?"

Judy stubbed out her cigarette on the bench, setting the half-smoked remainder aside for later as she rose dutifully from her bench seat.

"I used to push your daddy on these exact swings when he was your age," she told the child.

"Did you give him underdogs?"

"Of course."

"Will you give me one?"

"Oh, Bella, I'm an old lady. I couldn't."

"Please?"

Judy was not even sure she could bend down far enough to get under Bella, let alone duck out of the way in time to avoid getting kicked in the head. Add that to the growing list of things Judy couldn't do anymore. Like this town, like Davey, like the world at large, Judy was not what she used to be. Why couldn't they all just turn back the clock and have their old lives back? Back when V-Falls felt like the center of the world, back when Davey was in the newspaper for his athletic exploits, back when Judy could walk around town tingling with a sense of pride and accomplishment, back before everybody was discussing politics at all hours of the day and night, back when differences of opinion were still reconcilable.

Judy gritted her teeth, bent at the waist, and lunged forward, executing an underdog for the first time since 1988, though she pulled something in her back doing it. Still, she'd take any small victory she could get today, knowing that tomorrow morning Davey and Bella would be gone, and outside of her tiny sphere of influence once more.

"That wasn't really an underdog," said Bella. "You gotta go all the way under, Nana."

"Oh, Bella, honey, it's really tough on Nana's back."

"Okay," she said, a little sadly. "I understand."

Bella's deference, her willingness to accept disappointments, big and small, her impassive little face reminded Judy of Davey at six years old. Six-year-old Davey had aimed to please. He was polite, even-tempered, played well with others, minded his little brother, and made very few demands on her patience, unlike Travers, who was needy and tempestuous. Davey had very much been a first born: compliant, conscientious, if not a little on the earnest side.

She remembered the year after Wayne left, sitting at the vanity applying her eye shadow, a cigarette smoldering at her elbow, while the boys sat watching from the bed, awaiting the sitter, Travers restless, Dave resigned. Looking back, Judy felt guilty for wanting more. Like those two precious boys should've been enough. But they weren't. How could they have been when she never got a break?

"Who are you going out with?" said Davey.

"Just a friend."

"Mrs. Vance?"

"A different friend," she said.

"Mrs. Reese?"

"No, honey.

"The guy from the tow truck place?" said Davey.

"No. Davey, go see if that's the sitter."

Despite any confusion it might've caused Davey and Travers, Judy didn't regret trying to find companionship, whether it was Rudy, or Stan, or Walter. The thing she regretted was that she couldn't provide more for her boys, more security, more happiness, more opportunities. Twenty years ago, she hadn't had these regrets. Things had been working out reasonably well for Travers, and it looked like Davey was set to make the world his oyster. But he never got that far.

"Nana, you can finish smoking if you want," said Bella. "I don't need you to push."

"I'd hold on, if I were you, young lady," said Judy. "And keep your feet forward."

"Maybe you shouldn't," said Bella.

And probably Bella was right, but Judy bent at the knees this time, doing her best to ignore the vice-like pinch at the base of her right hip as she measured up Bella's backswing, then gripped her little butt, and pushed off with everything she had. She was directly under Bella when she let go, and she didn't even have to duck. By the time she turned to look at the girl, she was already on her way back, wide-eyed and grinning, and Judy was ready to execute ten more underdogs if that's what it took.

Faint Traces

———

Dave walked in the shadows as much as possible, limping slightly on his aching hip, eyes to the pavement, as he wound his way through the streets of his youth, the sidewalks a little dirtier, the houses a little more worn. In front of the library, he managed to dodge Wes Hayes, his high school student body president, and proceeded inside, directly to the children's section where he selected seven or eight middle grade books he thought might appeal to Bella.

Dave yearned for something to read himself, but had no idea what. Maybe something about physics, but why? He had zero interest in anything theological, along with an imperative aversion to anything political. So he chose horticulture and geology, two subjects that might help him better understand and master his new home.

At checkout, the librarian was perfectly fine with not chatting, limiting the entirety of their interaction to, "Those are all due back August twenty-eighth."

If only all his interactions in town could've been executed so painlessly and efficiently.

Walking past the high school, Dave doubled down on his efforts to ward off the past. But when he passed the football field it caught up to him. God, but he'd known that playbook inside out. As a halfback, he was patient to break and quick through the hole. He trusted his blockers. As a receiver out of the backfield, he had a tricky release, and ran crisp routes. He was good in space. Never mind that Tatterson couldn't hit the broad side of a barn. Walking past the western goal post, Dave couldn't help but wonder what Rolla, Missouri, might have been like.

Navigating the center of town with his backpack, he managed to evade those inquisitive eyes upon him, knowing what he must've looked like to them: at the very least a curiosity, at worst a nut job. Striding purposefully past the newspaper boxes, he avoided reading the headlines. Head down as he passed the crowded patio of Cascade Coffee, he all but tuned out the random snatches of conversation. He didn't want to know what was going on in the world. He could guess that already: the same old bullshit, but worse. Same old fat, white, incomprehensible madness. Same old orange menace. He didn't want to hear anyone's opinion. He didn't care what was being done to stop the madness. Let it burn.

At the credit union, Dave checked the balance on his savings account, which amounted to seven hundred and thirty-six dollars. He considered draining it for a fleeting instant, but instead withdrew a hundred and twenty dollars. Sooner or later, he would have to ask Travers or his mom for money if he was going to remain dependent on town to any extent, but that was a bridge he would cross when he got to it.

On his way out the door, Dave heard his name, but ignored it, proceeding briskly on his way. The voice followed him out the door, then down the sidewalk. Finally he turned to find Nadene's brother, Jerry, approaching. Before Dave could escape, Jerry locked him in an embrace.

"Brother," he said. "You're back. Glad you came to your senses."

"No," Dave said. "Just for the day."

Jerry held Dave captive at arm's length, inspecting him with kind, somber eyes, a smile playing at the corners of his mouth. Somehow, Jerry defied the diminishing effects of time. His face was as smooth and hairless as it was senior year of high school.

For years, throughout high school, and throughout his marriage to Nadene, Jerry had been like a big brother to Dave, at times more of a brother than Travers. Two years before Dave ever played varsity, Jerome

Charles was the best quarterback the Vigilantes ever saw. He could've been the next Sonny Sixkiller if it hadn't been for a torn labrum. It was Jerry who explained the finer nuances of offensive schemes to Dave freshman year, the same year Dave started seeing Nadene. Even when Dave was at odds with Nadene, Jerry always seemed to have his back.

Now, half a lifetime later, there remained nothing but the distance Dave had created between them, as if Nadene's life had been bridging the chasm all along.

"You don't look bad, brother," Jerry said. "What are you doing down here?"

"Supplies," said Dave, shrugging free of his brother-in-law's clutches.

"Ah, salt, I bet. You should be catching your fill of Chinook up there this fall. It's gonna be a good run."

"Built a smokehouse," said Dave.

"Smart," said Jerry. "You're gonna need the fat this winter. Supposed to be a cold one."

"They're all cold," said Dave.

"And how's my niece?" Jerry said.

"She's great, doing great."

Jerry searched him, eyes visibly doubting Dave.

"Really," Dave assured him. "She's great. She's healthy, she's happy, and she's smart as a whip."

"If you say so, brother. But sooner or later, they're going to come for her."

"I'll be ready," said Dave. "Look, I've gotta go, Jerry. It was really good seeing you."

"Don't be a stranger," said Jerry. "Maybe I'll come up this fall for a visit."

"Ok," said Dave. "I'll be looking for you."

"How will I find you?"

"I'm up past the falls, a couple miles south of the canyon. Look for a bluff above the meadow."

"Maybe I will," said Jerry.

But it was Dave's hope that he would not.

"See you around, Jer," he said.

Then he turned and walked off without looking back.

At Red Apple, Dave bought two Tony's frozen pizzas and licorice tea, along with five pounds of brown rice, five pounds of wheat flour, five pounds of oats, and ten pounds of sea salt. He bought honey, raisins, and walnuts in bulk. He bought a little pink brush for Bella, though there was not much hair on her head left to manage. He bought a deck of cards, four spiral notebooks, and a pack of twenty-four colored pens.

At the checkout stand, the woman with the nametag that said "Kiki" was snapping gum as she scanned Dave's groceries.

"Still camping, huh?"

"We're all camping," said Dave, packing the supplies directly into his backpack.

At the end of town, Dave was relieved when the sidewalk ended, and he could walk in the shadows once more. The town was haunted. Practically every square inch of the place still bore the faint traces of Dave's erstwhile footsteps. Everywhere he looked, he seemed to have a memory attached. All those good times with Nadene, and Fishel, and Wettleson, and Spaz. All those weekend nights driving around to no purpose, all those late-night breakfasts at Dale's, all that Friday night glory under the lights. When he thought of those times now, they only depressed him, for he could not help but compare them to what his life had become.

With forty pounds on his back, Dave walked as fast as he could back to his mom's house.

The following morning, when they were readying to leave, Dave's mom took him aside in the kitchen.

"Leave her with me, Davey, please."

"I can't do that, Mom."

"Why not?"

Dave knew he didn't have a good answer, at least not one that would persuade his mother. As though on cue, Bella arrived in the kitchen to save him.

"I want to go back, Nana," she said.

His mom eyed her doubtfully. Then she turned to Dave and searched his face, but Dave just lowered his eyes.

"C'mon, baby," he said to Bella. "Let's beat the rain."

Third Time Is the Charm

Midway through his first tour in Iraq, Dave began losing faith in the chain of command. The rule of three was a cruel math. In combat it tended to look a lot like subtraction. It didn't take too many patrols for Dave to see that his staff sergeant, whose name shall not be uttered, was a self-serving prick, routinely volunteering the lives of his platoon to make himself look good. And make no mistake: lives were sacrificed to this end. It was the grunts and the unlucky reserves who put their butts on the line, while the superiors used them like human stepping stones.

By the end of his second tour, Dave had not only lost all faith in the chain of command, but also his faith in military enterprise as a whole, which he began to see less and less as service, and more and more as political enterprise, an industry in which he occupied the most thankless of roles. But he took the twenty grand, and re-enlisted anyway.

By the end of the deployment, Dave essentially felt like he was serving out his contract. Any noble instincts that once attached themselves to his service had withered long before he was ever deployed the third time. His sense of duty was at an all-time low. The foundation of his marriage was already showing cracks. His drive was down sexually, professionally, and socially. His sleep was already tortured. But he was trying to beat it, trying to pull himself up by the bootstraps. He was finally making progress in his daily life: small steps in redefining his expectations for happiness, in resisting his impulses, in controlling his temper, in pretending to want to interact with people, in bridging washed-out inroads to his past, in blotting out an urgent, unresolvable history that came rushing back at him in feverish waves.

He was making small steps toward feeling human again.

Re-deployment was the worst thing that could have possibly happened to him, though his sense of duty was not entirely flagging. The night before Dave deployed in March, Nadene woke him in the middle of the night, her hot breath in his ear. And no sooner did he stir than she rolled him over on his back and began to straddle him. But before they could ever engage, Nadene broke down crying, and rolled off him, and Dave lay there frozen as his hard-on withered, aware that he was unable to comfort her.

It was a harbinger of things to come.

"It will be okay," he finally told her, half-believing it.

"I know," she said without conviction, her voice catching.

His third tour was the worst. The suffocating heat, and the dust. The shitty food. The sweating and chafing and burning. The jangled nerves and the dry throat. The ceaseless tedium of base life, playing cards and chess, and drinking vodka with blue food coloring out of mouthwash bottles. The restless ribbing, and the competing, and the constant shit-talking.

And then, without warning, a security detail, where it seemed nobody was innocent, where it seemed every Iraqi cowering behind a wall or skulking in a doorway wanted to kill you. Dave remembered just about every detail with the odd remoteness of a dream. By then, he was numb to the violence, though his nerves were worn.

Around week six, Dave started to come unhinged. Despite his frayed nerves, and scorched sinuses, his intermittently bleeding nose, his ears that rang at all hours of the day and night, Dave managed to persist. But persistence was a tenuous state of equilibrium. A half-dozen times Dave hallucinated on patrols. Once, on a security detail, he wasn't sure if he was asleep or awake for a good ten minutes. On five separate occasions, he heard persistent voices. Meanwhile, his head ached, his esophagus burned, and he shit his fatigues with increasing regularity. On patrol, Dave's thoughts scurried about his head looking for cover like panicked mice, while dark impulses arrived suddenly and decisively, manifesting just as suddenly into actions whose consequences were not even considered.

Somewhere in the heat of engagement, Dave lost his moral compass. He was in crisis, unable to sustain his actions without separating himself from the consequences. It was obvious. Coach Prentice would have read it in his body language immediately. He would have seen it in his eyes and sat him down. For that matter, so would anyone who knew him.

And yet, up the entire chain of command, officials, superiors, politicians, all of them looked the other way. They just kept throwing Dave out there, despite the fact he was clearly traumatized, and clearly a potential danger to himself or anyone else who happened to cross his path. And he kept showing up, not for country or honor or justice, but for the marine standing next to him. And isn't that precisely what Dave had learned on the gridiron? Wasn't that the message coach Prentice and all the other coaches before him tried to impart for Dave?

"Play for the guy next to you," Gordy told him.

And Dave had always been willing to surrender his will to some larger scheme or objective. A platoon, a team, a community, a family, they were all like a web, wasn't that the message? So, why is it that once Dave got home, all he wanted to do was separate himself from the team, extricate himself from the web, and completely avoid the rest of humanity? Why is it he could no longer be a team player? Why was the man next to him no longer enough reason to try?

Refuge

If there was one thing in Bella's life that became clear with the arrival of fall, it was that her dad needed her. She couldn't say why exactly, and she was not quite sure how to serve him beyond obedience, but she knew that if nothing else, her dad needed her to be near him, or he never would have brought her here. And though she was now permitted more freedom to wander, she stuck close to camp most of the time, rarely out of earshot, though there were whole mornings and afternoons when they hardly communicated with each other. So it was not that she felt particularly wanted, only needed.

The cats were her constant companions: Boots and Betty, Boris and Tito, Sugarfoot and Jimmy Stewart. She mimicked their feline mannerisms, their lazy grace as they slunk about the bluff, their lithesome stealth as they stalked the meadow for birds.

"Boris," she said, one day in the meadow. "Do you ever wish you were someone else? I'll bet you don't. I'll bet you can't even imagine being somebody else."

Boris seemed to consider the statement briefly, but soon turned away to lick between his legs.

"What about you, Betty? Do you miss your old life? Are you glad we brought you here?"

But Betty had little patience for these conversations. Motherhood had changed her, or maybe it was this place that had changed her. She'd lost her old playfulness, and she was not nearly as affectionate as she once was.

"I wish you could have met my mom," Bella said to Jimmy Stewart, curled in her lap. "I think you would have liked her. If it weren't for my mom, we would've never got Betty, and then there never would have never been a you, so I guess you'd have to like her."

Despite her ability to summon the ancient world of ice at will, Bella could no longer talk to her mother. Of late, when she thought of her mother, she thought mostly of her mother's empty closet, and the spaces she once occupied: the kitchen table, where she smoked by the window, and bit her nails, and did crossword puzzles; the green sofa, where she sometimes fell asleep with the TV on; the empty spot in the driveway where the Dodge used to be parked. It all seemed like part of a different life to Bella. Every day it seemed like the memory of her mother grew blurrier and a little more distant. If she concentrated really hard, Bella could remember what she looked like, she could recall her scratchy voice, and recall the feel of her calloused fingertips upon her cheek. She could remember her mother telling her stories before bed, but she couldn't remember the stories, just the sound of her voice washing over Bella as her eyes grew heavy. She could remember not crying at the funeral, and being just about the only one. She remembered knowing without a doubt that her mother was coming back. She remembered trying to explain it to the adults, and how they didn't know what to say in response. But now, Bella knew her mother was not coming back, and she felt dumb for ever having believed that she would. She only had the memories to keep her mom alive, and she could feel them slipping away. What would happen when Bella no longer remembered her?

"Daddy," she said, one evening, watching him clean the Winchesters by the light of the lantern. "Did Mommy die on purpose?"

He paused in his task and lowering the barrel of the rifle rested a hand on her shoulder, looking meaningfully into her face.

"No, baby, no," he said softly. "Mommy had an accident. Why would you think that?"

Bella averted her eyes.

"I heard a lady at the store whisper it when I was with Nana. She called it a death wish."

"Well, that lady doesn't know what she's talking about," he said. "She ought to mind her own business. Shame on her."

Bella retreated into silence momentarily, chewing on her bottom lip.

"Do you think about her every day, Daddy?" she said.

"Most days, yeah," he said.

"What do you remember?"

"Well," he said. "A lot of things."

"Tell me," she said.

"Like, I remember how good she was at Scrabble, how she'd always come up with a word I'd never heard of, and I'd challenge her, and she'd look it up in the dictionary, and she'd be right every dang time."

"What kind of words?"

"Well, like I think 'qanat' was one of them, with a 'q' and no 'u' in it."

"What does it mean?"

"Heck if know," he said. "I doubt I'm even saying it right."

"What else do you remember?" she said.

"I remember her laugh."

"It was scratchy," she said.

"Yeah," he said with a sad smile. "I guess it was kind of scratchy."

"Are you crying, Daddy?"

"Yeah, baby," he said. "Just a little."

"I'm sorry, Daddy."

"Me, too, honey," he said, gathering her in his arms and squeezing her.

Bella pressed her face into his itchy flannel shirt and clutched him as hard as she could as she felt her own eyes begin to sting. No matter how hard she clung to her mother's memory, it was already growing fainter by the day. How was she supposed to keep her alive forever?

U'ku'let

After searching the mountains far and wide, U'ku'let found his young family a suitable home; a narrow cleft in the mountainside, which opened up into a stone cavern, spacious enough for three, and nearly, but not quite, of sufficient height in which to stand up straight. The cave was six steps deep, tapering toward the rear. At its widest point, it was nearly five steps across. Ventilation was adequate for a small fire, and the daylight hours allowed for a narrow swath of light, just enough to see by.

The cave was situated high on a bluff, above a broad canyon, in the shadow of a soaring ridge, keen-edged, and marked at intervals by jagged pinnacles like the teeth of a canine. Beyond the canyon, the terrain flattened out into a scrubby forest of stunted spruce, dusted in permafrost, which sprawled to the north for miles. To the west, the bluff overlooked a frozen meadow, beyond which several abrupt valleys gave way to the ice, which spread out into eternity.

A short hike to the northeast of the bluff ended abruptly atop a ridge, overlooking a broad, grass valley, running north to south. From here, once the season was upon them, U'ku'let would be able to watch the game moving through the basin.

U'ku'let hunted with renewed courage, and a new determination, an impetus fueled by a force stronger than even hunger: responsibility. For the first time in his twenty winters, U'ku'let was more concerned with the welfare of others than himself, a state of affairs that he found to be both a burden and a relief.

Daily, U'ku'let appealed to the Great Provider, and in the end, the Great Provider did not fail him. After three days of hunger and driving snow, upon the first clear afternoon, with the sun glinting off the snow and ice, a hobbled bison cow and her calf came moping through the valley, clearly not long for the world. U'ku'let gathered his spears and dressing tools, and swiftly but stealthily worked his way down the craggy incline to the basin, tracking his target's progress through the trees.

When he reached the half-frozen grass, U'ku'let emerged from the reeds and stalked the cow and her calf for a mile through the valley, until the cow, beleaguered and exhausted, finally turned to him, expelling twin plumes of steam out of her nostrils, her huge brown eyes entreating him to get it over with, or that's how it seemed to him.

When U'ku'let reared back with his spear, making clear his intentions, the cow, miraculously, surrendered according to the Great Provider's plan. Not that it had ever gone that way a hundred times before. Oh, no, U'ku'let had watched his own father trampled to death by bison, saw his older brother stomped, maimed, and rendered speechless by a stampede. There's a good reason U'ku'let never wanted to be a hunter. If he could have stayed back with the women, mending hides and hollowing spear tips, and tending to the fire, he would have jumped at the opportunity. Why invite such danger if you had no appetite for it, if somebody else could do it for you?

But that was the old U'ku'let. The new U'ku'let knew exactly what he was fighting for. As the cow lay there dying, speared cleanly through the neck, the twin plumes of her nostrils now discharging a thin spray of blood that pocked the snow with its warmth, the calf sought out its mother's prone body, and not comprehending her state, nudged it with his head.

"I am sorry," he said to the calf. "You will not survive without her."

And then the calf, lolling his head up to make eye contact with U'ku'let, surrendered, too.

Sometimes the things of this world know when they are beaten. Sometimes they don't fight to the bitter end because they know better. U'ku'let had seen it many times before, and it would not be the last time.

Not yet convinced of his good fortunes, U'ku'let began dressing the animals immediately, a bloody and rigorous affair he undertook with the utmost haste. Now that blood has been spilled, who knew what wolf or cat or bear lurked in the wings to challenge him for his kill? He would not die in the name of greed. No, he would survive in the name of knowing when to stop. As much as he wished it were so, he could not possibly claim the whole kill, anyway. He had neither the time to carve it into anything manageable, nor the ability, given his crude tools.

Thus, U'ku'let left something for the others. His only hope as he carved away savagely at the carcasses was that those other ravenous suitors in the wings were patient enough to wait for his offering. When he concluded his crude butchering, sawing and hacking the meat off of the ribs, and tearing away the impossibly tough cartilage from the bone, along with the sinewy, bone-white connective tissue from the hide, he left the scene, dragging the great cow pelt across the ice, two hundred pounds, headless, and packed with the hearts and livers and soft organs torn, severed, and cleaved from around the stomach, in addition to what meat was left hanging in strings and bloody slabs from the mother's giant ribcage.

Smeared with the blood of the beast from foot to forehead, the grueling journey back to the cave was not so much a triumphant affair as a desperate and harried retreat to outrun any number of predators on his trail, the conspicuous swath of warm blood left blooming in his wake.

Only when U'ku'let the Hunter had returned to the safety of the fire, and the shelter of their cloistered cavern, did he bask in triumph.

He was grateful, and why not? For that which clung to life in these mountains: the grass, and the trees, and the shy, small creatures that skulked between the rocks were a revelation, a beautiful relief from the cruel outside world of ceaseless ice. It was madness for his clan to ever have left these mountains, to ever have turned their backs on the bounty that dwelled in these valleys, hard won as their survival might have been. And for what did they leave? For nothing more than to chase an empty legend, the slim promise of something more grand, something warmer and more fertile, something easier and less bloody that awaited them beyond the horizon.

Foolishness.

Not to boast, because nobody was listening anyway, but U'ku'let celebrated daily the fact that their little cave on the bluff was sheltered and vented well. Despite all the hunching, and the sore elbows, and bruised knees, and the fact that he'd bumped his head to the point of bleeding countless times at the narrow entry, U'ku'let deemed their burrow a perfect starter home for a clan of three, and perhaps someday four. Bear in mind, they had been there less than a moon, so the place was still a work in progress. With a rock here, a buffalo hide there, a found tusk, or gem, or string of sabre teeth placed tastefully about, maybe some crude charcoal drawings on the wall, the possibilities for their cave seemed endless.

And for this shelter and security, they found themselves beholden to no one. Who was the boss? U'ku'let was the boss. U'ku'let with the harelip, and the patchy beard. U'ku'let, who never got a fair shake from the clan, U'ku'let who could have taught the elders a thing or two if they would have ever listened to him. It was not always the tallest and the hairiest that made the best leaders. Sometimes it was the guy cowering behind the tanning hides.

But all of that was irrelevant now. U'ku'let's day had arrived at long last. Finally, he was the leader of a growing clan.

At night, the small space was warmed by the fire, as the frozen wind bellowed, ravaging the world outside their shelter, carrying upon it the cry of the slathering, half-starved wolves. U'ku'let shivered at the memory of the clan's hapless weeks on the ice, which ended in banishment, and by extension his union with S'tka.

Surely, their wayward clan would all be dead by now, what with the lack of leadership, and their foolhardy commitment to pursue the non-existent, when the fruits of the world were right in front of them. It was a blessing to be banished from such an idiotic quest.

He looked to S'tka, bathed in the light of the flames, sleepy-eyed but content, the swaddled infant suckling at her breast, and suddenly his appetite for her was irrepressible. Squatting, he sidled around the fire on his heels to S'tka's side, pressing his face into her neck, where he nibbled at the flesh.

"Ooooh," he groaned softly.

"U'ku'let, stop," S'tka said, giggling as she fended off his advance.

Her laughter only aroused the hunger between his legs as he redoubled his effort, nibbling down her neck to her clavicle, toward her swollen breasts.

"Ech," she said, just as the baby lost its purchase on the nipple, and immediately began to fuss. "Tsk," S'tka scolded U'ku'let, scooting away from him.

Little N'ka managed to find his mark with a slurp and a whimper, his tiny fingers grasping at the soft flesh of her shoulders.

"Bah," said U'ku'let, who began to sulk, staring into the fire.

Who provided the meat, that helpless, suckling thing groping at you? No! I provided the meat! It is I who saves our naked carcasses from this frozen world, I, who makes sure we don't become meat ourselves. Bah, no gratitude, no respect.

But when U'ku'let looked back up and saw S'tka's placid face smiling across the fire at him, he felt humbled, and ashamed of the thing between his legs.

"Ech!" he said to it, with a healthy thwack. "Ech!"

S'tka laughed sweetly, though her expression showed a certain concern, too.

"It has a mind of its own, eh?"

"Ay," he said, even as the thing began to wither, pasting itself to his inner thigh, a pale, wrinkled nubbin compared to its former glory.

Immediately, he began to berate himself. *He was not worthy. He was but a failed warrior and spineless follower, with a harelip, and wide, feminine hips. Worse, he was an outcast of a doomed clan, the stupidest of clans, and thus doomed himself to be loveless, no matter what meat he presented to whom. It was a fluke that he was with S'tka.*

But before U'ku'let could brood any longer, S'tka scooted in closer to him, perhaps an act of mercy, her placid eyes still smiling, and the infant still suckling at her breast.

"Look," she said, staring down into its face. "He looks like his father."

U'ku'let smiled, looking down into the pinched face of the infant, eyes big, and alert, and calm.

"You think so?" he said.

"Yes," said S'tka, pulling back the hide to reveal his nakedness, his little dingus standing at attention.

Gently in the Darkness

At night, Dave fought off the nightmares by lying awake, distracting himself with plans about improvements for their insular existence. There was storage to be improved upon, portage to be streamlined, warmth and water and grain to be conserved, along with various best practices in order to avoid their dependence on town. But some nights, as he distracted and deflected and avoided, his sleep-deprived mind wandered in spite of his efforts, and in the orange glow of the embers, in the dry whistle of the coals as they surrendered the last of their moisture, Dave intimated jug-eared Lyle Abbot from El Paso, hanging out of the hummer, stock still when he caught it, still staying upright somehow, like a scarecrow on fire, the Kevlar melting to his skull.

One night in the cave, somewhere between asleep and awake, he screamed without even knowing it, raging at the dying fire until Bella awoke terrified. Only then did Dave realize that he'd lost his shit momentarily, and that Bella had borne witness. Liberating himself from his sleeping bag, he scurried across the uneven ground on his hands and knees in the darkness to comfort her.

"I'm sorry if I scared you, baby. I was having a bad dream."

"I thought it was real," she said, sobbing. "I didn't know what was wrong."

"No, baby, it wasn't real, it was just a dream."

"I'm scared," she said.

"Don't be scared, honey. I'm right here."

Wrapping her in his arms, he felt her body go rigid.

"But, Daddy," she said, "I'm scared of you."

And a cold hand gripped Dave's heart, even as he clutched Bella tighter, rocking her gently in the darkness.

S'tka

For many days and nights, S'tka and U'ku'let managed a peaceful existence on their bluff, overlooking the canyon. U'ku'let hunted with increasing skill and continued good fortune, while S'tka cured hides and tended their camp, the infant harnessed to her chest. If not content, she felt purposeful. The pride of making their new life happen was fuel for her fire. Had her transgression not saved them? Were they not better off without the clan? Were they not better fed, and better rested, and more appreciated? She no longer wished ill will on the clan for her banishment, for it had led her to a better life.

In recent weeks, the air had begun to warm, promising some degree of relief from the snow and ice. Each year, the warm air seemed to arrive a little earlier. How could this be a harbinger for anything but good? Without the clan around their necks, they would continue to thrive.

As for baby N'ka, he was cow-eyed and alert, with a dark shock of hair sticking straight up off the crown of his little head. Already his neck could support the weight of it. He kicked his arms and legs. He babbled and cooed and laughed at nothing discernible. He watched his mother and father eat with keen interest, chin slick with drool. He grasped futilely for their food and whimpered at their amusement when they wouldn't allow him to partake.

His father claimed N'ka would be a great hunter, and that someday he would lead his own clan. His mother thought not. She saw, in the bottomless depths of his eyes, someone who would do much grander things than toil with spears, things she could only guess at, things that had never been done. Perhaps he would devise a way of life that would render the clan forever obsolete. Perhaps he would discover a new world where the others before him had failed.

"Bah," said U'kulet. "Like what? Shall he lead his clan over the ice in search of legends, like that muscle-head Ok'eh? No, he will be a great hunter. The greatest on ice."

These were the prosperous futures they contemplated as they warmed themselves by the fire. The Great Provider had smiled on this family. She had brought food and shelter and good health to these mountains. She had brought hope where formerly there had only been despair, she had brought a future to where there had once only been a present.

Until, one day, their good fortune ran out.

The men arrived boisterously from the southern corridor, up the narrow, snow-packed sluice, announcing themselves with their hooting and cackling and their coarse laughter.

"Woot!" one of them hollered, his guttural voice echoing across the valley.

S'tka did not have to see the marauders to guess at their brutish natures.

The dialect was a familiar one. They had long been the enemy of her clan, bloodthirsty savages from the south, the great mastodon hunters, though they were well known to eat human flesh when the game got scarce.

S'tka and U'ku'let exchanged anxious glances across the fire.

"Go," he said.

Without hesitation, S'tka bolted to the cave with the sleeping infant. Swaddling him tightly, she stowed him without awakening him amongst hides in the deepest, darkest alcove. She piled an additional heap of hides in front of the recess to dampen the sound should anything threaten to awaken N'ka, and he should begin to whimper or cry.

By the time she re-emerged empty-handed, the ravagers had already landed, kicking the fire, and taunting U'ku'let with their spears. Backpedaling against their advance, U'ku'let fell backward onto his butt, where immediately he tried to muddle back to his feet, much to the amusement of his tormentors.

The largest and dirtiest, the foulest of the bunch—though that distinction was worthy of debate—took hold of U'ku'let roughly under the arms, dragging him to his feet.

"Let's go, ugly," he said, exposing his rotten teeth. "Time to play."

"Stop!" S'tka protested to the amusement of all.

The giant man pushed U'ku'let forward, propelling him into the arms of another brute, who immediately pushed him back to the bigger man, grinning stupidly.

One of the looters ducked into the cave. S'tka watched helplessly, fearful of displaying her concern, lest she compromise N'ka, tucked away in the depths.

"Please protect him," she prayed, beneath her breath.

And this time, finally, the Great Provider heard her entreaty, as the brute emerged moments later, his arms heaped only with hides and half-eaten hindquarter.

"Not much," he announced.

Meanwhile, the youngest and smallest among them, no more than a boy of twelve or thirteen, had begun to circle U'ku'let, razzed and encouraged by the others, amused by his antics.

U'ku'let continued to backpedal until he reached the edge of the bluff, where he nearly slipped and lost his footing. Cornered by the young man, U'ku'let darted to one side, eluding him by several feet, only to find himself backed up against the rocky hillside.

"What are you waiting for?" said one of the spectators. "Finish him."

Eyes stuck to U'ku'let, the boy stooped to collect a jagged stone the size of his fist. Wielding it like a weapon, the young man charged. Lashing out, he struck U'ku'let across the forehead, and sent him reeling backward into the side of the mountain, where he immediately began to cower, covering his head with his arms.

And as U'ku'let cowered, the boy struck him again and again.

U'ku'let wobbled dazedly, swiping at his bloody head, before crumpling to the ground unconscious, where his blood began to redden the snow.

The others erupted in laughter. One of the stinking brutes grabbed S'tka by the arms and forced her onto her back. Straddling her, he hefted one of her breasts from beneath her hide, then the other, impressed by their weight. S'tka's biggest fear was not that he would hurt her, but that he would connect her heaviness of breast and her swollen nipples with the infant stashed in the cave, that her breast might ooze milk and blow N'ka's cover. Her next biggest fear was that N'ka would awaken and announce his presence.

But this one was too stupid to make connections. His eyes held all the light of a dead squirrel. His lips were chafed and blistered. His brown, crooked teeth were worn to nubs.

The brute leaned in with his putrid breath.

"Relax," he whispered.

S'tka struggled against his weight, tried to wriggle her wrists free of his grasp, but her efforts only amused her assailant, along with the rest of the band. When he pressed his face to S'tka, she forced her head to the side to elude his abscessed lips, where she saw U'ku'let, splayed out lifeless at the base of the hillside, a slash of crimson from his head sullying the snow.

The filthy goon redoubled his effort to kiss her, finally succeeding. He tasted of rotting flesh and offal. It took all the strength S'tka could muster not to bite his face. But she knew she must weather this assault without a fight if she hoped to ever see her N'ka again.

Her assailant bore down on her with all his weight, forcing himself inside of her. His breathing was wet and labored. The stink of him was unbearable.

Just as the filthy sloth shunted one final time and emptied himself inside her, her attacker climbed off hastily and scrambled for his spear, as the others, too, abandoned their lounging and scurried for their weapons at the trumpeting of a mammoth from the valley below.

"Giant!" one of them shouted.

"Giant!" they all chanted, as they raced down the hill, leaving S'tka half-naked on the ground.

S'tka clambered to her feet and hurried to U'ku'let, bleeding in the snow. Turning him over on his back, she found him conscious, but dazed.

"Where is N'ka?" he inquired, glassy-eyed, blood congealing around the gash on his forehead.

As if on cue, the infant began to cry in the depths of the cave.

S'tka rushed to the cave and retrieved the infant, shushing and consoling him as she made her way back to U'ku'let. She squatted once more above her partner, brushing his blood-matted hair away from the gash on his head.

The cries of the maulers were distant now, their figures tiny against the ice as they circled the great beast, and taunted him, two hundred feet below, hooting and hollering at their good fortune.

S'tka gathered a handful of snow and began cleaning the wound on U'ku'let's head, which was three fingers wide and half-a-knuckle deep. Even the snow could not stanch the bleeding. S'tka gathered up a stone and began chipping at the ice at the base of the hillside. When she'd loosed a large chunk, she pressed it to the wound, and held it there, as U'ku'let slipped into unconsciousness.

Of all the perils and pitfalls you've foisted upon us, Great Provider, none is equal to the thoughtless cruelty of man. For only man among all the beasts worked so hard to cultivate the worst of his nature.

Salty Sweet

———————

One afternoon, when Bella was stationed beneath the lonesome willow amidst the high grass, Boots, curled beside her, suddenly tilted his head, raised his hackles, and then rose to his feet, arching his back.

Bella sprang upright, clutching her bear spray as Boots circled nervously. When Bella heard the crunch of footsteps behind her, she swung around, expecting to confront an animal. Though relieved, she was equally surprised at what she saw there.

"Uncle Travers?" she said. "You scared me."

"Shh," he said, holding a finger to his lips, as he swished toward her through the grass.

"Why are we being quiet?" she whispered.

"We just are," he explained.

Thrilled to see him, Bella smiled despite her confusion. Boots, meanwhile scurried up the willow, where he watched the scene unfold.

"What are you doing here? Is Bonnie here, too?" Bella said, hopefully. "Where's Daddy?"

Uncle Travers kneeled and wrapped her up in a bear hug. He was a good hugger, Uncle Travers; he made hugging feel natural. She liked the way he smelled, too, the salty sweet mix of sweat and underarm deodorant.

"I came to take you home," he said softly, patting her back. "Bonnie and Auntie Kris are excited to see you."

"But . . ." said Bella, trailing off.

Still kneeling at eye level, Uncle Travers held her shoulders at arm's length and smiled into her face.

"You're gonna stay with us, now," he said. "You'll have your own room."

"But what about Daddy?" she said.

His smile faded, but not altogether. "Honey," he said. "This is about what's best for you."

"Did Daddy say it was all right?"

"This is about you," he said, like she hadn't heard him the first time. "This isn't about Daddy. Bonnie can't wait to show you her new bike. She says you can have her old one."

"But all my stuff," she said.

"We'll get you new stuff. Better stuff."

"But I need to tell Daddy," she said. "He's fishing down at the river."

"I left him a note," he said. "He knows. We need to get going soon, though, before it gets late. Here, hop on," he said, offering her his shoulders.

"But what about the cats?" she said.

The truth, she knew, was that the cats could take care of themselves, and that they'd come if they wanted to come, or stay if they wanted to stay.

"Daddy will take care of the cats," he said.

"You're sure it's okay with Daddy if I go?"

"It's all in the note, honey."

"When are we coming back?" she said.

"C'mon," he said playfully, as though he hadn't heard her, and began loping through the tall grass. "We'll go out to Westside for pizza tonight."

"Can Nana come?"

"Of course."

And through the meadow and into the tree line they galloped, while Boots, from his willowy perch, warily watched them go.

Bella began to laugh as Uncle Travers weaved between the hemlocks, jumping over downed trees, yet she sensed something in his brisk pace that was not so playful, after all.

"Uncle Travers? When will we—"

"Ssh," he said.

A Real Home

Dave returned from the river triumphantly in the afternoon with a string of early Chinook, their silvery skin glimmering in the sunlight. No need of rice, or bullion tonight. No, tonight, they would feast.

"Bella!" he shouted. "Look what I've got! C'mon!"

But she neither called back, nor came running.

Dave set the fish aside and ducked into the cave.

"Baby, you in here?" he said.

His heart skipped a beat when he saw the note on the ground near the entrance, pinned beneath a stone. Snatching it up, he studied it furiously, pacing the bluff as he read:

> Dave,
>
> As you can see, I came for Bella. It's for her own good, and if you love her, you've got to see that. I suppose there's a more official way to go about this, but somehow I knew I couldn't count on you complying, and who knows how long it might take the paper-pushers to figure all this out. You could argue that I have no legal right, but if you want to make this a legal thing, Kris and I like our chances, given the circumstances. Family is family. I've already pulled some strings with the school administration. Before you lose your cool, or do anything stupid like come after her, just know that Kris and I have Bella's best interest in mind. School started last week and she needs to be there. She needs to be living in a real home, with a real bedroom, and have friends. Winter is right around the corner, and this is no place for a little girl in winter. Know

that she'll be safe and taken good care of, and we will in no way try to turn her against you. When you're ready to come back to town and stay, we've got a place for you, too. And once you get back on your feet, and prove you can take care of Bella, we can go from there. I know you're going to be very angry at me, and I'm okay with that. Eventually, you'll see the wisdom in it. Whatever you do, Dave, don't come back for her unless you intend to stick around. This is all for Bella's good, and if you can't see that, well, I guess things are even worse than anybody thought.

> *Your brother,*
> *Travers*

Dave's first instinct was to head them off at the bottom of the canyon. They couldn't be more than a couple of hours ahead of him. He'd be wise to catch them before town, knowing there'd surely be a scene. Little Brother had a lot of damn nerve. The fact that Travers had somehow managed to find Bella up here, and catch Dave unawares, led Dave to believe that Travers had been spying on them all along, hatching this plan for weeks. Maybe months. He must have followed them up here at some point. Dave ought to hurry down the mountain and kick Travers' ass right in front of Bella. So what was he waiting for? Why couldn't he take that first step?

Because, he reasoned, Travers was right.

He walked to the edge of the bluff, and looked out over the abyss, where somewhere below his daughter was snaking her way out of his life. He wanted to shout out something to Bella, something that would echo down through the steep corridors and reach her, a few words that would acknowledge that Daddy had been wrong, and that he hoped she would not be mad at him. But all he could think of was the obvious.

"Baby, I love you!" he shouted, eyes burning as the words echoed through the canyon.

II

———

The Book of Doubt

Cave Dave had no wife,
Cave Dave had no life,
Cave Dave had a daughter,
Cave Dave never taught her,
Cave Dave thought he was boss,
Cave Dave ate crazy sauce."

—Second-graders, Nelson Elementary,
Vigilante Falls, WA

Sean Halligan; Bartender, Doc's

———

"Oh, I knew who he was, all right, but really only from a distance. He was like Bigfoot, sort of a legend around here. The day he took that little girl up there to live was the day he became almost like a myth. Mostly what I knew about Cave Dave is what I heard from other people, and that comprised a lot of opinions, and a lot of stories, some of which were a stretch if you ask me. Max from down at the tackle shop swears that Cave Dave broke into his hunting cabin up by Dead Man's Falls two winters ago. Stole his ghillie suit and his rain gear, canned food and batteries, then dropped a deuce in Max's skillet just to add insult to injury. But it's well known in this bar that Max is a talker after two or three Wild Turkeys, so take that for what it's worth.

"Seems like nobody could ever quite agree on Cave Dave. But they never got tired of talking about him. For everyone in this town who treated him like he was some kind of ghoul, seems like there was always two folks ready to call him a hero.

"Dave Cartwright was not much of a drinker, so far as I know. He was only in here once on my shift. The time I saw him must've been shortly before he took to living up there, maybe a month after his wife went over the falls. It was the middle of the afternoon when he came in. The place was dead. Only a few hardcores I won't mention by name. But one of them is on the city council.

"Anyways, Cartwright sat right down there by himself at the end of the bar under the antlers. Ordered bitters and soda, no ice. Didn't take two sips of it the whole time he was here. Just sat there like he was made of stone, gripping the glass real tight, not making eye contact with anyone, and staring mostly at the bar top in front of him. I tried my hand at small talk, but he wasn't having it, and I know better than to push. My impression of the guy wasn't crazy, and it wasn't heroic, either. He just seemed like a blank slate to me. Like he wanted to be left alone."

A Real Home

———

Bella was hardly ever cold, that was one thing she appreciated about living at Auntie Kris and Uncle Travers' house. And the refrigerator was always full. Here, she was surrounded by comforts: thick carpet and fluffy pillows, a kitchen that was always clean, and a dining room that was never cluttered. The house was only four years old, a big house, but not huge, not like the houses Uncle Travers had been developing up on Raven Ridge, houses he called "McMansions." Uncle Travers always wore cowboy boots with slacks, and a shiny buckle, and a big leather cowboy hat that didn't look like anything a real cowboy would wear.

"These people have no taste," he complained almost nightly at the dinner table. "They want all those corny flourishes that they think make them look rich—wrought iron gates, and circular driveways, and goddang pergolas and bird baths in the garden. And for godsakes, swimming pools—here! They won't use them but three weeks a year. It's like pouring money down the drain."

"Then why encourage them?" said Auntie Kris.

"Because that's the market. They can afford it, and that's what they want. But they're gonna ruin this town, you wait and see."

"You brought them here," said Auntie Kris. "The Ridge was your idea."

"And it was a good one, obviously," he said. "We're already at seventy percent capacity, and half the houses aren't even framed yet."

"Well," said Auntie Kris. "You can't have it both ways, Trav."

"What am I supposed to do? They want to buy here. Somebody's gonna build those homes. We've already tripled our investment in less than two years. I don't hear you complaining."

"I wasn't complaining before the Ridge, either."

"But what's so great about this place, anyway, Kris? What is it we're preserving here? You're not even from here. It's about time this little backwater town saw some progress. We've been living in a bubble for forty years. Damnit, if I—"

"Honey," interrupted Auntie Kris with a flick of her eyes to indicate Bella and Bonnie.

"Pardon my language, girls."

At least the food choices were five million times better than at the cave: grilled chicken with mashed potatoes, and tiny little steamed carrots; tacos you could make yourself, so that you didn't have to put in stuff you didn't want, and chicken fingers, which was a really dumb name considering chickens didn't even have fingers, and even if they did they wouldn't be so big.

Also, it was nice to use a real bathroom. It's funny how Bella never thought she'd ever like taking baths, but the bathtub was just about the only place anyone left her alone anymore, even though she wasn't allowed to lock the door. Lying on her back, head submerged, Bella would gaze up at the ceiling tiles until they disappeared, until the world as she knew it ceased to exist, and she was back out on the ice. Sometimes she stayed in the bath for forty-five minutes before Auntie Kris made her get out.

Second grade at Nelson Elementary wasn't so bad. Bella liked Miss Martine better than Mrs. Rundgren. Bella had hated first grade. She found Mrs. Rundgren to be just like her name sounded, kind of all ground-up like gravel. Mrs. Rundgren had never seemed excited by anything she was trying to teach. Everything was a paper handout. You never got to decorate anything, or make anything up, or play any learning games. Bella never saw Mrs. Rundgren eat lunch, but she always imagined she must eat something dry, like a cheese sandwich without mayonnaise, or a sleeve of soda crackers. And when Mrs. Rundgren walked with her class down the hallway after the final bell, she always looked tired and hungry, and about a hundred years older than she did first thing in the morning. Her hair had always fallen off to one side, and her jeans looked droopy.

Miss Martine at least tried to have fun with the class. She was extremely patient, especially with the boys. They rarely did handouts, and when they did, you were allowed to decorate them. Miss Martine had a sneaky way of teaching. And at the end of the day, after the final bell, Miss Martine looked proud walking down the hall with her long, blonde, straight hair, all silky and still in place, and her perfect posture, and her skinny but muscular legs, and her chunky high heels swinging fluidly one in front of the other. Miss Martine was glamorous next to Mrs. Rundgren. Uncle Travers usually tried to find some excuse to talk to Miss Martine in a flirty way on the days he picked Bella up, but Miss Martine never indulged him for too long.

Beyond Miss Martine, Bella had only one ally at Nelson Elementary: Hannah B, whose last name Bella couldn't remember but it was different from Hannah G, whose last name Bella couldn't remember, either. Hannah G was pretty in the same way that cousin Bonnie was pretty, in a storybook princess way, so that people must have been telling them how pretty they were all the time, which gave them more confidence. Hannah G always raised her hand in class, whereas Hannah B—who sat at Bella's table— never once raised her hand. Hannah B was what her dad used to call a contrarian, which meant she was sometimes too clever for her own good.

Almost every day, Hannah B claimed she saw something called the Green Guy, who crawled through her window at night, or walked across her front lawn while she was eating breakfast, or peeked through the window of the classroom and looked right at Hannah. Nobody else ever saw the Green Guy. But Bella believed what Hannah B said about the Green Guy, believed it without reservation, though Bella knew she would never see the Green Guy with her own eyes, any more than Hannah B would ever met S'tka.

They usually sat together at recess, Bella and Hannah B, on rainy days in the darkest corner of the covered play shed, telling stories.

"Why would they attack them?" Hannah B wanted to know. "It doesn't even make sense."

"Because they were brutes."

"What are brutes?"

"Brutes are people who are like animals. They do things just because they can."

"I think my dad is a brute," said Hannah B.

"I think a lot of grown-ups are," Bella said.

"So, did the U'ku'let guy die when they cracked his head?" said Hannah B, nibbling at a cuticle. "Did the brute people come back?"

"I don't know yet," said Bella.

"Well, what's gonna happen?"

"How should I know?"

"It's your story."

"But it's not. It's their story. I don't even hardly understand what half of it means. I don't know where it comes from."

"The same with the Green Guy," said Hannah B. "I'm the only one who sees him. My brother makes fun of me for it, so I don't even try to explain him to anyone anymore."

"Maybe I could see him," said Bella. "I could come to your house."

"My dad doesn't really let me have friends over," said Hannah B.

"I get it," said Bella. "I don't really wanna have friends over to my house."

When Bella first came to live with Auntie Kris and Uncle Travers, she was excited to be near Cousin Bonnie, but somehow their relationship wasn't the same as it used to be. Cousin Bonnie went to third grade at the Seven Acres School, which was private, and must have cost a lot of money, because Bella overheard Uncle Travers complaining about it to Auntie Kris.

"That's two car payments," he said.

"Really, Travers?" she said. "Is that how you quantify your daughter's education? My God, who are you anymore?"

"Well, it's not exactly fair to Bella."

"Bella's not your daughter," she said.

Bella barely saw Bonnie at breakfast, since Bella had to leave early for the bus. Then she didn't see Bonnie again until right before dinner, because most days Bonnie had violin lessons or ballet lessons or a playdate. The weekends were when she spent the most time with her cousin, who, unlike Hannah B, didn't care much about stories. Bonnie wasn't very abstract. She liked things she could touch. She liked activities. Bonnie liked to arrange her hair in different ways, and line up all her shoes, and ask Bella which ones she liked best.

"Those ones, I guess," Bella said.

"Ew," said Bonnie. "Nana bought me those. They look like something a waitress at Dale's would wear. Why would you pick those?"

"I dunno," said Bella. "Because you could walk far in them, I guess."

"That's not a very good reason," Bonnie said.

All in all, life at Auntie Kris and Uncle Travers' was pretty good. But Bella missed the cats, and she especially missed her dad, the way she had his undivided attention at dinner, and at night by the fire. The way he patiently explained things, and rarely got annoyed with her questions, like Auntie Kris and Uncle Travers and even Nana sometimes did.

In bed, the night Miss Martine emailed Uncle Travers and Auntie Kris about Bella's frequent daydreaming in class, she heard Uncle Travers and Auntie Kris talking across the hall in their bedroom.

"Well, what if he doesn't come back down?" said Auntie Kris. "We can't keep her forever. What about your mom?"

"Kris, you need to be patient with this. This is my niece we're talking about. We're in a position to help, and that's what we're going to do, for as long as it takes. We agreed on that from the beginning."

"Well, I hope he comes down soon. I think it's hard on Bonnie."

"On Bonnie? How the heck is it hard on Bonnie? She gets a companion out of the deal."

"If you haven't noticed, they don't have much in common, Trav."

"They're cousins," he said. "What else do they need in common—they're family."

"You read the email," said Auntie Kris. "Bella's teacher says she disassociates. There's some kind of deficit. She doesn't have many friends, Trav. So why does Bonnie have to be her only friend? That's an unfair burden to put on an eight-year-old, don't you think?"

"Bonnie can handle it," said Uncle Travers. "It builds character."

S'tka

For two days and three nights, S'tka ministered to U'ku'let, cleansing his wounds, icing the ugly gash on his head, feeding him what food and water he could hold down. Despite the cold, his body was burning up. He was easily confused, and hardly spoke at all when not addressed. It was like M'ka'ta's son, Tay, who was kicked by a bison calf and was never the same. Too feeble to hunt, too stupid to launder hides, Tay could not even be trusted to mind the children. If this should be the fate of her husband, they'd both be better off dead. S'tka could little afford two children without a helper.

Yes, a second child was growing inside of her. She knew it from the second it happened, and she was as powerless now as she was then to stop it.

Upon the fourth day of his convalescence, U'ku'let was finally holding down his food, and beginning to speak a bit more. His thoughts remained jumbled and confused, and he complained of a crushing headache. Still, there was much reason to hope: he was clearly more alert to his surroundings than he had been three days ago. And suddenly he was an emotional creature, sometimes crying for no discernible reason.

On the fifth day, S'tka trusted an improving U'ku'let to hold the baby, and the connection seemed to do wonders for his health.

"N'ka, my son, someday a great hunter," he said, gently pinching a cheek. "Isn't that right, eh? Isn't that right?"

Coaxing a smile out of the infant, U'ku'let smiled in turn, though the very act seemed to cause him pain.

"I pity the band of marauders that would ever cross N'ka, the great hunter, N'ka the great chief, eh? Isn't that right, boy? The great N'ka would strike them down with the sound of his voice."

By the fifth night, things had almost returned to normal except for the intermittent headaches. The wound was beginning to grow new skin at the ragged edges, the old skin beginning to flake off. The center of the wound remained pink and inflamed, but no longer stunk.

Laying atop their few remaining furs at night, the baby sound asleep beside them, S'tka snuggled in close to U'ku'let for warmth, resting her head in the crook of his arm, and looking up at his face in the darkness.

The shadows hid his harelip and strengthened his chin somehow. And even if the shadows weren't enhancing the effect, S'tka saw him as handsome and courageous, loyal and capable. How did it happen that they ended up together? How could she not have seen this union coming? How could she have never felt the force of U'ku'let's intention? How could she have been surprised by his defense, his willingness to be cast out with her? Had she never filched that damn femur bone, fate might never have forced U'ku'let's hand, and she would not be lying beside him right now.

"You belong to me," she whispered. "I'm glad you are okay."

"Aye," he said.

"I'm sorry they hurt you."

"Bah. Next time I'll be prepared," he said.

"Let's hope there is no next time."

"Next time, we'll be prepared."

She clutched his arm tighter. "Goodnight," she said.

"Goodnight."

In the pale glow of the coals, S'tka watched him sleep, relieved that he was on the mend, but worried still about a future. What if he was not the man he was previously? She'd yet to see him walk. What if his spirit was broken along with his head? What if the marauders did come back? Or another band of savages happened along their path? Suddenly, at less than full strength, they were so vulnerable. How were they to protect N'ka until such time as he became the great hunter his father predicted?

U'ku'let snored fitfully now. S'tka continued to grasp his arm tight against her chest.

In the morning, when S'tka awakened, U'ku'let was cold beside her, his brown eyes wide open as if death had come as a surprise. His final repose was a toothsome rictus that made him look like a half-wit.

"Ahhheeeeeeeoooooo," she groaned.

The baby awakened now, demanding nourishment. So desperate and onerous were his little cries that S'tka was forced to nurse him there beside her dead husband, his terrible grinning countenance staring right at her from beyond the veil.

U'ku'let

In his dream, U'ku'let lopes through a field of mountain grass, grass green to the waist, and free of ice; grass un-trampled, grass warmed by the sun. The ground is unimaginably soft beneath his feet, softer than the shaggiest hide. He feels his heart pulsing in his naked feet, as though up through the soil from the center of the world. He feels it beating double-time in his toes.

This is what it means to have your feet on the ground.

There is no ice in U'ku'let's dream, no ice anywhere. No snow, no blistering wind, no dank caves swirling with smoke and dust, no baying beasts crouching in wait, and licking their chops beyond the shadows. There are no shadows, no constant hectoring from the unforeseen. The world of U'ku'let's dream is a world of light.

Before him he sees N'ka, his son, the great hunter, skin bronzed in the sunlight, joyously leading the charge of men.

What charge, U'ku'let does not know. He only knows that they will follow N'ka to the ends of the earth.

In his dream, U'ku'let finally sees the grand design of the Great Provider, and he laughs and laughs and laughs as he bounds through the high grass. Along with the flora and the fauna, the mountains and the ice, the Great Provider gave him an idea, beautiful, malleable, and ultimately indestructible: the idea of belief.

Castoffs

Judy could hear the clatter of Travers' diesel engine halfway down Cascade Lane. Standing at the kitchen window, she watched the big black pickup pull up the drive. Travers hopped out, leaving the motor running.

Never any time to visit, either one of her boys. Never mind that Dave was at large in the wilderness, dead for all Judy knew. Travers was less than two miles away, but there was always a contractor to meet, a parcel of land to appraise. Thank God for her granddaughters.

Judy watched Bella clamber down out of the cab with her sad little backpack full of colored markers and books, and hopefully a sweatshirt.

"Where's Bonnie?" said Judy, greeting them at the door.

"Playdate," said Uncle Travers. "Then she's got a recital in the afternoon."

"Well, then," Judy said to Bella, with a pat on the head. "We'll have our own playdate."

"Okay, then," said Uncle Travers, mussing Bella's hair. "I'll see you tonight, sweetie."

"Bye," said Bella.

"I like your shoes," said Judy, as Travers hopped in his truck.

"You got them for Bonnie," said Bella. "They're a little too big, but I like them anyways. They build character."

The poor thing, Judy thought. Look at her, living off Bonnie's castoffs. And so plain-looking next to Bonnie, with that staticky hair, and those thin lips, and sad eyes. But Bonnie didn't have half of Bella's personality.

How could she? Everything came easy for Bonnie. Bonnie's whole path was laid out for her. You could hardly blame the girl for taking certain things for granted; Kris and Travers had practically taught her to expect the world. Meanwhile, motherless Bella scraped and scrambled up the crumbling hillside of a life she never asked to climb, never complaining, never demanding, never expectant. Judy knew it was wrong to play favorites with her granddaughters, but she couldn't help but favor Bella, her little underdog.

"Would you like to go to the farmers' market?"

"I'd rather stay here," said Bella. "We could play Life."

Judy did her best to suppress a sigh. Whoever said life was short never played the board game; the ceaseless doling out of money, and all those cards, and bonus spins, and those elusive little pink and blue pegs, forever finding their way onto the floor to frustrate her vacuum cleaner.

"Okay, honey, we can play Life," said Judy.

"We don't have to," said Bella. "We could just do nothing."

"Honey, we'll play Life; that sounds like a great idea."

"It's kind of long, actually," said Bella. "We can do whatever you want, Nana."

Always submitting, the dear girl. Never wanting to inconvenience anyone. It was heartbreaking to watch a child bear the brunt of life's disappointments, when she could control so few of them.

"Whatever you want, sweetheart," said Judy. "You get to choose today. Nana is game for anything."

"Anything?"

"Within reason, darling. Nana has limited resources."

"Can we hike up and see Daddy?"

It's like somebody kicked Judy right in the heart.

"No, honey, we can't do that," she said.

"Please?" said Bella.

Judy bent down and wrapped Bella in a hug. The child squeezed her so tight that it just about took Judy's breath away, as she felt the girl's desperate little sobs muffled against her chest.

And damned if Judy didn't start crying, too.

Untethered

Not a single day went by that Dave didn't contemplate returning to town, if only to visit Bella for a few precious hours. Hardly an hour passed that he didn't think of her. Really, why didn't he go get her and bring her back? Was this really his plan unconsciously all along? Twice he started down the trail to get her back, once proceeding as far as the foot of the canyon, only to turn back. He couldn't stay in town, and he couldn't bring Bella back, so he stayed on the mountain. Probably better for her in the long run that way.

Dave kept himself busy to fight off the loneliness, and ward off his demons. As usual, there was plenty to keep him busy. The Chinook were plentiful, and the last of the wild berries were still ripe. Soon there would be venison in the little smokehouse. Thus he had no need of provisions. And though he felt the call of the outside world at times, though he sometimes yearned for connection, for company, if only silent, for another human presence, he continued to exist in isolation.

God, how he missed Bella's tireless curiosity, how he longed for the melody of her sweet little voice, and for her living warmth and curiosity. If only to field her endless litany of ice age questions around the fire, to correct her grammar, or to hear her read anything aloud to him. And selfishly, too, Dave yearned for the focus and purpose Bella had once provided him.

Without Bella, Dave came untethered from the world. Often in his isolation, his mind wandered, usually into the past. Knee-deep in the river, dancing his fishing fly reflexively on the surface of the water, Dave thought of his wedding day, the fullest and happiest day of his life by a wide margin, a single afternoon that seemed to undo all the damage he suffered his first tour in Iraq. What a day, what hope! What a glorious and fulfilling future that day portended.

Travers, his mom, Barlow, Coach Prentice, nearly all his old teammates and boosters, practically all of Vigilante Falls was there at the Valley Foursquare Church to hear Dave and Nadene's vows. It was like all the people in their lives were witnesses, like Nadene and Dave were making their vows not just to each other, but to the whole community. And it felt, too, like in hearing those vows, the community was acknowledging their commitment to Nadene and Dave, vowing to help them, and protect them, and support them in sickness and in health. On their wedding day, it was like the community was absorbing Dave and Nadene, and their hopes, and dreams, and fears all became part of the fabric of the community.

We're so excited for you, they said.

You were made for each other, they told them.

When can we expect those little ones (*wink wink*)?

Now, when you get ready for some life insurance . . .

When you're ready to buy a house . . .

If you're ever looking for work . . .

Afterward, at the Sons of Norway Hall, Dave must have hugged a hundred people, and each one of them felt like an ally in his marriage, a resource and a partner. Theirs was a union that was built to last, like this town was built to last, like America was built to last. Dave had never felt more certain of anything in his life. So how could such a community ever fail them? How could Nadene and Dave fail each other? How were the resources not enough to save them?

There were occasions now when Dave talked to Nadene, and Bella, and Coach Prentice as though they were standing right there beside him in the current, or across the fire. It was a comfort just to hear his own voice.

Sometimes he walked loudly through the brush, scattering birds, or belted out a few verses of something—the Doors, or Pearl Jam, or an old church hymn—in a booming, off-key tenor, just to hear a human sound amidst the great, indifferent expanse of the wilderness.

S'tka

And what have you in store for me now, oh, Great Provider? What fresh misery could you possibly concoct for me that I haven't already endured? You gave me life when I never asked for it. Here, in this place, this frozen wasteland teeming with perils. You made me a woman, consigning me to a thankless life of service and drudgery. You starved me half to death with my baby inside of me, and then had me excommunicated from my people. You had me raped and brutalized, then took my husband from me right before my eyes.

Will you take my child next? My limbs? My eyesight?

Is this a sign, Great Provider, that you want me to leave this place? Is that what you're trying to tell me by leaving me here, bereft of hope or security, by abandoning me with no help to eke out an existence? If that is so, then I will disobey your will, Great Provider. I will not leave this place. For this is the place I shall put my husband, and the father of my child, in the ground.

I shall no longer solicit your help, Great Provider. I shall pray to nobody or nothing. I shall depend only on myself.

The site S'tka chose for U'ku'let's burial was a half-mile east of the cave, on a little shelf atop the ridge, overlooking the broad, grass valley of the giants, who had been traveling this corridor for all time, feeding on wheat grass and buttercups, scratching their wooly shoulders on the great pillars, wearing their stone surfaces shiny and smooth. This valley was perhaps the one worthwhile place the Great Provider had ever bequeathed her people. Never again would S'tka leave it.

It took two days to dig U'ku'let's grave in the frozen earth. And for two days his lifeless form lay pale and rigid for his infant son to gaze upon, eyes gaping, as he leered from some unfathomable place beyond this world. When S'tka had fought through the worst of the ice with a jagged stone, she dug with her bare fingers until they were ragged and blistered and frozen.

Though it shamed S'tka to admit it, she had never much cared for U'ku'let before he'd inexplicably come to her defense and attached himself to her. Why had he not made his intentions known at the edge of the wallow, upon the occasion of their one and only coupling? There had been nothing in the reckless thrust of his hips, nor the panicked look in his eyes, no tender utterances on his hot breath that had made S'tka think that U'ku'let felt any more deeply than the others. She was not at all sure they were even capable of emotional expression beyond the blunt theater of fear and anger, beyond the hooting and yammering of the hunt, or the grunt of carnal release. Throughout time, while the men trifled to perfect their hollow spear points, their crude carving implements, and their tasteless jokes, the women were left to grieve and remember. And what was the product of all this grieving and remembering if not the story of the people? Who was more qualified than a woman to tell the story of humanity?

The grave was not quite waist deep, but it would have to suffice, for soon the sun would sink below the ice, and S'tka must get N'ka back to the cave before dark. The best she could do was roll the body shoulder over shoulder into the pit, where it landed face down with a thud.

Climbing in after him, S'tka turned U'kulet over on his back, and straightened him as best she could, brushing the dirt from his face, and wrapping his hide snugly about him.

Climbing back out of the pit, she looked down at the bloated shell of U'ku'let, leering stupidly up at the slate gray sky, eyes bulging, gums swelling around his soft, yellow teeth. Surely there was nowhere to go from this world, thought S'tka, but at least the wolves wouldn't get him.

"Goodbye," she said.

And that was all.

Just as N'ka began to fuss, S'tka dropped to her knees and started pushing dirt into the grave.

Don't You Even Care?

———————

The days ran into weeks without any word from Bella's dad. Every day, Bella enjoyed school less. It didn't help that Hannah B, without warning, went to live with her mother in Blaine. Nobody but Bella missed her, apparently, because everybody started calling Hannah G just plain Hannah, like there never was a Hannah B. Miss Martine seemed to want less and less to do with Bella, whom she began sending to the specialists in the other building for part of the day: Mrs. Dunwoody, who was really fat, and Mr. Caruthers, who had breath like garlic and fish. It's not that Bella minded either of them so much, it's just that they sometimes smothered her with their attention. Always wanting to know what Bella was thinking, or how she felt, or trying to get her to focus on stuff in tricky ways. She liked it better in the classroom with the others where she could feel more invisible, and everybody just left her to herself.

"Do you think about your mom a lot?" Mr. Caruthers wanted to know.

"Sometimes," said Bella.

"Is that what you're thinking about when you're losing your focus?"

"No," she said.

"What are you thinking about?"

"Stuff that happened a long time ago."

"Anything you want to talk about?" said Mr. Caruthers.

"No, thank you," she said. "Not if I don't have to."

"Can you tell me how thinking about those things makes you feel?"

"It all depends," she said. "Different ways. It depends what's happening."

"Do you ever talk to your mom?"

"How would I do that when she's dead?"

"Oh, I don't know," he said. "Just pretending she's there."

"No," said Bella. "I never do that."

"There's nothing wrong with doing that, you know."

"I know," she said. "I've seen my dad do it."

"Do you miss your dad?"

"Very much," she said.

"How does it make you feel when people say things about him that aren't nice?"

"I don't listen," she said. "They're stupid, anyway."

Bella's home life was a fruit salad of mixed signals. Sometimes it seemed like Auntie Kris and Uncle Travers wanted her to stay, then sometimes it seemed like Bella had stayed too long already. Sometimes they talked about Bella's long-term future like they were already planning it, and sometimes they talked like it might end soon. The spaces between her and Bonnie seemed to grow wider by the week. As little as they had in common, Bonnie did not hesitate to make Bella do things to serve her.

"I need you to get something out of Mommy's purse," she said.

"What?"

"Twenty dollars."

"Why do you need twenty dollars?"

"Because she won't give it to me."

"But what are you gonna use it for?"

"I haven't decided yet."

As often as not, Bella complied with Bonnie's directives, and when she was resistant, Bonnie could be very persuasive.

"Since you've lived here," said Bonnie. "I've had to give up half of basically my whole life. The least you can do is help me once in awhile."

And Bella supposed her cousin was right, though she was beginning to despise her.

From this remove, life in the mountains seemed refreshingly simple to comprehend.

"Uncle Travers," she said one day at the breakfast table. "Can we go visit my dad?"

Uncle Travers glanced up from his real estate papers, then quickly back down again.

"He'll come down soon, Bella. Don't you worry."

"But he won't," she said. "You keep saying it, but I know Daddy, and he won't come down. He's too afraid of the world."

"He'll come down," said Travers without looking up.

"She's right," said Bonnie. "Uncle Dave won't come down. He's too crazy already."

Bella glared at Bonnie with the first flash of real hatred she'd ever felt for her.

"Finish your breakfast, you two," said Auntie Kris.

"But we should at least see if he's okay," said Bella, her tone pleading.

Uncle Travers looked up from his papers and held Bella's gaze this time.

"Bella," he said. "Your dad will come down when he's ready. If he wanted to see us, he would have come down already."

"I know he wants to see me," said Bella, a little more forcefully than she intended. "You're lying."

"Bella," scolded Auntie Kris.

"Don't you even care?" said Bella.

"Of course we care," said Auntie Kris.

"Then, why won't Uncle Trav take me to visit him?"

Auntie Kris appealed to Uncle Travers with a meaningful look.

"Bella," he said. "I know you miss your dad. I know you're worried about him. But I've known him a lot longer than you, and I know he's fine up there."

"How?"

"Because he's been through a lot harder things."

"He needs us," said Bella. "It's not fair."

"You're right, Bella. He does need us. But see, sweetie, that's something he has to realize on his own. Trust me, I know."

Bella left for the bus even earlier than usual that morning, abandoning her half-eaten cereal despite Auntie Kris's protests. Bella preferred getting to the bus stop before the brothers Tyler and Kyle who were invariably obnoxious in all the ways boys are usually obnoxious: clowning, bragging, hitting, spitting, and making factual claims and observations about stuff that obviously wasn't true. If she got there early, Bella could prepare for them in her head. Sometimes, only one of them showed up, and of course, like all boys, they were easier to endure when they were alone. The younger one, Tyler, was actually reasonably polite in the absence of his brother, though not very interesting.

Some days, neither Tyler nor Kyle showed up, and as far as Bella was concerned, those were the best days of all. The world was a noisy place, full of Tylers and Kyles. It was always a relief to get on the bus and press her face to the window and watch the world roll by.

Most days Bella had a hard pit in her stomach as she walked to the bus stop, a sort of nervous dread attached to the day ahead. But this morning, foggy and cold, as she ambled along the broken sidewalk, Bonnie's brown backpack from last year slung over her shoulder, Bella was seized by a sense of clarity. For the first time, it occurred to her that nobody could control her, that no matter who tried to plan her life, or tell her what to do, no matter how good, or how misdirected their reasoning, no matter how convincing their argument, Bella would always be in control of herself. They could boss her around, and they could ask her questions and try to correct her, but they could never change what she wanted.

When she got to the bus stop, she walked right past it and crossed the street. She kept walking south past the gloomy streets at the edge of town, and past the gray middle school, until she reached the highway, where she walked east along the shoulder for a quarter mile as the occasional car whizzed past. She walked until she arrived at the familiar spot past mile marker 62 where she proceeded to jump the guardrail and the culvert, and picked up the soggy trail into what her daddy called the bottomlands.

Where I Should Be

Alone, the same old hike felt longer than it ever did with her dad, and a lot scarier. All the way through the wooded flats, Bella was certain somebody, or something, was following her, a sensation that hurried her progress and kept her glancing over her shoulder at every turn. Had Bella known when she left the house that morning that she was making this journey, she would have worn rubber boots, but instead she was putting her brown hand-me-down shoes to the test.

Following the trail was easy enough through the forest, despite two small washouts along the river. It wasn't until partway into the canyon that things got confusing, and Bella began second-guessing her progress. She couldn't decide whether certain things—a grove of cottonwoods, a steep rise, or a bend in the river—were familiar or not. In places, the trail was broken and hard to follow. Halfway into the canyon her concern nosed toward panic, as she was quite sure she had arrived at an unfamiliar place.

Before panic could get the best of her, Bella remembered what her dad told her: That in a crisis, the most important thing is to stay calm and rational. Because she would be making very important decisions, maybe even life or death decisions.

In a sunny portion of the basin, out from under the cover of the forest, Bella halted her progress. Standing on a stony rise, she surveyed the landscape in every direction, taking inventory of the peaks she had named herself, as she tried to calculate the position of the bluff accordingly. This exercise only served to confuse her more. The distances were too hard to measure. And no trail would offer a straight path. But she stayed calm, reasoning that the best course of action would be to backtrack to the last place she recognized without a doubt, a trek that took her a mile-and-a-half back down canyon to the point at which the trail departed the river and began to gain elevation. Near the bottom of the rise, she arrived at a fork in the trail and recognized immediately where she'd lost her way.

With renewed confidence, she started up the right path, and within two hours reached the butt of the canyon. Once she was up and over the final hump, everything was once again familiar in spite of the season: the wide canyon behind her, and the meadow before her, its waist-high grass brown and rain-trampled. When she drew within a couple of football fields of the bluff, Boris appeared suddenly to welcome her, and on his heels came Boots.

Bella arrived at the bluff five minutes later, where she found her dad sitting by a dying fire to no apparent purpose.

"Daddy . . . ?" she said.

He swung around jerkily, looking like a ghost of himself, skinnier, paler, a gray-tipped beard drooping halfway to his collarbone.

"Baby, wha—what are you doing here?"

"I came back," she said.

He looked stunned.

"Where's your uncle?" he said.

"Working, I guess."

"Baby, is something wrong? Why are you here? You came all by yourself?"

"Yeah," she said.

That's when he bent down and squeezed her so tightly she could hardly breathe.

"Did something happen?" he said. "Talk to me, baby."

"I missed you," she said.

"Bella, baby, does anyone know where you are?"

"No," she said.

He squeezed her tighter, and Bella pushed herself against him as if her life depended on it.

"Baby, we gotta take you back to town," he said. "This isn't good."

"No," she said. "I want to stay here."

"Bella, I gotta take you back," he insisted. "They're probably already looking for you."

"I'll be with you," she said. "That's where I should be, right?"

He held her at arm's length and looked at her sadly, and Bella's heart sank at what looked like his uncertainty.

"Baby, I'm not so sure anymore," he said.

"Don't make me go back, Daddy."

"They've gotta know you're okay, baby. Everybody's gonna be worried. Imagine how Nana must feel."

"Make them find me," she said.

"We can't do that, Bella."

"Then, I'll hide."

"You can't do that, baby, it wouldn't be fair."

"Then, I'll go somewhere else," she said.

"Bella, slow down," he said. "You're not going anywhere."

"That's what I've been telling you," she said.

In a single breath, his expression slackened, and he seemed to give in, though Bella could still see the distress and indecision in his knitted brow, as he mentally took stock of the situation.

"It won't be long before they come for you, Bella."

"Don't let them take me, Daddy," she said.

"Why, baby? Why do you want to stay?"

Her eyes began to burn, but no matter how she tried, she couldn't keep the tears from filling them, which only made her angry with herself.

"Daddy, I don't like it down there," she said.

He wrapped her up in an embrace once more.

"I don't either, baby," he said.

S'tka

Finally, the blistering winds out of the north abated. The stunted spruces studding the mountainside had at long last shed their snow and stood straighter and prouder, shimmering green in the sunlight. Down in the long, broad valley below the bluff to the northeast, the frost had lifted. Everywhere life pushed itself through the ice; grasses and sage stirred in the breeze, poppies and buttercups rimmed the basin where soon the giants would come to graze, as they always did.

S'tka, too, felt as though she was pushing herself up through the ice. For many days and nights after U'ku'let left the world, S'tka retreated into her cave and deep into herself—so deep she could hardly see her way out. The very prospect of a future was beyond her reach. For days on end, she did not eat. Her ears had been deaf to all but the most plaintive cries of her infant son, who, watching her in her moments of abject despair, looked up at her with perplexity and a hint of concern in his brown eyes. But like all things, her grief ran its course, and the blood in her veins began to warm once more.

N'ka was her constant passenger, wrapped in hide and lashed to her chest, as she hunted ground squirrels and collected roots, and scoured the forest for firewood. In her busy state she no longer felt alone. As long as she had an immediate objective in front of her, the dark thoughts did not crowd in on S'tka. But in the quieter moments, as when the day was drawing to a close, and S'tka squatted in the dusky cave with N'ka sleeping soundly beside her, swaddled in fur, the pangs of isolation still visited her.

People were not equipped to live alone, not among this barren landscape, besieged by monsters, beset by fang and tusk and savage claw. Only in their numbers did people enjoy any kind of advantage; only in cooperation could they ever thrive. So how was S'tka to thrive if she had nobody with whom to conspire, nobody to carry the other end, or to hold the other side fast when she was bereft of allies with whom to surround her prey? How was she supposed to maintain her humanity with nobody to hear her voice?

S'tka ached for N'ka to come of an age when he could speak to her and share his thoughts. Even now, as a matter of course, she talked to him as though he could understand her. She would not let the frigid isolation penetrate the warmth of her child as it had penetrated her. So she populated N'ka's life with stories, implanted his burgeoning awareness with memories that were not his own, memories across time and space.

"We were not always alone in these mountains," she told him. "There was a time when our people thrived and struggled here in accordance with the great cycle of life. It was a hard life, but a good one. But the people grew impatient with struggle, and they broke the cycle, and left their dead behind in this place."

And the boy took it all in with his curious brown eyes, though it was far beyond his comprehension.

"The people, they fled these mountains at the behest of their elders, leaving it for the promise of a new world. It was a foolhardy plan, destined to failure."

The infant would tilt his head in wonder.

"So your father and I returned to this place to preserve the old ways," S'tka told him. "For we knew in our wisdom that the season of bounty would always follow upon the heels of the long, cold winter, such was the great cycle of life. The ice would recede, and the bison and the mammoth would return to the valley. This is why we stay, child. And we are not alone here, we live amongst the ghosts of our ancestors."

But no matter how S'tka populated her stories, no matter how she attempted to embellish the connectivity of the clan across time, she was still haunted by an emptiness that even this bountiful season of life could not fill. She thought she might die of loneliness.

One afternoon, as S'tka was gathering wood at the edge of the basin, she spied beyond the brush a lone stranger trudging tall through the valley, dragging a bloody pelt in his wake.

Crouching for cover among the reeds, S'tka watched his steady march south, at once heartened and distressed by the appearance of this stranger. Her pulse quickened as she watched his purposeful stride. How long since she had spoken to anyone other than her uncomprehending child?

Who was this stranger, and why did he travel alone? What if this person had news of her clan? Was he an outcast like her? Had he a family somewhere for whom he provided? Though S'tka was compelled to call out to him, perhaps even to cast her meager lot and join forces with the stranger, she reasoned that it would be unwise. She knew nothing of his nature, of where he came from, or what his customs may have been. She couldn't take the risk. God, what she would have given for some adult conversation, another body to occupy the space next to her. Her chest ached for intimacy.

Stealthily she crept closer in the reeds, tracking the loner's progress through the high grass, which was trampled and besmirched by blood in his wake. Soon, S'tka drew to within a stone's throw of him, until her shifting weight snapped a twig, drawing the stranger's attention. He instantly halted his progress and looked around, sniffing the air like a bear, until it seemed he was looking directly at S'tka.

S'tka froze. A frigid hand gripped her heart as she recognized the stranger, the flat nose, the brutish brow, the rotten teeth, the stupid expression. For a long moment it seemed that he held her gaze, that he must have seen her crouched in the reeds. S'tka stopped breathing, closing her eyes as though it might render her invisible, praying that N'ka did not fuss, or budge, or make a peep.

In that terrible moment, as the dead-eyed brute gazed directly into her reedy cover, S'tka summoned the Great Provider for the first time since her husband's death.

Please, let him go on his way.

And breathless, S'tka awaited her fate.

At last, the stranger stopped sniffing at the air and shrugged before promptly resuming his bloody march south.

But Not for Me

As usual, her dad was right: it didn't take long for Uncle Travers to track her down. The day after Bella's arrival, when she and her dad returned to the bluff with a half-dozen Chinook on the line, they were greeted by Uncle Travers, pacing the bluff, clad in sweatpants and hiking boots, and a baseball cap instead of his usual fake cowboy attire.

"That was quite a stunt, Dave," he said. "The whole goddamn county is looking for her. Least you could've done was leave a note like me. Might have saved everybody a lot of heartache and trouble."

"She came on her own, Trav," her dad said, like she wasn't standing right next to him. "It's not like I kidnapped her."

"Bella, you had us worried sick," Uncle Travers said. "Why'd you run off like that? You had us up all night looking for you, the police, everybody. We thought something terrible had happened."

"I'm sorry," she said, casting her eyes down.

"Why'd you run away?"

"Because you wouldn't let me come," she said. "I kept asking."

"Well, c'mon," said Uncle Trav. "It's time to go back, sweetie."

"Not so fast," said her dad.

"Listen, Dave. I'm here to take her back. If you want, I'll come back up in a couple weeks with all the right papers and the rest of it and we can make it official. But I'm not leaving here without her."

Bella clutched her dad about the waist.

"She was just starting to sink back into some sort of a normal life, Dave," said Uncle Trav. "The specialists at school have been working with her. She's been getting counseling. You can't set her back, Dave, it's not right. You've got to let the kid grieve properly. Damnit, Dave, you owe her some stability."

"Stability is one thing I do give her, Travers," said her dad. "It may not look like much to you—"

"Me or anyone else, Dave."

"Well, Trav, I can't account for your lack of imagination. You're just thinking like everybody else down there, and that's fine for you. But not for me."

"And not for Bella, either."

"It's not that I don't like you and Auntie Kris," Bella said, still clutching her dad. "I just want to be with Daddy. Please, Uncle Trav."

When Uncle Trav reached out for her, her dad stepped between them and straightened himself up in a threatening way.

Though Uncle Trav was an inch taller, it was hard to look tough in sweatpants and hiking boots.

"What have you got in mind here, Trav?" said her dad. "We always knew I could lick you if it ever came down to it."

"But you never did, did you, Dave? You did the right thing, because you were a good big brother. And now I'm asking you to do the right thing again and be a good father."

"Please," said Bella. "Let us be here, don't make us go back."

"He can't make us do anything, baby."

"What about winter, Dave? What's that gonna look like? How are you gonna eat? How are you gonna stay warm up here?"

"If you think I haven't given full consideration to those things, well, then, little brother, you don't know me too well. And maybe you put too much faith in modern conveniences. How do you suppose folks got by for the last two hundred thousand years?"

"It's true," said Bella. "The ice people did it."

Uncle Travers looked at them both in turn. When her dad locked eyes with him, Uncle Trav seemed to shrink a little.

"This isn't over yet, Dave," he said. "Anybody can see this ain't right."

"You get moving, now, little brother. You tell everybody we're just fine up here."

"Well, it sure don't look that way."

"Well, it is," said her dad.

"It is, Uncle Trav," said Bella. "I promise, it is."

"It ain't natural, Dave."

"Or maybe it's the most natural thing in the world," said her dad. "Maybe it's life down there that ain't natural. Maybe everybody's so checked out, and distracted, and scared, and disconnected from real life that they've lost their way. Of all the trouble in the world, all the suffering, how much of it was caused by folks living the simple lives they were intended to live?"

"Intended by whom, Dave? That's what I don't get. By God?"

"Not by God, little brother, by nature," he said. "By the natural order that governs all living things."

"No way you're gonna make living in a cave with a little girl sound natural to me, or anyone else, let alone have us believing it's a noble thing."

"Doesn't matter how it sounds to you," said her dad. "You can see yourself that Bella's made up her own mind."

Uncle Trav looked at her meaningfully, and Bella averted her eyes, clutching her dad's waist tighter.

"Well, that don't mean she's right," said Uncle Trav. "She's a kid, Dave. She loves her dad, which is the only natural thing I can see about any of this."

"I love you, too, Uncle Trav," she said. "And Bonnie and Auntie Kris. But I don't want to go back, really I don't."

"You're gonna change your mind this winter, darlin', believe me."

"I won't," she said.

"Go on, Trav," said her dad. "You heard her. Get along back to town. You let everybody know we're just fine up here, and we want to be left alone."

"Oh, I'll let them know," said Uncle Trav.

N'ka

———

The world was resplendent with light and color; every leaf, every cloud, every shaft of golden sunlight slanting through the trees, every speck of dust swam with life. Only the child's mobility depended upon his mother's whim. When she toted him about, his eyes and ears and impressions were free to wander.

Every moment of every day, N'ka catalogued a new sensation: the burbling of his own laughter, the trilling of squirrels from high in the canopy of trees, the trickle of water beneath the ice. This world was a feast for the eyes, inviting his touch, begging for his observation; it sung, and whispered, and nudged him; it nourished him with its warmth.

Above all else in this world, above the golden sunlight, and the bottomless blue sky, N'ka prized the shelter and attentiveness of his mother, delighting in her gentle touch, her adoring gaze, and her endless patience. There was no greater music than the sound of her voice.

"You are everything to me," she told him, as he drew his nourishment.

The child cooed, and smacked his lips, and beamed up at her, his little heart full.

"I live for you," she said, stroking his head.

N'ka did not know the meaning of her song. He only knew that it would last forever.

The Toll

———

Bella dreaded Uncle Trav's inevitable return. If she knew anything at all about her uncle it was that he was a doer, not a talker, just like her dad. Maybe the expectation of his return was taking a toll on her dad, too. There was a nervous energy about him, a new shortness of tone. Bella had begun to feel as though she was in his way much of the time, like he wanted to be alone.

"You don't want me here," she said, watching him craft a fishing fly.

"That's not true, baby," he said, looking up from his work. "Why would you say that?"

"I can tell," she said.

"Nonsense," he said, resuming his task.

"It's because you're worried, isn't it? When you're worried you don't talk as much."

"Mm," he said.

"See, you are worried."

He paused to inspect his work.

"Look, I am a little worried, okay?" he said. "It's part of being an adult, baby."

"But there's plenty to eat," she said. "We have enough wood. We can go back for more supplies whenever we need them."

"It's not that," he said. "It's just . . . sometimes I worry I'm not doing the right thing keeping you up here with nobody your own age. Maybe your uncle is right."

"No," she said. "I want to be here, Daddy. I keep telling you that."

"Okay, baby, I hear you."

But Bella still didn't believe him. She could tell he was ambivalent, like he was trying to convince himself something he wasn't really sure about.

"You want me to go back, I can tell."

"I didn't say that."

"You think it."

He left off tying his fly and looked her in the eye.

"I just wonder if maybe it would be better for you to be with your friends, and your grandma, and your cousin."

"I don't want to be anywhere else. I want to be with you," she said.

Bella remembered being at her dad's side constantly the days right after her mom died, following him about in a haze, clinging to his side as he tended to his daily business. She sat quietly at his side as he made phone calls, and waited outside the door when he went to the bathroom. She clutched him for dear life when he broke down to grieve. For nearly a month, she couldn't sleep at night unless she could hear his breathing. She was afraid that the world might take him away, too. And now, all these months later, she was still afraid. But now it seemed a new anxiety muddled her every thought and polluted her every action: the fear that he didn't want her.

"I don't know, baby," he said. "Maybe it'd be better for you in town. You'd have all your old stuff back. You'd have your friends. You could eat pizza any time you wanted."

"You said yourself you didn't like it down there," she said. "You said the world was going to S-H-I-T. So, why would I want to go back there?"

"Aw, baby," said her dad. "I shouldn't have said that. I'm sorry. I was just frustrated with my own life."

"Please don't make me go back," she said. "I don't want to. I want to be with you."

"Okay, baby, I won't," he said.

"Promise me."

"Baby, I'm not sure I can promise that."

"Promise, Daddy," she said, gravely.

He looked up from his work and searched her face long and hard from across the fire, as Bella watched his ambivalence harden into something that looked like resolve.

"I promise," he said.

S'tka

———

The new moon had come and gone, and the bulge in S'tka's abdomen continued to grow. For weeks she moved about her daily tasks in a fog of preoccupation, vacillating between denial and disquiet, until finally she was forced to accept the terrible, unavoidable fact of her condition. For the better part of two days afterward, to N'ka's frequent and obvious consternation, S'tka hunkered in the depths of the cave, succumbing to grief, sobbing the hours away. It sickened her both physically and mentally to feel her body changing, knowing with chilling certainty, as she'd known from the very moment of conception, that the bulge belonged not to U'ku'let, but to the dead-eyed marauder.

Just when it appeared that the Great Provider had heaped every torment in her arsenal upon poor S'tka, she had bestowed this unthinkable curse upon her. What design was this? Those barbarous acts on the bluff had begotten a cruel arithmetic; that one life was taken senselessly, and another added, was something less than a zero sum.

In the weeks that followed, as the unwanted thing continued to grow inside of her, and the pressure on her abdomen seemed to increase daily, S'tka agonized about her untenable future. What about five and six moons from now, when the ice had returned with its deathly grip on the landscape, and the food was scarce, and her stomach was out in front of her like an obstacle? Somehow, once before, she'd managed to survive under such duress. But recalling those cruel months of servitude on the ice, ravaged by hunger, exhausted beyond her capacities, S'tka knew she could not, and would not, endure such agony again, especially not for the monstrous thing growing inside of her.

Late one afternoon in the meadow, seven days thawed, and blazing purple and yellow with wildflowers, S'tka set aside her bundle of sticks. Unfastening N'ka, she laid him in the high grass, where he immediately began to fuss. Kneeling, S'tka leaned down and put her face near his so he could feel her breath. Within seconds, the boy settled back into sleep, and S'tka began to survey the vicinity for a means to solve her problem.

At the edge of a tiny stream, only recently liberated from the grip of the ice, she found her means in the form a rock, the size of N'ka's head.

"It has to be done," she said beneath her breath.

Hefting the stone, S'tka took a deep breath, releasing it quickly, like something unwanted. Gritting her teeth, she held the heavy stone at arm's length, and proceeded to pummel her abdomen again and again, silencing her agony so she wouldn't wake the baby. If that didn't sum up parenthood, what did?

After five or six blows, S'tka doubled over in the grass, and began to retch and cry at the same time.

Why was this happening to her? Was this the price she paid for her disobedience to the clan, for sneaking a leg of meat, the price for wanting to nourish a child she never asked for, for wanting to eke out a meager existence on this forsaken ice, for having to accept a man she never chose, for having to learn to love him, only to watch him humiliated, then die brutally by the hand of savages?

And what of their recompense? What about the men who accounted for all this trouble and strife? How did those brutal savages pay for their inhumanity? And what of the elders before them? Did they suffer for taking liberties with S'tka whenever the mood presented itself, only to turn their backs on her when she was pregnant and starving? What price did the clan pay for depriving her, then casting her out onto the ice? Was it the victim's legacy to always pay?

When the baby began to stir, S'tka, her stomach still in full rebellion, her breath strangled by the awful cramping, cleared her watering eyes against her forearm, and resolved herself to continue her life, as little as she was compelled to.

First Offering

———

It was early afternoon, though you wouldn't have known it. You wouldn't have known that it was raining in sheets, either, except for the trickle of ground water leaching in through the volcanic rock. Were it not for the pale blade of light knifing in slantwise from the mouth of the cave, you couldn't tell night from day. It had been nearly three weeks since Travers' visit, and by Dave's count it had rained practically every day since.

He was losing Bella. And though he sensed her unhappiness, though it seemed to hang in the air between them at all times of late, neither one of them spoke of it. Once again, he was failing her as a parent.

Sugarfoot slumbered fitfully in the dirt near the mouth of the cave, his burr-tangled belly rising and falling uneasily with each breath. Sometimes Sugarfoot didn't come home for days. And when he did, only warily did the white-pawed loner sink into domesticity.

Tito curled in the corner, his orange and white legs scissoring the air as he groomed himself with a sandpaper tongue.

Betty sprawled nearest the fire, green-eyed and black as night; so baggy and deflated after her last litter that she almost looked like a rug.

Jimmy Stewart curled in Dave's lap, purring like an air compressor, though Dave had done nothing to encourage him.

Bella was sitting stiffly at the foot of the bed, as she had been for an hour, alert but unresponsive.

"What say we bundle up and go outside?" he said.

"I don't want to," she said.

"C'mon, Bella."

"Coco," she said. "My name is Coco."

"You're not a damn cat, Bella."

"You said damn again, Daddy."

It was true, he ought to watch his mouth, though they had nobody to impress up here. Isolation had whittled his vocabulary down to the coarse and rudimentary. So little remained in his life that required the nuances of language. It was getting to where he hardly recognized his own voice.

Mirabella, once verbally irrepressible, once relentless in her curiosity, had hardly spoken to him in the last week, and he knew it was his own fault. Despite their proximity, or maybe because of it, they were growing apart.

The week before last she'd taken to hunting with the big Toms: Sugarfoot, Tito, Boris, and one-eyed Stinky. She took to slinking around in the bear grass below the plateau, stalking mice in the woody debris beneath the canopy of fir, pouncing on anything that moved.

Her first offering was a tiny vole, its little severed head lying nearby. Dave didn't say anything about it, nor did he say anything after the second. Now a week later, she insisted on being called Coco.

"But your name is Bella," said Dave.

"I can call myself anything I want," she said.

Dave had gone along with the cat thing for a few days. It was child's play, after all. It demonstrated a healthy imagination, right? But as Bella grew more silent and watchful, moving about the periphery of Dave's life each day, coming and going as she pleased, engaging him on her own terms, even hissing at him on several occasions, Dave began to entertain concerns.

It wasn't until she started licking her hands and feet, though, that all bets were off.

"You're not a cat, Bella. Stop it," he said.

"Sssssssss," she said.

"I mean it, stop."

"Ssssssss."

She was still hissing when a foreign sound penetrated their burrow. All at once, Sugarfoot and Tito were on their feet, backs arched, tails stiff.

"Hello?" said the voice. "Anybody there? Mr. Cartwright?"

Jimmy Stewart immediately sprang off Dave's lap as Dave reached for the Winchester, though not before he considered the Magnum. Bidding Bella silence with a finger to his lips, he crept toward the mouth of the cave.

Peering out through the narrow cleft in the mountain, Dave immediately saw the interloper standing out in the open on the edge of the brush.

"Who is it, Daddy?" said Bella.

"Shush," he said.

He was a miserable looking sonofabitch, whoever he was. Wet glasses, and wet hair. His windbreaker, woefully inadequate for the rain, looked like it must've weighed twenty pounds by now with all the water it had absorbed.

"Who are you?" said Dave, clutching the rifle.

The stranger held out his soggy valise like an offering, when he ought to have been hiding behind it.

"My name is Tristan Moseley," he said.

"So?" said Dave.

"I work for the State of Washington," he said. "Family services division."

"Yeah?" said Dave. "What do you want?"

The poor guy had begun to shiver.

"May I please come in, Mr. C-c-cartwright," he said miserably.

"No, you may not, sir, I'm sorry."

"Let me explain, Mr.—"

"Go, away," said Dave.

"Mr. Cartwright, we need to talk about your daughter."

"My daughter is my business," said Dave, leveling the .22 at the stranger.

"Sir, I—"

"She's not my brother's business, and certainly not yours. So, I'm gonna ask you nicely to move on."

Clutching his soggy folio, the stranger began backing slowly through the brush. When he reached the clutch of stunted hemlock at the edge of the ridge, he turned and retreated cautiously down the hill.

Back in the cave, the cats were still on edge. Bella squatted by the glowing embers of the fire as Dave shook the rain off, setting the Winchester aside.

"You should have let him in," Bella said without looking at him. "He seemed nice."

"Things aren't always what they seem, baby. What he wants is to take you away from me. Is that what you want?"

"But he looked cold, Daddy. You said the rain would get us before any bear. You said that—"

"He's not us."

"But what if—?"

"Put a log on the fire, baby."

She cast her eyes down and fetched a dry wedge of spruce from the rear of the cave. Gently, she set it open-faced on the coals without stirring so much as an ember. In a matter of seconds, the little quarter round flamed up around the edges, setting the shadows to dancing.

Looking at Bella in the glow of the fire, perched lithely on all fours, the shadows cutting hard across her impassive face, her big green eyes calm, her thin lips pursed, Dave thought—not for the first time—that she actually looked like a cat.

"Stay here," he said, and went out in search of the miserable social worker.

Travers Cartwright; Brother

———

"There had to be laws, right? There had to be culturally acceptable guidelines. There was a social contract to consider. You couldn't just raise the kid in a damn cave, with no lights, no electricity, no bathtub, could you? Somebody, somewhere had to be regulating this stuff, right? We were a civilized culture. You couldn't just opt out of society completely, could you?

"Bella, she was just a kid, a really bright kid, actually, whose life got needlessly complicated by my brother's bad decisions. I'm not saying Dave wasn't doing his best, but sometimes I had to wonder. The strain of losing Nadene, that's understandable. Something like that is always going to be a tough transition. But if having to live in a cave in the damn mountains, away from everything you ever knew, and everybody who ever loved you, if that wasn't neglect, I didn't know what was. No matter if Bella was safe up there with Dave, even if she thought it was neat living in the wild with a bunch of feral cats, that didn't make it right, did it? Safe to say, an eight-year-old wasn't going to see the big picture.

"Obviously, there wasn't much more I could do, not personally. I'd gone that route already more than once. And it didn't work out. But there were checks and balances in place for this kind of thing."

Estimates

"So, then, you'd estimate that you return to town once a month?" said Tristan Moseley, the thawed out social worker, glasses fogged, pen poised over his clipboard in the murky light of the cave.

A soothing voice softened Moseley's inquisitive manner, but Dave wasn't buying.

"I don't see where our comings and goings are any business of the state," he said. "You can see by looking at her, the girl is just fine."

Please don't talk about being a cat.

"Do you miss your friends?" said Tristan Moseley.

"My friend moved away. Her name was Hannah B. But I have friends here," said Bella.

"Oh?" said Tristan Moseley. "Like who?"

"Like my dad," she said. "And the cats, and my stuffies."

"Do you have a favorite cat?"

"I like them all the same," said Bella. "But I pet Sugarfoot and Boris most. That's only because they like it best."

"Do you like it here, Bella?"

"Yes."

"Do you feel safe here?"

"Yeah," she said without hesitation.

"Of course she feels safe," said Dave. "She *is* safe."

"What about school?" said Tristan Moseley.

"What about it?" Dave said.

"Is there a plan in place?"

"Look," said Dave. "Everything she needs to know, I can teach her. I'm not under any obligation to answer to anybody. But while you're making notes, write down that Bella can name every tree or animal you're likely to come across in this wilderness. She can tell you how these mountains were formed millions of years ago. She's a proficient reader and writer. She can recite Nooksack folklore, and Salish, too. She can build a fire, catch a fish, and tell you if it's a coho or a sturgeon. She can gut it and cook it over that fire. You go find me another eight-year-old that can do all that."

"Tell me, Mirabella," said Moseley. "What are your favorite things to do?"

Please don't say hunt with the cats.

"I like to eat honey with a spoon," she said. "And sometimes I just like to sit and think."

"Do you ever get lonely up here?"

"Why would she get lonely?" said Dave irritably. "We have each other. We have people like you and my brother dropping by unannounced. We go to town. We see plenty of people."

Dave had just about run out of hospitality. He had half a mind to pull up camp in the morning and move deeper into the mountains, so deep that nobody would ever find them.

"And you've got plenty to eat?"

"Yes," said Dave, an edge of aggression in his voice. "More than enough. Look, we're warm, we're healthy, we're happy, and we've got plenty to eat. Bella is learning daily, okay? And she brushes her teeth every morning and night. I think we've about covered everything, Mr. Moseley. Be sure and let my brother know as much. I'm sure it's him who put you up to this little visit. And now that the rain has let up, it'd probably be best for you start making your way down the mountain."

"You're probably right about that," said Tristan Moseley, de-fogging his glasses before replacing them on his face. "To be perfectly honest," he rejoined, "your life up here seems rather idyllic. Not that I could ever pull it off."

"Yeah, probably not," said Dave, looking him in the eye.

"A guy can dream, can't he?" said Tristan Moseley.

"Used to be that way, anyway," said Dave.

Dave couldn't help but soften slightly toward the stranger. Not that he welcomed the company, but it was tolerable, and Bella seemed to have taken a shine to Mr. Moseley. She liked the questions, Dave guessed, enjoyed the engagement and the attention, yearned for the connection. It's not that Dave didn't try.

"What's your favoritest thing, Mr. Moseley?" she asked. "Do you like honey?"

"Very much," he said. "I like it with peanut butter."

"Hmm, I like it plain. Did you know that ravens can whisper?" she said, as though the two things were somehow connected. "They can whisper so soft, Mr. Moseley. I've heard them with Daddy at night in the woods."

"What do you think they were whispering about?" said Tristan Moseley.

"I think they were telling each other secrets," said Bella.

Moseley looked impressed.

"What kind of secrets?"

"If I knew that," she said, "they wouldn't be secrets, silly."

"I guess you've got me there."

"Well," said Dave, filling the very brief silence. "Thanks for the visit, Mr. Moseley."

And Tristan Moseley took his cue to stand but seemed a bit unsure how to proceed.

"I'll walk you out," said Dave.

Out on the bluff, the two men stood side-by-side, peering out over the rim of the canyon, as the fog began to lift, and the low clouds moved swiftly past on their northern route.

"A lot to admire about this view," said Moseley.

"Mm," said Dave.

"Mr. Cartwright," he said. "To be frank, at this point, I don't see Mirabella as being at risk, or in imminent harm, provided she's supervised. It surprises me to say it, but I don't see it. She appears physically and emotionally secure, adequately provided for, and ostensibly healthy. If I were you, I'd go to town and file a declaration of intent with the school district. My understanding is, you've still got a permanent address."

"Bank will be taking it soon, if they haven't taken it already."

"Perhaps you could use your brother's address?"

"I'll consider it," said Dave.

"I'm afraid you have to," said Moseley. "After age seven, you're legally obligated."

"By whom?"

"By the state."

"Like I said, I'll consider it," said Dave. "But I don't like it a damn bit. Nobody ought to have the right to control a man's children."

Tristan Moseley's face bore an expression that almost looked like pity.

"In some cases, Mr. Cartwright, you might be surprised. Some kids, they don't have an advocate. They have a parent that's neglecting them, or even abusing them, sometimes sexually. There are children out there that wouldn't be eating at all if it weren't for the state, and that's a fact. Unorthodox as your methods are, I'd say Bella's got it better than a lot of kids, which is why I don't intend on making any trouble for you, so long as you make it legal."

"The only laws I'm interested in anymore are the laws of nature."

"That may be," said Moseley. "And I'm not gonna argue the wisdom in that. I'm just telling you how it is, Mr. Cartwright. I'm trying to help you."

Looking him in the eye, it was not hard for Dave to believe the man. He seemed like a decent guy. In fact, Dave was already willing to trust him, probably more than his own brother at this point.

"I believe you're intent on providing for, and protecting your daughter's best interest," he said. "But Mr. Cartwright, supposing something were to . . . ?"

"Were to what?"

"Supposing something happens to you up here. What happens then?"

"Nothing's going to happen."

"How do you know?"

Dave looked at him meaningfully.

"If something was going to happen to me," he said, "it would have happened already, in Fallujah or Mosul, or some other goddamn place. Nothing is gonna happen to me in these mountains."

Looking out over the rugged country surrounding them, Tristan Moseley nodded, though none too convincingly.

"Goodbye, Mr. Moseley," said Dave, offering a hand. "I'll look into this statement of intent business."

Tristan Moseley shook his hand. "And I'll file my report," he said.

A moment later, Dave watched Mr. Moseley scramble clumsily down the hillside toward the meadow.

A Different Life

———

Sometimes Bella envisioned a different life back home, not with Uncle Trav and Aunt Kris and Cousin Bonnie, but a life with her dad, the way he used to be, in their own house. Maybe not their old house, but a new house near Nana's. Maybe a blue house, with a white fence, and a big yard for the cats to prowl. Maybe there was another Hannah B somewhere down there in town, a new girl, someone who liked the things Bella liked, someone who didn't boss her around, or bully her. She longed for connection, for activity, for an otherness beyond her ancient visitations.

It was almost as though her dad could read her mind.

"What do you say we go to town?" he said, waking her from her reverie.

Her face brightened, but then faded just as quickly.

"This is a trick," she said. "You want to leave me there."

"No, baby. I just want to get some stuff we need. Hey," he said, "we can go to the library and stock up on books."

"What about Nana's?"

"No, baby, we can't go to Nana's. We'll have to camp."

"Why not?"

"We just can't, honey. It's best that Nana and Uncle Travers don't know we're there. Not unless you plan on staying. Do you wanna stay?"

"See," she said. "I told you it was a trick."

"No, baby, I promise it's not a trick," he said. "We don't have to go if you don't want to."

"I want to," she said.

And so, within the hour, they donned their empty packs and fled their isolation. For twenty minutes they trudged through ankle deep autumn snow, their breath fogging the crisp air in front of them, until they reached the snowline at the head of the canyon, where they began wending their way down the basin, as the great wooded canyon walls closed in on them, and the sky tapered to a narrow swath of blue.

They proceeded mostly in silence, Bella retreating into her thoughts, savoring the anticipation that welled up inside of her. God, but she missed TV. She knew it was bad for you, that it could rot your brain if you watched too much, but it was one of the main reasons she wanted to go to Nana's: *Teen Titans, The Powerpuff Girls, Johnny Test.* That and frozen pizza, cut into little squares like Nana did it. If she was really being honest, part of Bella, the part that didn't feel inextricably bound to her dad, really did want to stay in V-Falls, and go back to school, at least for a while.

As much as Bella liked routine, she yearned for newness, and, at the same time, oldness: her old toys, the way she kept them scrupulously organized in green plastic bins from the Home Depot in Bellingham, a fact that always seemed to impress the adults in her life. She missed her old stuffies, the ones she couldn't bring, piled against the headboard, and along the edges of her bunk bed: Hopper and Daisy and Mr. Beaver, now in a closet at Nana's. Bella missed the mobile, the circus animals slowly circling with the slightest draft, even if it was kind of babyish. She never in a million years thought she'd miss taking baths. She missed, too, the patience and enthusiasm of Miss Martine, and her playful way of teaching. And she missed her mother, who now felt almost like a figment of her imagination.

Then there were the things she didn't miss about town, the things she didn't miss about her old life: the awkwardness of being motherless, the anxiety of being social, the bossy ways of her cousin, and the whispering that forever seemed to trail in her wake.

As they plodded through the soggy bottomlands, all was still beneath the canopy except for the gentle swishing of the treetops. Bella loved this vast wooded landscape because it asked nothing from her. It sheltered her from the complexities of her life. The silence of these wilds, the vast unknowableness of the mountains and valleys calmed her, even as the worries crowded in on her.

When they finally reached the highway and jumped the culvert, Bella was flush with equal parts dread and excitement. The march along the shoulder of the highway was her least favorite part of the journey. She hated the cars that slowed in passing, the craned necks, and curious looks from the passengers that accompanied them. She felt like she was under a microscope, with her ragged blue jeans and her dirty backpack. She knew how she and her dad must look to them. She knew they must be judging them.

As always, it was a relief to see the old familiar library, with its smudgy windows and mossy brick facade. As awkward as town could be, the library was the only place that Bella didn't feel like she stuck out. The librarians were always well intentioned and helpful, even when they were kind of weird and rude, possessing what her dad called "bad social skills." Though Bella would never tell him as much, his own social skills could have used some work, lately. For example, the way he looked straight ahead when he walked down the sidewalk, and never seemed to notice the people he passed. Most of the time he didn't even notice if they nodded or smiled at him. Also, the way he never smiled in public. And the way he never chatted like other adults did, about the weather, or the price of gas, or anything else.

Arriving in the children's section, Bella headed hungrily for the low shelves, past the puzzles and the baby toys, past the early readers to the chapter books, where she began running her fingers over the spines, each one a little doorway to another world. Unless, of course, the writing was crappy. Like when they overexplained things, or talked to the reader in a parentizing way, like the reader wasn't adult enough, or too dumb to understand something. The really important thing about stories was not the writing, though. What was important were the lives of the characters in the story, how we recognized ourselves in them, how we connected with them, how we cared about them, how they became real. People who weren't us, people who were maybe nothing like us. People that did and said things we might never do or say. Reading a good story was like seeing into another person. At least, that's how Bella understood it, and Bella had actually been inside of other people, or at least, they'd been inside of her.

"Hey, you go to Nelson," said a voice.

Bella's stomach was aflutter when she turned and immediately recognized a girl from Mrs. Gaskill's third grade class, though she didn't know the girl's name.

"Hey," said Bella, suddenly self-conscious about her appearance.

"You were in Miss Martine's," said the girl. "I had her for second. She used to give out gum on Fridays."

"Not for us," said Bella. "She just gave out stickers."

"That's lame," said the girl.

"I dunno, maybe, I guess," said Bella to the empty-handed girl. "So, are you getting books?"

"Nah," she said. "My mom's just here to use the computer. What's your name, anyway?"

"Bella."

"I'm Grace," she said. "So, what are you doing?"

"Getting books."

"We just get videos," Grace said. "Have you seen *A-X-L*?"

"No."

"What about *Ice Dragon*?"

"No."

"What have you seen?"

"I've seen *Wall-E*, and *Ratatouille*, and *Frozen*. And I've seen *The Iron Giant* like five times."

"Those are ancient," said the girl.

"I don't watch too many DVDs because I live in the mountains," said Bella.

"Duh. Everybody in V-Falls lives in the mountains."

"I mean way in the mountains. We don't even have a TV, or electricity, or a lot of stuff."

"That sucks," said the girl. "Is that why your clothes are all dirty?"

Bella felt the heat rush to her face.

"Yeah, I guess," she said. "I must've got dirty walking down here, or something."

"Is your dad that guy with the beard, the one with the big pack?"

"Yeah."

"He must've got dirty, too," said Grace.

Before Bella could formulate a reply, Grace's mom, who looked pretty proud of herself for somebody checking their internet at the library, and maybe a little too made up for the occasion, suddenly walked up, looking down her nose at Bella in an unpleasant way, as she shepherded Grace away by the wrist without a word. Not until they were halfway down the 700 aisle did Grace's mother quietly reprimand her daughter.

Bella's heart hardened into a little fist. Maybe her dad was right, maybe it was a disease, maybe people really were getting worse.

S'tka

———

Five winters had passed since S'tka committed U'ku'let to the frozen ground. Five years of ice and hunger and solitude, of strain and worry and sometimes terror. Five mostly joyless cycles of isolation, and habitual survival. Five years serving her son. Five years hiding in the reeds from strangers. Five years wondering why the world did not offer her more.

And yes, five years wondering nightly what had become of the clan who forsook her to this desolation. Did they die out there on the ice in their quest for something more? Did they weaken, day-by-day, moon-by-moon, as the wolves patiently stalked and menaced them to the feeble end? Perhaps, beleaguered and half-starving, her clan was sacked in the night by another. Knowing Yq'mat, Kt'ak, and Ok'eh, they might just as easily have eaten themselves.

Or maybe, just maybe, they found their new world beyond the ice. If so, what did it look like? What did it promise? Was it everything they ever dreamed of? Was it their destiny, after all? If so, why, oh why, did the Great Provider set it so far out of reach? Why the perilous, frozen wasteland to traverse?

Whatever the possibilities, S'tka would have liked to believe that world was out there, if not for her own sake, for N'ka's. Were it not for the need to sustain N'ka, surely she would've walked out onto the ice and given herself to the wolves winters ago. But N'ka demanded her survival. And as ever, S'tka did what was demanded of her.

Not to say that N'ka was not a revelation. N'ka the irrepressible, N'ka, spry and endlessly curious. N'ka, furiously awake to the world. See him sharpening his sticks and beating his chest like a man, though he's never seen an actual man within a half-mile that he could possibly remember. See him sulk when his pride was hurt. See him crouching silently behind rocks, biding his time, saving his breath, not answering his mother's call, only to leap out and startle her. See him laugh, see him scratch himself, see him empty his bladder as though it were a celebration. This is the spirit that men work so hard to preserve, to remain boys. And frankly, S'tka couldn't blame them. When did she ever celebrate a piss?

What little joy S'tka experienced, she experienced vicariously through N'ka, who was like the grass pushing up through the ice. Each day S'tka could feel the child longing to stretch out, to pursue his curiosity, to cast himself toward the light of the world.

"Where are all the other people?" he asked, sitting in the glow of the fire.

"They are spread out everywhere," she said. "Here and there, as far as the eye can see."

"Why don't we see them then?"

"You've seen them, N'ka. Moving through the valley."

"But we never talk to them. We never stop them."

"Not all people can be trusted," she said flatly.

"But some people can, can't they?"

"Go to sleep, N'ka."

She could not shelter him forever, this she knew. Five, maybe six more winters, if she could sustain the two of them that long, before his jaw dropped, and he began breathing out of his mouth, before he started growing the first downy hairs on his chest, and between his legs, and asserting his manhood. Whatever she owed N'ka, whatever she wished for him, whatever she tried to build or preserve for him, would be irrelevant when that time came. Like his father before him, N'ka was certain to cast his own lot, no matter how foolish.

S'tka wished she could say the same for herself.

The Stranger

———

Dave had been tracking the stranger's progress since he crested the green lip of the canyon, a thousand feet below. From his perch at the edge of the bluff, Dave watched the lanky figure switch-backing up the incline for a half mile, pausing intermittently to catch his breath, and drink from his water bottle, carabiners glinting like mirrors in the weak autumn sunlight.

He was coming from the west, so Dave knew he likely came in on FS 1220, the old logging spur out of Lundgren. Still, it was a pretty decent hike from the end of the road, maybe three miles and two thousand vertical feet. Dave stood at the edge of the bluff, partially obscured by the great, gray outcropping of rock, monitoring the stranger's progress as he disappeared behind the hump, then reappeared minutes later on the near side of the saddle, walking with purpose through the meadow.

Before the top of the stranger's head ever broke the upper plane of the meadow, before his khaki shirt and pea green pants emerged into plain view, Dave had already made him as a ranger. Retreating to the fire, still smoldering from breakfast, Dave propped one boot casually on the ring of the pit and awaited his visitor, hoping that Bella would not return from her wanderings to complicate matters.

As he crested the edge of the bluff and stood upright, Dave could see that the stranger was quite tall, maybe 6'4", rangy, and a little stooped, like a guy who never wanted to be tall.

"Howdy," he said, approaching the fire pit.

He was maybe forty years old, with some acne scarring on his cheeks, which were slick and ruddy with exertion. He wore a shiny badge, but Dave couldn't read the name, nor did he care to know it.

"Saw your fire," said the trespasser, pulling up short of breath. "Decided I should check it out."

"There a burn ban I don't know about?" said Dave.

"Not at present. Just playing it on the safe side," said the ranger, perusing the camp. "How long you been up here?"

"Four days," said Dave.

"Four days, huh?" He pursed his lips, nodding his head in consideration. Just then, Bella appeared out of the brush. The ranger turned twenty degrees and offered her a nod, doffing his cap.

"I heard voices," said Bella.

"Hello, young lady," said the ranger with a pleasant grin. "What's your name, darlin'?"

"Mirabella," she said. "But nobody calls me that."

"Ah," said the ranger. "Kind of late in the season to be camping out, isn't it?" he observed.

"Maybe for some," said Dave.

"Hunting?"

"Nah."

The ranger continued to look around the camp, considering the neatly stacked wood beneath the tarp, the well-worn chopping block, and the row of plastic water bottles, tucked tidily against the face of the rock hillside.

"Where you from?" he said, at last.

"Just down the canyon in V-Falls," said Dave.

The stranger registered the information

"So, just camping then?" he said.

"That's right," said Dave. "Been camping in these woods my whole life."

"In a cave?"

Dave hinted at a smile.

"On this occasion, yeah." He said. "Pretty convenient, right? Gets awful windy up here sometimes. Not the best for tent camping."

"Looks like you've made some improvements," he said, indicating the furrowed soil.

"Not my work," said Dave. "But it's a good spot. Others have been here before."

"Looks like you're fixed pretty well, all right. You armed?"

"Yessir, I am. A pair of .22s and a .458, all licensed," said Dave. "Teaching my girl how to shoot—with the .22, of course."

The ranger nodded his head.

"Looks as though you're dug in for a while," he said. "How long you plan on staying?"

"Not long," said Dave. "About a week."

The ranger set his hand on Bella's head.

"Well, aren't you a lucky girl?" he said, mussing her hair. "I didn't realize school was out."

"I don't go to school anymore," she said.

"Is that right?" said the ranger.

"She's homeschooled," said Dave.

"Ah," said the ranger. "Well, can't argue with that. My sister down in Lacy did as much with my nephew. And she says she's glad she did it. He just graduated from Wazu."

Just then Boris and Boots emerged from the depths of the cave, the latter pausing to splay her spotted arms and white paws way out in front of her, bow her back, and stretch extravagantly, while Boris, black and shiny as his mother, began to push himself up against the ranger's ankle, purring like a sump pump.

"They were already here," said Dave, referring to the cats. "They could probably tell you who was working that soil."

"Hmph," said the ranger, apparently not convinced. "It's a wonder they can survive up here."

"Cat's a resourceful creature," said Dave. "Especially next to a dog. A dog can't seem to keep himself out of trouble."

"I've got two beagles," said the ranger. "They wouldn't last two hours up here before they'd run off and get themselves in some kind of trouble. Probably corner a wildcat, or nose their way into a bear den."

The ranger squatted down to scratch Boots behind the ears. The imploring cat all but collapsed at his feet, exposing her nippled underside.

"Doesn't act like any feral cat, does she?" he said.

"Guess not," said Dave. "Long as they don't follow us home, I'm okay with them."

The ranger left off petting Boots and rose to his feet.

"Well, anyway," he said. "You two stay warm. And keep that fire down to a reasonable size."

"Yessir, we will."

"Looks to me like you're the responsible type," said the ranger. "What'd you say your name was?"

"You never asked. But it's Cartwright."

"You register for a backwoods permit, Mr. Cartwright?"

"Not a designated wilderness area, as I understand it—not like the park. Am I wrong?"

"You're not wrong," he said. "Always a good idea to let folks know you're out here."

"My people know right where I'm at," said Dave.

"That's good. You'd be wise to get back to town before the weather blows in. Could get nasty."

"We're paying attention," said Dave.

"And just so you know," said the ranger, as though it were almost an afterthought. "Thirteen days is the limit for camping up here."

"Is that so?" said Dave. "Never heard that before."

"That's the rule," said the ranger.

"Heck, thirteen days is more than I need out here at a stretch. I reckon I'd get a little stir crazy after two weeks," said Dave.

"A week's about all I can take, myself," said the ranger. "All the same, thirteen days is the limit. Just so we're clear."

"I'll keep it in mind," said Dave.

"You do that, Mr. Cartwright," he said. "Good day, Mirabella. You be good at homeschool, you hear? I'll probably be back through in a couple weeks, but I imagine you'll be long gone by then. Right?"

Bella flashed Dave an unsure look.

"Like I said, we'll be clearing out of here in a week or so," Dave said.

"Okay, then," said the ranger. "Last thing I need up here is another squatter."

"I'm no squatter," said Dave.

"Glad to hear it," said the ranger. "You take care, now."

And with that the ranger began making his way down the face of the bluff, and was soon crossing the meadow, with one final look back over his shoulder. Dave waved cheerfully, though the ranger's sudden appearance had gone a long way in darkening his mood.

"Daddy, you lied," said Bella, once the ranger was out of sight. "We're not only staying a week."

"It's no business of his how long we're staying, baby."

"But he's a ranger. Doesn't that make it his business?"

"No, baby, actually it doesn't."

"He said we can only stay thirteen days."

"He's wrong, buddy," said Dave. "It's not up to anybody but us where we stay, or how long we stay for."

S'tka

Slogging ankle deep through the snow on a downhill course, her ragged breaths sawing at the frozen air, S'tka observed the signs of another early spring all around her. The valley was no longer strewn with ice. The saplings propagating along the edges of the corridor had begun to crowd in on the grassland. These seedlings were not stunted in permafrost, nor bowed beneath the weight of the winter's snow. S'tka saw life awakening all around her amidst the sprawling white world, saw it tentatively peeking through the ground, almost but not quite ready to commit.

In the deepest folds of the basin there was mud like she'd never seen before, mud gathering in wallows, mud running like rivers, mud oozing down the hillsides, where it gathered in great, gloppy marshes. It was perilous, this mud, it could mire you, pull you down and suffocate you. It could bury you alive.

But today, the mud was not their adversary. Today the mud was their ally.

N'ka struggled to keep pace with his mother through the wet snow, his outsized spear further impeding his progress.

"Are we almost there?" he said.

"Almost," she said.

Down the slushy hillside they progressed, the snowpack vanishing as they descended, until they reached the bottomlands, dappled golden and green.

"Are we here?"

"Not yet," she said.

They marched north through the basin, sticking to the reedy edges for concealment. It had been nine years since S'tka had spoken to another human besides N'ka, and should anybody cross her path now, she was not about to start.

"You said we were almost there."

"Shush," she said.

For a half-mile, they trudged north with their spears, the great serrated peaks of the high country scraping the blue sky. Were it not such an unforgiving place it might have been beautiful.

Finally, they arrived at the edge of a muddy morass near the foot of a sluice-like slide.

"There," she said, indicating the shaggy red masses near the center of the quagmire, where a mother mammoth sprawled on her side, mired in the mud, lolling her great shaggy head uselessly, as her listless calf huddled nearby, nudging her. For three days it had been thus. S'tka's hope that the mother would finally expire, and the calf would weaken, had not fully come to pass, though it appeared that the end was close at hand. The mother was lethargic, her eyes distant and unblinking.

The calf was growing restless.

"Stay," said S'tka to N'ka.

"But Mom, you said—"

"Get back," she clucked, quelling his resistance.

Bad enough that N'ka should end up like the calf, watching his marooned mother suffocating in the mud. She would not see him gored or trampled.

S'tka began collecting bundles of grass and piling it at the edge of the mud.

"Look, look," she said, holding the tufts of grass high for the calf to see.

"Mom, he can't understand you," said N'ka from the sidelines.

"Silence!"

S'tka didn't dare venture into the mud herself, for fear it might swallow her.

"Food, food," she said, to the calf. "Eat, eat!"

"You're supposed to kill it, Mom. Not feed it."

"Shush!"

"Well," he said. "It's true."

"Come, come eat the nice grass, baby!"

"This is never going to work," said N'ka. "Let me do it."

"Ha!" she said. "You, who can barely hike two miles, you're going to feed us? Ha! Do not forget your place."

Before long, S'tka had piled up half her weight in grass, managing finally to arouse the calf's curiosity, if not his appetite.

"See, see?" she said to N'ka. "He's coming."

"Get him in the neck," he said.

"Good, baby," she said to the calf. "Look at all the grass I have for you."

As S'tka lured the sluggish calf to the edge of the wallow, she bent at the knees, reaching back for her spear in the grass, slinging it low in her grasp, so as not to discourage the beast.

Though only a yearling, the calf was already huge; his shaggy shoulder a half-foot above S'tka's head. And even in its feeble condition, S'tka knew he was incredibly powerful.

The calf ambled slowly through squelchy earth, mired halfway to its knees. S'tka prayed it would not get itself stuck beyond her reach. At the edge of the marsh, it dully registered the heaping grass, S'tka met its plaintive, dull-eyed gaze. "That's it, baby," she said. "You stay put."

As though warning her calf, the mother mustered the weakest of trumpets.

"Thank you for coming," said S'tka, inching closer to the calf.

"Now, Mom!" hollered N'ka.

On cue, S'tka threw herself headlong at the calf, striking it in the neck with all her strength. The calf instantly reared back into the mud, and nearly lost its footing, spear still buried in its throat. S'tka slipped backward in the mud and scrambled to her feet, as the dazed calf righted itself, and appeared as though it were readying itself to charge her, when something fleet streaked past S'tka in her peripheral vision.

N'ka was but a blur as he hurled his spear upward, lodging it in the throat, just below the first spear with a force and accuracy that caused the calf to buckle at the knees and rear back once more, before toppling at the edge of the marsh, where it wheezed and burbled toward its final breaths, blood spewing out of its punctured throat.

N'ka, the mighty hunter, barely seven years old! What strength and accuracy! What courage! How proud his father would be!

The Law of Diminishing Returns

During Dave's second tour his unit was outside of Mosul on an advise-and-assist, doling out candy to a scrum of kids in front of a clapboard market, Dave razzing Pope about his tireless Christian charity.

"Aren't you gonna make them sing some hymns or something? Isn't it how that works, Pope? You offer the poor sonsofbitches the straw of life, but only after you convert them?"

Pope shook his head. "Man, you got it all wrong, Dave. These kids are innocents. They're already saved."

"Maybe they're innocent, maybe not."

"They're innocent, man. They ain't nothing but children."

"Old Reverend Pope," said Dave. "Doin' the good work. Savin' souls, one Tootsie Roll at a time."

"Tootsie Roll, my ass," said Pope. "That shit would melt out here in ten seconds flat! You gotta have hard candy."

"You got it all figured out," said Dave.

"You know the problem with you, Cartwrong?" said Pope. "You know why you say and do some of the sick shit you do?"

"Do tell, Reverend."

"Because you're afraid, man. You're scared shitless. More scared than any one of these kids."

"Scared of what?" said Dave.

"That's a question to ask yourself, dog. But if you ever wanna talk about it seriously, you know where to find me."

"You think I'm afraid of dying out here? Is that it?"

"Did I say that?"

"What, then?" said Dave.

"Not my place to say," said Pope, as they made their way down the dusty, stinking boulevard, seemingly casual but at the same time alert to peripheral movement every step of the way.

"But if I was guessing," said Pope, "I'd say you're scared of a general lack of meaning in the universe."

"Why the hell should that scare anyone, Pope? Just means that the stakes are lower."

Pope pursed his lips and swiveled his head a few times in apparent disillusionment.

"Dave," he said. "That's where you're wrong, man. The stakes are higher than you may ever know. Your life, man, it's a reflection of everything. Everything that ever was. You're a link in the chain, but it's more than a chain. It's like a whole gigantic fabric. A huge quilt. And God, God's like the needle. God sews it all together. God connects us. It's a crazy ass quilt, and every square is different, see, but God connects us."

"Give me a fucking Tootsie Roll, Pope. You're full of shit, you know that? Connect? Really? Look around you. Is this place a reflection of everything that ever was? Is it? Those little ragheads tugging at our pockets for penny candy? This blown-to-shit backwater? This stupid fucking business we call security detail? Where's the meaning in any of this shit? Where's the fucking connection? These people didn't ask for this. This war is about money, Pope; this war is about goddamn oil. There ain't a damn thing holy about that. Why would God require anybody to endure this bullshit? That's the question, Pope. If there's a merciful God like you say, then what are we doing here in the first place? Why does this place even exist?"

Pope got real quiet after that. Dave knew he was percolating a thoughtful answer, but he never did get in his last word, not that Dave would've ever let Pope convince him. Three minutes later, as they patrolled a narrow side street on opposite sides, a rat scurried out from under the carcass of a dead dog and they both nearly jumped out of their armor. Wide-eyed, they caught their breath again in tandem, locking eyes across the street with a palpable relief, as Pope began to kick the dead dog aside.

In that instant, right before Pope kicked the dead dog, Dave entertained the idea that just maybe Pope was onto something. Maybe the stakes were higher than Dave was ever willing to admit. Maybe the oppressed, and the humiliated, and the abused had something to teach us. Maybe they would inherit the earth, after all. Maybe they would save us. Maybe our suffering really was all connected somehow.

Dave was looking right into Pope's eyes when the poor sonofabitch kicked the dog carcass and took the hit. Before Dave could hit the deck, he was blinded by a spray of gravel to the face, which was a lot better than Pope ended up—in several pieces, his boot coming to rest in the middle of the street, half his lower leg still intact.

Once Dave got to his feet and scrambled to Pope's aid, he found the Reverend blown half to shit, and his face full of shrapnel. His goddamn blood-filled eyes implored Dave to do something.

At the sound of laughter from across the street, Dave swung around and started spraying off rounds indiscriminately, watching the children scatter. He didn't kill anybody, but in that moment, he wished more than anything that he had.

Innocents, my ass. There was no innocence left in that goddamn desert.

Dave got down on his knees in the dirty street and propped Pope's head in his lap, then took a grim inventory of the situation, trying not to reveal the gravity of the situation to poor Pope.

"Pope, man, look at me," said Dave.

Pope was in shock, losing a lot of blood from the leg, and from a deep side wound. Dave was gonna have to tie off the leg fast if there was any hoping of saving him.

"You're gonna be just fine, Reverend. Just hang tough, now."

Pope just looked up at him with imploring eyes.

"I love you, Dave," he said. "Everything is gonna be all right."

Dave was practically hyperventilating.

"I'm gonna fix you up, Rev, hold tight. We're gonna get you out of here, okay, pal?"

"Relax, brother," said Pope. "I'm good."

Counting Days

———

Bella kept waiting for something to happen. Every morning, a fresh dread of the unknown fueled her anxiety. And all she could do was wait. And wait. Even the cats seemed to sense her edginess, and they did their feline best to comfort her, or more accurately, they forced her to pet them whenever they felt like being petted.

Today was thirteen days since the ranger came, with no sign yet of his impending return. No sign of Mr. Moseley, or Uncle Travis, or anyone else either. And yet she knew somebody would come. She was certain that at any moment her life would change again.

Her dad did not seem concerned, a fact that both buoyed her optimism and inflated her anxiety. Despite his incessant reading, and apparent interest in such a wide variety of subjects as geology, forestry, para-something-ology, and dentistry, there was a lot that no longer seemed to concern her dad. A whole world, in fact. How could he possibly think everything was just fine when somebody was sure to come for her? His generally not worrying about anything of late was something she was beginning to resent.

Finally, Bella confronted him in his customary repose, huddled around the dead fire, his face buried in a book, his hand fussing absently with his long, gray-tipped beard.

"What about the thirteen days, Daddy?"

"What thirteen days, baby?" he said, glancing up from the page.

"The ranger said thirteen days was the limit for us to stay."

Dave dog-eared the page but didn't close the book. He scratched his beard once last time for good measure.

"Today is the thirteenth day," she said.

He started to say something, then stopped himself, scratched his neck, and looked down absently at the book in his lap, before looking back up at her.

"Look, Bella, honey, that rule is . . ."

He trailed off to heave a sigh.

"Well," he continued, "it's bullshit, okay? Sometimes the rules are bullshit, baby. In fact, a lot of times they are."

As whenever he swore, Bella was dubious. It was usually in anger, and it usually involved saying something he would take back later.

"But you always told me to follow the rules," she said.

Her dad clenched and unclenched his fist the way he did when he didn't know what to say, as if he could squeeze out an answer. Finally, after a moment's thought, he offered her an explanation.

"Baby," he said. "There are principles, and then there are rules. There's a big distinction."

"What's 'distinction'?"

"Distinction means a difference," he said. "There's a big difference between your principles—what you know is right—and the rules, which can sometimes be arbitrary."

"What's 'arbitrary'?"

"Arbitrary means, well, random, I guess."

"Like a guess?"

"Kind of like that, yeah. Something that doesn't always have a good reason for being the way it is. The point is, that it's important to stick to your principles."

"What are my principles?"

He clenched and unclenched his fist again, scratching at his beard reflexively with the other hand.

"Well, let's see. Be a good person, that's first and foremost," he said. "Don't do wrong to others. Always take the high road if there's a decision about right or wrong. And don't be greedy. Take what you need in the world, but not more. Basically, just live an honest life."

"Is that what we're doing here?"

"Yes," he said. "Exactly."

"Are there rules against that?"

He clenched his fist again but didn't unclench it this time.

"Yes," he said. "More and more every day."

"Why?"

"Because the damn greedy power-mongers want to own us."

"You can't own a person," she said.

"What do you think a slave is?" he said.

"There's no more slaves," she said. "Miss Martine told us they stopped slavery a long time ago. In the eighteen-hundreds."

"Of a certain kind," he said. "But there's different ways of enslaving people."

"Like how?"

"Well, like rules that don't make sense, rules that say a person can't live where a person wants. There're laws that aren't fair, laws that say certain people can't do certain things. And debt, debt is a kind of slavery; it's kind of like a chain that keeps people tied to a life they can't afford."

"Do we have debt?"

"Not anymore, baby. What we owe, we owe to the earth."

She knew such a vague answer was insufficient. She hated it when he parentized her.

"What if the ranger comes back?"

"We're not doing anything wrong," he said. "We have as much right to be in these mountains as anybody. Nobody has jurisdiction over nature."

"What's 'jurydiction'?"

"It means nobody can own nature. The world doesn't belong to anybody. Baby, the ranger can't do anything. He won't do anything, okay? So don't you worry."

"Will he come back?"

"It doesn't matter if he comes back," he said.

"Maybe we should move somewhere else," said Bella.

"Like where? You want to go back to town? Because if you really want, I can take—"

"No," she said.

"You could live with—"

"No," said Bella. "Just somewhere different."

"Baby, any town we go to will just eventually—"

"I mean farther into the mountains," she said.

He finally unclenched his fist.

"I've thought about that," he said. "A lot. But we can't just keep moving around, Bella, that's no way to live. We're not nomads. This is our home now. We have shelter. Everything we need is here. And besides, winter is coming any day. Nobody is going to stop us from making our lives here. They can't, and they won't, baby."

"Even if we're breaking their rules?"

"We don't live by their rules, understand?"

"I dunno," said Bella. "It seems like a bad idea to stay if we're not ortherized. What if they put us in jail?"

"For what?"

"For staying past thirteen days."

"The worst they can do is fine us a couple hundred bucks," he said.

"Promise?"

"I promise."

But the truth was his promises were no longer a comfort to Bella. It used to be she could trust him. It used to be he was always right. Lately, though, more and more, his judgment failed to inspire confidence.

As though he could sense her unease, her dad pulled her in close, trapping her in a hug.

"Everything is gonna be all right," he said.

And for the moment, at least some of her anxiety fled.

If Not Remote

———————

Judy awoke with a start, the clock on the nightstand glowing a red 3:40 a.m. What jarred her from her sleep was not a dream, rather a sudden, sharp certainty that could only be likened to a premonition. Once awake, she knew better than to pursue sleep again. Rising from bed, she slid into her slippers and padded to the kitchen to boil water.

Her first such jolt of foreboding arrived when Davey was only seven weeks old, and she was sure he'd stopped breathing in the night. Just as now, back then she'd risen from bed, hurrying to the crib where she discovered that Davey had somehow managed to roll over onto his stomach, though he was breathing when she found him. She kept vigil by the crib the remainder of the night, and in the morning drove all the way to JCPenney in Bellingham to purchase a crib wedge. She started having the bad omens again regularly in 2003, when Davey was in Iraq. There must have been a dozen nights where she awoke in a sweat, convinced that Davey was in trouble. It was an incredible weight off her back when he returned in the fall, at least physically intact.

When the kettle began to hiss, Judy poured a mug of water and plopped a tea bag in to steep. She had half a mind to dial Travers, but resisted the impulse. What could she say to him? What could he do? All Judy had to offer was a terrible impression that something was wrong, somehow, somewhere with Davey or Bella. And there was absolutely nothing anybody could do about it.

Judy sat at the kitchen table most of the night, with the little TV on, muted, oscillating between dread and grief, volleying between frustration at her powerlessness and anger at Davey for putting her in such situations, time and again. What good was she as a mother, or grandmother, if she could not protect them? What good was anybody to anybody once they were beyond arm's reach?

Finally, when Judy surmised that the hour was no longer indecent, she switched from tea to black coffee, and promptly dialed Travers, who was already awake and eating breakfast.

"I'm not going up there again, Ma. Dave made it abundantly clear I was not welcome."

"What if something's wrong?"

"He's a big boy."

"Bella's not," she said.

"We've already sent CPS and a ranger up there," said Travers. "There's not much else we can do."

"You can go up there again."

"I've been up there twice already, and neither time has done a damn bit of good. Remember, Ma, I got her back once already. Frankly, I can't promise he won't shoot me if I go up there again."

"Something is wrong, I can feel it."

"I don't doubt something is wrong," he said. "But I wouldn't worry for their safety. They're pretty dug in up there, and pretty well stocked. Dave knows what he's doing."

"Travers, please."

"There's just no way, Ma. I've got like fifteen meetings this week: the housing authority, three different contractors, the bank, the ownership group, four buyers."

"So you're too busy, is that what you're telling me? You've got bigger, more important things to worry about than your brother, the one who taught you how to throw a football? The brother who—"

"That's not fair, Ma," said Travers. "You know I love Dave, and you know how much I care about Bella. I tried, Ma. I brought her down here,

I put her back in school, I fed her and clothed her. And all she did was run back to him. Bella and Dave are outside my jurisdiction at this point."

"Will you at least go to church with me on Sunday and pray?"

"I'm in the city all weekend. I'll pray from my hotel. Look, Ma, I've got an eight-thirty up on the ridge with the roofers, so I've gotta run. I love you."

Travers was right, of course. There was little if anything to be done that hadn't already been attempted. But Judy would've been lying had she said she didn't wish that Travers were more like Davey. Davey would've gone up there, she knew it.

Judy was restless after she got off the phone with Travers. She didn't want to be alone. If not with somebody else, she wanted to be around other people. She thought about going to Dale's for breakfast, but the food gave her heartburn every time. She thought about calling Carol Trembley from church, but Carol could be so exhausting sometimes. Finally, Judy decided to go to Red Apple and do her shopping for next week.

She dressed without showering, then put on lipstick, and made sure her checkbook and reading glasses were in her purse before she walked out the door.

The hour was still early enough that Judy got one of the non-handicap spots right out front of Red Apple. The Elfendahl girl was working the only open register. As Judy trundled her cart down the cereal, baking goods, and convenient breakfast aisle, a large, familiar, slightly obese gentleman, roughly Davey's age, addressed her.

"Hey, Mrs. C."

God, it had been twenty years since anyone called her Mrs. C.

"Who's that?" she said.

"Joe Wettleson, from Ace Hardware. Dave's pal from high school. I played right guard for two years for VFHS. I blocked for him. Dave got all the glory. But hell, he deserved it. Dave was a stud."

"Oh, of course . . . Joe," Judy said, though she still couldn't place him.

"What do you hear from Dave?" said Joe. "Last I heard, he was living in the mountains or something."

Judy could feel herself blushing. She never knew what to say in these situations. Was she supposed to make Dave's life up there sound like something more than it was? How could she possibly spin the situation to play the proud mother? It was impossible. *Oh, he's still living in a cave. They've got a wonderful view.*

Perhaps Joe sensed her discomfort, for he quickly filled the silence.

"I've got a ton of respect for Dave's service," he said. "I'll bet he was a hell of a soldier."

"Don't ever let him hear you call him that," she said, relieved to re-frame the conversation. "He was a marine."

Joe smiled. "I never did understand their beef with each other."

"Me neither," said Judy.

"Well, if you see him, tell him I said hi. Tell him he should pop into Ace sometime. He owes me that much for all the punishment I took clearing his path every Friday night. Be great to see him. I'd love to buy him a beer and hash out old times."

"I certainly will, Joe," said Judy.

"See you around, Mrs. C."

The brief exchange left Judy feeling better somehow. She guessed it was just the knowing that there was still some good will out there for Davey despite everything. Her spirits were buoyed somewhat as she wheeled past the pharmacy toward the deli counter.

By lunchtime, with a little help from prayer, and her now daily cigarette, smoked surreptitiously on the back porch so that nosey Rose Van Hooris from across the street couldn't see her, Judy was able to ward off her anxiety.

All she could do was pray.

S'tka

That spring, for the first time in S'tka's lifetime, the giants did not lumber south after the thaw, they did not amble down the broad valley to graze on the green grasses, their tusks digging at the soft earth, their big, shaggy ears twitching against the onslaught of mosquitoes. S'tka and N'ka waited on the ridge north of the bluff, spears sharpened and at the ready for the appearance of their ancient benefactors. They clung to their hope, they braced their ears for trumpeting in the distance, but their patience was not rewarded. Where were those restless bulls, ready to stomp them to smithereens? Where were those tusky upstarts to challenge the alpha, while the calves were left to wander the ice alone, vulnerable and unsuspecting? Surely they would come eventually, as they'd always come since the beginning of time. Perhaps the mild early spring offered no sense of urgency. Perhaps they would come yet. Perhaps the giants were simply taking their sweet time getting there.

Oh, how S'tka wished she could take her own sweet time, schedule her own existence, as though the endless progression of day and night was something she could ever bargain with. That their adversary and unwilling patron should never arrive was unthinkable. For the coming of the giants was an absolute, like the inevitable dawn of day, and the inexorable shroud of night. And yet, when the wildflowers exploded in the valley, and the days grew longer and warmer, the giants were still not to be found scratching their backs on the great pillars of rock, or idly trumpeting in the meadows.

For days and weeks and months, S'tka and N'ka awaited their arrival with mounting unease, routinely checking the wallows and muddy sluices of the bottomlands. And when they were not scouring the basin, they roosted at the edge of the bluff, waiting.

"What if they don't come?" said the boy.

"They will come."

"How do you know?"

"Because some things never change."

This assurance rang hollow even to S'tka's own ears. Because all around her she saw change: the shortened season, the melting ice, the proliferation of forests and grasses in the hollows once mired in ice. One might've easily suspected these symptoms were harbingers of life, not portents of starvation.

"Maybe we should go to them," said the boy, leaning upon his spear as he stared out over the bluff into the long, wide valley sprawling north.

"No, we will wait for them," she said. "Trust me, nothing good ever came of going."

And so they continued their interminable wait. Anxiously on the bluff, restlessly, desperately, hopelessly they waited, until the warm season began its not-so-gradual retreat, and S'tka was forced to acknowledge that once again the Great Provider had failed them. Had she failed the giants, too? Had they starved? Had the weather prevented their migration?

"What if they never come again?" said N'ka.

"Shush," she told him.

"Are we to wait again in another year?" he said. "Just sit here and starve, and hope for something that may never come?"

"That is what hope is," she said.

"Bah!" he said. "Why must we always wait? You say no good comes from going. But I say no good comes from waiting."

"That is because you are still a child, still impatient," she said.

Were it not for the roots and ground squirrels and the sloths, were it not for the lone mule deer, mangy and half-starved that wandered into the meadow below the bluff, S'tka and N'ka might themselves have starved that winter. But they soldiered on doggedly, huddled about the fire in the shelter of the cave, sustaining themselves on the promise of stories, the stories of the mighty herds that once sustained them, and the great choreography of the hunt, which joined their feeble spirits and puny bodies into a single entity, greater and more intelligent than any giant.

And so, as another lean winter beat down upon them, they took refuge and comfort in their stories.

When the Great Provider created this world for the people, she made it out of mud, and ash, and ice. She formed the rivers and the mountains to shelter them. Then, she made the sun and the moon to protect them, and watch over them, and count their days for them, so they could mark the eternal march of time. There was a rhythm to the world, and that rhythm was a human heartbeat.

But that is not to say that the world was made for people alone. The Great Provider imbued all the things of the world with a spirit: the wind, the clouds, the rocks. Even the ice.

The Great Provider made a promise to the things of the world, and that promise was that so long as the sun and the moon circled the horizons, she would provide for all things. For the plants she would provide nourishment from the soil, for the great, roaming beasts of the lowlands, she would provide grasses and roots and shrubs in abundance. And for the people, she would provide fire and water, and those same furry beasts in endless supply to feed and clothe them on the ice.

And that was the promise of the world, passed along through the epochs on the tongues of men and women.

We are not alone. We are watched over and cared for. So long as the sun and the moon circle the horizons.

The Damage

B ooks, books, and more books. Books in stacks, and toppled piles, books
dog-eared, face-down, and spine-split, books morning, noon, and
night. Here was Dave, in the grips of a mania that apparently no amount of
knowledge could appease. He no longer busied himself about camp, stowing and organizing and preparing for eventualities. Where he once cut and
stacked, sawed and plowed, he now read and read and read, pausing only to
feed his daughter, and relieve himself, one area in which he had grown lazy
in recent weeks, for the mouth of the cave was beginning to stink of piss.
The weather was getting colder, and Dave could feel the change of seasons
in his aching hip, which lately took half a day to warm up.

Their most recent trip to the public library, nine days ago—upon which
occasion Bella insisted on combing her hair, and wearing her least muddy
pants, and walking thirty feet behind Dave who lugged a lumpy, construc-
tion grade garbage sack in addition to his stuffed backpack—had yielded
some twenty-three dollars in fines. Bella had gone to great lengths to keep
her distance from Dave during their visit, as though she was embarrassed
by him. And frankly, Dave didn't blame her. He wasn't so old, nor so
checked out, that he couldn't remember the indignities and insecurities of
childhood.

They left with no less than thirty-five pounds of books, on subjects
ranging from genealogy to meteorology to quantum mechanics to cat
breeding to football. There was hardly any room left in his pack for supplies, though he managed to squeeze in bouillon cubes, multi-vitamins,

iodized salt, herbal tea, a pound-and-a-half of raisins, and, for the first time in his life, a pair of reading glasses.

In the dank of the cave, or by the light of the fire, reading glasses perched upon the bridge of his nose, Dave comprehended wormholes, waded through epochs of geologic strata, wondered at the miracle of genetic design, and experienced Super Bowl III through the eyes of Broadway Joe.

But most of Dave's reading was reserved for his new favorite subject: Iraq. Not Iraq as Dave came to know and abhor it. Not the hellish nursery of his worst nightmares, or the sandy course of his psychological and spiritual undoing. Not the Iraq of blasted cities, and maimed children, and improvised explosives concealed within the carcasses of dead animals. Not the sight of global trauma, and misplaced ideologies, and craven greed, but Iraq as the fertile crescent, the Garden of Eden that the Sumerians had once deemed it; a land of wheat on the edge of the great sea.

Of all the mortal sins, of all the human follies, it seemed to Dave that greed had done the most damage.

Reacting and Pretending

————

Dave had been home from his final tour in Iraq less than twenty-four hours before he officially lost his shit. No excuses, but looking back, maybe he could have used a palate cleanser between six months of combat, a week in the hospital, and full immersion into a domestic life he had lost all familiarity with. It was almost like having amnesia, like having to learn everything all over again when it came to dealing with other people, particularly civilian people. So Dave mostly defaulted to a rusty auto-pilot in which the world was a dull blur of reacting and pretending.

When he deplaned, hobbling down the jetway stairs on crutches, and saw Nadene standing at the edge of the tarmac in Bellingham on that unseasonably dry afternoon in late fall, her a good ten pounds skinnier than when he'd left, all made up with her red shoes and a print dress he didn't recognize, Dave's heart seized up like a pulled muscle. Though there was fifty yards between them, time enough for him to prepare, it felt like the journey was over in three steps, despite his crutches. But when Nadene threw her arms around him, Dave's whole body went stiff as a cadaver.

Of course, he was happy, at least as much as the idea of happiness was still discernible to him. Of course, he was relieved to be out of that stinking hellhole desert. Yes, Nadene should have been a sight for sore eyes. Yes, Dave should have crutched those final steps a little faster to reach her waiting embrace. But something, or many things, perhaps, all of them beyond his comprehension, held him back.

God, he prayed for some kind of transition, for a week of decompression alone in the wettest, furthest-from-Iraq environment possible: Cameroon, the Hoh Rain Forest, Equatorial Guinea. A motel room, a hut, anywhere wet and alone with a stack of books, and a TV, and a bottle of Advil. Christ, even a rubber room somewhere for a couple of days might have helped.

The town of Vigilante Falls, the house he remodeled with his own hands—everything felt smaller upon his return. Every interaction with Nadene seemed to start off benignly enough, but quickly elevated to a dangerously charged state before anyone knew what happened. Chalk it up to nerves, or combat fatigue, or just the unattainable imperative of being alone, but Nadene's voice, her questions, even her physical closeness became nearly unbearable.

Dave couldn't even remember what had started them arguing that first night back, but by the time it was over, the quarrel covered a dizzying amount of ground, and looking back, it did irreparable damage. In the end, Nadene stormed out of the bedroom. He literally remembered seeing red. The whole goddamn world had been bleeding red. How dare Nadene give him hell for being absent after what he'd just been through. As though he'd had any damn choice in the matter.

After their quarrel, Dave and Nadene each had apologized, and Dave had cried like a damn baby, until Nadene held his head close to her chest and stroked his hair, and Dave promised he'd get a handle on himself, and tried through his sobs to articulate what was going on inside of him. And then it had been Nadene's turn to cry, and Dave's turn to hold her close, and stroke her hair mechanically.

"We'll get past this," he said.

"I know we will," she said.

But two hours later, they were at it again, and Nadene stormed out of the house before he could stop her. And when she returned, somewhere around noon the following day, eyes bloodshot, hair tangled, Dave remembered distinctly wishing that she hadn't come home.

Jerome Charles; Brother-in-Law

———————

"My little sister was soft-hearted, always had been. She hardened up in the end, I suppose, but before that, she always tried to save things, ever since we were kids. Taking in stray dogs, watering dead plants, tending to injured squirrels. Nadene trapped spiders in glasses and released them outdoors. Wouldn't even kill a mosquito if it was biting her. In summer, she'd stop in the middle of the road, didn't matter whether there was a car coming or not, just to transport a caterpillar safely across to the shoulder, even though the caterpillars were a pestilence. She'd cup her hands and strain a wet moth out of her bathwater, and blow its wings dry for ten minutes, hoping it might fly again. Nadene went about springing mouse traps, and freeing houseflies from spider webs. She didn't like to see things end, I guess.

"It was the same with broken things, whether it was toys, or knick-knacks, or favorite mugs. Nadene never wanted to throw things away. She was convinced everything could be fixed. And that included Dave. Didn't matter that it wasn't easy. And it didn't matter how anyone tried to talk her out of it. I'm not the first to point out that Nadene was stubborn, but she was patient, too, and maybe to a fault. My sister was slow to give up on anything. It was both a blessing and a curse."

N'ka

![separator]

The world as N'ka knew it was written on his mother's face, all the struggle and endless worry could be read there in the blue crescents beneath her eyes, in the crow's feet at her temples, and in the dual creases running deeply down her cheeks, as though they were there to contain her smile.

Then, there was the world as N'ka yearned to see it, a world of possibilities beyond the tedious business of mere continuance, a world of glorious, lusty hunts, and unimagined adventures, a vibrant world of other people, a predictably bountiful world, teeming with giants, a world that adhered to certain expectations, that could be counted upon to provide. Or better yet, a world that surpassed all expectation, a world that did not test their fortitude, or strain their belief at every turn.

What would it look like? Beyond which horizon would this new world lie? These were the speculations that occupied N'ka, these were the reckonings that soothed his restless spirit in the face of limited experience. For long were the winters alone with his mother, ever watchful, ever restricting and amending his freedom as she saw fit. Longer still were the thaws, the interminable, hopeless days when the giants no longer fulfilled their promise. Who knew, perhaps their shaggy allies had left in search of their own new world. Perhaps the long valley brimming with buttercups was no longer enough for them. Perhaps this restlessness, this impulse to change and adapt, to seek out new places and new means was the true nature of the world.

"Maybe the elders were right," N'ka dared to suggest, bracing himself for the inevitable blowback.

But his mother said nothing; she only stared distantly into the fire, working one hand inside of the other, as though for warmth.

"Maybe there's another place," N'ka pursued.

"Bah," S'tka said. "You're a dreamer. Our place in this world is not our own to decide. What do you suppose got us in this mess in the first place? I'll tell you what: thinking there was anything more than what is in front of us. Look around you. What you see is what you get, child. The better you understand this, the more equipped you will be to survive it."

"What do you know?" he said. "What have you ever seen but these mountains?"

"I've seen the ice," she said.

"So have I, Mother."

"You've seen nothing, boy. Have you ever seen a man ripped to shreds by a pack of wolves? Have you watched your husband beat to death by savages who looked no different than you and me?"

N'ka cast his eyes down.

"No," she said. "You haven't."

But N'ka found it increasingly difficult to accept his mother's limited concept of the world. He refused to believe that the possibilities were finite, that what you saw was what you got. His appetite could no longer be sated by the bland offerings of his mother's limited belief system and experience. Ground squirrels and tree sloths were no longer enough to satisfy N'ka's appetites.

Still, like a reasonable ten-year-old yearning for adulthood, the boy complied, a half-willing accomplice to their gradual surrender: hunting squirrels, stalking sloths, listening to stories that went nowhere but further into the past.

But all the while, N'ka's mind was busy working on a plan. Someday, even if it took years, he would convince his mother to leave this place.

A Big Pat on the Back

When they were finally discharged, soldiers got a big pat on the back, maybe even a Purple Heart if they were lucky. Marine brass told them to keep their noses clean, they told them to stay away from drinking and drugs and gambling. They told them to mind your angry impulses, not to visit frustration on your spouse or kids. They told them that they were marines, that they would always be marines. They told them to drive on.

Never mind Dave's hip. Never mind that his nerves were so severely fried that he actually thought he could smell them smoldering inside his head. Never mind that his emotional faculties were in ruin. Never mind that there were no official resources in place to help him integrate or re-orient himself to civilian or domestic life, no counseling to help prepare him for his forever changed life moving forward. They ran him back into the regular world, just like they ran him out there on patrol after patrol.

Never mind that his marriage was crumbling at the foundation, or that guilt was his relentless passenger. Guilt over the acts he'd committed, traumas that belonged to Dave alone. Guilt over his failure as a husband, his failure as a marine, his failure as a normally functioning human being in a hundred little ways every day. Guilt was the only meaningful connection Dave could seem to make once he rejoined civilian life. He couldn't even make himself return phone calls from his war buddy Duane Barlow, and the voicemails stacked up:

You all right, buddy? Give me a call.

Hey, buddy. We need to talk.

Cartwright, you sonofabitch, don't leave me hanging.

In his four months back in V-Falls, Dave hadn't accepted a single invitation, not for a cup of coffee, or a game of darts, not from Jerome, who had reached out on a half-dozen occasions, not even from Coach Prentice, who was courting Dave for his new offensive coordinator and assistant coaching position. To call Dave anti-social was an understatement. Not only did he routinely duck old classmates and acquaintances in Red Apple and Vern's, he avoided his own mother and brother. Just about every time somebody did manage to stop Dave, they thanked him for his service, and each time Dave fought the impulse to ask them if they had any earthly idea what they were thanking him for. What Dave wanted anymore—beyond quietude and dim light—was beyond his conception. On so many levels, he was no longer the man he once was. No longer was he sure of himself, no longer was he confident, no longer was he hopeful. His hands shook to where he could hardly hold a nail gun, or a cup of coffee. His sleep was tortured. He was wary of crowds. Christ, he hardly drove anymore because he was so terrified of being blown to shit, still haunted by the sudden blast of IEDs glittering along the shoulders, the wreckage and the remains scattered across the roadway. Arms and legs, and pretzels of twisted steel.

On only one occasion, when pressed, did Dave open up to Nadene about his experiences in the desert. It was an incident involving a Shiite boy, maybe ten or eleven, standing on the side of the road with no shirt on, and a green bandana over his face, who may or may not have been phoning coordinates ahead of their convoy.

"I could've given him the benefit of the doubt," Dave said. "He was just a kid. A skinny little runt of a kid with his ribs poking out like a washboard."

"You couldn't take the chance," said Nadene. "You had to protect the others."

"But what if he wasn't, Dino? What if he was just some kid, fooling around on the side of the road? What if that bandana was just to keep the dust out?"

"You did what you had to," Nadene said.

"I did more than I had to, Dino. He couldn't have weighed a hundred pounds."

Dave's voice began to waver, as he clenched and unclenched his fist.

"Dino, that kid wasn't fifteen yards away when I laid into him."

"Shush, baby," said Nadene.

"I nearly tore him in half," Dave said.

"It's over now," she said reassuringly. "It's not your fault."

What else could Dave ask of Nadene beyond that? Not only was she willing to withstand his unpredictable moods, his days on end of silence and evasion, she was willing to forgive him for taking the life of a child. So why had he been pushing her away?

The night Dave told Nadene about the boy in the bandana was the same night Bella was conceived. For two hours in bed, they talked themselves into it. Maybe the only way to forget the dead left behind was to bring somebody new into the world. What could heal death, if not life? They could finally have the family they'd been putting off. That would put them back on the right track. If it was a boy, they could call him Gordy, after Coach Prentice.

"But no football," Nadene insisted.

"Fair enough," conceded Dave.

And so, after eight years of marriage, though the proceeding days had been some of their darkest, Dave and Nadene, against their better judgment, decided to start a family. And they left little margin for error that night. They would not leave the bed for the next eight hours, making love on no less than three occasions during the night, and again shortly after sunrise, Nadene rousing Dave from his sleep to mount him.

Breakfast was eggs and toast and coffee. Dave and Nadene ate on the back porch, looking out over the greenhouse to the studio. That was the first time since 2003 that Dave remembered feeling hopeful.

But Dave and Nadene didn't even make it to lunch before Dave blew a gasket over something, and soon they found themselves in another shouting match, until Nadene finally ran off to her mother's house. Dave stayed in bed for two days after that.

N'ka

They sat by the fire, mother and son, picking their teeth with slivers of spruce, unloosing the stringy flesh caught there. For nearly a week, they'd been feeding on the big buck that N'ka ambushed in the meadow.

N'ka, the mighty hunter, and still only a boy.

They spoke less and less as the seasons passed, though often their thoughts seemed visible to each other. They were twelve winters removed from U'ku'let's death, now but a distant memory to S'tka, and nothing more than an old story to N'ka, one told less and less frequently with the passage of time. Any mental picture he'd once had of his father faded long ago. Gone were the days when N'ka plied his mother for details about his father's exploits.

N'ka looked the part of a man now, lean and sinewy and hard. He walked with his shoulders straight and his chin up. The downy hair of his face had grown coarse and dark, the hair of a man, not a child. And like a man, he'd grown restless. And who could blame him? Every winter seemed to grow leaner.

The giants had never returned from the north to gorge on the grasses and scratch their wooly backs. They had become legends, like his mother's clan. This was the valley of the forgotten, the valley of the dead and the forsaken.

"Mother," he said. "You must listen to me. The time has come."

"The time for what?" she said, irritably.

"The time to leave this place. To find our clan."

"Bah," she said. "Our clan is nothing but so many ghosts on the ice. Follow them and you will only share their fate."

"You don't know that," he said.

"I heard it on the wind," she said. "They are ghosts, boy, dead and gone."

"They are alive."

"Bah," she said. "Don't delude yourself, child. They are nothing but bones strewn on the ice by now."

"What makes you so sure?" he demanded.

"Because they are fools."

"So, what if they are gone?" he said. "That doesn't mean there's not somebody or something else out there for us."

"There is nothing for us," she said.

"Says you," he said.

The young man stared into the embers, his thoughts troubled. This was not a life. Somewhere out there, beyond the ice, men were gathered in a circle, hollowing the tips of their spears in readiness, talking nervously amongst themselves before the hunt, their hearts beating fast, their nerves buzzing, eyes and ears and hearts attuned as they hollowed their points.

And when the hunt finally commenced, they would relinquish their fear and give themselves whole to the heat of the pursuit, throw themselves at the necessity of the kill, risking life and limb. They would hoot and they would holler. They would besiege and taunt their massive adversary, their hearts beating in their throats, their arms and legs electric, all of them in concert together like one living thing.

That is what it meant to be alive. And N'ka had yet to feel it.

III

———

The Book of the Living

Darla Dayton; Dale's Diner

———

"Did Dave Cartwright really lose his way up there, mentally speaking? I really can't say for sure. Really, nobody had a way of knowing, beyond the few people who actually made contact with him. It sure seemed to be the consensus around town that he was crazy, I mean that he was writing some kind of manifesto, and letting that little girl wander off untended, uncared for. That part I find hard to believe, personally. I saw him thirty different times with that little girl over the years, and it was pretty clear he was a good daddy. Not like some. He talked to her like an adult. He really took the time to explain things to her. I once heard him explain to her the difference between a diesel engine and a regular engine. Compression, ignition, injection. Wasn't any wonder that child was so smart.

"But you know how people talk, especially people around here, nothing to do. Heck, half of them's unemployed, or too old to work, and none of them's very good at minding their own business either. And more than a few of them are just plain mean-spirited. I can't count how many times I've caught customers talking about my mole—which is exactly why I don't do nothing about it. So I can't say whether he went bonkers up there, like they say.

"Sooner or later everything gets exaggerated. Stories just move from one person to another, and they have a way of growing. But usually, there's a little bit of truth to them, don't you think? This place here, it's like the nerve center of V-Falls in a lot of ways. Nothing really happens that somebody isn't talking about it at the counter, or in one of these booths. If I had a dollar for every time I heard someone say "Cave Dave," I could take Thursdays off. But who's to say how much of it's fake news, and how much of it's the truth? Doesn't even seem to matter anymore."

The Pull of the Unknown

———

Among recent changes in her dad's behavior was the fact that he no longer obsessed over order and organization around the camp. Bella found tools lying carelessly about, firewood piled up willy-nilly, and tarps left unsecured to flap in the wind. The fire pit was heaping with ashes. The pots and pans were in disarray. The cave was a mess, with books strewn everywhere.

Her dad read ceaselessly, often muttering under his breath, or scribbling notes in the margins of library books, an offense that would have been unthinkable a few months prior. Unnerved by these new habits, Bella forced him to engage in frequent conversation.

"Maybe he won't come back," she said.

"Who?" said her dad, slumping before the dead fire.

"The ranger."

She was standing at the edge of the bluff, scanning the canyon south to north for movement, just as he taught her.

"Maybe so," he said, like he didn't care one way or another.

"I hope Mr. Moseley comes back, though," she said.

"Be careful what you hope for," he said. "Mr. Moseley is not our friend, Bella."

"He's my friend," she said. "Even if he's not yours."

All afternoon, Bella found that she was especially restless, and unable to focus.

"I'm bored," she said.

"Go down to the meadow."

"I'm sick of the meadow."

"Then read a book."

"I'm tired of reading. I've read all my books a gazillion times."

"Hmph," he said.

Bella felt the pull of the unknown, as though something out there was calling her. So, she ventured east beyond her dad's set boundaries, winding through the stunted forest for a half-mile until she emerged from the trees onto a bald ridgeline, high above a broad, deep valley. She recognized the place immediately. Here, the great herds of mammoth once came down from the steppe to graze. Here, people had once eked out an existence until the place would no longer sustain them, and they began their journey west, across the ice.

How different would her own life in the mountains have looked had she never known anything else, not known her own bedroom, her friend Hannah B., whom she hardly remembered anymore, her Cousin Bonnie, her Auntie Kris and Uncle Travers, and Uncle Jerry. What if she had never known the thrill of the bustling playground, or the comfort of her grandma's well stocked refrigerator? Bella wished she'd never known her mother's embrace. She wished she'd never known a dresser full of clothing, or the satisfaction of a warm, dry, orderly house on a rainy day. She wished she'd never known the luxury of sitting in her pajamas in front of the TV on a Saturday morning watching Cartoon Network for hours at a time, eating Pop-Tarts and Rice Krispies. What did Saturday even signify anymore? It was no different than Monday or Tuesday or Wednesday. If only she'd never experienced what it was to look forward to something.

The prospect of being seen by someone as she stood atop the ridge was thrilling. There were days when Bella was sure she was invisible, when even her dad didn't see her, and days when she really, truly did wish that she were a cat, instead of merely acting the part. Yes, she'd gone whole days without uttering a word, licking her hands, and scratching her back on trees. But it always felt like pretending.

Bella lingered all afternoon on the ridgeline, giving herself to the otherness. When she awoke from her reverie, she began working her way back toward the cover of the forest. She was halfway to the tree line when something at her feet seized her attention. She stooped to pick it up with both hands. The object was lighter and more delicate than she expected, bleached, and smooth with age, but well preserved, the mandible still fixed precariously below the bun: a human skull, its forehead marred by a three-inch cleft, as though struck with blunt force by a hatchet, or a rock.

"U'ku'let," she whispered beneath her breath.

S'tka

Now in his fifteenth year, N'ka was moodier than ever. Half of the time he wouldn't do as S'tka instructed, and on those occasions when he complied in executing the simplest of tasks—tending the fire or getting water—the act was usually accompanied by a plaintive sigh or some form of grumbling protest. Some days the boy slept until the sun was directly overhead, frequently awakening with a persistent erection. He usually spent a good portion of the afternoon hours skulking and grousing and lounging about the cave, lazily scratching his chest.

Beneath the surface of his boredom, S'tka could see that he was restless. His yearning was only natural. It was her own resistance to change, her own aversion to risk that kept them from a more expansive life.

"Are you just going to sit around all day?" she said.

"Why not? What am I missing?" he said. "Shall I go hunt some more squirrels? We've already got more than we can eat. The more I kill them, the more they breed."

He was right. At present, there was nothing terribly pressing to demand their energy. But somehow, S'tka still found it hard to forgive her teenage son his recent and uncharacteristic lack of industry, his growing disinterest in their survival, as secure as it seemed.

From his earliest youth, N'ka had demonstrated his overconfidence in a hundred ways, from his casual sure-footedness in navigating the high country, to his certainty of achieving desired outcomes, to his unwavering convictions about things with which he had no experience, the brutality, fickleness, and disloyalty of other people, for instance.

Perhaps S'tka was wrong to doubt his confidence; maybe N'ka was more of a man than she was ready to admit. Maybe after all these years she still wanted to view him as helpless. Maybe she needed to see him as dependent. But why? After all the years she had single-handedly accounted for their survival, shouldn't her son's blossoming manhood have been a welcome development? Wasn't this what she'd been working toward all along?

It was true from very early on that N'ka possessed surprising strength for his stature, and an undeniable physical grace. It was also true that his tact and prowess as a hunter was already far superior to his father's. And for all N'ka's apparent carelessness of late, he had been nothing if not decisive and resourceful in the past. Were these not the qualities of leadership?

No wonder he was restless.

What would become of her son, once she could no longer regulate him, once he refused to live under her dominion? She was beginning to suspect that they were already beyond that stage.

Maybe S'tka had it backward all this time. Maybe it was she who had become dependent upon N'ka. Maybe her welfare was the very reason why the boy didn't follow his appetite for the unseen out into the white world. Because he felt obligated to protect her. Because he couldn't leave her alone, and he knew she would never go along. The thought was at once a comfort and an annoyance.

Never had S'tka felt dependent on anyone. Since she was a little girl, since the day the mountain swallowed her mother, she had made her own way in this world, a world that had shown her nothing but hostility, granted her little in the way of kindness, bequeathed her nothing but a legacy of fear, and solitude, and anxiety. The Great Provider had strewn her path with obstacles at every turn, burdened her with worry, starved and raped and forsaken her long ago.

"Perhaps you are right," he said, tending the fire one night. "It's possible our people have been erased. Then we should seek out a different clan or start our own."

"We already have," she said.

He stared sullenly into the flames.

"But what about the others?" he said. "We've seen them, time and again, passing through. Why couldn't we join them?"

"Pssh," she said. "They'd just as soon kill us as join us."

"How do you know?"

She shot him a look so pointed that he was forced to avert his eyes.

"Experience," she said. "That's how I know."

Still unsatisfied with the explanation, N'ka resumed his moody gaze into the fire.

"Two people are not a clan," he said bitterly.

"And what is so great about a clan?" she said. "What do you know of clans? What do you know about anything beyond what I've taught you? What have you experienced that I have not shown you? You're not yet a man. So what makes you so smart?"

She could see him clenching his jaw in the glow of the flames.

"Boy, you must understand that in a clan you are nothing," she explained. "You are beholden to the will of others. You have no choice but to do as you are told, to eat what you are given, to accept the responsibility you never asked for."

"How is that any different than my life?" he said.

"What did the clan do for me when I was starving to death with you in my belly?" she said. "Where was my clan to protect me when your father had his head staved in?"

"But you said yourself," he said, looking her in the eye, "the Great Provider made us small."

"Yes, she did. Then, she abandoned us here among the giants. In a place where you can't trust anybody, in a place where your own people will throw you out onto the ice just for trying to stay alive."

Precious Oil

———

It was dusk when Bella returned from the ridge, clutching U'ku'let's bleached cranium. Apparently her father was not overly concerned about her prolonged absence because she found him asleep in the cave, his chin on his chest, a book still open in front of him. Beside him, the lantern was still burning precious oil.

Bella paused a moment to see whether her presence would rouse him, and when it failed to do so, she squatted down and dimmed the lamp. When she gently touched his shoulder he awoke with a start and looked up at her, momentarily befuddled.

"Oh, hey, baby," he said in the half-darkness. "I fell asleep."

"I noticed."

He rubbed his neck groggily.

"Where've you been?" he said.

"The usual places," she said.

"Baby, you gotta check in more often."

"Okay," she said.

He neither inquired about the skull in her hands, nor seemed to even notice it.

"Man, I'm bushed," he said, snapping the book shut before rolling over onto his sleeping bag.

He didn't used to be so tired all the time. He used to wear Bella out. It was hard to see how he was getting so tired.

"Are you feeling sick, Daddy?"

"Nah, baby, just tired. It's cumulative, I think."

"What's 'cumatalive'?"

"It means things add up. Like, maybe I was pushing a little too hard before, so now the tired is catching up with me."

"I get it," she said.

"I love you, baby. I'm glad you're back," he said, covering his head with a pillow. "Could you turn the lantern off all the way if you're not gonna use it?"

"Yeah," she said. "Goodnight, Dad."

"Goodnight."

Turning off the lantern, Bella retreated to the bluff as the last vestiges of daylight faded. She set the skull aside and gathered kindling, then began reviving the fire just as the stars came out to keep her company. The night was windless, and eerily calm. The thin air seemed to hold no life. Below, the canyon seemed bottomless in the darkness. Sitting there under the night sky, the cold, uncaring stars wheeling above her, Bella was visited by a profound, almost absolute loneliness, which she understood to be eternal, the loneliness of separation. Not separation from her mom, nine months in the grave, nor from her father, an apparition of his former self, nor from Nana or Uncle Travers or Hannah B., but the unmitigated state of being separate from everything. For the first time, Bella comprehended with aching clarity the ultimate estrangement of being human.

And she began to weep, not for herself, but for all of humanity.

When her grief was finally spent, Bella sat by the fire, the bleached skull cradled in her lap as she ran her fingers over the ancient wound as though she might somehow heal it.

N'ka

_____

N'ka could not help but notice his mother growing weaker and more passive as the weeks went by. She no longer moved about with her former urgency. Every task seemed a chore. She slept late in the day, sometimes even later than he did, and often she nodded off in the evening around the fire, where once they had cheerfully made conversation. His mother also had grown thinner and more fragile. At times she was forgetful. She no longer scolded N'ka for his pride or ignorance, no longer ordered him about day and night, or sought to exercise any influence over his actions whatsoever. It was as though she'd given up. It was this passivity that was most unfamiliar, and frightened him the most.

His mother was growing old. Yet many times she had told him of men and women living past the age of fifty winters, their hair grown white, their teeth falling out of their head, their eyes clouded blue like glaciers. N'ka had seen with his own eyes a strange little hairless man shuffling across the ice, draped in furs, muttering and hissing to himself. Surely he must have lived too many winters to count.

This place, it haunted you. It froze the life out of you. It wouldn't allow you to grow but one way, and that was older.

"Mother," he said, as she was about to nod off in front of the fire. "This place is stealing your future. If you stay here, you will only become a white-haired ghost. Or shrunken, like the little nightwalker."

"I shall never lose my hair," she said.

"Really, Mother. This place, this changeless existence, it's draining the life out of you. You need a challenge, you need purpose."

Though N'ka expected to be met with his mother's customary resistance, this time she did not dismiss him with a wave, but stared fixedly at the coals, a hint of a smile playing at the corners of her mouth.

"I have already outlived my purpose," she said. "My purpose was your survival, and your development. Apparently that's all the Great Provider had in mind when he created a woman—to carry men. Carry them in their wombs, and on their backs, and in their hearts, to carry their burdens, and bear their disappointments until such time that a man no longer needs them. And you, you are a man now. You no longer have any need of me," she said.

"That's not true."

"Go," she said. "Like you're always talking about. Go test your fortune on the ice. Go find your new land of promises. Maybe you'll find the giants there. You can ask them why they abandoned us. Maybe you'll find our clan, and you can ask them the same."

The next morning, as they were huddled around the fire, his mother stood without a word of explanation and wandered off into the snow to the north.

"Where are you going?" he said.

But she paid him no mind, and continued on her way, trudging deliberately but purposefully through the ankle-deep snow.

N'ka went after her, following her tracks across the bluff, and down the slight incline, and into the forest. He meandered through the trees, until the terrain opened up on a familiar vista where he found his mother kneeling at the edge of the great snowy ridge overlooking the Valley of the Giants.

"What are you doing here?" he said. "They are gone, Mother. They're not coming back."

But she did not answer. Instead, she looked straight at the snowy ground upon which she was kneeling.

"This is where I buried your father."

How long since N'ka had even thought about his father as anything more than a name, a word, an abstraction? For the formative years of N'ka's life, his father had hung over their lives like a shadow, an invisible third person in their otherwise unpopulated world. For the first half of his life, it seemed like this invisible father was the standard by which N'ka had been measured. But now he was a specter, a legend. Until that moment, which N'ka knew to be significant, though he was not at all certain as to why.

"Why did you never tell me he was here?" said N'ka.

"Would it have made a difference?" she said.

They withdrew into silence, as the wind moaned through the valley.

Looking at his mother kneeling in the snow, N'ka could only guess at her sacrifice.

"You didn't make a peep," she said. "With all the hooting and hollering and excitement. Not a peep. Even when they ransacked the cave, you stayed silent, though you were awake when I came back for you. I sometimes think you were awake all along."

N'ka knelt beside her and draped his arm about her.

"I can't remember."

"Of course you can't."

"I'm sorry," he said.

"I'm sorry, too," she said. "The world is sorry."

She plunged her hands into the frozen earth and clutched two handfuls of snow, which she sifted through her fingers.

"He has never left us," she said. "He's still here in this place. If only we could reach him."

"You're afraid to leave him," he said.

"Yes."

"So, this place really is haunted."

His mother stood and dusted the snow from her knees.

"The whole world is haunted," she said.

This Time

————•————

His clothes were beginning to hang funny, like they belonged to somebody else. His beard, which now hid his neck completely, came to a pronounced point shaped by his endless fussing. His every movement was jerky, mannequin-like. It seemed like his hip was bothering him more than usual. But mostly he seemed like someone who might be going crazy. Yesterday Bella found him standing wild-eyed over the fire, ripping the pages out of a book and burning them one at a time.

"Daddy, you can't do that!"

"It's all rubbish," he said. "History is a fairy tale."

"It's the principle," she said, snatching the remainder of the book from his hands.

"We stick to our principles," she scolded. "That's a library book. You can break the rules if they're dumb, but stick to your principles. You told me that."

He looked up at her, his eyes softening in recognition.

"Yeah, baby, you're right," he said.

The next morning, Bella awoke before him for the third day in a row, a development impossible to imagine even a month ago. Out on the bluff, Bella started the fire and made them a breakfast of rice mixed with a precious spoonful of brown sugar, wishing she'd had some raisins. Though she expected her dad to appear at some point once he smelled the fire, she had to go in and shake him awake, at which point he lashed out at her reflexively.

"What the—?"

"Daddy, it's morning," she said. "I made breakfast."

It took him a second to get his bearings, as he squinted up at her in the dim light.

"Aw, baby, you scared me."

"Sorry," she said.

With a little encouragement, he limped out to the fire, where, to Bella's relief, he inhaled his rice, and even seemed to relish it for the first time in days. The minute he set his tin aside, his foot started tapping.

"Should I make more?" said Bella.

"No, no, baby, I'm good, I'm good."

But it wasn't long before he began twisting at his beard, crossing and uncrossing his legs.

"Let's go fishing," he said, at last. "We can't live on rice."

What a relief to hear him say it.

"Okay," she said brightly.

After they rinsed their plates, they gathered the tackle and the rods, and scrambled down the steep bluff to test their fortune. Soon they were crunching through the meadow over a half-inch of fresh snow. The peaks all around them were already frosted with snow, surrounding them like a giant crown, so near, yet so far away. The sky was blue, the bluest it had been in weeks.

Her dad was talkative in that nervous way. He didn't even seem to notice how big and crystal clear and beautiful the world was all around them.

"Plenty of trout still in the high lakes," he said. "Not to mention they stock the reservoirs, not that we'll need to go that far. And once spring comes, well, there will be food everywhere."

He kept talking like he was trying to put Bella at ease, but really she figured he was trying to put himself at ease. If he wanted to put Bella at ease, he'd start shaving, and stop sleeping so late. If he wanted to put her at ease, he could start inspiring her confidence again.

When they reached the east fork of the river, they meandered south for a half-mile or so along the banks, navigating snags and deadfall. When the bank became impassable, they cut through the alders and into the evergreens, leaving the river as they gained elevation.

"Where are we going?" said Bella.

"I know there's a little lake out here somewhere," he said.

"What's it like?"

"It's bluer than the sky," he said. "And sort of diamond shaped, as I remember."

"The river is closer," she said.

"Yes, it is," he said.

After a half-mile of gaining steady elevation, they found themselves straddling a green saddleback, dappled with snow, the river far below to the west, its roar barely perceptible.

"Gotta be down there," he said.

They descended to the south, opposite the river, her dad offering intermittent commentary. Bella could sense his creeping anxiety. The more he talked, the more unsure he sounded.

"You sure this is the way?" she said.

"Yeah," he said. "It ought to be."

Bella grew less confident with each stride. Though she was pretty sure she knew where they were, it was troubling that she simply couldn't trust her dad unconditionally like she once could. Especially the way he twisted his beard to a point and muttered half the day. It was a relief when twenty minutes later they arrived above a little oblong lake, desolate, and impossibly blue.

"Boom," said her dad.

"Um, it's not shaped like a diamond," said Bella. "It's more like a peanut."

Her dad was giddy scrambling down the hillside to the shoreline, more like a boy than a man in his eagerness, When he reached the edge of the lake, where the scrubby brush gave way to a strip of silty marsh, he immediately set his fly and readied himself to cast.

Bella picked her own spot along the marshy shore, thirty yards north of her dad, where she cast her line into the shallows, a little less than hopeful.

A half hour later, when nothing had bitten and the temperature began to drop, as a frigid wind started blowing down from the north and the sky darkened, her dad still held out hope, or at least pretended to.

"This here is the spot," he said, a hundred feet south of where he started.

The temperature continued to drop, and the wind picked up, flecked with snowflakes.

"I'm not feeling so lucky, Daddy," said Bella.

"It's not about luck, baby, it's about probability."

"Well, I'm not feeling so probable, either."

"Hang tight," he said. "Be patient."

And Bella tried. But she couldn't quite escape a sinking feeling, any more than she could escape the chill that took hold of her bones. Still, with each cast she went through the motions, watching him out of the corner of her eye.

Eventually, his optimism began to wane, long after Bella's had begun to edge toward panic.

"They've gotta be in here somewhere," he insisted.

"Maybe we should have tried the river," said Bella.

"Too late," he said.

"Maybe we could try tomorrow," she said.

"We could," he said.

Finally he agreed to give up, and they started back up the incline empty handed, Bella glad to get her blood pumping again.

"I have a good hunch about the river, Daddy," she said. "Tomorrow we'll catch a bunch."

But she was just saying it. Tired, famished, and sick with worry, a tin of rice and a campfire never seemed so good. A cave never sounded so cozy. When they reached the saddle, they descended back toward the river, the light snow turning to sleet. When it seemed Bella couldn't possibly be more miserable, the sleet turned to rain as they reached the bank. They wended their way along the bank of the river, over and around the deadfall, around the snags, until the shoreline all but disappeared, and the narrow bank became impassable. They proceeded for several minutes, ankle deep in the river.

Bella was sopping wet by the time they took to the shelter of the woods again, blazing a trail through the cluttered understory. After a mile or so, something began to feel wrong. It felt like they needed to be up higher, over the ridge to the east, and maybe a bit farther south.

"Daddy, I don't think this is the way," she said at last.

"This is east," he said.

"It feels wrong," said Bella. "The first time we were on the other side of this hill. We need to go back."

Even as she said it, she hoped she was wrong. She wanted her dad to be right, as he so often was. But the instant she saw him question himself all the warmth drained from her body.

"I think you're right," he said. "Maybe we did come a little too far north."

The concession did little to warm Bella.

"Let's head back toward the river," he said, turning as though to lead.

"The river is that way," she said.

And suddenly she knew without a doubt that they were lost. Her dad had finally failed them.

"Actually, yeah, I think you're right," he said. "Good work, scout."

Funny how those words and that encouraging pat on the head emboldened Bella. What started as an intuition now unfolded clearly in her mind as a course of action, a route home. She knew the way back. After backtracking a mile, they arrived at the cut they'd missed at the bottom of the hill.

"Now, we go that way," she said.

"You've got this, baby," he said.

Various Discomforts

———

Aside from the various discomforts—the swollen ankles, the pressure on her lower back, the irritable bladder—Nadene claimed that she liked being pregnant. She slept well. She said she felt more relaxed, more hopeful, and more purposeful from the moment she awoke every morning. Even when she wasn't doing anything, she felt productive and content. There was no denying she had a glow about her, a slight flush in her cherubic cheeks, a light in her green eyes, at once playful and self-assured. And the bigger Nadene got, the more she radiated. Dave thought her most adorable late in her third trimester, as she moved laboriously around the house with diminutive steps, her cumbersome belly jutting out in front of her, a constant hindrance. He could not resist stopping her occasionally to set his hands upon her precious cargo.

"Who's in there?" he would say. "Are you a little boy, or a girl?"

"She's a girl," Nadene would say with perfect conviction.

"How can you be so sure?"

"I just am," she would say.

"Is that right?" he would say to the bulge. "Are you a little girl?"

In those moments, it seemed certain that the precious little life taking shape inside of Nadene would save them and would keep their marriage whole.

Dave was helpful throughout the pregnancy. He did most of the dishes. He baby-proofed the kitchen, and the dining room. He did the laundry, and folded it as best he could. Sometimes he rubbed Nadene's aching feet at the end of the day, as they sprawled on the sofa in front of the television.

"I still think it's a boy," he would say.

"It's a girl," she assured him.

And when the day arrived at last, and Dino began her labor in that very spot on the sofa, they barely had time to get her to the birthing center before the baby began to crown.

"It's gonna be okay, it's gonna be okay," he assured her in the car.

"I know," said Dino.

Dave pulled right up to the front entrance to the center and double-parked. Circling the Dodge in a mad rush, he helped her from the passenger seat and led her in by the hand.

Dave was a wreck through the delivery, pacing wildly about the birthing suite, too anxious to remember his breathing prompts, while somehow Dino managed to remain calm in the face of her agony.

"It's gonna be okay, it's gonna be okay," he assured Dino.

But really he was assuring himself.

And when the child emerged, pinched and blue, and he heard her phlegmy cries, Dave nearly fainted.

Six hours later, they brought Bella home, swaddled in a terrycloth blanket.

As during the pregnancy, Dave was helpful through the first year of infancy. Not that he changed too many poopy diapers, or took too many night shifts with the baby, but he held Bella frequently, and gave her the bottle, and strapped her to his chest, and pushed her for hours on end in the stroller so Nadene could catnap or catch up on laundry, or spend a precious few minutes in the greenhouse tending her peppers. Dave loved taking Bella on errands, to Vern's, or Ace, or Red Apple, or the post office. People sometimes commented on his fatherly glow. Indeed, Dave beamed when people pointed out the resemblance between him and Bella. Times like those, parenthood felt like a noble calling.

Dave and Nadene were happy for a while with their new family. Their lives were like their finances, small and a little strained, but they made do.

In the evenings they would watch TV together on the couch, while the baby nursed, or slept in Nadene's arms. They still had time between them to cook a decent dinner with the baby sleeping so much. They even managed to have something of a sex life.

But once the baby stopped sleeping so much, and started requiring more and more of Nadene's attention, their sex life evaporated, their intimacy got pushed aside. Looking back, Dave was ashamed to admit that he might have grown a little sulky. It felt like Nadene had run out of time and energy for him, and for a lot of other things, including herself. The laundry piled up. The dishes were stacked next to the sink. The garbage was overflowing with dirty diapers. Often as not, dinner was frozen. Evening conversation, once playful, was limited to practical concerns.

Eventually, Dave started sleeping on the couch.

As bad as it got those first couple years, as much of a blur as it had become looking back on it, Dave never regretted having Bella, not ever, not even for an instant. Though he regretted the world he brought her into, regretted that he couldn't provide better for her, regretted that he had trouble controlling his temper, and his impulses, and could do little to deter the dark moods that fell upon him without warning, any more than he could control the ringing in his years, Bella had always felt to Dave like his greatest accomplishment. There were moments of crystal clarity when peering down into her bottomless gaze, Dave was filled with a sense of wonder that he'd managed to help create something so pure and perfect and innocent.

Still, there were times when Nadene went to town and left Dave alone with the baby, when Bella's crying became so urgent and inconsolable as to be disconcerting, times when he felt so frustrated by his own helplessness that he was visited by the momentary impulse to throw the child out the window. But he didn't, of course. Instead, he laid her in her crib and walked out of the room long enough to gather the wherewithal to go back and scoop her up, and attempt once more, with varying degrees of futility, to calm her.

N'ka

In the spring, after two years of pleading and hectoring with his mother, two years of all-you-can-eat squirrel but little else, two years in the same ragged hides, N'ka finally persuaded his mother to leave the mountains behind. And much to his surprise, she acquiesced calmly, albeit against her better judgment.

"We will not find them," she said impassively. "But you're right about one thing: there's nothing left for us here."

And so, on a chill, clear morning, the air so crisp and alive with possibility that it caused his skin to tingle, N'ka and his mother set out on their journey, crunching over a fresh blanket of snow. To the west, the wind was stirring up an icy vapor that hovered inches above the ice, stretching on for untold miles toward the horizon. Suddenly the world was boundless and full of mystery.

With their spears lashed to their backs, five pounds of charred squirrel, a satchel of roots, and all the furs they could shoulder, they left behind the only home N'ka had ever known.

The young man thrilled at their prospects, as they moved steadily across the white expanse, the saw-toothed mountains receding in their wake. Finally he was determining his own future. As they trudged over the blinding ice toward the edge of the earth, it was as though his mother could hear N'ka's thoughts.

"Well, at the very least, perhaps this new world will provide us something to eat besides squirrel," she said.

"There will bison in great numbers," he assured her. "Like it used to be. And the giants will be there, too, lazing about in the meadow."

"And where among all this ice will we find such a place?"

"Farther than the eye can see," he said. "But it will be green where we are going; everywhere grasses, and rivers, free of ice."

"Mm," she said. "A paradise."

"Yes, a paradise."

"Will there be no death there, no starvation, no brutality?"

"Those things I cannot promise, Mother."

"How can you make promises at all?" she said, the old bitterness creeping into her tone. "Certainty is the game of fools. Ask the Great Provider. What promise has she ever delivered on?"

"You will see, Mother. This new place will save us."

"Bah," she said, embracing the fullness of her gloomy nature. "I'll more likely be eaten by wolves."

N'ka smiled. "What a dreary old woman you've become."

"And you," she said. "What a foolish dreamer."

"You're wrong," he said.

But he knew, as they slogged across the eternal ice, encountering no sign of life along their way, that it would take a long time to convince her. Though nothing about the barren expanse surrounding them seemed to hold any promise, nothing about the blistering wind that assaulted their faces hinted at paradise, N'ka's hopefulness could not be tempered.

In the waning light, they made camp near a clutch of stunted trees at the edge of the ice, where N'ka constructed a fire destined to be small.

When the cloak of night descended, and they were awash in the light of the stars, spattered cold and white across the bowl of night, the world seemed all at once larger and more mysterious.

"It will be a good life for us," N'ka said aloud, mostly to reassure himself.

But his mother, exhausted, had already succumbed to sleep, head bowed, hands tucked under her arms for warmth.

N'ka covered her in furs, then bundled himself up, and resumed huddling over the pale flames. A vein of ice ran the length of his spine, as the distant baying of wolves shattered the silence. All of his newfound confidence and swagger drained from N'ka in an instant, as he huddled even closer to the weak fire, pulling his fur snug across his shoulders, a half dozen spears near at hand.

The Right Thing

B ella never thought she'd miss fish skins and rice, or the weak broth that barely sustained them through the latter part of fall, but here they were at the beginning of winter with no more raisins, no more nuts, no more fish skins. No oats, no honey, not a scrap of meat. Not so much as a bouillon cube. And yet her dad seemed unconcerned. But why should he worry? He hardly ate anymore. God, but Bella would have given anything for a frozen pizza. She knew better than to complain, but midway through yet another breakfast of lightly salted rice, eaten in the weak winter sunlight puddled near the mouth of the cave, she could no longer help herself.

"Daddy, we need to go to town," she said.

"We can't do that," he said.

"But Daddy, it's hardly even snowed."

"Baby, we just can't. There's things th—"

"Don't call me 'baby' anymore," she said. "I'm not a baby."

"Honey, there's things that—"

"Stop parentizing me," she said.

"Well, I'm your parent!" he exclaimed. "What else am I supposed to do?"

"Just because you're my parent doesn't mean you have to talk to me all the time like I don't understand anything."

He almost managed to smile.

"Baby, you mean patronizing—stop *patronizing* me," he said.

"See, you're doing it again."

"I'm sorry," he said, running his fingers through his beard. "Fine, you win. You're right. We could use some stuff."

"So, then, we can go?" she said. "We can go see Nana?"

"We can run for supplies," he said. "And maybe the library. But that's it, baby."

"Why can't we go to Nana's?"

"Because if we do," he said, "one of us is not coming back. And it's not me."

"I knew it," said Bella. "It was your plan all along. Why did you even bring me here, if you just wanted to get rid of me?"

"No," he said. "Never, baby. I'd never want to get rid of you."

"Well, I don't believe you," she said. "I'm not going."

"Fine," he said. "We won't go."

"Fine," she said, folding her arms across her chest.

"Baby," he said. "Listen to me: I don't want to get rid of you, okay?"

While there was a ring of truth to it, Bella feared that it was only because he'd come to rely upon her. For two weeks, it had been she who had prepared the rice, and stoked the fire, she who had straightened up the cave and kept the camp tidy and the tools dry. Even this change in routine seemed to be lost on her dad, who lived in a nearly unreachable state of pre-occupation. It was Bella who kept daily vigil at the edge of the bluff, scanning the canyon for intruders, a task her father once committed himself to with determination. Now, when Bella scanned the canyon, she actually hoped she would spot somebody. If only for a little company, another voice, for something to disrupt their isolation.

Thus it was a relief to see Mr. Moseley crest the lip of the bluff shortly after breakfast.

"Daddy," she called out. "It's Mr. Moseley!"

When her dad shuffled out of the cave, shielding his eyes from the sunlight, Bella's relief edged toward anxiety. Had she known Mr. Moseley was coming, she would have made her dad shave.

When he crested the hillside, Mr. Moseley brushed off his knees and stood upright. The instant his eyes fell on her dad, Bella could see the concern written on Mr. Moseley's face.

"Good morning," he said.

"If you say so," said her dad.

Moseley extended a hand, which her dad left hanging in mid-air.

"Been a spell," he said, withdrawing the hand.

"Has it?" said her dad.

"Did you bring honey?" said Bella, brightening.

"Sorry, buddy, not this time. But I brought you some chocolate," he said, producing a Hershey's bar from his pack. "Okay with you?" he said to her dad.

Her dad consented with a nod, even as Bella snatched the chocolate greedily.

Once Sugarfoot, Boots, and Boris converged on the bluff, Mr. Moseley's arrival was officially an event.

"I brought you something too, Dave," he said, fishing a card out of his wallet.

"What the hell is this?" said her dad.

"My cousin Randall, he did six tours between Iraq and Afghanistan," said Moseley. "Special forces. It really messed with his head, nearly ruined his life. His wife left him, his kids stopped talking to him. He almost lost his house."

"And?" said her dad.

"Dr. Pete is great," said Mr. Moseley.

"Says right here he's an LPC," her dad said. "Last time I checked, that wasn't a doctor."

"Everybody just calls him Dr. Pete," said Moseley.

"You mean, like Dr. J?" said her dad. "Or Dr. Scholl's?"

"He really did wonders for Randy," Mr. Moseley said. "He totally turned his life around."

"Thanks, but no thanks," said her dad. "That why you came up here? To try to save me from myself?"

"Don't get me wrong," said Mr. Moseley. "I just thought that maybe—"

"I don't need saving," said Dave. "And we don't need your gifts, either," he added, snatching the chocolate out of Bella's hand and tossing it at Moseley's feet.

"Sorry, if . . . look, if I overstepped my bou—"

"Thanks for dropping by," said her dad, cutting him short.

"Daddy, you're being rude," scolded Bella, who promptly retrieved the candy bar out of the dirt and began dusting it off.

"Would you like to come inside, Mr. Moseley?" said Bella. "We could play Uno."

Her dad flashed her a threatening look.

"Not today, sweetie," said Mr. Moseley. "I've got work to do. I just came to talk to your daddy."

"Well," said her dad. "We're done talking. Goodbye, Mr. Moseley."

"Daddy, stop being so rude!"

"Look, Dave," said Mr. Moseley. "There's something you need to know."

"I know all I need to know, Mr. Moseley," he said.

"The sheriff's office has been asking questions."

"About what?"

"About you and Bella."

"And what'd you tell them?"

"I didn't tell them anything," said Mr. Moseley. "Dave, look, they know you don't plan on vacating this place."

"So, what are you telling me?" said her dad.

Moseley looked down to his hiking boot, toeing the gravel.

"I'm telling you that I think you should go back to town. To stay."

"Is that right? And what do you suppose is waiting for me in town? A parade?"

"A house, for starters," he said.

"Wrong," said her dad.

"Some companionship for your daughter," said Mr. Moseley. "Some support. Family. Friends, medical services, schools. You want me to keep going?"

"No," said her dad. "You've made your point. But you're missing my point: there's an awful lot that's wrong with the world, a lot more wrong than right. Hell, it's not even a contest. You, Moseley, you're a do-gooder, that's admirable—few are anymore. But you're also part of the problem."

"Go back to town, Dave. It's the right thing to do."

"Safe journey, Mr. Moseley," said her dad, spitting on the ground. "Sorry you wasted your time coming up here today."

"Think about it, Dave," he said.

"Goodbye, Mr. Moseley."

Clearly discouraged, Mr. Moseley turned and started down the incline.

"Mr. Moseley," Bella called after him.

"Yeah, sweetie?"

"Next time could you bring honey?"

"I'll see what I can do, sweetie," he said.

N'ka

———•———•———

For two days, they'd progressed steadily, mind-numbingly, over the ice, passing nothing, encountering only the wind that ravaged their faces, the ice that threatened their footing with every step, and the weak sun that failed to warm, but succeeded in blinding them. They stuck to the scantily wooded edges wherever possible, though where could they be safer than the middle of the nothingness, where the element of surprise was impossible?

This frozen wasteland could not go on forever. Somewhere the ice ended, surely, and the frozen world gave way to a more plentiful place. Squinting his eyes against the blinding glare, N'ka held a picture of the place inside his mind—green and gently rolling, mild in temperature—even as the icy wind stung his face.

On the afternoon of the fourth day, having recently dined on the last of the squirrel, N'ka and his mother encountered a dark form huddled on the ice, some quarter mile to the west. Pausing in their tracks, they watched the dark mass for movement.

"What is it?"

"I can't tell."

"Is it alive?"

"How should I know?"

Only once it was apparent that the form was both motionless and defenseless did N'ka dare to investigate.

"Stay back," he told his mother.

Armed with a spear, N'ka crept warily over the ice toward the unknown mass, awake to the slightest movement, his scalp tight, as though the temperature had suddenly dropped ten degrees. What if the beast was only sleeping, or lying in wait? N'ka clutched his spear tighter and forced himself to proceed.

What he discovered on the ice was the bloody carcass of a wolf, singed by fire, a substantial length of broken spear sticking quill-like out of its neck. How hard had he struggled to break that spear? How far had he run in his desperation, nipping hopelessly at his flaming backside?

But the gruesome scene was not a harbinger of death so much as it was a promise of life. Finally, other people amidst the boundless ice, humans undaunted by claw or fang. Perhaps, like N'ka and his mother, they were nomads, searching for a home.

Though the blood was no longer warm, the carcass was not yet frozen. Surely, these others could not be far. But the further N'ka pursued his eager speculations aloud, the more his mother attempted to buffer his eagerness.

"We know nothing of them," she said. "Their ways, their natures. They could be violent. They could be cannibals for all we know."

And just like that, her gloomy forebodings cut his youthful confidence down to size. For all his vigor and enthusiasm, for all his yearning and desire, hunger and curiosity, for all that he presumed to know, he had little experience in this world beyond the shelter of the mountains. Not like his mother: abandoned and forsaken, raped and left for dead.

Still, N'ka could not help but entertain his yearning to be part of a clan, to belong to something bigger than himself. And there was something else, too: a strange and unfamiliar sensation that churned deep within him when he imagined a mate, a stalwart companion to walk beside him, who looked in his mind's eye something like a younger version of his mother. For who else had he to compare this other person to?

"What is it like to be with somebody?" he said, huddled over the coals amidst the reeds, where the great cloak of night was sprawled out above them.

"You are with somebody," she said.

"Not like that," he said, stirring the coals. "To . . . have somebody. To choose somebody, like you chose father."

"He chose me," she said.

"What was it like to be chosen?"

She looked up from the fire, engaging his eyes for an instant. Then, abruptly she looked back into the flames.

What had she seen in his eyes? Had she recognized something there? Hope, fear, vulnerability?

"Spare yourself," she said.

But N'ka was determined not to spare himself any consequence if it might make his life fuller.

"You're a coward," he said, regretting his words immediately.

"How dare you," she said.

N'ka hid his eyes in the fire.

"I'm sorry," he said.

"Bah," she said, looking away. "Sorry for what? You don't know any better. How could you?"

"You're right," said N'ka. "I know nothing."

And it pained him to admit it. Between what he wanted and what he knew to be true lay a world of ice.

"Don't listen to me," said his mother, waving him off. "You're right to call me a coward. I would have the whole world suffer for my misfortunes. And just to tell them I told them so. You have courage, child. Trust your vision."

Clipboard Jesus

———

The day, which started clear and sunny, which seemed to promise a respite from winter's onslaught, soon wrapped its hands around Dave's throat. At midday, Bella called him out to the bluff, where he emerged just in time to see a lone figure striding through the meadow below. Not ten minutes later, the same ranger, his pocked face patchy with a week's growth of beard, scrambled up the incline, clutching an aluminum clipboard box, a Glock holstered at his waist.

Dave met him near the edge of the bluff, close enough to finally read the nametag on his green jacket: Paulson.

"Mr. Cartwright," he said, none too brightly.

"Mr. Paulson," said Dave, spitting on the ground.

"We talked about this, you and I. I'm gonna have to ask you to move on," he said.

"Oh?" said Dave.

"That's one option, anyway," said Paulson.

"And what's plan B?"

Paulson glanced at Bella, then back at Dave.

"We're not there yet, son," he said. "For now let's just call this a friendly nudge. We went over the rules last time. There's a limit to how long you can squat on this land. You hit that limit weeks ago."

"You still haven't told me about plan B," said Dave.

Paulson held Dave's eye steadily, until he couldn't anymore, at which point he promptly flipped open the lid of his silver clipboard, unfastened the pen, and began scrawling.

"Ah," said Dave. "Paper."

"Bit more than that," he said. "It's what we call a consequence, Mr. Cartwright."

Paulson finished scribbling in a flurry, ripped a yellow slip from his clipboard, and foisted it at Dave.

"A consequence of what exactly?" said Dave.

"It's all right there on the paper."

"Save me the time, will you?"

"Class B misdemeanor," he said flatly. "We went over this. I issued a warning and told you I'd be back. Well, here I am."

"We left before thirteen days," said Bella.

"Come again, darling?" says the ranger.

"We left before the thirteen days were up," she said. "Last time. We left for like a bunch of weeks, and we just came back four days ago."

"She's right," said Dave. "We've only been here for a couple days."

Paulson looked him in the eye again, briefly.

"Well, your beard, and about a half dozen folks down in Vigilante Falls say differently," he said. "It's a known fact you've been up here since spring."

"It wasn't contiguously," said Bella.

Paulson hoisted an eyebrow and tilted his head like a terrier confronted with a wind-up monkey.

"Say again?"

"Contiguously," Bella says. "We were never here for thirteen days contiguously. That's what the rule is, right? You can't be here thirteen days in a row. You didn't say anything about not coming back again."

Paulson gave Bella a look that seemed at once admiring and pitying.

"Sweetie, I think you mean continuous," he said. "And you've been here a lot longer than that."

"You can't prove that," said Dave.

"Look, you're welcome to contest that citation," he said. "Take a look at it and you'll see I went awfully easy on you. Maximum punishment for this offense is five grand and six months incarceration. It's time to think about relocating, Mr. Cartwright."

"Why is there a limit, anyway?" said Bella. "I thought everybody owned this land."

"I didn't make the rules, darling," said Paulson. "I just enforce them."

Dave forced a laugh.

"I did three tours in the sandbox in the service of my country," he said. "I still file my taxes. You talk to Anne Marie Wright down in Vigilante Falls about that."

"I thank for your service," said Paulson. "I'm not from the IRS, Mr. Cartwright."

"How about you?" said Dave. "You ever put your butt on the line for your country, aside from the Smokey the Bear routine?"

"I'm not trying to diminish your service or your sacrifice here, Mr. Cartwright, I'm just doing my duty. Duty, that's something you understand, right?"

"No sir, not like I used to," said Dave. "My sense of duty isn't as far reaching as it once was."

"Whatever the case may be, I'm gonna need you to move on," said Paulson. "Pains me to say it, but looks like you haven't been taking care of your business much, lately, Mr. Cartwright, with all due respect."

"You have no idea," said Dave.

"I see a sweet little girl living in a cave," said Paulson. "And to my eyes, that looks like neglect. But again, that's not for me to decide."

"Ask her something," said Dave. "Go ahead, ask her. Then tell me if there's something wrong with that sweet little girl living in a cave."

"Are you gonna arrest us?" said Bella.

"He can't arrest anybody," said Dave. "He's just a ranger."

"I'm not here to arrest you," said Paulson. "You have sixty days to pay the citation. But in the meantime, I am going to need you to relocate. Look, Mr. Cartwright. Let me lay it out for you: we both know you've been up here with your daughter for at least eight months. I've talked to Fish and Wildlife, and they're not convinced you haven't been poaching."

"That's a lie," said Dave. "We take what nature gives us, and nothing more."

"Nothing natural about a man living in a cave with his daughter, Mr. Cartwright. Especially not in winter. But whatever the case, you're gonna need to move on. That's the law, and I'll see to it that you're in compliance."

"And if I'm not in compliance?"

"Do yourself a favor, do your daughter a favor, Mr. Cartwright. Whatever it is that brought you out here, whatever life you think you're gonna make for yourself, it's not gonna work. Go home. The next time I come up here, it won't be to write a ticket."

"Is that a threat?"

"That's a warning, Mr. Cartwright, your final warning. I'm gonna leave you now, but I'll be back, and when I come back, I can guarantee you I won't be alone."

Ed Paulson; Ranger

———————

"I didn't like it, not one bit. Seemed to me like we were headed toward some sort of standoff. It just felt that way. Something told me that Cartwright would never give in, no matter how hard anyone tried to force his hand. He was determined to have his way, no matter what the rest of the world had to say about it. It's a quality I might have admired in a different situation.

"But as it stood, it made me uneasy. For all I knew, he had a couple screws loose. He seemed pretty stable on the one hand, lucid enough. Didn't display any behavior I'd characterize as too erratic. But to hear folks in town talk about him, you might have guessed otherwise. At the very least, he had some misgivings about many things in the world, and I was no doubt one of them. He wasn't interested in the law, that much was clear. He was the law, so far as he was concerned. But I had a job to do, and when push came to shove, I knew I was gonna have to do it, and I also knew that the time to take action was approaching. I couldn't risk letting the thing escalate, and I couldn't let Cartwright dig himself in up there any deeper.

"The troubling part of it was knowing he was armed. How armed, I couldn't say, but I knew he was armed just as sure as I knew something awful was liable to happen to that little girl, sooner or later. We had to get them out of there."

N'ka

———◆———

The relentless wind blasted their faces raw, froze their eyes half-shut, and turned their feet to blocks of ice as they trudged onward, half-starved, N'ka's mother growing weaker by the hour.

On the seventh morning the wind finally subsided, and the sun managed to burn through the fog. They awoke on the ice, stiff and aching.

"Are you okay, Mom?" said N'ka.

"I'm alive," said his mother. "Unfortunately."

With nothing to eat, and nothing to burn, they did not linger. They hefted their hides and resumed their interminable journey toward the horizon. A half-mile into their progress, N'ka spotted a small plume of smoke in the distance, trailing toward the north.

"There!" he said. "There, what did I tell you?"

"It could be anybody," she said.

N'ka hurried his pace.

"C'mon," he said.

But his mother was unable to keep up with him.

"You go," she said. "I'll catch up."

"I can't just leave you behind. What if the wolves come slinking around?"

"Bah. It would be a relief," she said.

A quarter mile later his mother was but a distant spot on the ice, as N'ka finally arrived at the source of the smoke: a flat, smoldering smattering of coals, recently abandoned. How long? An hour? Maybe two?

He scanned the area for further evidence, finding the hollow point of a broken spearhead, a few measly bones which he recognized as squirrel, a patch of yellow snow, but no footprints, no further indication of which direction the mystery people had proceeded.

N'ka swept the coals into a pyramid, then huddled over it, awaiting his mother. She arrived, hobbled and winded, squatting wordlessly beside him to warm her extremities.

"We will find them," he said.

"Mm," she said.

By afternoon, the sun off the ice was blinding. N'ka and his mother were forced to shield their eyes as they plodded along into the glare. It was not long before his mother developed a piercing headache, and they were forced to pause in their progress, as she squatted on her haunches and buried her eyes in the crook of her arm, until N'ka could no longer suppress a sigh.

"Oh, forgive me," she said, registering his impatience. "I forgot. We're in a hurry."

Before N'ka could defend himself, she was already upright again, still shielding her eyes from the light.

"Well, c'mon, what are you waiting for?" she said.

"Mom, we can rest," he said. "If you need some more time to—"

"Oh, no. No, no. You're so eager to meet other people, why should we wait? Let's go see what you've been missing your whole life. Let's go see how your imaginary clan greets us. Maybe they'll have a feast waiting."

"Or maybe we'll be the feast," he said wryly.

She lowered her arm slightly to hide a grin.

Hard and bitter old woman that she'd become, it heartened N'ka to know that she was still soft in there somewhere. For all that he didn't know about her previous life, N'ka understood intuitively that his sustenance, his well-being, his very existence in this world accounted for much of what he considered her hardness. He suspected also that it accounted for the bulk of what he considered her softness. It seemed that she allowed N'ka to shape her. She had given the raw material of herself to his survival. For this, a debt he could never repay, he would forgive his mother anything.

In silence, they maintained a brisker-than-usual pace, their breath sawing at the frigid air as the sunlight off the ice consumed their eyes. For hours they encountered no life along their way. But N'ka knew they would catch up to the others eventually, they must. If not in a day, in two days, or a week. Despite the lack of recent evidence, N'ka sensed that they were not so far off. He trusted that the route he forged was likely the same as theirs, for he imagined that they were on the same quest as him, the quest for a new world.

As the sun gradually dipped on the horizon, N'ka began looking for a suitable campsite somewhere, but saw nothing promising to the north or the west, which stretched out flat and white forever. The south looked more promising, with a group of low hills huddled together at a distance of two or three miles, a smattering of vegetation along their lower fringes.

Beyond the hills there were real mountains, craggy and sudden, though not so high, and not so abrupt as the ones they left behind. They would camp in the green at the base of the hills, N'ka decided. He should have begun veering south an hour ago instead of daydreaming. The instant he shifted their course southerly, his mother slipped on the ice, landing flat on her back with a sharp exclamation.

N'ka swung around so fast that he nearly lost his own footing shuffling to her aid.

"Are you okay?"

She groaned.

Kneeling down, it was obvious from her dull and uncomprehending gaze that she was not okay.

"Mama," he said. "Talk to me."

She only groaned again.

He sat her up.

"Where are you hurt?" he said.

"I'm fine," she said. "Help me up."

He helped her to her feet.

"That's one way to get rid of a headache," she said.

He held her under the arm for a step, as though aiding her in her forward progress.

"I can walk myself," she said impatiently, pushing him off.

In spite of her insistence, the incident slowed her pace markedly. The farther they walked, the more her tempo slackened, the more evident it became that she was injured in some way.

Halting his progress, he turned back to her.

"Where are you hurt?" he said. "Is it your back, your leg?"

"Bah," she said. "I'm fine. Just stiff."

"You're limping," he said.

"I'm cold," she said. "I'm tired, I want a fire. Now, keep walking."

Though their progress remained excruciatingly slow, and his mother continued to refuse assistance, they managed to reach the wooded fringe along the base of the hills and located a small clearing before the sun had sunk completely below the horizon.

N'ka began hastily setting up camp, first scavenging sticks from amongst the scrubby trees that lined the perimeter of the clearing and heaping them in a pile. Next, he laid the ragged hides out, his mother watching, grimacing through her pain and exhaustion.

As N'ka tended to the fire, a sudden movement on the periphery caught his attention. When he turned to look, he saw a brown blur dart behind the measly cluster of trees to his left. He fixed on the trees momentarily, looking for further movement.

Rising slowly to his feet, he began to creep in the direction of the trees.

"What is it? Where are you going?" said his mother.

"Shhh," he said.

Stealthily he moved out past the perimeter of the clearing into the brush, which dropped down into a swale ten or twelve feet deep. There he discovered a figure crouching in the brush at the bottom of the gulley.

She was just a child, maybe ten or eleven years old. The hide she wore was unlike any hide N'ka had ever seen, fitted and cinched about the waist with a strap of leather, unlike his own baggy, crudely cut garment.

"Hello," said N'ka.

Though the child hardly stirred, N'ka saw her green eyes darting about for a possible escape route.

"It's okay," he assured her. "I do not wish to harm you."

But the girl only looked at him uncomprehendingly.

"Where do you come from?" he said. "Are there others near?"

Still she could not apprehend his meaning.

As soon as N'ka reached out to take hold of her wrist, the child clambered up the far side of the gulch and darted off into the brush.

N'ka gave chase, twice losing his footing up the incline. When he reached the top, heart pounding, he furiously scanned the vicinity for the girl, but found no sign of her, or any indication as to which direction she might have proceeded.

"Come back!" he called out.

Though she left no discernible tracks through the underbrush, N'ka proceeded west for a quarter mile, presuming the girl belonged to the same band of westbound travelers who had been leaving signs in their wake all along.

He hurried along, dodging trees and boulders, eyes frisking everything he passed. Why did she run? Was it because she, too, had a mother somewhere teaching her to be wary of outsiders? Or was she alone and frightened? Lost on the ice? Every possibility only exacerbated N'ka's sense of urgency. He must find her. But where? Where did she go, this girl, this other person, the only other person beside his mother that N'ka had ever been within arm's reach of?

Before he could locate the girl, the light began to fade, and N'ka was forced to abandon his pursuit, hurrying back to camp in the gathering darkness.

He found his ailing mother huddled over the weak fire.

"And?" she said

"A little girl," he said.

"Eh?"

"Her clan must be nearby," he said.

"No doubt they've seen us coming for miles," his mother said. "You'll see, they're trying to lure you away from me, and then—*snap*," she said, with a whacking gesture.

"That must be it," he said. "They must be afraid of you, the fierce old pessimist, so their plan is to lure me away from you. That makes sense. Surely, whoever they are, they can see they're no match for a bitter old woman the likes of you. Now that I think about it, I'm sure that's what's been keeping the wolves away, too."

"Bah," she said, rubbing her feet. "Laugh at me if you want. But you will see."

As she looked back into the fire, her eyes were smiling.

Travers Cartwright

―――――――――

"I kept telling myself to stay out of it, just let them be. Kris and I, we already tried to help, and it didn't seem to do any good. Bella just ended up back where she started anyway. If anything, it turned her against us. It's gonna sound like I'm making excuses, and that's fair, but if there was one thing you should know about my brother, he was a capable guy, a lot more capable than me. He could hunt, he could fish, he could build, and he was just generally resourceful as hell. He could make a little go a long way. Look what he was able to do on the football field at five-nine and a buck-fifty. And on top of that, he survived three tours in Iraq, and the death of his wife. More than I ever survived by a mile. So if anybody could do just fine up there in the dead of winter, it was Dave.

"That's what I kept telling myself.

"The thing that worried me more than the weather conditions was the talk of the sheriff's office getting involved, which was probably my fault without getting too far into it. Anyway, the thought of cops up there made me nervous. Because I knew how proud Dave was, and I also knew that slow as he was to anger, if you pushed him too far, hell, he was likely to blow his top.

"In some ways, winter may have been a blessing."

Almost Perfect

———

Finally, the heavy snow came falling in languid sheets, big, fluffy flakes like cotton fiber, ghostly in their descent. They settled on the little plateau above the canyon, gathering in drifts, muffling sound and reshaping the world. Confined by the plunging valleys, buttressed by the hulking palisade of the front ranges, the serrated edge of the Pickets seemed to pierce the living sky. The North Cascades truly were a wondrous place.

Bella was giddy with the arrival of the snow. Dave saw her crunching through it, saw her sliding upon it, saw her digging and burrowing, piling and flattening, and rolling in its white wonder. He watched her form it into bricks to stack into misshapen igloos, saw her rolling it into balls half the size of herself.

"Oh, Daddy, it's the best snow!" she cried. "You can do absolutely anything with it! I made a throne for Boris, and he actually sat on it. You should have seen it! I tried to make a crown, but it wouldn't stick together."

Her joy awakened Dave. After weeks of simmering apathy, he finally knew vitality once more, a heat in his blood, a hopeful beating in his chest. And for the first time since fall, he was motivated. He shoveled a clear passage in and out of the cave, and carved a path to the pit toilet, fifty yards downwind. No sooner did he set his shovel aside than he was drilled in the chest with a snowball.

"C'mon, Daddy!" she said. "Try and get me."

And just like that, Dave was ducking and diving, crunching and rolling, and firing off snowballs.

"Time out," he said, winded, holding up a hand to catch his breath, the grin on his face irrepressible.

To be alive again, God, but it was glorious! The rush of adrenaline, the crisp air filling his lungs, the glowing face of his daughter.

"C'mon, hurry up and rest," she said, already leveling her aim.

Soon they agreed to an armistice, but only long enough to build opposing walls, and stockpile their arsenals. When the tips of their gloved fingers were numb, they charged at each other again and again, hurling and dodging, until finally they collapsed on their backs next to each other in the middle of the snowy meadow, where, panting and heaving, they looked up at the slate gray sky.

"Can we make a sled?" she said.

"Let's do it," he said.

And together they fashioned a sled made of cedar slats left over from the smokehouse, with a deck big enough to hold two bodies, and runners of bowed green hemlock, Bella holding the last runner fast, with numb fingers, as Dave fastened it. They hauled it out past the pit toilet, and through the woods past the smoke house, to a bald incline.

"You go first," said Dave.

"Can we go together?" she said.

And so, with a running start, Dave launched them down the hill, and jumped on deck behind Bella, the sled holding up much better than Dave had imagined, the runners not bogging down as they swished down the side of the mountain toward the tree line, Bella squealing with delight. The runners started to mire at the foot of the hill, but not before they rode halfway up the berm and tumbled off into each other's arms, laughing.

"Let's do it again," she said. "Oh, please, please, please."

Dave would have stopped at nothing to preserve her joy. They launched themselves down the hillside again, and again, and again, Bella, red-nosed and panting, as Dave, light headed and short of breath himself, towed the sled back up the incline each time, until finally the runners were too wob-bly to attempt another run.

"We can fix it tomorrow," he said.

"Promise?" she said, just as the snow started to fall again.

"Promise."

"Or we can build a faster one," she said.

God, it thrilled Dave to see the sparkle back in Bella's eyes, to hear the old singsong in her voice again! He looked at her smiling, cheeks red and chafed, lips ravaged from the frigid air. She was so exhausted on the hike back that Dave was forced to abandon the rickety sled and carry her the rest of the way, her warm, satisfied breath against his neck, her little arms clutching him securely. This day was as good as any he'd ever envisioned for the two of them: happy, healthy, connected. And all it took was a foot of snow.

Back on the bluff, back aching, heart full, Dave set Bella down by the pit and promptly started a fire, as Bella watched on.

"Don't fall asleep. Just hang on a few more minutes, baby," he said. "I wanna get some food in your belly."

Dinner was a broth of squirrel, seasoned with a smattering of salt and rosemary, along with a tough hunk of jerked salmon. Dessert was a palm full of frozen blackberries. Afterward, Dave set the kettle on the glowing coals.

At dusk they ducked into the cave, Dave clutching the sighing kettle as Bella lit the lantern. Reinvigorated for the moment, she wrapped herself in a blanket and awaited the licorice tea that Dave had been saving for months, unbeknownst to Bella.

Dave poured the hot water out into their enamel cups, and Bella blew impatiently at her steeping tea.

"Let's read," she said.

"Whatever you want, baby."

And so they took turns reading aloud in the pulsing lamplight. They read about Nepalese holidays, and orangutans in Borneo, and about Jupiter's great red spot, ten thousand miles across, Bella plying Dave with questions at every turn. Then they read about mandala sand paintings, and elephants of the African savanna, until Bella grew so sleepy she could hardly keep her head up. However, the moment Dave dimmed the lantern and they lay down side by side in the darkness, Bella immediately caught a second wind.

"Today was a perfect day, Daddy," she said.

"I'm so glad," he said.

"Except for maybe dinner," she said.

"We can do better tomorrow," he said. "There's still a little venison in the smokehouse."

"I love venison."

"I know you do," he said.

"Can we have licorice tea again?"

"It might be a little weak."

"That's okay," she said.

With that they fell silent for a few minutes, until Dave was certain that Bella had fallen to sleep. But soon, to his dismay, he heard her muffled sobs.

"Baby, what is it?"

"I don't want to die," she said, her throat catching.

Dave's heart ran like wax into the hollow of his stomach.

"Baby, you're not gonna die," he said, propping himself up on an elbow. "Not for a long, long time. Are you worried about something?"

She sniffed and swallowed.

"No," she said.

"What made you think that, baby?"

"I don't know," she said. "Because today was so much fun, I guess."

"Baby, you're just a little girl. You're gonna live a long time."

"But it seems like just two minutes ago I was five," she said, fighting back a sob. "And now I'm eight already."

Dave rolled over and clutched Bella.

"It goes faster when you're younger, baby, I promise," he said softly. "I hardly even remember anything before I was your age. Think about that. I've got like ten memories before I was eight. It's like my life hardly started until then. And now I'm forty, and eight seems like three lifetimes ago."

"But Daddy, I don't ever want to die," she said. "I love life."

S'tka

———•———

For the second day in a row, S'tka's movement over the ice was measured and excruciatingly slow. Her fall the previous afternoon had taken a toll. With each step, she winced, as the pain of her injured hip ran down her leg to the back of her knee, and up her spine to the base of her skull.

N'ka had grown irritable and impatient with her limitations. He worried, though never aloud, that they would not be able to keep pace with the elusive others as they moved west.

As always, she could guess at his thoughts.

"Leave me behind," she insisted. "Go on up ahead, I will catch up to you eventually."

"And leave you to die?"

"Go," she said.

But N'ka refused to abandon her.

Time, however, was running out, and they both knew it. They hadn't eaten in three days, and there was no sign whatsoever of game. Looking west, through the haze, over the frozen wasteland, there was still no discernible end to the ice, no hint of anything different, nor the tiniest whiff of N'ka's paradise. Meanwhile, the cruel conditions of this perpetual winter showed no signs of abating.

Finding the elusive others seemed their only hope for survival.

With each mile, S'tka's condition worsened. Each step seemed to require more effort than the last. Still she trudged on mechanically, too tired to think or reflect, her only impetus the dim promise that the cover of darkness would force them to stop eventually. The trail had long gone cold where the mysterious others were concerned. The best they could hope for now was sleep.

For hours, they found no sign of life, nor any sign of recent habituation, neither footprint, nor distant voices on the wind, nor the cooling embers of a cooking fire. Finally, as afternoon waned, they made camp amidst a lonely stand of spruce at the base of the hills, with the craggy, ice-strewn mountains rising abruptly to the south, promising nothing in the way of comfort. Sometimes it was hard not to wonder at the Great Provider's design. Why not give the people fur, like the beasts, if she intended for them to live in such an inhospitable place?

S'tka watched dully, massaging her aching joints, as N'ka built a fire for warmth. Only now did her thoughts resume with any lucidity, and the first among them was the thought of starvation. How much longer could they go before the ravages of hunger weakened them beyond the point of further progress? And what would they do then, just lay down on the ice to die? Hunker in a gulley to freeze to death?

N'ka, meanwhile, somehow managed to remain upbeat, as he busied himself making camp.

"Have you noticed it's getting greener?" he said. "A little bit, anyway."

"Yes," she said, though in fact, she had noticed no such thing. At this point, they could have been walking in circles and she wouldn't have known better. Her only meaningful guidepost the whole journey long had been the mountains they left behind days ago. All the rest had been sameness to her eyes, until the appearance of these new mountains to the south.

"We're getting close, I can feel it," he said.

"Mm," she said, huddling closer to the flames.

She could no longer afford to doubt him. Either he was right or they would both perish on the ice.

Please, oh, Great Provider, let him be right. Let there be something better. For his sake, if not mine.

When darkness had fallen, mother and son leaned wordlessly into the fire, their gnawing hunger hunkered conspicuously between them like a physical presence. Somewhere in the distance, under cover of the moonless night, the wolves were yelping and baying, letting their own hunger be known, as N'ka fed more sticks to the fire and tried to rally some optimism.

"Someday the struggle will be over," he said, as if he actually had any insight into the cruel machinations of this world, let alone any control over it.

N'ka understood that if he was to lead effectively, to guide them responsibly to safety, he mustn't betray the full depth of his doubts, though he knew, too, that his over-confidence could prove to be their folly. The foundation of N'ka's certainty was beginning to show cracks, and more troubling still, it seemed that fear was starting to seep through those cracks.

They'd lost track entirely of the others onto whom N'ka had pinned all their hopes. The little girl was gone like an apparition, and with her the promise of belonging. N'ka had only the vaguest of idea where he was leading them. But the landscape did appear to be getting greener; N'ka was sure he was not imagining that. The shrubs and scrubby vegetation at the edge of the ice seemed to be growing denser. The trees, though still scattered and few, seemed to be growing heartier, their trunks thicker and their canopies fuller. N'ka looked for reason to hope in every exposed rock, every sliver of green.

That night he dreamed that the sky and the ice were as one vast and seamless space. N'ka found himself alone amidst a boundless nothingness. He had no visible form, nothing by which to differentiate himself from the endless iteration of sky. There was no amplitude to define his position. He did not know if he was moving, or if he still existed within the space. He did not know if anyone or anything else existed in this place.

In this dream, N'ka felt lost, adrift in a meaningless eternity. He yearned desperately for something perceptible, for anything or anyone, a sound, a movement, the tiniest spot of color.

Abruptly, the stillness gave way to a deafening disturbance, like the grinding retreat of glacial ice, slow and steady, through mountain rock. A crack opened in the nothingness, as a zipper-like tear formed in the fabric of the sky.

And then, silence again. The space was no longer seamless. There was now depth by which to navigate. Cautiously, N'ka's formless self approached the breach, a sliver of pale blue sky, and slipped through the breach.

When he arrived on the other side, N'ka occupied his human form once more. The world around him was verdant and swimming with life. Trees of unimaginable size reached toward the sky. Strange creatures, never imagined, hoofed and horned and winged, populated his dream world.

N'ka found himself in this new world, standing on the banks of a river that was somehow itself a creature, with quivering silver ribbons running just beneath its surface.

S'tka awakened at sunrise, with N'ka still snoring fitfully beside her. Sunrise was a bit of a misnomer, since the dawn was shrouded in the same inexorable fog that had obscured much of their travels. The fire was all but dead. Her bones were all but completely numb, her blood running thick and slow through her veins. Crystals of ice had formed in her eyebrows. Certainly they could not last much longer under these conditions. How many more hopeless dawns could she endure before her spirit and her body quit on her?

When S'tka attempted to move in order to set about reviving the fire, she found that she was so stiff that she could not even manage to assume a sitting position. It was as though she was truly frozen, like old O'qu'a, when they found his body, pale blue and stiff as wood, in a field of snow.

Too weak to budge, S'tka lay helplessly at the edge of the smoldering embers, waiting for N'ka to awaken.

Somewhere deep in the cloak of fog, maybe a mile off, maybe less, she could hear the restless yammering and yipping of a wolf pack.

When N'ka finally stirred from sleep, S'tka immediately solicited his help getting up.

"Here we go again," she said.

But even with N'ka's assistance, she still hadn't the strength to stand, let alone walk across the frozen wilderness for untold miles.

A dark pall seized them both as the realization took hold. She could go no farther on her own power. N'ka fed the fire, taking inventory of the grim possibilities.

"Leave me," she said once more, reading his mind.

"Shush," he said, furrowing his brow in concentration as he scoured the fire for answers.

"You can come back for me."

This time N'ka did not even offer a reply. Instead he stared intently at the lapping flames, as though he could coax some answer from their warmth. After a moment, a possible solution presented itself and N'ka immediately set to work. The stunted stand of spruce proved to be a saving grace, as N'ka constructed the crudest of sledges from limbs gathered and claimed. Lashed together with strips of hide, the carrier was surprisingly sturdy, and should be sufficient for sledding his ailing mother over the ice. Though the endeavor cost them two hours of valuable light, the effort allowed them to proceed, albeit slowly, over the ice.

As the fog began to lift, N'ka rolled the dead weight of his mother onto the contraption and covered her in a mound of piebald hides.

"Leave me in peace," she pleaded.

"This is not peace," he said, even as the restless wolves repined somewhere in the distance.

"I will only hold you back," she said.

"So be it," he said.

He took hold of the crude leather reins, fashioned from strips of hide, and began conveying her ponderously over the ice.

Today was the day, he told himself. Today their journey would end, for better or for worse.

No Quit

B y the dawn of the new year, the winter landscape had lost its cheer, and the bruised sky pushed down upon them, turning the powder to ice, while the frigid wind from the north howled up the canyon to savage their encampment on the plateau. Once again their food stores had dwindled to practically nothing. The sallowness of Bella's cheeks was a daily reminder to Dave that circumstances were now more dire than ever. Town was all but inaccessible in these conditions, and the game had months ago fled the higher elevations, while the salmon run, not the bonanza Dave had hoped for, had petered out in the middle of December. Lately, all Dave had managed to pull out of the river was a few measly cutthroat, hardly enough to sustain them through the heart of winter.

At night, huddled in their dreary cavern in a puddle of lantern light, Dave and Bella heard the wind whistling through cracks in the rock, as it roared past the mouth of the cave. And when the icy squalls finally relented, a deathly, frozen silence fell upon the high country. Not so much as the restless stirring of a chipmunk or the trilling of a marmot broke the stillness. The little creek east of the bluff froze solid. The path to the pit toilet was a skating rink. The whole world was ice.

What firewood remained was mostly green. At the risk of his fingers, Dave split the wedges as thin as humanly possible, but they still resisted the flame. With little to eat, and little to warm them, and spring still months off, something had to give. For the first time since they began their life in the wilds, Dave began to entertain the possibility that he was beat. Everybody had been right: Jerome, Travis, Paulson. The mountains were no place for a man and a little girl in winter.

Still, Dave simply didn't have the quit in him, and never had, not even in the fourth quarter against Mount Vernon, so gassed from playing both sides of the ball that he was sure he didn't have another snap left in him, and not when he was flat on his back in the desert, paralyzed by his own apathy as the cries of his brothers reached his ears. He always found a way, if not a reason, to keep going. He never abandoned the cause.

And so he awoke at dawn one still morning, and in a flurry of industry he split and stacked and shoveled. He built a fire, and warmed the broth, and doled out the last stringy shreds of salmon jerky. Then, donning his snowshoes and retrieving his pack, and the .458, freshly oiled, Dave committed himself to a hunt that was bound to be fruitless, though he had no choice but to convince Bella and himself otherwise.

"I'm going after game," he said to Bella.

"Can I go?"

"No, baby, you've got to stay here and guard the camp."

"Guard it from what?" she said. "You're just saying it that way to make it seem like it's a real job."

"Baby, please."

Bella crossed her arms and stared iinto the flames.

"Same old story," she grumbled.

"Now, c'mon, sweetie," he said. "We're a team. We depend on each other. I'll be back before dark, okay?"

Bella continued to stare sullenly into the coals.

"Okay?" he said, once more.

"Fine," she said, spitting into the fire.

Poor kid, thought Dave as he began descending the face of the bluff. Ought to have let her come along, though God knew it could only diminish the already astronomical odds of finding any game this late in the season. He'd have to go clear to the bottom of the basin to have any luck at all.

Halfway down the face of the bluff, Dave lost his purchase on the frozen hillside, and began sliding down the incline, his heart beating furiously, before he finally managed to stop himself with the drag of his snowshoes. Dusting himself off, he tramped through the deep snow of the meadow, then proceeded ponderously up and over the hump, short of breath by the time he descended the leeward side and dove down into the upper river valley.

When he finally reached the east bank an hour later, he progressed downriver through the canyon toward the bottomlands, where, in another twenty minutes he emerged in a wide, snow-covered pasture at the foot of the basin. Here, to his disbelief, he picked up a group of tracks that numbered at least two deer, possibly three. He began pursuing the tracks north until they disappeared into the wooded fringe at the base of the hillside. Ducking into the forest, Dave wended his way up the incline, between the trees, trampling fern and salal. The snow was shallow beneath the canopy, and the tracks were nowhere to be seen.

Dave was discouraged by the time he crested the hill, and the terrain dipped down toward a narrow swale. No sooner had he begun to ease down the incline when a sudden movement stopped his heart. Not thirty yards to the north, frozen in their tracks, Dave spotted a doe and two yearlings. Such good fortune defied reason. After luckless seasons of endeavor and unrewarded patience, weeks spent squatting motionless in the meadow, whole days spent lying in wait amongst the tall grass, here, at this desperate hour, Dave had somehow bumbled into his deliverance in this seemingly lifeless frozen hinterland.

Deliberately, he crept forward so as not to startle the animals, until he was within fifteen yards of the nearest fawn. It would probably take a headshot at this distance, even with the .458. Breathlessly he leveled the barrel and held the fawn steady in his sight, until he quieted his heartbeat to a faint pulse. When he pulled the trigger, the report shattered the chill silence, echoing through the basin with a whip-like crack. The yearling dropped instantly, as the mother and the other fawn scattered up the wooded incline in a ruckus of hooves.

Dave scrambled through the understory to his kill, where he set the rifle aside and unburdened himself of his pack, then dropped to his knees and set his gear out beside him. With one long incision up the belly, he began dressing the carcass, working quickly and efficiently through the paunch, and dredging the organs out through the windpipe. When the cavity was clean and patted dry, Dave wrapped the carcass in the big, green tarp, and immediately began the long journey back to the bluff.

The going was slow, as Dave dragged the hundred-pound tarp up and out of the gulley, then through the cluttered forest with its countless snags and uneven ground. The wide pasture ahead granted him a half-mile reprieve, but soon he was fighting his way up the canyon over uneven terrain. Despite his exhaustion, Dave's heart thrilled at this miraculous good fortune, his mouth watered at the prospect of a steak, his stomach turning somersaults in anticipation.

"Hahaha, yes!" he cried aloud, letting go the tarp with one hand to pump a fist in the air. "Goddamn right!"

He paused to look up and over the first range, with its wedge-shaped valleys, to the rock-studded ridge running north-to-south like the spine of a dragon, five thousand feet above. It was truly immense, this wilderness, its breadth and grandeur almost impossible to conceive. It could crush your fortunes and bury your body and erase you for all time. It seemed to care little for the life that dared to populate it, yet it was not entirely heartless.

How pleased Bella would be, the poor thing, to gorge herself on fresh meat! The little fawn had saved them; it represented a new beginning for Dave and Bella, a harbinger of prosperity to come. They would no longer freeze, or starve, nor hunker in despair. From now on they would own the winter, they would beat the frozen world into submission. These were the thoughts that warmed Dave's blood and hastened his progress through the canyon and over the hump, and across the meadow to the foot of the bluff.

Snags

———•••———

Bella passed the morning mindlessly out on the bluff, stirring the fire and petting the cats, moving fluidly between her worlds. Around noon, she took to scanning the canyon for the prospect of her dad's return, hopeful that any moment he would crest the hump, triumphantly dragging his kill.

But he did not appear.

By afternoon, she began to worry. What if he'd lost his way again, without her to right his course this time? What if he was injured, or worse? Her anxiety steadily gained momentum as the day wore on. At least a dozen times she called out to him, only to have her own voice echo back through the canyon. She debated going after him but deemed it wiser to stay put as he'd instructed her. Such was her distraction late in the afternoon that she could no longer seek refuge in the otherness. She stationed herself once more at the edge of the bluff and surveyed the canyon obsessively.

Finally, a half-hour before sunset, she spotted him, plodding across the meadow, just as she had hoped, dragging the hump of his green tarp, trailing a swath of blood through the snow.

"Daddy!" she called out as he neared the bottom of the bluff.

He waved to her and she could see him smiling from a hundred yards away.

He did it. Of course, he did. How could she ever have doubted him, when he had yet to fail her?

From the lip of the bluff, she watched on eagerly as he began his ascent, hugging the snowy hillside as he strained to haul the cumbersome tarp up after him, cussing frequently beneath his breath.

"What if we tie a rope on it," she called down to him.

"Haven't got enough rope," he managed between grunts.

Halfway up, he halted his progress momentarily to re-gather his strength.

"Talk about heavy," he called up to Bella. "I hope you're hungry, baby. We should be eating good for weeks."

Before Bella could answer him, everything went suddenly wrong. Bella watched on helplessly as her dad lost his footing, and instantly began a rapid slide down the face of the bluff. Letting go of the tarp, he fumbled desperately with his arms and legs to stop himself as he picked up speed.

"Daddy!" she hollered.

Twenty feet from the bottom, his slide came to an abrupt stop when his snowshoe snagged a rock, and his downhill momentum catapulted him backward, head-over-heels, to the bottom of the embankment. He landed with a dull thud on the snowy ground, not twenty feet from the twisted deer carcass, which had been thrown clear of the tarp. There he lay perfectly still, his right leg jutting out at an impossible angle, as the agitated snow settled back to earth around him.

With little thought of her own peril, Bella clambered crabwise down the hillside without incident, where she found her dad conscious but dazed, his face covered with cuts and scraped raw on one side. Below his right knee it looked as though the bone had been sheared in half, with one bloody end jutting out through a gash of bloody flesh and muscle. Already the tissue was discolored. The sight of it caused Bella to retch.

"How bad is it, baby?" he said calmly.

"Really bad, I think," she said.

"Okay," he said. "Don't worry. It's not as bad as it looks, okay? It doesn't hurt much. But Daddy's gonna need your help."

"What do I do, Daddy? I don't know what to do!"

"Stay calm, baby, that's the first thing. Do some star breaths."

Bella inhaled deeply through her nose, held her breath for a beat, then exhaled slowly.

"That's it, baby, again."

Bella repeated the sequence three times, until she felt her tummy begin to soften and her shoulders slacken.

"There you go," he said. "Now, baby, first I'm gonna need you to wrestle this pack off my back so I can lay down flat. Try not to move me too much, okay?"

Getting the strap over the exposed arm was not difficult. It was the arm pinned under him that was tough. But after a few minutes she managed to get the pack free of his body, and helped him to lie down flat.

"Now, I'm gonna need you to prop Daddy's head up so I can see, okay? I want you to put your hands under Daddy's head and lift it up just a little."

"Daddy, I should go for help."

"No, baby, it's gonna be dark soon. We gotta stay right here. I'm not gonna be able to move just yet, baby. I'm gonna need you to bring me some blankets, can you do that?"

Bella nodded.

"And some water."

Again Bella nodded, even as her chin began to quiver.

"Baby, don't worry," he said. "Everything's gonna be okay. We just need to stay calm."

"Okay," she said, fighting back the tears.

"Be careful going up and down that hill, it's really slick, baby. Don't try to carry everything at once. Just take it slow and steady, okay? Really dig your feet in."

Bella scrambled up and down the hillside twice without faltering. Not only did she procure water and blankets, but a tarp full of kindling, along with the first aid kit. At the conclusion of her second trip, her dad met her with a weak smile, grimacing through his pain.

"Okay, baby," he said. "You're doing great, baby. I'm so proud of you. Now comes the hard part. We're gonna need to set daddy's leg."

"What does that mean?"

"It means we have to straighten my leg out how it's supposed to be."

"Daddy, I can't," she said. "I can't hardly look at it. I'll get sick, I promise."

"Bella, you can do this, I know you can. Don't think of it as my leg, just think of it as a thing that needs to be fixed."

"But, Daddy . . ."

"First, you need to go to the edge of the meadow and find two sticks—about this thick, and this long," he said, demonstrating. "And they gotta be really straight, baby, and green, so they're not brittle, you got it?"

"Yeah," she said.

"Take the big knife out of the pack, and the bear spray—you might need it. And be very careful. Cut with the serrated part—the side with the little teeth at the bottom, okay? And always keep your hand clear like Daddy showed you."

"But I don't want to leave you," she said.

"You have to, baby. You won't be long. You gotta go quick while there's still light. Take my headlamp, just in case."

Bella dug the knife, still streaked with blood, out of the pack and hurried toward the meadow.

"Don't run with that knife!" he shouted after her.

It only took Bella a matter of minutes to find two bare fir boughs low to the ground. Both limbs were a half-inch thick, and about three feet long, neither one tapering much.

When she arrived back at her dad, it was nearly dusk.

"Okay, baby. There's a rope attached to the tarp, I want you to cut it off, then I want you to cut in three even pieces, okay?

Bella nodded.

"Use the toothy part of the blade, okay?"

Sawing the rope free of the bloodied tarp, Bella laid it out, and began cutting it in two-foot lengths.

Her dad's breathing was scratchy and shallow, and he was paler than she'd ever seen him.

"Look at the rope, baby," he said. "Not at me."

Bella could feel the hot lump rising in her throat once more as the tears began to blur her vision. Once the rope was at the ready, next came the dreaded task of confronting the leg again.

"Okay, now," her dad said. "Remember what I said: it's just a thing that needs to be straightened out. I'm gonna help you. I'm gonna hold the upper part of my leg steady, and you're gonna put the two ends so they're lined up again."

"I can't do it, Daddy, I can't."

"Baby, look at me: you have to. Daddy can't do it by himself."

Wiping away her tears, Bella took firm hold of his calf and deliberately guided the bone until the muscles seemed to pull it in place. Her dad gasped in pain through the ordeal, but when it was over she saw a little of the color come back into his face.

"That's it, baby," he said in a breathy voice. "Much better."

It was all but fully dark as her dad guided her through the process of splinting the leg, securing the apparatus tightly with the rope at the ankle, then both above and below the knee.

"Perfect, baby," he said. "You did amazing. Almost as good as new."

But her work was far from done. Next she gathered up the kindling and started a fire, and when it was burning sufficiently to leave untended, she returned to the meadow by the light of a headlamp, where, at once electric and numb with dread, the darkness crowding in around her, she collected heaping armloads of limbs and hurried them back to her dad, her heart racing.

Each time, he seemed a little weaker upon her return. By the final trip, he'd given up greeting her with encouragement. For ten minutes he fell silent completely, eyes wide open, much like the deer.

"You must be starving, baby," he said, at last.

Indeed, she was famished enough to drag the deer carcass across the snow to his side, where, propped on one elbow, sweating, and still looking pale in the firelight, he managed to butcher two steaks from the loin.

"Now, baby," he said, his arms bloodied to the elbow. "You're gonna need to drag the rest away and cover it with the tarp."

"Back to where I got it?"

"Farther," he said. "We don't want to attract company."

And even after she'd dragged the bulky thing the length of a football field, her work was not done. Before she lay down next to him, she made three additional trips to the forest and back, arms loaded with more downed limbs, until there was enough fuel for the fire to get them through the night.

Her dad, who had not touched his steak, grew weaker as the night wore on, his body wracked with shivering. She covered him with blankets, tucking them tight beneath his torso, and fed the fire to warm him. Eventually, he slipped into a fitful sleep, his breaths ragged and uneven.

Still, for hours afterward, despite the heaviness in her bones, Bella's thoughts raced, as her senses remained on high alert. Her tears did not return. Instead her emotions hardened into a state of relative indifference, as her fear assumed a different shape, less a hindrance, and more an instrument of her survival. This, she imagined, must be what it felt like to be an adult.

Somewhere in the middle of the chilly, starlit night, sleep finally came for Bella, and when it did, it came suddenly and completely.

N'ka

If their journey was arduous before, it had become almost unbearable now. N'ka's hide boots were beginning to deteriorate, and his feet, purple-toed, blistered, and numb, were beginning to swell. Though the makeshift sled was miraculously holding up, it was beginning to bow beneath the dead weight of his mother. Though a little antagonism might have boosted N'ka's energy, his mother remained silent until he finally coaxed her out of her shell.

"Why aren't you complaining?" he said, over his shoulder.

"Why should I complain?" she said. "This is better than walking. Pick up the pace, would you?"

"Let me know when you're ready to pull," he said.

Such banter heartened N'ka, but all the while he found himself fending off a relentless anxiety that his mother would never be the same, and that moving forward into their new lives she would be dependent upon him.

They'd been moving steadily southeast all morning as the sun burned through the fog. By late morning they were again skirting the hills, as the mountains behind them began to peek through the clouds, a stout and craggy range, though not quite the equal of the mountains they'd left behind. The place, as much as any place along their way, reminded N'ka of home. The thought was almost comfort enough to stave off the hunger gnawing at his insides.

He knew they should have eaten the wolf carcass. They could've made good use of the pelt, too, for that matter. But N'ka had refused to lose time on such an endeavor. How thoughtless he had been.

If only their fortunes would change suddenly with the appearance of a stray calf, or a mangy mule deer. N'ka would swiftly rise to the occasion. Surely his flagging senses would snap back into sharp focus, if only the opportunity would present itself.

By afternoon, the sun had caught up with them and was shining just over N'ka's shoulder.

"I thought for sure today was the day," he said. "I felt it in my bones."

"The day's not over yet," she said.

But the words were no comfort to N'ka, as the grim reality of starvation settled in. If they didn't starve, they were liable to freeze, or worse. N'ka's mind followed this dark path for hours, until suddenly a vaguely familiar sound from the south gave him pause, setting his neck hair on end.

What was this? Listen. What was that sound? Low and steady it came beneath the wind. Is it . . . ? Could it possibly be . . . ?

N'ka redoubled his effort over the ice. A dozen steps more and he paused once again to listen.

"Haha! Listen, mother! Listen to it!" he said.

Now, the sound was unmistakable to N'ka's ear, a sound he only ever heard in late spring, a sound that never failed to evoke joy in this frozen world. Yes, yes it was, the mighty rumble and hiss of rushing water.

"Do you hear it?" N'ka said breathlessly.

"Hear what?" his mother said weakly from the sled.

"We're here," he said. "We made it."

Without further pause, he began trundling the sled furiously across the ice toward the thunderous drumming that grew louder with each step. When he arrived at the edge of a snowy rise, he released the sled.

"Stay here," he said.

"As if I have a choice," she said.

N'ka plowed forward through the knee-deep snow toward the drumming of the water, his heart thumping madly. As he approached the top of the rise, he began laughing aloud.

Haha, yes, he knew it! He knew in his bones, knew it all along!

Still, it would be impossible to overstate N'ka's relief as he crested the rise and glimpsed the other side. He was moved almost to tears as he beheld the torrent of water roaring out from beneath a shelf of ice as though it were in hurry to get somewhere.

And something else soon aroused his senses as well, a faint but comforting odor riding on the breeze: the acrid aroma of fire.

"I told you!" he hollered down the incline to the tiny, prostrate figure of his mother, strapped to the sled. "Didn't I tell you?"

That was the exact instant when a terrible flash of movement caught his eye. His entire body turned suddenly to ice. His voice seized up so that he could not so much as call out to warn his mother about the five specks of brown and gray, noses to the ground, scuttling four-legged across the ice toward her helpless form. The beasts were already fanning out as N'ka began barreling down the incline. Losing his footing almost immediately, he tumbled end-over-end twice through the snow.

As he scrambled to his feet, N'ka could hear the snarling brutes take hold of her. The scrum was so sudden, so vicious and chaotic, that N'ka could not see clearly what was happening to his mother as he charged down the hill. But he could discern her agony readily enough in the quick, clipped desperation of her cries, as the beasts ripped at her from all sides, yipping and biting at one another in a snarling frenzy.

As he neared the bottom of the slope, N'ka regained his voice, and began taunting the beasts at the top of his lungs, waving his arms about wildly, though the wolves paid him little mind.

When he finally reached the besieged sled, N'ka threw himself in the thick of the pandemonium, where instantly, he felt the crushing scissor-grip of a jaw as it clamped down and began to tear at the muscle and tendon.

N'ka kicked and flailed madly, lashing out with his free arm. He cried out, though his agony was all but drowned out by the bloodthirsty thrall of his assailants, ripping and tearing at him.

Even as he fought for his life, N'ka feared the worst for his mother. Close on the heels of this revelation was the realization that he, too, was going to die a violent death, though he was determined to go down fighting.

N'ka managed to get one of the fiends by the scruff of the neck, but no sooner did his hand find a purchase than another had attached itself to his shoulder. He managed to wrest one arm free, but almost immediately another beast seized it in its snapping jaws. He tried to roll over on his stomach, and ball up for protection, but he couldn't seem to get there.

Then, something inexplicable happened, something so far beyond the realm of probability that N'ka believed it could not possibly be real: all at once came a fiery blur of orange and black, as the wolves released their ferocious grips and scattered in an instant, whimpering and gnashing their teeth.

"Mother," he said, groping blindly to his right with the one arm he could still move.

But his mother's body was twenty feet from where it began, torn free of the sled and dragged across the ice, now spattered with blood.

"Mother," he said, overcome with grief.

But his mother did not budge, nor make even the weakest response.

Like a vision, out of nowhere there descended a second fiery limb of blackened spruce, tracing orange through the chill air, followed immediately by another. Both torches landed on the snow near the sled with a hiss, while the wolves, still slathering at the jowls, teeth and gums bared, still dripping his mother's blood in the snow, retreated farther with mincing back steps, whining and whimpering at the flames.

Before N'ka could assign any reason to these events, a blurry figure emerged out of the trees in front of him, wielding still another torch, howling as it came, screaming words unfamiliar to N'ka's ears.

Soon, the figure stationed itself directly above N'ka, and looked down upon him with concern.

"Oosah vita!" it shouted. "Oosah vita!"

Distant voices responded.

The stranger looked kindly down into N'ka's face and spoke, her words incomprehensible to N'ka.

"I do not understand," he managed weakly.

Only then, dazed and bleeding, did N'ka recognize the face looking down at him as none other than the face of the little girl, she of the neatly cinched hide whom N'ka chased futilely through the forest two days prior. She whom he was certain they had lost forever.

"I am N'ka," said N'ka, his mouth filling with blood. "She is S'tka."

But the little girl could no more decipher N'ka's words than he could decipher hers.

Instead she placed a cool hand upon his forehead and looked deeply into his eyes, as if to reassure him.

"At last," he whispered through parched lips.

But the girl only smiled sadly and stroked his forehead once more.

Soon a second, and then a third face joined the girl, crowding in to look down upon N'ka. Like the girl, they were clothed in cinched hides, their faces smooth and hairless. Gravely, they spoke amongst themselves as they considered his condition. Unlike the sharp-edged, guttural articulations of N'ka and his mother, the language streamed musically and un-haltingly from their mouths. The sound of their voices was hypnotic.

Expecting the worst, N'ka attempted to turn his head to the side in order to check on the condition of his mother. No sooner did he begin the maneuver than a bright light flashed behind his eyelids and he slipped into oblivion.

Duane Barlow; Marine

"You can argue that Dave should have never stopped taking his meds, and you can argue that he never should have been on them in the first place, but you can't say Dave didn't have foresight. Because once Dave came back from his third tour, just about everything he feared would happen did happen. Did he bring some of it upon himself? Sure, it's what we do as human beings. Dave wasn't unique in undermining his own self-interest. He wasn't the first guy to push away the people that loved him most, or the first guy to quit going to counseling, or the first marine to stop eating his benzos, and he sure as hell wasn't the first guy to make questionable life decisions—and yeah, some of the decisions might look pretty damn bad from where you're standing.

"But that doesn't mean Dave deserved what he got. You want to point your finger at somebody, point it at Bremmer, point it at that knucklehead Bush and his overlords. Point it at neocon interventionism, or Islamic fundamentalism, or the UN, or the Kurds, or point it at the damn mirror, but don't you dare point it at a kid who didn't know any better. Dave and I and the rest of us, we were just doing as we were directed to do—that's what we signed up for.

"We were serving some purpose beyond ourselves, though the nature of that purpose became more and more elusive every day. We were blunt instruments in the wrong hands—hammers, that's what we were. Hammers for the Coalition, hammers for the politicians, hammers for all the shoppers back in America. And so we hammered. We hammered cities to dust. We hammered the shit out of those poor sonsofbitches—men, women, children, didn't matter. Because when you're a hammer, everything looks like a nail."

Dale Duvall; Owner, Dale's Diner

———————

"As a general rule, we take care of our own here in V-Falls. But if I'm being honest, we've had our blind spots, like everybody else. The plain truth is, after his third tour, a lot of the hero polish started to wear off of Dave around here. He wasn't quite the same guy, and neither were we. We weren't prosperous anymore. We weren't relevant; at least that's how it felt. I guess a lot of us, we started looking the other way when it came to the wars over there. They seemed a long ways removed from where the whole thing started. Maybe we just didn't want to see the collateral damage. Like we didn't want to share the responsibility for what happened to Dave, or the rest of those kids. I suppose maybe we didn't want to connect the dots between our lifestyle and the price of gas, and the cost of living, financial and human, and where Dave fit into making it all possible. And I was as guilty as the next guy of looking the other way.

"But not anymore. Everything that happened up there really put it all in perspective for me. It really made me think about what Davey Cartwright must have gone through in his life, and what could drive a man to go up there and try to make some kind of life and end up the way he did. And that little girl. Well, she just breaks my heart."

IV

The Book of Healing

Tristan Moseley; Caseworker

———————

"Everything is relative when we talk about the care of children—culturally, financially, spiritually. Sure, there's some baseline indicators of abuse and neglect, some comprehensive standards a caseworker adheres to, but there's no universal golden rule regarding the proper raising of children. A situation isn't always what it appears from the outside. I've seen Vietnamese kids with their necks and backs rubbed raw from silver coins. Abuse, or dermabrasive therapy? Depends on who you talk to. I've heard it actually cures a cold.

"The point is, profiling will only take you so far. For instance, there's this myth that neglect and abuse hardly exist in higher income families. It's just not true. It may look more palatable on the surface, but sometimes it's worse, particularly in the muddy realm of what we deem emotional neglect. I've interviewed teenagers with every financial resource available to them, virtually every academic or professional opportunity wide open to them, who were completely disaffected, and in some cases, sadistic.

"Personally, I think we put too much emphasis on where a person lives, and how they present themselves on a superficial level. Did Bella Cartwright walk around with a dirty face and knots in her hair? Yeah, okay, she did. Did she lay her mattress on a dirt floor at night? She did—she and a billion other people around the world. Did she face an unusual set of hazards living in the wilderness? Sure, she did. Were they any more damaging than the hazards that might have been waiting for her in town? Who's to say? Did she sometimes disengage from her immediate surroundings? Yes. Did she have an unusual imagination? Yes. Did she sometimes talk to cats? Apparently so.

"But you tell me how she was less of a person because of it."

Exposed

M orning arrived unwanted, gray and penetrating, bringing a bitter wind out of the southeast to ravage their crude camp at the base of the bluff. Her dad looked terrible, pale and frightened. His leg looked even worse, swollen and split like a hot dog left too long on the grill. The splint was still holding, but the bloody lengths of rope had begun to tighten against the swelling. The mere sight of it caused Bella to retch.

Bella immediately stoked the fire, feeding it sticks, fanning and blowing it back into a respectable state. With considerable effort, her dad lifted his torso up far enough to support himself on his elbows, where he appraised his leg grimly.

Bella brought him the jug of water and he tilted it up with one hand and drank from it. After he swallowed it down, he drew a deep breath and exhaled in short, punctuated bursts like a sprinkler, the way he sometimes did when confronted with a problem at the workbench, or beneath the hood of the Dodge.

"We need to ice that leg," he said, setting the jug down. "I need you to gather snow, okay, baby? I want you to pile it up on both sides but keep it away from the wound. We want to keep that part clean."

Bella complied promptly, gathering unsullied snow by the handfuls, and packing it along the length of his leg, which was beginning to give off a sickly sweet odor, like the kind that wafted up from the garbage disposal at Nana's.

When the leg was packed tightly in snow all around the wound, Bella pulled the blanket back over him as far as the knee, which she left exposed.

"I'm going for help, Daddy."

"You can't do that, baby. The weather, it could change, and it's too far, and you're liable to lose the trail."

She leveled a steady gaze at him.

"I know the way," she said.

"It's too dangerous, he said. "I won't let you."

"You can't stop me," she said.

Before she took leave, she made two more trips to the edge of the meadow to gather limbs, which she piled beside him so he could feed the fire. She set the Winchester beside him, too, along with his pack, and the hardened mass of his uneaten steak. If only she'd been strong enough to drag him onto a tarp and pull him up the hill to the safety of the cave. Instead, she left him there at the bottom of the bluff, exposed to the freezing wind, and practically helpless.

Before he could talk her out of it, Bella scurried off across the meadow in the snow, without looking back.

"Bella, no!" he called after her.

When she reached the tree line she slowed her pace to a brisk walk, her footsteps crunching the snow as she wended her way westerly between the trees, knowing she had hours ahead of her, but convinced she had the stamina to make it to town as quick as usual, with no stops and a good pace. Already she was nearly through the first leg of the journey. Within ten minutes, she emerged from the cover of the forest and started up the bald hump.

Bella sang aloud nervously along her way, little snatches of songs she remembered: "Hot Potato," "Baby Beluga," "We Will Rock You," and a bit of an old lullaby she learned from her mom, half of it in a language she did not understand. She wasn't even sure if she had the words right. When Bella's musical memory failed her, she talked aloud to herself, lending voice to her scattered thoughts.

Within a half hour, Bella reached the rocky jumble at the head of the canyon, where she cautiously descended the twenty-foot incline, planting each foot firmly. She had no wish to repeat the grisly spectacle of her dad's leg. For surely another broken leg would mean death for of them both. Though progress was sluggish and nerve-wracking, Bella reached the base of the steep incline without a hitch and continued her gradual descent into the basin.

The wind picked up as she switch-backed down the canyon. She visualized the path before her, the fork in the river, the crossing of the trails, the long, relatively straightforward path through the bottomlands. Within a few minutes snow began to fall, the tiny flakes harried slantwise by the wind.

"It's hardly even sticking," she told herself aloud.

But minute-by-minute, step-by-step, Bella could see she was mistaken.

N'ka

———

B efore N'ka opened his eyes, he heard all at once the burble of water and the hushed chatter of voices. He heard the wind frisking the tree-tops. When he finally opened his eyes, the first sight to greet him was the kind face of the green-eyed girl looking down on him, her head framed in the swaying treetops against a background of blue sky.

"Amah," she said.

N'ka attempted to rise but couldn't quite manage through the pain. Seized by a cramping in his chest, an angry fist clenched his spine as the girl coaxed him back down. Both of his arms were caked with a mud-like poultice, half an inch thick. His right arm was splinted, the hand mangled badly, though mercifully, it had no feeling. It could just as well have been somebody else's hand.

She spoke softly to him, words he could not comprehend, and she gently brushed the hair out of his eyes.

Then she stood and walked away, returning quickly with a shaggy pillow of hide. Gently she propped it beneath his head.

Then she continued her melodic speech, as though he would eventually understand her meaning.

Looking around, N'ka saw that he was stationed on a mattress of hides at the edge of a fire, in the thick of a bustling camp that stretched along the riverbank, running swiftly beneath a canopy of green. The people who busied themselves around the camp were not his own people, but men with hairless faces and broad foreheads, and shorthaired women, lithe and graceful.

The camp was like nothing N'ka had ever seen, orderly and precise, with tidy shelters constructed of limb and hide, and a half dozen cooking fires strung out at even intervals. And there was something else, something beyond his wildest imagination: a sled-like vessel, long and slender, and made of wood, which moved effortlessly on top of the water.

What was this place? Who were these magnificent people with their miraculous water sleds, and their hairless faces, and their fitted hides? But N'ka's wonder was rudely interrupted when the thought of his mother suddenly took hold of him, and he strained to lift his head despite the pain.

As though she could read his mind, the green-eyed girl cast her eyes down somberly and shook her head.

"She dead?" he said.

Understanding his meaning, she lifted her green eyes briefly and nodded her head.

N'ka's grief was immediate and complete. How could it end like this, after all that his mother had survived? How could it be that she, who gave him life, she who nurtured and protected him, who had taught him all he had ever known, was gone? How could it be that she was no longer present to adore and instruct him, to mock and tease, to antagonize him?

N'ka could practically count the occasions he'd been out of his mother's sight. He had never faced the world without her, nor even envisioned a world without her. Every imaginary road he walked down, his mother was there doggedly beside him; moaning and groaning, and ever hiding her secret smile, lest N'ka deduce that she viewed life as anything more than the unglamorous drudgery of survival.

On top of N'ka's grief was the avalanche of guilt that immediately overwhelmed him. How did this happen? How could he leave her there at the bottom of the hill, helpless and exposed? How could he toss her life away so thoughtlessly? How could he dare lead her over the ice against her will, for days on end, away from all she had ever known, only to let her be torn to pieces by wolves?

"I am responsible," he cried out in anguish. "I did this."

The green-eyed girl tenderly took hold of N'ka's head and rested it once more on the hides, as wave after wave of the despair washed over him.

Miss Martine; Second-Grade Teacher

———•———

"Of course, as far as what I'm at liberty to discuss, there are well-defined perimeters. And they exist for good reasons. So I can only discuss Bella Cartwright in a general sense. Academically, all I can tell you is that at the time of her withdrawal, shortly after mid-winter break, she was performing at or above standard in every category but one. And no, I won't tell you what that category was. What I can tell you from my own observations is that Bella was a compliant student. She was even-tempered, somewhat reserved, and not very outspoken. She possessed what I would characterize as a shy curiosity. My instinct with Bella was to draw that curiosity out, though usually only in one-on-one situations rather than the group environment. I can also tell you that she responded favorably to this drawing-out process, and possessed a very healthy sense of curiosity, along with a vivid imagination.

"I try to visualize my kids at the best of their potential. I try to guess what they might grow into, what kind of adults they might turn out to be, given the resources and support they're likely to have. How they will navigate the awkward trappings of childhood in general, along with all the other specific factors, including gender, and upbringing, and financial circumstances, and the various, ever-changing social environments they're likely to confront.

"Interestingly, with Bella, I found this exercise difficult. But my instinct was that Bella was a strong girl, quietly willful and observant, and that somehow she would find her way, whether or not she was set up to fail.

"But then, my instincts weren't always right."

No Small Wonder

———·———·———

Shortly after the snow began its sideways assault, the trail opened up and then promptly disappeared in a small clearing where Bella halted her progress. While she could guess at the general direction, she knew that the wooded landscape would obscure her path. If she calculated wrong, even slightly, it could mean miles of backtracking, or worse, death. She must reach the fork in the river soon. From there, she would know which way to proceed. Having not yet strayed from the path, she knew the river must be near at hand. From this very clearing she'd heard it running high in spring. But it was no longer surging in the dead of winter. How could she ever locate it with the whole world blurred by this gauze of white?

In that instant, Bella nearly hunkered down in the gathering snow, and surrendered to despair. But wiping the tears from her eyes, she instead gathered resolve. Had she not known greater perils on the ice sheet? Had she not survived worse conditions in all her lives? Had she not heard the very whisper of death in her ear? It was no small wonder that she clung so dearly to this life.

With three star-breaths, Bella managed to allay the stampeding progress of her anxiety. If life through the epochs had taught her anything, it was that our senses were not the root of consciousness, our brains not the true seat of awareness. There were many ways to hear, and many ways to know.

And so, face to the stinging wind, Bella closed her eyes and listened for the steady progress of water somewhere in the howling white world.

N'ka

___

There was life here hitherto unknown, including waters teeming with the miracle of fish, shimmering, silver grace incarnate. Fish hurrying upstream, fish whispering beneath the water. Fish, beautiful, reliable fish that did not gore, or trample, or disfigure. Fatty, meaty, oily fish, guileless and nutritious fish that practically surrendered themselves to the people, sustaining them through the seasons.

And for their trouble and sacrifice, these fish were worshipped.

There were forests, thriving green forests not forever frozen in the grip of ice. There were green, grass-bottomed valleys cut through with murmuring streams. There were canopies alive with birdsong. The world brimmed with possibility. The forest, like the river, like the grass-bottomed valley, was alive with spirits. Not gods, or ghosts, or creators, but allies, and teachers, and ancient reminders.

The world was not a frozen wasteland, but a vast, living thing.

Here, at last, was paradise.

Farther to the west, where the mountains began to taper, folding themselves into the flatlands, the river grew wider and flatter, until it emptied itself into the sea, a frothy, undulating expanse more vast than the ice shelf, a vastness the likes of which N'ka could never have previously imagined. When he first set eyes on this miraculous sea, tears welled up at the thought that his mother would never gaze upon its grandeur.

And then there were the magnificent people, those noble souls that saved N'ka and took him in, those who nurtured him back to health, who sheltered him, and taught him how to live in this new world.

There was Reka, the young man with the jagged scar upon his cheek, Reka, who was tasked with the job of teaching N'ka to weave a fish trap and paddle a canoe. Good-natured, patient Reka. Quiet, companionable Reka, like the older brother N'ka never had.

There was Alma, a strikingly tall, breathtakingly beautiful, dark-eyed woman of indeterminate age, placid of face, with impeccable posture. Alma, minister to those who ailed, tender to all wounds and maladies. Alma, mistress of mud and magic. Alma, who blended so seamlessly into the natural world that one did not hear her coming, she simply appeared.

There was Amon, to whom everybody except old Olta, the muttering man, deferred. He won their deference without trying. He won it not because he was the biggest, or even the wisest, but because Amon inspired confidence and engendered cooperation. How could there possibly be a more competent leader than Amon? Strong, thoughtful, even-tempered, and never quick to judgment. He who could be trusted to measure and weigh all considerations, to navigate any scenario. Amon the fair, Amon the practical.

There was muttering Olta, the white-haired old man, stooped but irrepressible. Stubborn, impatient Olta, who would accept no help, nor bow to any directive. Olta, who consented to live among them, but not without misgivings, who foraged his own wood, and hunted his own game, and tended his own traps downriver, invariably sharing the resulting bounty without reservation, while accepting nothing in return. Of all the people, Olta reminded N'ka the most of his mother.

There was Iku, and Ando, and Elay. There was Tiam, and Tanta, and Rami.

Finally, there was Bayla, kind and fearless, wise and playful. Bayla, who saved N'ka from the horrible fate that claimed his mother. Bayla, who was the first to grasp his language, to glimpse his experience, the first to penetrate his isolation, and the first to welcome him into the fold. Bayla, the green-eyed girl.

Extremities

After crossing the clearing, Bella plodded blindly through the snow, groping her way between trees, late into the afternoon. Still, the river eluded her. Harried by the fear that time was running out for her dad, Bella doubled her pace until it felt as though her lungs would burst.

Pausing to catch her breath, despair once again began to crowd in on her. They would die alone in this white hell, both of them, separated by miles. Bella could not think of a worse fate. As she began to lose feeling in her extremities, a profound sorrow took shape in the hollow of her chest. There was no end to the loneliness of the world. It stretched across time and space like a boundless sheet of ice.

Just as her eyelids began to feel heavy, something flashed through the trees to her left. Straining her eyes against the wind and snow, she glimpsed it again.

Could it be, at last? Was it . . . ? Yes, yes, it had to be!

Lungs cramping, Bella galloped toward her savior, giddy with relief. Within a quarter mile, she met the river, two hundred feet downstream of the fork. She wanted to drop to her knees and weep with gratitude, but there was no time to spare.

Minutes later she picked up the trail again and began the final stretch through the bottomlands, pushing her pace to the limit. Never in all the trips she'd made between the cave and town had this stretch of forest seemed so long. As if to taunt her, the trail just went on and on. If she didn't reach the highway soon, it would surely mean the death of her father. Though it seemed that every muscle in her body was ready to give out with each step, Bella hurried on toward town.

By the time she arrived at the deserted highway, her hands and face were numb, her feet frozen. It was already dark when she jumped the culvert and began bounding toward town through a half-foot of snow.

Sheriff Harlan Dale

"When that little Cartwright girl came dragging into the Sheriff's Department around 8:00 pm that night, all wet and half-frozen, with her hair all matted, and her face scratched up, one look at her and I knew we were dealing with a dire situation, whatever it was. Poor thing nearly collapsed right there in the lobby. When I scooped her off her feet and carried her to my office, she didn't weigh but forty pounds, seemed like. I set her on the sofa and fetched a cup of water for her.

"She wasn't making a whole lot of sense at first, like she was trying to tell me too many things at once. Something about her daddy falling, and a dead deer, and somebody named Mr. Paulson, and somebody else named Mr. Moseley.

"I said to her, 'Relax, now, sweetheart, start at the beginning, nice and slow.'

"Within about ten minutes I was able to get the story straight, and I called the ranger station and nobody answered, so I phoned every Paulson in the county and managed to track down the right one—Edward— though I didn't have luck with anyone named Moseley. Ed Paulson was a Fed ranger. He'd been up to their encampment and said he could take us to the spot Mirabella described.

"We were gonna need a few bodies to move him, and what's more, we had to move right then, or Dave Cartwright probably wouldn't make it through the night, if he was still alive at all. We were gonna need an airlift, and that was a hell of a dicey proposition considering the weather and the fact it was long past dark. We had power lines down and outages all over the county, so you knew it had to be howling up on the mountain.

"No matter what happened to her dad, that little Cartwright girl, she was the hero in all this. Can you imagine an eight-year-old girl finding her way nine miles down that mountain in a blizzard trying to save her daddy's life? I would've never believed it if I hadn't seen it with my own eyes."

N'ka

For days on end, Bayla sat by N'ka's bedside during his convalescence. She was a soothing presence in the pale glow of the fire, the shadows falling across her face when sleep finally came to take him each night. And she was still there, alert and attentive when he awoke in the morning. She brought him water, and fed him, and tended his fire. N'ka could not help but wonder at her kindness.

Thrice daily Bayla redressed his wounds, dabbing the sweat from his forehead as he winced against the pain of her ministrations. She spoke soothingly to buffer his agony, and smiled kindly down upon him. She listened patiently, hour after hour, as N'ka gave voice to his guilt and anguish at the fate of his mother.

And Bayla's kindness extended still further, for she did her best to teach N'ka the ways of the world as her people understood them. Though N'ka may not have been the quickest study, he could not imagine ever tiring of the beautiful language, the soft vowels and rolling syllables that flowed out of her mouth with the fluidity of a stream. How ugly and unnatural his own brutish dialect must sound to their ears, so sharp and angular, so stark and abrupt, like the mountains that inspired it. But here was an altogether more fluid landscape of rolling green hills, and flowing water swimming with life. Of course their language was beautiful.

Bayla taught N'ka the word for river, and the word for sky, and the word for mountain. As for this place where N'ka found himself, this tidy, bustling camp strung out along the river, it had no name. And N'ka would learn that it was not the only home of Bayla and her people. Twenty miles to the west, away from the mountains, on the shores of the great sea, lay a second home for the people, and it was called *Sala*.

Upon what must have been the sixth or seventh morning, once N'ka was well enough to move about on his own power, the ones called Amon and Reka came for N'ka in his tent, where steadfast Bayla was at her post.

Amon addressed him with words he still could not comprehend. Beside him, Reka with the scar across his face nodded solemnly.

They led N'ka from his tent—Amon, Reka, and Bayla—west along the pebbly bank of the river, then south through the ferns and yellow-leafed trees to a steep, grassy rise. At the top of the rise, they came upon what could only be his mother's figure, packed in the snow, presumably for preservation. Her body was wrapped in hides and hooded in leather. N'ka had only to imagine her disfigurement, her ravaged body, her gouged face, wrapped beneath what amounted to a water skin, so nobody was forced to look upon it.

Two young men that N'ka did not recognize attended his mother's body, both of whom nodded solemnly and respectfully, in the same manner as Reka.

Adjacent to his mother's cloaked form, a hole four feet deep had been dug to host her remains. The sight of the pit, even more than the sight of her body, was too much for N'ka to absorb, and he broke down immediately.

Amon spoke at length in his lyrical tongue.

Heartbroken, N'ka stood on the hill, his splinted arm dangling lifelessly, his face to the wind as the grass whipped his bare shins, while Reka, the quiet young man, and Bayla, his green-eyed savior, flanked him on either side, Bayla clutching his good hand firmly.

Amon stood facing them, tall, straight, and somber-eyed, buffered by the wind at his back. Following a considerable silence, Amon said a few words, and though N'ka could only guess at their meaning, the words were delivered gravely, and in a deliberate tempo. The one word N'ka recognized at the time, a word that was invoked on no less than four occasions, was *sho*, river.

Perhaps Amon likened his mother's life to a river, vital, steady, flowing into the unknown. Or perhaps by summoning the river, Amon was asking the river to take his mother's spirit and deliver it to the place behind the sky. Or maybe the idea was that life flowed like the river into the horizon. Or maybe Amon was just commenting on the view, for his mother's final resting place indeed offered a view of the river.

N'ka let Amon's words wash over him as he gazed down at an elbow of the river, running swift and turbulent over the rocks, disappearing through the trees, winding its way to yet another new world farther west.

Once Amon concluded his speech, he nodded in turn to N'ka, and then to the body of his mother.

N'ka understood this as a cue and stepped forward to look down into her hooded face, wishing he could look upon it one last time. As sure as he stood there on the grassy hill, grief-stricken, N'ka knew that he would move forward in dutiful compliance with the laws of survival. He would carry out the tasks of living, he would hunt, and fish, and rage, he would dream, and wonder, and ache, and even love, should he be fortunate enough. He would measure the days and the seasons as always by the sun and moon, as his mother had taught him. He would think of her often, he would hear her voice, he would speak to her in times of doubt and tribulation. He would hold her close as long as he could. She would always be a part of him.

"If only you could have seen this world with your own eyes," he said to her hooded visage, as they lowered her into the pit. "You would have to believe, Mother."

Mercy

Judy was already in bed, flipping through TV channels, when her phone vibrated on the nightstand.

"Judith Cartwright?"

"Yes."

"Sheriff Dale, here, ma'am."

Judy bolted upright. "What is it?"

"Mrs. Cartwright, we've got your granddaughter down here at the station."

"Bonnie?"

"No, ma'am, Mirabella."

"Wha—is she okay? What is she doing there?"

"She's fine," he assured her. "Little bit of frostbite, but she's thawing out fine. She straggled in here about an hour and a half ago, half-frozen."

"Where's her father? Is he okay?"

"We can't say at this point, ma'am. He's somewhere up beyond the canyon, east of the river. Injured, apparently, but we don't know how badly. We're sending up a party within the hour. Suppose there's any way you could see your way down here to pick her up? I'd bring her by myself, but as you might imagine, I've got my hands full with search and rescue."

"Yes, of course," said Judy. "I'll be right down."

"Take it easy on those roads, ma'am," he said. "It's slick out there."

Judy hopped off the bed, snatching her keys off the kitchen counter on her way to the foyer, where she donned her puffy winter coat, and stepped into her fur-lined boots.

The snow was still falling, flakes the size of postage stamps sparkling in the porch light. The crunch of her feet over the snowy walkway seemed the only sound in an otherwise silent world. Somewhere, miles and mountains away from Judy, her firstborn was in mortal danger, and there was absolutely nothing she could do to save him.

There must have been ten inches of snow on the hood of the LeSabre, which Judy began clearing in wide swaths with the sleeve of her coat. She ought to have called Travers to come pick her up in his truck. Truth be told, Judy also didn't see too well after dark anymore. She actually made it a point not to drive after sundown if she could avoid it. But she was impatient to get her arms around Bella, to serve her poor Davey the only way she could. Besides, Travers tended to be overbearing in crisis situations.

Judy's heart was a clenched fist as she scraped the ice from the windshield, her breath fogging the air. She always knew it would end badly for Davey and Bella, no matter how hard she prayed for their safe return. It always ended badly. At every turn, life tested her faith. When the world wasn't punishing the ones she loved, it was taking them from her. First Nadene, now her Davey. God have mercy on their souls, she thought, and God show mercy to their poor orphaned child.

Stop that now, she scolded herself. Don't start putting anybody in the grave yet.

LeSabre idling, Judy sat in the driver's seat as the back window defrosted. She fidgeted with her icy fingers, warding off anxiety. After a minute or so she cranked the heat with a warm blast and almost turned on the radio, if only to warm the frozen silence. Once the back window cleared, she squinted into the rearview mirror and backed into the dim red puddle her rear lights afforded her.

The back roads were dicey around corners, with the LeSabre's front wheels spinning out on several occasions, but the highway had been recently plowed. White-knuckling the wheel, Judy hunched forward in the driver's seat, as though her comportment could somehow enhance the performance of the car. The snow coming right at her in the headlights was hypnotic, and also a little disorienting.

The thought of her Davey up there in the mountains somewhere, marooned, frozen, life hanging by a thread, was almost too much to bear. Forty years, and not a day went by that Judy didn't worry for her oldest. Forty years, and she could remember infant Davey like it was yesterday. Hardly crying, hardly eating, not pooping for days on end. She could still visualize toddler Davey clear as day, waddling around in his OshKosh overalls she bought at the Saint Barnabus rummage sale for two bucks. Putting every damn thing in his mouth, including his boogers, a habit that would prove harder to break than Judy ever imagined. She could see him at twelve, wearing his Seahawks jersey, Toughskins jeans riding halfway up his ankles, a little peach fuzz mantling his upper lip. She could see him in his pee wee uniform, the shoulder pads and helmet comically outsized. She could see him at sixteen, buffing out the smudges on the hood of that old Buick. It was damn generous of Gordy Prentice to gift him that car. Heaven knows Judy couldn't afford to buy him one. And it was hard for Davey to manage a job during the school year, what with football and wrestling.

Judy fishtailed, nearly putting the LeSabre in a ditch as she veered off the highway onto Yew. The center of town was deserted, the traffic signals flashing yellow on either end of Cedar. Judy crawled past Dale's, and Ace, and the shuttered-up video store, then past Doc's to the west end of town, where she pulled into the Sheriff's Department and parked, then crunched across the snowy lot to the entrance.

Bella was sprawled on a bench in the reception area, wrapped in a blanket, sleeping fiercely under the glare of the fluorescent lights. It only took one look at her pinched-up little face, the red rings under her eyes, and the homely little mop of dark hair pasted to her forehead, before Judy began to weep.

A bearded deputy stepped out from behind the counter to greet Judy.

"Just crapped out, mid-sentence. Like somebody turned out the lights. She's had quite an adventure."

"What about her father?" said Judy, wiping away her tears.

"They sent a chopper up there as of about twenty minutes ago. Ranger named Paulson thinks he knows where to find him."

"What happened to him?"

"Listen, ma'am, I don't want to get your hopes up. The chances that he's still alive are pretty—"

"What happened?" said Judy.

"He had a fall, broke his leg pretty bad from the sound of it. We really don't have a lot of details right now. You want I should carry the girl out to the car, ma'am?"

"No, it's all right," said Bella, groggily coming to. "I'll walk."

The instant Bella got to her feet, Judy stooped down and wrapped the child tightly in her arms, refusing to let go, as Bella sobbed into the puffy folds of Judy's coat.

"Is he alive, Nana?" said Bella.

"We don't know, yet, honey. But we have every reason to hope," she said.

Ranger Ed Paulson

———————

"See, that's exactly why you don't do it. You don't just opt out of society one day and go out there in the backcountry with the idea of making a free life for yourself, whether it's squatting in the National Forest, or the Trust Lands, or DNR land, or anyplace else you haven't got a deed to. It's not 1840, damnit. We're not treating influenza with leeches, or tanning our hides with urine anymore, either. The frontier is not wide open. Heck, there is no frontier. We have regulations and policies for good reasons, to protect what's left of the wilds, no matter how much some people want to rail against that fact. We're a republic of laws. Without regulations, it would all be gone. That's just human nature.

"But never mind the politics; it's just damn dangerous living out there in the backcountry. Just look at Dave Cartwright and that poor little daughter of his. A person can get themselves in a lot of trouble out there. And nine-hundred-and-ninety-nine times out of a thousand, there's not going to be anybody out there to help them. Especially not at four thousand feet in the middle of a damn blizzard. You can die out there, a fact that ought to be obvious. Forget the modern conveniences, and the social benefits, it's the emergency services that keep people living in bunches, instead of out there by themselves. If we didn't have an organized way of taking care of one another, everybody would go the way of Dave Cartwright eventually."

Lights in the Sky

————————

When he wasn't brushing the fresh snow off himself, or feeding sticks to the fire, Dave lay on his back, trying to conserve his waning vitality. Time, such as it even existed in his current state, was impossible to gauge, though if Dave had to guess, he would've ventured that it was moving slower than usual. Lightheaded and sluggish, he tried to eat; gnawing on a mouthful of cold venison for what seemed like an eternity, until, unable to swallow it, he spit the masticated lump into the snow. He was bleeding from the mouth, but that may well have been from biting his numb cheek; he had no way of knowing.

The weather was only growing worse, if that was possible. The snow, not so much falling as churning and swirling, clouded the air in flurries. Visibility couldn't have been four feet. Dave could only hope it was better through the canyon, otherwise Bella was liable to break her own leg out there, or get lost, or fall off a cliff. Over and over, Dave cursed himself for his own carelessness. Even now, in this most dire hour, the parental instinct to manage his child's risk, with no thought of his own peril, kicked in. More than his own life force, Bella was his imperative. It seemed in those interminable moments of uncertainty, with the snow assaulting him and his own flame growing dim, that his life only had meaning insomuch as it related to Bella's.

The pain in his leg had subsided entirely, which he knew was not necessarily a good thing. His thoughts, still mostly clinging to Bella's welfare, raced despite his waning energy and his efforts to remain calm.

A dark line of questioning suddenly imposed itself upon Dave: How would his death obligate and entrap others? Where would the nine grand for his demise come from? Who would make those arrangements? Would they even be necessary? Perhaps it was better this way, him getting buried in the snow, lost to the world. But what would become of Bella when he was gone? Who would protect her? Whom would she cling to when he was gone? And his mom wasn't going to be around forever to look out for Bella, either. He should have never brought Bella up here to begin with, and she never should've come back, either. Somehow even that was his fault. Dave should never have turned Travers away when he came back for her. He should have just gone back down the mountain himself and started rebuilding his life out of the rubble.

Shining the headlamp down his leg, Dave took a grim inventory of the damage; the wound swollen, inflamed, horribly discolored, and likely crawling with bacteria, or worse. Goddammit, he was gonna lose it—assuming he even got out of there alive. Imagine him surviving three combat tours only to lose his leg, possibly even his life, to an icy mishap. But that was the least of his worries. If anything happened to Bella, he wouldn't want to go on living anyway.

Now, more than ever, Dave wished he had a God to pray to. But how could he, given the state of the world, or the condition of his own failed life, or the hopelessness that seemed to weave its way into the very fabric of humanity? Time, gravity, mortality—these things were tangible, these things were real, but faith was a mirage. And yet there was his mother, and a billion people like her, clinging to the impossible. Or maybe it wasn't impossible after all, maybe it was a force, just like gravity.

He could hear them, Pope, his mother, Reverend Hardy, the chorus of the devout: *God has a plan for everybody, Dave, His grand design is beyond our conception. Everything happens for a reason, Dave. Every obstacle, every pitfall, every tragedy that befalls us is a gift from God. His strength is made perfect in our weakness. We are stronger because of our suffering.*

Bullshit, thought Dave, gritting his teeth. What of the weakness that was unchecked greed; how did greed benefit the world? What of the weakness of willful destruction, or the subjugation of other living things, or the architecture of injustice that seemed to govern the world? If you could pretend to find meaning in senseless tragedy and destruction, you were lucky—among other things. But no sensible design would ever ask as much of a little girl, an innocent who did nothing to earn her measly lot, who understood so little, but was forced to withstand so much in the ways of the world.

His Bella.

And now she was out there alone, beholden to the only force whose cruelty could rival God's, or the condition of humanity itself—the whim of nature.

As the hours wore on, the fire began to die out, until there was nothing left to feed it. At some point, Dave lost consciousness for an indeterminate period of time, which amounted to a half-inch of fresh snow blanketing him when he awoke. The world was still dark, his entire body was numb, the wind continued howling up the canyon, and the snow played havoc.

At some point, Dave swept the snow off his blanketed torso and checked his right leg with the headlamp. The wound looked no worse than upon his previous examination, which might have been consolation, were it not for the fact that he was bound to die of exposure anyway. It hardly seemed to matter if his leg went first. All that mattered was Bella, and yet, moment by moment, he felt his control slipping away.

Eventually Dave surrendered to his fate, and a warmth suffused his body. It came as a profound relief to relinquish control, to let the fear and anxiety drain from him. All that remained was grief and anguish for the world at large, a sad sense of the inevitable disappointment that awaited the individual in a wilderness beyond measure.

When the numbness took over completely, Dave's torrent of thoughts slowed to a trickle, and was replaced by memories that came seemingly out of nowhere, shards of moments, sprite flashes like snowflakes in the headlights.

Thirteen-year-old Travers, clutching the fence at Dave's varsity practice, unable to conceal his admiration as he watched Dave ball out.

Dave's mom, senior year, asleep in her La-Z-Boy, her achy feet propped up after a double shift working the register at Vern's, the TV on, but unattended.

Coach Prentice, late at night, scheming on the whiteboard in the glaring overhead light of his office, a half-eaten sandwich on his desk.

Bella, weeks after Nadene's death, clutching him desperately in the darkened living room, refusing to let go.

Pope in the dusty outskirts of Mosul, his kind eyes smiling out from beneath his helmet.

The images flooded Dave's mind arbitrarily, with no discernible pattern. Not at first, anyway. But then a pattern did emerge: people. All of those flashes, every one of them, was a person who loved him, who protected him, and supported him, and sacrificed for him. A person who depended on him, whatever that might mean. In coming to this remote place to wallow in his isolation, Dave had turned his back on every single one of them, even Bella, whom he had failed in almost every way.

The whole rickety bulwark of Dave's defenses were crushed to splinter beneath the realization that even if he could manage to survive his current conditions, he still could not guard Bella from grief or harm, any more than he could deprive her of love and meaningful connection. Bereaved, we were but orphans, dispossessed, impoverished in our solitude. Our only buffer against the cold, cruel world was one another.

The snow began to come even faster now. His heart beating sluggishly, his blood beginning to slow, Dave watched the flakes appear suddenly out of the darkness, three feet above him. He felt them settling upon his face. Never had he tasted the fruits of such loneliness.

Then something completely incongruous disrupted his lull. Dave left off his sobbing abruptly, and with all his strength propped himself up on his elbows, suddenly alert. It was not a sound exactly. It was more of a sensation. It fluttered in his chest, though its source was nowhere close at hand. His first thought was an avalanche. But as the thing grew closer, its flutter revealed a sharply punctuated arrangement, and the din of it began to rattle Dave's bones. In an instant, he was besieged by a mechanical whirring, as the world all around him exploded in a flurry of snow. And filtering through the shroud of white, came the inescapable glare of light.

A Prayer

———

Half-asleep in the back seat of Nana's car on the drive home, Bella basked in the forced-air heat as much as her guilt would allow her, knowing that her dad was still out there freezing.

"They'll save him, Nana," she said.

"They will," said Nana.

"It's not too late."

"That's right, sweetie," said Nana. "All we can do is have faith."

Bella took comfort in the idea, though faith, like luck, had never served her particularly well.

"What about the cats?" she said.

"The cats will be fine," said Nana.

And Bella supposed she was right. If anything could take care of itself it was a cat.

When they arrived at Nana's house, Bella ate two bowls of Raisin Bran and an English muffin with raspberry jam. Then Nana ran Bella a warm bath and kneeled by the tub as she washed and conditioned Bella's hair, combing out the snarls while it was still wet.

"Gracious, what a mess," Nana said.

But for the fierce tug of the brush when it snagged in her hair, Bella could hardly stay awake.

"You poor dear. You're falling asleep," said Nana, blow drying her hair.

"I'm sorry," said Bella.

"Sweetie, who can blame you after what you've been through? We'll get your jammies on and put you straight to bed."

"Do you still have my polar bear jammies?"

"Of course," said Nana. "If you can still fit into them."

"I can fit," said Bella. "Can I sleep with you tonight, Nana?"

"Of course, sweetie," she said.

After Nana finished blow-drying her hair, she fetched Bella the clean fleece polar bear jammies. Though the jammies were indeed too small, they were still cozy, and Bella loved the way they smelled like Nana's house.

"Goodness, you've grown," said Nana. "Looks like I'm gonna have to make a trip to Target for new jammies."

"I like these ones," said Bella. "I don't care if they're tight."

Bella climbed under the covers with Nana, and Nana turned off the light.

"Nana, can I hold your arm?" she said.

"Of course," said Nana, rolling over on her back, so Bella could take hold of her arm.

The soft flab of Nana's arm was a comfort, and Bella not only clutched it, but pressed her face to the warm, mole-speckled flesh, drinking in its familiar scent of old lady soap.

"Can we say a prayer for him, Nana?" she said.

"Of course we can," said Nana.

"Will you say it?"

"Of course, sweetie," she said.

Nana lay there quietly in the darkness for a moment, gathering up her prayer.

"Dear Lord," she began, finally. "Please protect our Davey, the father of this precious child. Lord, they've both seen so many trials."

Nana's familiar voice was a salve. As much as Bella wanted to hear her prayer, she fell asleep before Nana got any further. And she slept straight through the buzzing of Nana's phone three hours later when the Sheriff's Department called with the news of her father.

In her dream that night, Bella sat in the grassy meadow below the bluff one final time. It was summer, and there were only a few puffy clouds in the sky, drifting lazily south. The grass was high, and winged life flitted about in the sunlight.

Though Bella thought at first that she was alone beneath the willow, she soon sensed a presence beside her. And when she felt a cool hand upon her bare knee, she found that the hand, slender-fingered but rough, and as dark as her own, belonged to Bayla, the green-eyed girl.

Sean Halligan; Bartender, Doc's

—— • ——

"I was getting ready to start closing up shop the night they went up there after Cave Dave. The snow here had finally let up by then, and the roads in town were mostly plowed. There were more people in here than you might expect at that hour on a Wednesday night—about ten, I'd guess, more than half of them regulars.

"Brady from the Sheriff's Department ducked in just in time for last call, which made a few of my regulars nervous, if you want to know the truth. Brady ordered a Coors and a bourbon, then took his coat off and draped it on the empty stool next to him and set his hat on the bar.

"When I brought Brady his Coors, he told me they'd just brought Dave Cartwright in, and then sent him on an airlift to the trauma center in Bellingham. Brady wasn't sure whether he was gonna make it, or what shape he was in exactly, but it sounded kind of rough. One way or another that was the end of Cave Dave.

"'What about the girl?' I said.

"'It was the girl that saved his butt,' Brady said. 'You know the man?' he asked me.

"'Not personally,' I said.

"'Me neither,' he said. 'My kid thinks he's some kind of bogeyman, my boss thinks he's a nutter, and my neighbor thinks he's a goddang folk hero. I don't know what to think.'

"'Guy had some moxie,' I said. 'That's for certain. Livin' in a damn cave all year long.'

"'Maybe so,' Brady said. 'But not half the moxie of that little girl.'"

A New Coat of Paint

Pink wasn't Bella's first choice for the walls. In fact, it wasn't even her tenth choice, but she didn't have the heart to tell Nana. It was enough just to have her own room again, with a ceiling high enough not to bump her head on, and flat, carpeted floors, and a mattress that didn't feel like there were rocks piled underneath it. All of her old stuffies lined the window sill, though some of them, like Teddy Ruxpin and Mr. Beaver, now seemed to Bella a bit infantile for a going-on-nine-year-old. Still, the familiarity of them was a comfort.

Though Bella had slept in this very room at least two hundred times before, the new paint was intended to make the room Bella's own, and for that she would endure pink walls, and frilly curtains, too. Maybe in time she could make some changes without hurting Nana's feelings. But even if she didn't, she knew the room would eventually feel like her own.

She was back in Miss Martine's class, and she was only with the specialists for half the day on Tuesdays, which wasn't so bad, except for Mr. Caruthers' breath. Sometimes Bella still drifted off in class, but never for long, and never very far, not so far as the icy, ancient past. Somehow, the otherness was beyond her reach now. Maybe it no longer needed her, or maybe Bella no longer needed it.

Bella made friends in class with a new girl named Jonnie. Sometimes they read the same book at the same time, and sometimes at recess they played What Time Is It, Mr. Fox? with Aria and some of the other girls from Mrs. Darling's class. Jonnie and Bella both agreed that What Time Is It, Mr. Fox? was a bit infantile, but it was still something to do under the play shed when it was raining.

Bella also made friends with a native boy named Jacob, from Mr. E's class. Jacob wasn't loud like the other boys. He also didn't make things up just to impress her. What Bella liked most about Jacob, though, was his calm energy, and his holey shoes, and the fact that he was just himself.

Only a few times did anybody ever tease Bella about her dad, or about having lived in a cave, and having her dad cut her hair, or having pretended to be a cat. And anyway, it was usually just the fourth grade boys who were talking, and they were not half as clever as they thought they were.

On the bus ride home, Bella usually sat alone, but that was okay, too, because sometimes she liked it that way.

No Place Like Home

————•————

Dave was plating Bella's waffle and fake-sausage patty when she walked into the kitchen and plopped down at the breakfast table, groggy-eyed, her sleep-tousled hair grown down past her ears.

"Good morning, baby," he said, wheeling around ninety degrees to table her plate.

Niftily, he spun back around on his rear wheels and opened the fridge door and fished the syrup out of the door rack. Then, wheeling with his left hand while holding steady with his right, he pirouetted back toward the table, setting the bottle in front of Bella.

"Where's Nana?" she said.

"She's at church."

"It's only Thursday," said Bella.

"She's getting ready for the bazaar this weekend. Now, eat up, baby, you're gonna miss the bus."

"Can you walk me to the stop?"

"I don't have time this morning, baby. The van's on its way."

She made a pouty face, stabbing at her waffle.

God, but it was good to see her pout, good to see her admit to any disappointment, any imbalance in the universe, because life on that mountain had just about frozen it out of her. If nothing else, he'd made a stoic out of Bella, a fact he was not proud of. That she forgave him for it was almost miraculous. The sad reality of the world was that nobody was quite as resilient as a child, and nobody paid a higher price for it.

"Will you still be at work when I get home?" she said.

"I'll be home around 5:30, like usual."

"Can we watch a show?"

"Of course," he said. "Make sure you eat your whole sandwich today. And your carrots."

"What kind of sandwich?"

"Ham."

"Aw," she said. "Can't I just buy for once? Aria always buys."

"I checked the schedule, today is beefy nachos, and you don't like them," Dave said.

"The meat is like cat food," she said.

A moment later she stood abruptly, leaving her waffle half-eaten on her plate. Still clutching her fake sausage, she hoisted her pack off the counter.

"Bye, Daddy," she said, and scooted out the kitchen door and down the wooden ramp before he could kiss her, before he could tell her for the two-hundredth time—in a gesture, at least—how sorry he was.

"You didn't brush your teeth!" he called after her.

"I'll brush them twice tonight," she said.

"That's not the same thing!" he said.

Not two minutes later, as he scraped the remainder of Bella's waffle into the garbage and stowed the plate in the dishwasher, Dave heard the access van pull up in the driveway. Snatching his own pack off the counter, he straightened his empty pant leg before wheeling out the kitchen door and down the ramp.

Arnie was already lowering the lift as Dave rolled down the drive.

"Mornin', Dave," he said.

"Yes, it is," Dave said. "Lived to see another."

"I hear that," said old Arnie, flashing a long-toothed, tobacco-stained smile.

Dave's heart beat just a little bit stronger as he buckled himself in. He never would've believed it three months ago, but sometimes people really were made stronger through suffering, and sometimes losses actually could make them whole again.

On the bus ride to town, Dave looked out the window as the clouds began dispersing and the sun crested the mountains, spilling orange and yellow into the valley. In six months or so, they could afford their own house somewhere closer to town. Though it was awfully nice of Travers to offer Dave and Bella his rental, Dave wanted to build his life back on his own as much as possible. He had learned, though, finally, that nobody could ever do anything all by themselves, and that they ought not to try. But his pride was still too strong.

Arnie dropped him behind Ace, and Dave wheeled off the lift into the sunny morning chill. Out in front of the store, Joe Wettleson, his manager, and a heck of a pulling guard in his day, was already busy carting out the barbecue grills, and placing the signage. Dave started across the lot in the sunlight, his pack dangling off the back of his wheelchair, ham sandwich and carrots inside, same lunch as Bella, his red work apron rolled up in his lap.

Halfway to the garden center, Dave waved to Angie as she carted out the perennials. Angie, who had two teenagers, also worked weekends at the Lowe's down in Lundgren. Angie, who was going to be a naturopath if she could ever finish her online courses. Angie, who was going to get an FHA loan and buy a four-and-a-half-acre Christmas tree farm once she got out from under her credit card debt.

Just in front of the handicapped spots, Dave paused to look up at the mountains in the light of morning, ghostly streamers of mist clinging to their wooded faces. Somewhere invisible to the eye the river was burgeoning with the thaw, rushing forth from beneath the frozen ground, gathering force as it wended its way down the green valley and into the yawning canyon, still mired in shadows.

Mountains and valleys, shadow and light, the pitiless freeze and the merciful thaw. Change was ceaseless, the seasons countless, the outside forces of the world relentless, and yet nothing was permanent, not Ace Hardware, not Vigilante Falls, not even the North Cascades.

Dave slipped into his apron. Leaning forward in his wheelchair, he tied it off, cinching the knot firmly in back. Puffing up his empty pant leg once more, he straightened his name pin before pushing through the double glass doors.

Just another day in the life of a legend.

Acknowledgments

————————

I would be remiss in writing a book set in the North Cascades without acknowledging the legacy of the people who inhabited the region long before the arrival of European Settlers: the Chilliwack, the Nooksack, and the Chelan, as well as the people of the Upper Skagit, and many other groups from the Columbia River Basin to the western lowlands of Puget Sound. Before we had Mt. Baker, we had Koma Kulshan; before Mt. Ranier, Tahoma. Being a Washingtonian, this is something I never forget.

I would be also remiss in writing a book concerned centrally with child-hood trauma without acknowledging those who have had to endure such circumstances. I extend my gratitude as well to those of you who have put your lives on the line in service of your country, and those of you who may have lost part of yourselves in doing so. And God bless those who never found their way back, and all the rest who made it back but could not find the help that they needed. As much as it may seem, you are not forgotten.

Thanks to my longsuffering partner and wife, Lauren, for her boundless patience and unyielding support, not to mention all her early reads and reliable feedback. Thanks to all the usual suspects at the Gonk: Lauren Moseley, Elisabeth Scharlatt, Betsy Gleick, Michael McKenzie, Randall Lotowycz, Debra Linn, Brunson Hoole, Frazer Dobson, and all those who make me look good.

Thanks to Kurtis Lowe and Phoebe Gaston at Book Travelers West for always having my back. Thanks to Jon Cassir at CAA for putting my books in the right hands. A huge thanks to my early readers: Jarrett Middleton,

Kurt Baumeister, Jenny Shank, Brock Dubbles, Jamie Ford, Jason Chambers, Marilyn Dahl, Thomas Kohnstamm, and Paul Bang-Knudsen.

And an extra special thanks are due to my longtime partners in crime Mollie Glick and Chuck Adams, who with every book push me to do my best work.

LEGENDS
of the
NORTH
CASCADES

Love on Ice
An Essay by Jonathan Evison

Questions for Discussion

Love on Ice

An Essay by Jonathan Evison

———•—•—•———

I have three kids, ages three, eight, and eleven, and make no mistake, I want them to be confident and curious. I want them to experience life to the fullest, and be independent and adventurous, and discover things on their own, and I want them to take risks—once they're adults.

I can't help it. I'm a helicopter parent and have been since day one. That's me walking behind my infants and toddlers as they climb, then crawl, then waddle up staircases; that's me standing below my grade schoolers, ready to catch them when they're scrambling up trees; that's me riding on the outside anytime we're biking around traffic (even the mere possibility of traffic); that's me barely out of arm's length in the swimming pool.

I'd like to think I'm not suffocating about it. I go out of my way to offer them extraordinary experiences and opportunities. I give them space, I really do. I don't try to influence their every move or discourage them from exploring the world; I just keep my eyes peeled for trouble at all times. I've seen firsthand how fast an accident can happen to young people, and the irreparable damage it can do.

My helicoptering is by no means limited to the realm of physical safety. I constantly worry for my kids' mental and emotional well-being, especially when they're away from me at school, or out playing, or staying at a friend's house—anywhere and anytime they're out of my sight, really. While I am mostly powerless in these situations, I can't stop trying to prepare them for heartbreaks, or reassuring them that they are loved, and respected, and seen. I don't want them to get bullied, or hurt, or ever question their own worth, or feel depressed about climate change or rampant human suffering. As fanatical as it may sound, I'm guessing most parents feel the same way. And yes, our motives are selfish. Because we love them so damn much that the idea of anything bad ever happening to them is unthinkable. It would break us completely. Without them we wouldn't want to live.

When I write a novel I always try to get out of my own way and give myself to the characters, which can make it both a painful and revelatory process, but always expansive. Invariably I feel like I come out the other end a better, more experienced person somehow, a better husband, a better dad, a better friend, having learned lessons and overcome obstacles not just on the page, but in my heart and mind, just as sure as if the experience of the novel were real life. That's why I write in the first place, to live beyond the purview of my personal experience. And for the whole enterprise to work, I've got to allow myself to be vulnerable.

The toughest thing about writing *Legends of the North Cascades* was imagining situations where children were in peril, particularly Bella. Like my own kids, Bella is precocious, and extremely thoughtful, and empathic, and tends to take the world a bit personally at times. She asks the questions and says the things my kids might say or ask. She's got an active imagination and a voracious curiosity. But unlike my kids, Bella was born into a lousy situation, one that keeps getting worse, forcing her to confront things beyond her years, and as a result she's compelled to start acting like an adult long before she should ever have to. Likewise with Dave's character, I have a lot in common with him, in terms of his passion, yearning, and disillusionment, and especially in his intense love and sense of responsibility for his child. But as an Iraq war veteran, Dave's baggage is heavier than mine, his situation much more dire than my own, and it gets progressively worse, in part by his own doing. Who knows what decisions I might make under the same circumstances as Dave, suffering trauma, irredeemable loss, financial ruin, and constant physical peril? For Dave and Bella, while it seems like the ultimate solution, living in a cave in the high country of the North Cascades only exacerbates the issues already tormenting them.

It was heartbreaking living inside Dave and Bella under such circumstances. But what carried me through and ultimately saved me was the same thing that saved them: their fierce love for each other, their dependence on each other, their unshakeable faith in each other despite how bad things might get. While the novel is unquestionably an adventure story, at its core it is the story of the love between parent and child, a love that is tested at every turn. And so it is with Dave and Bella's Ice Age counterparts, S'tka, the young mother, and N'ka, the fatherless child, as they try to eke out an existence alone in an icy world that seems intent on forsaking them.

I wrote *Legends of the North Cascades* in 2018, so when I chose self-isolation as a theme I wasn't being prescient. I didn't see what was coming for all of us in 2020 (and most of 2021). The fact is, no matter how different each of my novels may seem on the surface, I've got only a few themes that preoccupy my work as a whole. I've always written about self-isolation. Whether overtly or not, nearly all my characters are in one guise or another dealing with the fundamental conflicts that comprise the dictates of self versus humanity, individual versus collective, alone versus together. But never have I explored these themes quite so directly as in *Legends of the North Cascades*.

I love adventure stories. Having grown up on a heavy dose of Jack London's Yukon, I always wanted to write a novel with a rugged northern setting, and I have dabbled there in the past, such as in portions of my 2011 novel *West of Here*. But *Legends* offered me the perfect opportunity to fully immerse myself in a frozen wasteland, to virtually experience the thrill and urgency and peril of isolation and survival in a harsh environment, and to explore how these extraordinary conditions might test the love and trust of a parent and a child. The result, I hope, is a timeless story that will stick with readers for a long while and leave them altered in some small way, as I myself was changed by the act of writing the novel.

Because of Dave and Bella, S'tka and N'ka, and the brutal and unforgiving forces that shaped and tested them, whatever obstacles life might throw at me as a parent going forward, whatever circumstances fate might ask me to navigate to ensure the well-being of my children, I feel more prepared than ever to face them.

Questions for Discussion

————

1. Do you think Dave is a good father? Though his actions are dangerous in many ways, does a part of you sympathize with Dave's decision to take Bella to live a life he feels is more authentic? Why or why not?

2. Have you ever dreamed of living off the grid? Where would you go? How do you think you would fare?

3. How would you characterize Dave's political beliefs? Where do you think he fits on the political spectrum?

4. Do you think Dave regrets enlisting in the Marines?

5. How do you feel Dave and Bella will adjust to their return to society?

6. The individualist ethos is deeply embedded in American history. At the same time, many Americans also hold it in deep suspicion. Why do you think that is? What are your own feelings about individualism?

7. Some parts of American culture also champion the idea of supporting our troops. How do you feel we as a nation treat our military veterans in reality?

8. Why do you think the author decided to make Dave a former high school football standout?

9. Why do you think the author included the interview snippets from Dave's friends, acquaintances, and neighbors?

10. What do you think is the nature of Bella's connection to S'tka and N'ka?

11. What do you see as the common threads between the modern narrative and the Pleistocene narrative? Why do you think the author included both?

12. For you, what resonated as the major themes of *Legends of the North Cascades*? What did you find yourself thinking about the most after you finished the final pages?

13. Are you familiar with any of Jonathan Evison's other novels? How does this book compare? What does it have in common with, and how is it different from, the other work(s) you've read?

14. Have you read other stories of survival, adventure, or living off the grid that you would like to recommend?

KEITH BROFSKY

JONATHAN EVISON is the *New York Times* bestselling author of six novels, including *West of Here* and *The Revised Fundamentals of Caregiving*. He lives on the Olympic Peninsula in Washington State with his wife and three children.